Karen Viggers was born in Melbourne the Dandenong Ranges riding horses and writing stories. She studied Veterinary Science at Melbourne University, and then worked in mixed animal practice for five years before completing a PhD at The Australian National University, Canberra, in wildlife health. Since then she has worked on a wide range of Australian native animals in many different natural environments. She lives in Canberra with her husband and two children. She works part-time in veterinary practice, provides veterinary support for biologists studying native animals, and writes in her spare time.

The STRANDING

Karen Viggers

A&U

First published in 2008

Allen & Unwin
83 Alexander Street
Crows Nest NSW 2065
Australia
Phone: (61 2) 8425 0100
Fax: (61 2) 9906 2218
Email: info@allenandunwin.com
Web: www.allenandunwin.com

National Library of Australia
Cataloguing-in-Publication entry:

The stranding/author, Karen Viggers.

ISBN 978 1 74175 401 8 (pbk.).

A823.4

Cover and text design by Christabella Designs
Typeset in 12/16 pt Bembo by Midland Typesetters, Australia
Printed and bound in Australia by Griffin Press

10 9 8 7 6 5 4 3 2 1

For David
For his infinite love, patience and support

He left the house in the eerie light of the moon and walked barefoot to the end of the road. Here the cliffs fell sharply into the sea and most nights the waves foamed over the rocks and crashed against the walls. But tonight was calm, and the sea collided with the rocks less violently, and despite the constant movement everything seemed unusually still. The moon sailed large and round, illuminating the wisps of cloud that drifted across the sky.

There was something else in the night. He could feel it. A presence. He was sure it had a name, and he was not afraid of it. Looking out across the flickering silver sea he watched the swell rolling in, ever moving, rising, falling, rising, falling. He felt his breathing slowing, deepening. The rhythm calmed him. The rhythmic emptiness of the endless sea.

Then he heard it. A loud huffing sound. Below and not far out. His eyes swept over the surface of the water, seeking. There must be something . . . The water slid quietly, rolling in towards the cliffs. Then he could see it, the smooth back of a whale, slick and glistening, black and silver, as the sea rippled over it. An exhalation came again. He could see the vapour spout this time, drifting fine spray lit by the moon. Then another, a smaller puff, a calf, wallowing alongside. His heart raced. He wondered if they had seen him too, whether they knew he was there, watching them, alive and present in the night, bearing the weight of existence.

For a long time he stood there, breathing with the whales, watching the sea slide over their sleek backs, listening to the slow puffs of their restfulness. In the long, moving quiet, he found emptiness, and the joy contained within it. He dwelled in the essence of now, away from pain, until he was cold and soaked with dew.

PART I

Patterns and Tides

ONE

A month after he moved to Wallaces Point, Lex Henderson burned all his clothes. He burned every last item, except what he was standing in. And he did it deliberately. It was an irrational moment and nothing could have stopped him.

He'd arrived with wounds that were deep but invisible. He'd packed his Sydney life into a suitcase and driven south, leaving chaos behind, but also carrying it within. As the highway hours stretched behind him, the trepidation and doubt that had followed him from the city began to ease, and his hands rested more steadily on the wheel. When, finally, the Volvo shuddered to a halt on the grass outside his new home, the sound of the sea entered him and he was calm.

He spent the first few weeks at Wallaces Point drifting along the beach by day and drinking himself into oblivion at night. He passed the daylight hours trying to erase the ugliness of the night before, and the night trying to erase the past four months when his life had turned upside down. Daytime, it was easy to immerse himself in the lonely wild world of the beach. The wind swirled through his soul, the spring sun warmed his head, and he walked, leaving footprints in the sand then sitting up on the rocks to watch them dissolve as the tide crept back up the beach.

In those first days, he saw large things, like the waves shaping the beach, the swans on the lagoon, the crushing blue of the enormous sky. Then, gradually, over hours and days, his focus sharpened and he began to see other things: the rippling patterns left in the sand by the receding water, a sea eagle floating on the breeze above the cliffs, sooty oystercatchers poking among the rocks, honeyeaters scattering in dogfights over the heath.

After that, patterns started to emerge, like the time of day the eagle appeared and where it roosted in a skeletal tree on the headland, the timing of the tides, the gradation of sea creatures on the rocks, when to expect the honking of swans just after dusk as they flew low towards the lagoon. He watched the waters and learned to read the rips, sat for hours watching gannets fishing out to sea. Along the high tide mark he fossicked for seashells and rocks, tiny bird skulls, cuttlefish floats, driftwood, crab claws, tendrils of pink seaweed. On the rocks just below the cliffs, he spent hours sitting, watching the waves roll in. Over and over. From low tide to high. The roar and rhythm were just enough to anchor his sanity.

In the laundry cupboard he found a wetsuit and fins, and on calm days he took to the sea. After that first gasp of cold water trickling through the suit, he plunged out and bodysurfed, kicking like crazy down the waves, then pulsing with the thrilling rush of being picked up and surged towards the beach. The waves shot him skywards before dumping him in a tumbled confusion of foam and sand. It did him good, the physicality of it, striding out against the incoming waves and then swimming to catch their ride in.

But nights were not so easy.

Each evening, he went inside, scrubbed clean by the wind and the sky, and stood by the window, watching the light fading from the heaving face of the sea. His new home stood fifty metres from the finish of the road, flanked by waving grasses and the stiff skeletons of a few hardy banksias bent rigid by the onshore winds. It was the last house in the line and its elongated face of glass looked out over the cliffs and the slow roll of the sea. The house faced north, gathering light, and the windows stretched in front of him like a wide-angled lens, collecting as much sea as they could grasp. From where Lex stood, the view reached far and long, passing the hummock of the darkening headland and arcing east across the water to the murky horizon. Whoever had built the house had only two things in mind: glass and sea.

To Lex, it seemed the house was waiting, as if it was watching for something.

When the sun had set and the silver waters had sunk to grey then featureless black, Lex would sit on a cane chair in the lounge room, staring out into darkness, wondering what he had done in coming here. When he had first seen it, the house seemed neutral enough—all straight lines and simplicity, an open plan kitchen and living area, just the essential furniture: a wooden kitchen table, a cane couch and a few armchairs facing the sea. But sometimes he thought perhaps he could feel someone else in the house. Someone else lifting an old book from the shelf and leafing through the musty pages. Someone else staring at the photos on the walls of old boats and salted fishermen. It seemed that the house was reminiscing on a past that had nothing to do with him.

The bookshelves were laden with books he would never have bought. A few were potentially useful: seashore guides, fishing manuals, a tattered handbook of birds. The rest were of dubious interest; mainly cheap shiny-backed novels, a few biographies and a handful of old books about whaling. Each night, determined to avoid the stash of grog in the pantry, Lex would pull a book from the shelf and flick through it, trying not to feel the dark pressing in through the windows, trying not to feel his skin creeping with desire—the desire for the emptiness that came with the bottle. But soon his will would wither and, with shaking hands and bitter self-contempt, he'd find himself at the cupboard again, pulling out a glass, pouring a drink, enjoying the tart burn of whisky. And there he would be once again, rollicking in misery, drowning the flood of his thoughts, burying them in staggering inebriation. Another night lost.

A few weeks into this ritual, when he was three or four whiskies down, the phone rang. Lex knew it could only be his mother. No one else had his number.

'Mum,' he said, hooking the receiver on his shoulder and pouring another drink, taking care not to clink the bottle against the glass.

'Darling. How are you? Just thought I'd ring and see how your holiday was going.'

'It's not a holiday, Mum.'

She didn't like to think of him moving away, he knew that.

'Let's be realistic, darling,' she said in her fruity voice. 'You just need a little break. After what you've been through, that's only natural. Then you can come back refreshed and sort everything out.'

'Yes, Mum,' he said.

But after all that had passed, there was nothing to go back to.

'I *do* understand that you've had a bad time,' his mother was saying. 'Jilly's been terrible and the funeral was awful . . .'

Lex walked to the window, gripping his glass tight. He didn't want to think about the funeral, or Jilly.

'Mum, I'm fine. I'm just settling in.'

'Lex, you're in the *country*. There's nothing you can do there that would be remotely interesting for you. Why don't you do what I suggested? Have a few more weeks' rest then I'll come down and visit. We'll have a chat.'

Lex tossed back the rest of his whisky and emptied the remnants of the bottle into his glass. His last bottle.

'You've been drinking, haven't you?'

He said nothing.

'I knew it. Darling, you need some help. It's not shameful to need help. We all do at times. Why don't you rent the house out and come back here where you belong.'

Lex didn't feel like he belonged anywhere.

'Jilly's very upset,' his mother said.

'She threw me out.'

'I'm sure she regrets that. We all do silly things sometimes.'

Lex said nothing.

'You didn't give it very long, did you?'

Four months of hell.

'These things take time to work out,' his mother continued. 'Both of you had such a traumatic time. Perhaps you should come back and give it another go. Persevere longer. Jilly's very distraught. Just tell me when you're coming. We can find you a flat, or you can stay here until you and Jilly patch things up.'

Nausea swept through him and he realised he was sweating.

'. . . I know about what happened just after Isabel died,' his mother was saying. 'I know what Jilly did . . . Her mother told me.'

'Mum, I don't want to talk about it.'

'I understand that it was terrible for you. I miss you, darling. I'll come and visit in a week or two. Things are very busy here, as you know.'

'Fine. Just call me before you come.'

Lex put the phone down. For a moment he leaned against the kitchen bench, exhausted. Then panic took him and his chest curdled in its grip. With tight hands he clutched the bench, holding himself up, struggling to breathe. In one ragged gulp he drained his whisky, then crashed open the kitchen drawer and snatched out the bottle opener. With the whisky all gone, he'd have to drink wine. He pulled a bottle from the pantry, but his hands were shaking so much he couldn't pierce the cork, so he threw the opener against the wall and held the bench tight until the panic passed.

At last, the black swamp of it left him and he wobbled to the couch and slumped there. He had forgotten how these attacks left him ripped open and empty. He lay down in a foetal curl and tears seeped out.

Later, cold, stiff and horribly sober, he went to bed.

He dreamed he was in the kitchen of his Sydney home, making breakfast. He could see the bowls of cereal laid out before him on the bench. On the wall, the clock was ticking, measuring time. Jilly and Isabel were both sleeping in.

At the bench he sliced strawberries, one at a time, until Jilly came out, all fluffy with sleep. They both looked at his hands, still cutting strawberries, and then Jilly looked at the clock and jolted when she saw the time.

'It's eight o'clock,' she said.

Lex heard his own voice, distant and hollow, as if he were far away. 'What time did you feed her?'

'I don't know. Two o'clock, maybe.'

Jilly disappeared down the hallway to wake Isabel and Lex put down the knife. He could hear floorboards creaking. He looked at the clock, stared at it, watching the numbers rippling as if the clock was underwater. The second hand didn't seem to be moving and Jilly's footsteps were slow in the hall. He wanted her to get to Isabel's room, but it seemed she'd never get there, and the second hand on the clock was still not moving.

There was silence, then Jilly's voice, strangled, panicked.

'Lex. She's not breathing.'

The pile of strawberries started rolling into the sink, one after another, and then a flood of them, filling the sink and overflowing onto the floor.

'Lex.'

He pulled up feet like lead and tried to run down the hallway. The ticking of the clock became the beating of his heart, and he ran and ran. But the hallway stretched forever and it seemed he'd never reach the end, never arrive in Isabel's room.

Then he was there, trying to drag back the curtains.

'Hurry,' Jilly said.

His heartbeat was in his mouth, thundering. Then he was at the cot, looking down.

Isabel's face was slack. Her mouth was open, her lips blue, like plastic. He lifted her out, rolled her out of the wrap—everything happening fast now. He placed her on the bed. She was still and cold. All loose and floppy.

'Call the ambulance.' His breathing was loud, and his voice was strange, like it was someone else speaking. Someone far away, using a megaphone.

He closed his mouth over Isabel's face and exhaled into her. Two small puffs. Two tiny airy breaths. Careful not to rupture her lungs. He watched her chest rise and fall and his heart thumped in his ears. Two of his fingers reached to Isabel's sternum. He beat out a string of chest compressions. Was he supposed to do ten or fifteen? He counted, pressed, breathed, counted, pressed, breathed. She could have been a doll in First Aid class.

Her eyes flew open, black and deep as wells, and she watched him as he worked on her. She was cold, so cold. And her lips were blue and flaccid. Panic surged in him. Why was she watching him? Why didn't she breathe? He didn't check her pulse.

Then he heard the siren. The ambulance was coming at last. Was it too soon or too late? In a minute he would know what he already knew.

They came in and ushered him aside. Their hands were kind and firm, slipping over Isabel, his baby, feeling her, touching her. Hands slipping, rolling, sliding, examining. Their hands seemed to be everywhere. He wanted to stop them. What were they doing?

'Keep up the CPR,' he said, panicky. 'Don't stop.'

They looked at him and the truth was in their eyes. He felt it in Isabel's cold lips. He knew it in his heart.

But why was everyone staring at him—the paramedics, Jilly, Isabel? Were they all thinking it was his fault? He could see it in their accusing eyes.

I didn't do it, he wanted to cry. It isn't my fault. But his voice wouldn't come. It was stuck in his throat, like a great lump of clay, and the words were buried.

Then there were Jilly's screams: hollow, echoing, like in a tunnel. His mind was telling him to reach for her, but everything was frozen. She was like an animal, contorted, red, wet. She was sobbing, sobbing, but he couldn't reach out to her. And there was another sound, an eerie moaning that wasn't of this earth, a grinding utterance of despair. It was coming from him. He was an animal too.

And then he and Jilly were falling into each other, clinging and grasping, like two strangers on a life raft. Holding each other up. It was physical support, nothing else. Everything was over.

Jilly took the baby. She sat on the couch in the lounge room, Isabel's dead body loose in her lap. Lex saw the arms swinging, the head fallen back. He sat in the corner and watched them, maybe for hours. He saw the baby's eyes watching him. And he wanted to reach for her. He wanted to tell Jilly the paramedics were wrong. That Isabel was still alive. But he couldn't move from the corner. He was weighted there, and it was as if Jilly had forgotten him as she wailed over Isabel's body.

Eventually, he crawled near, reaching for the baby. But Jilly was like a feral cat, snarling and hissing. He wanted to touch the baby. His baby too. But she clawed at him and he retreated to his corner again and again.

Then her mother came. Her long and haggard face looked at him, huddled in his corner. She went to Jilly and stroked her like a kitten, humming and cooing as she ran her hand over Jilly's head, rocked her. Finally she lifted the baby, all rag-doll loose, and brought her to him, helped him unfold so he could wrap himself around that little body and hold it close. She patted him, his head bent to Isabel's cheek. And then tears came, and wailing, chest deep. He was shaking with it, and it went on and on and there was no end to it.

When he woke, sweating, the night was large and dense around him. The dull roar of the sea reminded him where he was, and he lay in bed listening before he flicked on a light.

In the corner, his suitcase leaned lid-open against the wall. Everything he'd brought with him was still packed in there. The wardrobe remained empty. In truth, he was afraid of unpacking. Unfolding his clothes and hanging them up might signify ownership of this place. It might mean permanence of some sort. It might mean he had become someone else. Another person with another life.

But wasn't that why he had come here? Wasn't that why he had left?

He stared at the suitcase, feeling the sudden weight of everything. In the city, it had seemed important to keep something of himself, something from his past. But now these things were anchors. One month into a new life and nothing had changed. He was the same bruised person carrying the same scars. Still weak, broken and pitiful. He had thought things would improve by now. He'd thought the wounds might have begun to heal in this new place with its new sky and its cleansing wind.

The sound of the sea reinvaded him, and he remembered the incinerator in the backyard. It was near the crumbling chimney, all that was left of a previous house knocked down years before. He dragged on clothes and boots, grabbed an old newspaper from the box beside the wood heater and hauled the suitcase out the back.

In the dull shimmer of the outside light, and with shaking hands, he stuffed balls of crushed newspaper in the base of the incinerator, then struck a match and guided it to the paper. At first, the flames licked lazily, singeing the paper along its edges. He felt the warm glow against his face and the flicker of shadows at his back. Gradually the flames gained energy. He shoved in more paper, screwing it into balls, feeding the fire. Then he turned to the suitcase and pulled out a polyester shirt, dropped it in, his chest thrilling as it disappeared in clawing flames. He grabbed another shirt, neatly folded. Then three more. They were gone in seconds.

Later, it amazed him that there had been a strange sort of logic within his craziness. A definite structure to the burning. He managed to choose clothes in order of flammability. The shirts first. Then socks, jocks, fleece jackets, cotton T-shirts. The flames were tall and angry, leaping and roaring through the top of the incinerator like a great beast trying to escape. Flashing vivid streaks in the darkness.

He threw his jeans in last, then stood back, mesmerised, and watched the ripples of heat and flame rising into the dark dome of the sky. It was only then that he registered the hammering of his heart.

He was just turning back to the yellow glow of the house when a scrap of burning denim wafted down out of the night and settled at his feet. He watched it smoulder in the shadows. Then he thought he saw a wisp of smoke, and the grass crackled into thin flames. All around him, bits of glowing denim were floating and landing. Within seconds there were dozens of fires across the lawn. He ran from one to the next, jabbing his foot on the flames to choke them. But there were more chunks of material descending through the darkness, more quivering flames licking at the grass. Panting, he ran to the incinerator and closed the heavy lid. Then he dashed around the shadowy lawn, putting out fires.

Afterwards, he remembered this fragment of time in slow motion: a strange foot-stomping dance in the darkness, with orange flames glowing around him like torches illuminating his steps.

When it was finished, he hauled back the lid of the incinerator and peered inside. The last remnants of clothing were smouldering embers, slowly fading. He turned and went back into the house.

At the kitchen bench he stopped to look at the only possession he'd kept. A photograph in a frame. Isabel smiling out at him. All gums.

How did you come to terms with something as definite and infinite as death?

For a while, he stood staring at her, trying to hold on to the memory of her face. But he knew he was already losing her, knew that she was becoming as fleeting and ethereal as those leaping flames clawing their way out of the incinerator.

With his heart heaving, he pulled the magnet-torch off the fridge and went out the front door. Barefoot, he walked across the tarmac, over the moist pads of couch grass, among the sighing shadows of the wind-torn heath, down the uneven sandy steps, and out onto the open expanse of the beach. The stars cascaded across the clear sky like tiny flung jewels, right out to the black horizon where they seemed to fall into the murk of the sea.

At first the ocean seemed hollow and distant, but then the sound crept closer as he sat in a dent in the damp sand and the night swelled around him. He had never felt so small and vulnerable, so awash with loss, grief and desolation.

Dense with despair, he shrugged off his clothes and strode blindly into the breakers. He could see the wild white puffs of shredded manes as the waves dashed at him out of the dark. There was a sense of strength in pressing through the churn of the water, a sense of taking charge as the tingling cold smashed around his groin and splashed up his chest and back. There could be an end to all this. Everything could dissolve into blackness. But when he stumbled in a gutter and the waters surged over him, he realised that if he let himself go out there, sliding half-willingly into the surging night, Isabel's death would mean nothing. He foundered, panicky, trying to find his feet and drag himself away from the urgent pull of the rip. The dark suddenly seemed infinite.

In a lull between waves, he dug his feet into the sand, tore himself out of the suck of the waves, and lurched shorewards where a dull sheen of light from the moon glowed faintly on the wet sands. On his knees in the skittering shallows, his anger at himself subsided to shock and then grief which surged out of him in horrible racking sobs. He cried himself into exhaustion and emptiness.

TWO

When the old orange Kombi fizzled to a stop, the girl cursed. Usually the beast was reliable, but lately she'd been having a few problems. She ought to get rid of it, but she wouldn't be able to afford anything better, so for the time being she'd just have to put up with these unscheduled roadside delays. Leaving the keys in the ignition, she clambered out and jerked open the rear door where the engine was housed. Jordi kept telling her she should learn something about car maintenance to rescue herself, but she couldn't think of anything she'd dislike more. Changing tyres was about her limit. Mechanics was beyond her.

She stood on the roadside, wondering what it would take for somebody to stop. The wind shuffled her brown curly hair and she tied it back impatiently with a scarf. She had a pleasant rounded face, but the usual humour in her brown eyes was lost in her annoyance at being stranded. As she turned to look along the road towards town, a blue four-wheel drive flashed past. Obviously not a local. A local would at least slow down to have a look. Some of them may just wave and keep going, especially the church crowd. But most would be inclined to stop and give her a hand. She'd just have to wait it out. Pity it was a weekday. Everyone would already be at work.

Finally, an old F100 ute pulled up behind her. It was Barry Morris. He owned the local servo and was Jordi's boss.

'G'day, Callista,' he grunted, going straight for the engine.

'Barry. Thanks for stopping. I thought I was going to be here all day.'

He grunted again and poked about at the engine while Callista pretended to watch what he was doing. He was a big guy with a beer gut that hung over his belt like an advanced pregnancy. Jordi reckoned he was long overdue for a heart attack and Callista agreed with him. She could smell his BO from here. He caught her watching him as he turned and straightened up, holding a burnt-out spark plug between his oily black fingers.

'This one's had it,' he said. 'I've got another one in the cab.'

He flicked the old plug into the back of his ute and tugged a toolbox out from behind the seat.

'Here,' he said, returning with a new plug. 'I'll just put it in for you. But you ought to get this bloody thing serviced.'

'Can't afford to,' she said.

'You're just like your brother,' Barry said. Then he smiled. 'Only you're stylish and much better looking.'

'Don't go there, Barry.'

His smile widened. 'I wouldn't dare,' he said. 'You've got more prickles than an echidna. It's no bloody wonder you're single.'

'Thanks, Barry.'

While Barry replaced the spark plug, Callista kicked at the roadside gravel. She watched the stones skitter across the tarmac. Then she heard the back door of the Kombi slam shut. Barry climbed in the front and turned the key. The Kombi started like an angel and Barry hopped out, leaving the engine running.

'Going to the markets this month?' he asked.

'I might.'

'I'll look out for you there. Might even buy one of your paintings so you can get this heap serviced and give the money back to me.'

'Nice idea. But I'd buy a cask of wine instead.'

Barry laughed loudly. He was even more distasteful when he

threw his head back like that. He ought to try laughing in front of a mirror sometime. Callista stood back while he hauled himself into the F100 and slammed the door.

'Where are you off to now?' he asked.

'To see Joe Denton at the hardware. He gives me a discount on boards. For my paintings. And he keeps all the timber off-cuts for me. They're useful for making frames.'

'How about old fence palings?' he asked. 'They any use to you?'

'Could be. If they're not too damaged.'

'Mrs Jensen's having her fence done. She's got a whole pile of palings to get rid of. I could give her a call for you.'

'I wouldn't mind having a look. But come on.' Callista rolled her eyes. 'Do you think she'd give them to me—of all people?'

Barry smiled. 'Tough call. But I'll ask her.'

He dug around in his pocket to pull out his mobile phone then dialled a number.

'Mrs Jensen,' he bawled. 'You still trying to get rid of those fence palings? I've got someone here who might take some of them off your hands for you . . . You are. Good. It's Callista. The artist . . . Yep, that's the one. I'll send her around.'

He stuffed the phone back in his pocket and looked at Callista with a smirk on his face. 'Looks like she's feeling generous today.'

'Sure. But I have to go to her house now, don't I?'

Barry laughed. 'You'll survive. There's no such thing as a free lunch.'

He started the engine and the F100 throbbed loudly.

'Thanks for helping,' Callista said. 'I appreciate it.'

'Make sure you go 'round there,' he said. 'Old Mrs Jensen's a bit of a cranky old dame, but she doesn't bite.'

The wheels skidded briefly in the gravel as he pulled out and headed into town. Callista climbed into the Kombi and followed him.

Callista Bennett lived in a small A-frame home submerged in a deep gully in the foothills of the mountains. The house was surrounded by a token firebreak of slashed grass, and looked out over the twisted canopy of rainforest cradled in the gully floor. From the gully, where the heaped mounds of vegetation rambled and climbed, the scrub rose up the steep slope to meet the gangly eucalypts high up along the ridgeline. It was a quiet place where one season faded into the next. Most people would find it lonely but Callista liked the solitude and she revelled in the shifts of colour and light.

It was luck that she lived here. The owner lived in the city and had planned to retire here. But his whimsical wife had changed her changeable mind and decided that the humid isolation and the deep moodiness of the coastal bush were too difficult. So they lived in the city, close to the streetlights, theatre, restaurants, dinner parties and all the frenetic activity that Callista most needed to escape from.

Once, the wife had come to the gully with her husband when he was checking where the new water tank should be located. She had stepped out of the shiny white four-wheel-drive all beautifully made up and smart as a fashion magazine. Her careful image was entirely misplaced in the gully's wondrous perfect disorder. While her husband talked with Callista about the drought and the capacity of the new tank, the wife wandered around the dam looking bored and then retired to the car. Callista saw her preening in the mirror behind the passenger visor, tidying her lipstick. Primping wasn't something Callista had time for.

She liked her landlord though. He was tall and good-looking with tired blue eyes and an elegant longish nose. His face was ruddy and he was a bit thickset, probably from drinking too many beers trying to cope with the boredom of the city and his marriage.

Thinking of her landlord and his wife always reminded Callista of how different her own parents were in so many ways. When she was a child, her parents had been painfully embarrassing. Now, from adulthood, she admired their courage to be different and their strong stance on living what they believed. But it hadn't been so easy when she and Jordi were young. They had grown up isolated and sparsely clothed, running barefoot through the bush, scaling trees and devouring plates full of lentils, bean sprouts, brown rice and home-grown vegies. They hadn't known until they went to school that it was unusual to be vegetarian. At school, everything they did or wore was open to ridicule—their lunches, their home-made bright-coloured clothes, their wild unbrushed hair, the smell of garlic on their breath. All of it became a cause for shame. They were glaring exceptions in a conservative rural community—a town where dairy cows and timber-cutting were still the predominant sources of income. The other children jeered at them so that Callista longed for a pair of blue jeans, a sweatshirt and vegemite sandwiches so she could be like everybody else.

Over time things changed. Attitudes shifted and hippies became more socially acceptable. Eventually the children Callista had grown up with broke awkwardly into adulthood, and some tried to talk to her in the street—uncertainly, as if they weren't quite sure whether she remembered. It was too late by then. She and Jordi never could assimilate. Jordi lived alone in a shack in the bush up behind her parents' place, playing his guitar and smoking dope. He barely scraped a living from the meagre wage he earned pumping petrol down at the local servo. Callista couldn't merge with the local crowd either. She lived on a different fringe. Nobody could understand someone trying to make a living out of art. And, despite much encouragement from some of the young males, who fancied her curvy figure and exuberant curls, she just couldn't make it through the front door of the church to meld with their social group.

Over the years, she'd attempted a few dates with some of the local boys with no luck. Once or twice things had advanced to a fumbled kiss or an embarrassing grope in the back of a car, but that was it. They still considered her too weird, with the dabs of paint that were permanently on her hands and scattered through her hair, and the family that still lived by choice in a rough home embedded in the bush. She was just wired differently—she simply didn't think the same way as them. That was why she lived in her secluded gully. On her own at thirty-three.

Mrs Jensen lived with her husband in a large old home overlooking the river. It was one of the better bits of real estate in town. They had bought the house when Mr Jensen retired, selling his dairy farm to a big conglomerate that was buying up dairies in the district. The locals resented an outside company buying up their farms, appointing managers and taking the profits away from the community. And it was becoming harder for local owners to compete. But it was the way of the future and there was nothing they could do about it.

The sale of their farm placed the Jensens among the wealthiest people in town, as well as cementing their position as powerful members of the church. Their donations had helped finance most of the renovations at the church over the past few years, and they'd helped to put missionaries overseas in Africa and West Papua. Yes, the Jensens were held in high esteem by the church-goers of Merrigan. But Callista and Jordi reckoned the Jensens weren't being selflessly charitable. They were simply buying their tickets to heaven.

Callista parked the Kombi at the gate and sat behind the wheel for a moment staring at the big house and rambling old garden. She had never seen eye to eye with Mrs Jensen, and it was hard to come asking for hand-outs, although Barry had said she'd be doing Mrs Jensen a favour. She could see the palings piled up by the new fence. It'd be easy to just help herself and drive away, but she ought to do the right thing and go up and speak to Mrs Jensen first. She climbed out and trudged up the steps to the front door. The doorbell was loud enough to make her jump, and Mrs Jensen opened the door quickly, as if she had been waiting for her.

'Hello, Mrs Jensen.'

The old woman cocked her head back and looked down her nose at Callista.

'You've taken your time coming,' she said.

'I've had a busy week.' Callista couldn't help noticing the rough patches of foundation on the old woman's forehead and neck.

'You can take what you want,' Mrs Jensen said. 'I just want to get rid of them.'

'I'll have a look then. Thanks.'

Callista backed away, hoping that'd be the end of it. But Mrs Jensen followed her down into the garden.

'What are you going to use them for,' the old lady asked, watching Callista going through the pile.

'These ones that aren't too warped will be good for frames. They come up well with a few layers of paint.'

Callista started making a separate pile of palings she thought she might take. Some were too cracked and misshapen, but many looked like they'd be okay.

'What sort of things do you paint?'

Callista stood up and stretched her back. 'This time of year I focus on pretty basic things for the markets. You know, beach scenes, that sort of stuff. It's a money-spinner, keeps me going for the rest of the year. That's what I'll use this wood for.'

'And the rest of the year?' Mrs Jensen had her hands folded across her chest and was standing uphill from Callista so she could look down on her.

Callista frowned up into the wrinkled face. She really was a very ugly old woman, with those heavy features and mouth that sloped down in the corners.

'Well, if the inspiration takes me I get going on other things,' she said. 'But it's not particularly planned. Unfortunately inspiration isn't something you can buy from a shop and use when you need it.'

Mrs Jensen sniffed. 'What about portraits? Do you ever do any of those?'

'I'm generally a landscape person.' Callista bent over the pile of palings again to continue sorting.

'We need a portrait of our minister,' Mrs Jensen said. 'If you could do a good job we'd pay you well for it.'

Callista stood up again. 'I'm pretty busy at this time of year. But I'll give it some thought.' She didn't particularly want to paint the minister, but it was best to be polite.

'You should give it a lot of thought. It would pay better than your market art, and you'd be making a significant contribution to the community.'

Whose community, Callista wanted to ask. But she held her tongue.

'You should consider coming up to the church sometime to have a chat with the minister,' Mrs Jensen continued.

'About the portrait?'

'No, just to chat generally. He's a very good man. You should get to know him.'

Oh yes, it was coming. The call to religion. Callista should have known she couldn't get away with a visit to Mrs Jensen's house that easily.

'Bring that Jordi with you. He could do with some help from God.'

Callista threw a few more palings on her pile. 'I think Jordi can sort himself out.'

Mrs Jensen snorted. 'How long has it been? Seven years? Eight?'

Callista looked at the hard line of Mrs Jensen's mouth and thought perhaps her lips tweaked a little. Was she supposed to interpret that as an encouraging smile?

'These things take time,' she said.

But Mrs Jensen was persistent. 'This minister is very kind. I think he could help to show Jordi a path away from his troubles.'

Callista concentrated on sorting palings. She was feeling hot and cross now. 'Can we just leave Jordi out of this?' she said.

'I'm sorry you feel that way.' Mrs Jensen turned to go, arms still wrapped firmly across her large breasts. 'Do make sure you think about that portrait. We can talk more about it if you like.'

'Thanks, Mrs Jensen.' Callista struggled to muster politeness. 'I'll give you a call if I think I can fit it in.'

She watched the old lady stalk back up to the house. Old bag. Thinking she could run the lives of everyone in town. And there was no way Callista would paint a portrait of the goddamned minister. She'd rather starve.

It was Friday before Callista caught up with Jordi. She met him in the pub after the servo closed up, and tried not to grimace at the company in the bar. Friday was when everybody converged on the pub to tell stories and wash them down with beer. Callista rarely came because crowds made her skin prickle and she hated the smoke. By seven o'clock it was already beery and jovial. She noticed Jordi sitting at a bench with his Aboriginal mate, Rick Molloy. She bought three beers from Max Hunter at the bar, who smiled approvingly at her, and then she ferried the brimming glasses through the crowd.

Jordi nodded and pulled up a stool for her.

'Hey, Callista.' Rick was pleased to accept the beer she offered him. His white teeth flashed at her from out of his wide brown face. 'I hear you bin breaking down a bit.'

Callista passed a beer to Jordi and sat down. 'Just bad luck,' she said.

'That Kombi's an old heap. You gotta get something better to get 'round in.'

'I'm like you, Rick. No money.'

Rick laughed. 'That *is* bad luck,' he said. 'Not easy to change that.'

Jordi took a few sips of his beer. The froth clung to his shaggy moustache and beard. 'She just needs to get it serviced,' he said.

'Why don't you do it for her?' Rick asked.

'Don't like Volkswagens,' Jordi grunted. 'Barry does 'em best.'

'Reckon Barry'd give your sister a discount.'

'Reckon he's sick of bailing her out.' Jordi sucked the froth off his moustache. 'I might have a look at it next week.'

He finished his beer quickly and glanced at Callista as he set his glass down.

'I was up at Mrs Jensen's place this week,' she said. 'She wants me to bring you up for a chat with the minister.'

Jordi tensed. 'Why were you talking about me?'

'We weren't. She invited *both* of us up to the church, okay? To save our souls. And she wants me to do a portrait of the minister.'

'What did you say?'

'I said I was too busy.'

Somewhere in the depths of his beard, Jordi's mouth twisted into a smile.

'Good work,' he said. 'Hey, I saw Alexander at the servo the other day. Told him you were a bloody good artist and that he should give you a showing.'

Callista was glad to shift away from Mrs Jensen, even if the conversation had turned to Alexander. This was one of Jordi's causes—to set her up for an exhibition at Alexander's. It was hopeless of course, but Jordi wouldn't leave it alone.

'Come on,' he said. 'What do you think?'

Alexander was an art dealer from Sydney who owned a gallery off the highway south of Merrigan. According to local gossip, he'd moved south after his boyfriend died of AIDS. But there wasn't much sympathy for homosexuality in a town like Merrigan, and Alexander was considered to be a person to be avoided. Local mutterings flared every time he came into town, which wasn't often. And who could blame him? The way people talked was enough to make Callista's skin crawl. But she liked his gallery. It was an extension of the large, angular wooden house he'd built on a cleared hill overlooking the sea. She'd only been in the gallery once, and had been surprised by the airiness and spaciousness. Alexander had made clever use of tall windows to cast light in shafts across the room, and the walls were carefully placed so the light wasn't too harsh. Sure, she'd love to exhibit there one day. But right now it was beyond her.

'I'm not good enough for Alexander's,' she said.

'Yes, you are,' Jordi insisted. 'He said you should call him up when you want to show him your stuff. He was bloody nice about it, actually.'

'Look,' she said, 'he was just being polite. And anyway, I've got nothing to show him. The market stuff is a joke. And it's been a tough year.' She was gabbling and Jordi was still looking at her.

'Get to work then,' he said. 'I've half set it up for you.'

'It's not as easy as that.'

Rick stood up, uncomfortable. 'I'll get another round.' He slid off towards the bar.

'Don't worry about me, Rick,' Callista called after him. 'I'm leaving in a minute.'

She and Jordi sat in silence amidst the din of voices.

'Beryl sold the house,' Jordi said.

'What?'

'She sold it. Like I said.'

'What does she think she's doing? It wasn't hers to sell.'

'She's a cow. You know it. She wanted the money.'

'Who'd she sell it to?'

'I dunno. Some guy from out of town.'

'That's just great.'

'Yeah.'

'What do you know about him?'

'Nothing.'

'So how do we find out?'

Jordi shrugged. 'Nobody seems to know much.'

'Well, I'm going to ask a few people some questions.' Callista gave Jordi a five-dollar note. 'Buy yourself another beer. I'm out of here.'

THREE

When Lex finally decided to drive into town it was like breaking a spiritual communion with the sea. After the days he'd spent merging with the sky and the waves, and growing into the incessant roar of the ocean, the incinerator fire had shifted his centre of gravity and left him with a sense of being suspended in air. The only way he could ground himself was to climb into the car and drive.

He backed the Volvo off the grass, swung onto the gravel and started slowly along the pot-holed road, past the shadowy verandah of his unknown neighbour's house, past a row of holiday houses all shut up like faces in prayer, past a scatter of kids' bikes, and up over the rolling green hills that blended into the stringy-bark forest. Kangaroos grazed and lifted their heads to watch him pass. It was only three kilometres to the highway, but Lex felt so disconnected from civilisation it might have been three hundred.

Merrigan was a town that tourism had bypassed, despite its proximity to the coast. It was a place where people stopped for fuel or a newspaper or a quick cup of coffee on their way to the beaches further south. From the north, the highway ran into town too fast, disregarding the 80-kilometre speed sign near the caravan park on the outskirts. It passed the cemetery and the green flats dotted with Friesian cows placidly synthesising milk. To the west, beyond the farms, lay the jagged blue haze of the mountains in the dry wilderness of the national park. The final run into town was across the Merrigan River, which flowed coastward from the town and skirted south before dipping into the sea at the heads with wild desolate beaches visited only by fishermen.

Town consisted of the usual clutter of shops: a newsagency, butcher, milk bar, bank, coffee shop, real estate agent. In the middle of town, the highway took an awkward dog-leg turn and then ran past the hall, the post office, the supermarket, a few more shops, then the school and several rows of bland houses. After this it climbed a hill and that seemed to be the end of town, until the pub popped up out of nowhere, dingy and brown, followed by a small run-down cheese factory and the service station. Just before the 100-kilometre sign the church stood high on the hill, an imposing white icon frowning down on everything else.

Near the newsagency there was a sad-looking clothing shop. Lex had seen it the day he'd first cruised through Merrigan scanning shop windows for real estate. As he stepped through the door a bell jingled and he sensed stirrings down the back of the store, a shuffling of boxes.

'Be right with you,' a voice called out.

The store contained a collection of clothes hung on circular racks. Lex flicked through mouldy-smelling shirts—cotton and staid flannelette in red and blue checks. Not exactly his taste, but probably the local uniform. As he skimmed over a rack of football jumpers, a woman emerged from the shadows smoothing her skirt with fingers tipped by red nails.

'Need any help?' she asked.

She was quite a tall woman, not young, big without being fat, with strong features and a head topped by a mop of hennaed curls. Her face was carefully made up with red lips, puffs of rouge and sweeps of brown eye make-up.

'I'm right just now,' Lex said, feeling a flutter of tension.

Her eyebrows lifted just slightly as she took in his face and the armful of clothing he was gathering.

'I'll take those for you.' She reached out and whisked the clothes from him. 'Sing out if you want anything.'

Lex could feel her watching him from the counter. He hurried his selection, but paused at the rack of underpants.

'Do you have anything smaller?' he asked.

'Sorry, luv, just Y-fronts round here. It's all the locals wear.'

Her voice came close again as he shuffled through the packets to find something that might fit.

'Jumpers?' he asked.

'Back corner, luv. Army disposal stuff.'

Down the back he found a couple of jumpers, khaki and navy blue with elbow and shoulder pads. Ugly but functional. He held some camouflage pants up to his waist to check the leg length. There's a first time for everything, he thought, dumping his haul on the counter.

'You starting a new wardrobe?' she asked.

'Got tired of the old clothes.'

'You did? And what happened to your eyebrows? Got sick of them too?'

Lex had noticed their singed edges this morning. He must have been too close to the clothing inferno last night.

'Burned them,' he said. 'Nearly burned the whole Point.'

She was looking at him, concerned. 'It's dry round here this year,' she said. 'Drought year. You could get into serious trouble for burning like that. You new around these parts?'

'Yes.'

Lex watched her summing him up.

'Hey,' she said. 'Are you the guy who bought my house out at Wallaces?' She reached across the counter and offered a perfumed hand, all clinky with rings and bracelets. 'I'm Beryl Harden.'

Lex took her hand reluctantly. He was feeling shaky and the surge in his chest frightened him. He was terrified he might grasp her hand, fold it in both of his and lay his head on her ample bosom. Right here in the shop.

'You right, luv?' She tugged her hand away.

Lex couldn't arrest the flare of embarrassment on his cheeks. 'Bit shaky,' he said. 'Haven't had breakfast.'

She started ringing up the prices and folding the clothes. 'Take care of yourself out there. There's not too many folk around. Only old Mrs Brocklehurst and she's none too social. They say she's a nice old stick though. Not that she'd pass the time of day with me.'

She tucked the clothes into a plastic bag and Lex handed her his credit card.

'Wild place, isn't it? The Point?' she said as he signed. 'I used to love living out there when my husband was around for company. Too lonely and quiet on my own though.' Beryl passed the bag to him. 'Tell you what,' she said, 'I'll order in some men's briefs for you. What's your size?'

Lex flushed. 'I don't know.' Jilly had always bought his underpants.

'There's a change room down the back.' Beryl nodded.

When he came back, she made a note on a piece of paper.

'They'll be here in about a week,' she said. 'I'll see you then.'

Bag in hand, Lex walked down the street for a coffee at Sue's Café. He sat down at a small round table against the wall, sliding his hands across the plastic green-checked tablecloth. Unfortunately he was the only customer, so he picked up yesterday's newspaper and folded it around his face, pretending to read as he glanced around the room.

A woman emerged from the rear kitchen.

'Got a menu there?' she called out. 'Grab one off the table beside you.'

He leaned over and took a menu from the next table, then sat back and watched her regarding him as she wiped her hands on a tea towel. She was well rounded with a neat mushroom of brown hair streaked with grey. As she came forward to take his order, Lex saw that her eyes were brown too, sunken slightly in generous cheeks, and she had a wide mouth. She was thickset and sturdy, not young. He imagined she enjoyed her food.

'Are you Sue?' he asked.

'Yes, that's me. What'll you have?'

'A cappuccino, strong . . . and a toasted ham and cheese sandwich.'

'Passing through?'

'No,' he said. 'I'm local.'

'Not likely. I know everyone 'round here.' She paused. 'Ahh.' A small smile stirred on her lips. 'Are you the new-chum out at Wallaces?'

'Yes. I've only been there a few weeks.'

'Windy out there,' she said. 'Too windy for me. And not enough people about.'

'I bought the house from Beryl Harden.'

'Yes,' she said.

'Who owned the house before Beryl?' Lex asked. 'I don't suppose the whaling books on the shelves were hers.'

Sue raised her eyebrows. 'No,' she said. 'Those would have belonged to old Vic Wallace.'

'Wallace? After Wallaces Point?'

'Yes. The same. The house was in the family for years.'

'Have the Wallaces moved on?'

'No.' Sue's lips pressed flat. 'Some of them are still 'round here.'

Lex wondered how Beryl got hold of the house. He saw Sue glance towards the kitchen. The conversation was faltering.

'Did Vic Wallace have a bit of an interest in whaling?' he asked.

'More than a bit,' she said. 'It was his career. He took his family west to Albany to go whaling. Didn't return until the industry was closing down.' She moved off slowly towards the kitchen. 'I'll just get your order.'

Lex stared blankly into the newspaper. He was glad he hadn't known about Vic Wallace when he bought the house. Whaling was something he'd covered on radio each year when the Japanese fleets were sailing south for their annual 'research' catch. It was a controversial issue. And it made for good talkback. The phone always ran hot when they ran a whaling story. Whaling upset people. And the pictures in the newspapers weren't pretty either. Photos designed to arouse anti-whaling sentiment. Unfortunately it didn't seem to bother the Japanese.

He drank his coffee quietly then munched his toasted sandwich. He should have expected white bread in a country town. It was something he'd have to get used to.

When he paid his bill, he left a city-style tip on the counter.

'No need for that next time,' Sue said. 'I hope to see you a bit regular around here. A place like this can always do with some new blood.'

She pocketed the money and her eyes chased him to the door.

'You should get yourself down to the markets sometime,' she suggested. 'They're on every second Saturday. Lots of people to watch. A bit of local colour. It'll get you away from the Point too. Only birds for company out there.'

Back out in the street Lex peered through the front window of the butchery next door where meat glowed red in tidy arrays beneath the purple flush of fluorescent light. He should buy something for dinner. As he walked in through the plastic doors, a tall man with a shock of blond hair jolted out of the back room holding a bloodied knife in his hand.

'Can I help you with anything?' the man asked.

Lex could hear a dull thwacking sound out the back. There must be another person out there chopping meat.

'I'd like to buy some steaks.' He indicated towards the front window. 'Scotch fillets, please.'

The butcher looked down at the blood on his hands. 'Just a minute. I'll be right with you.'

He ducked back through the rear fly curtain and Lex heard the swish of a running tap and the rollick of a paper towel dispenser being roughly jerked. The butcher came out again and lifted a tray of meat out of the window display.

'How many would you like?' he asked, peeling back the plastic cover from the neat stack of fillets.

'Half a dozen. I'll freeze what I don't use tonight.'

'Meat's better fresh than frozen. No one ever taught you that?'

'Make it two then.'

Lex watched him jiggle out two fillets with big red hands and lay them on a piece of square plastic. He weighed them, then wrapped the meat in paper.

'You passing through?' the butcher asked, as he set the package on the counter.

'No, I've just moved in down at Wallaces Point.'

'Ah.' The man nodded as if he understood everything. 'I'm Beck. Henry Beck'.

A strong hand was offered over the counter. It engulfed Lex's hand, small and slender and city soft. The shake was too fast and jerky.

'Lex Henderson,' he said, dodging the butcher's piercing regard.

He opened his wallet and pulled out a fifty-dollar note. As he handed it over, he noticed a gaunt pale woman behind him. He hadn't heard her come in. She stood meekly with her eyes downcast, and her hands were fidgeting anxiously as if she were afraid of something. When Lex stood aside to allow her to move forward to the counter, her eyes darted nervously to the butcher's face then flickered away.

'I was hoping you might bring home some chops for dinner,' she said, her voice thin and quiet. 'The minister says he might drop around.'

The woman must be the butcher's wife. Lex wondered why she'd stood in line like a customer. He took his change and edged towards the door, but Beck raised an arresting hand in the air.

'One moment, sir,' the butcher said, 'I should introduce you to my wife, Helen. This is Mr Henderson. He's just moved in at Wallaces Point.'

Lex looked into Helen Beck's sharp angular face. She was as tall as him and had an intense gaze. Her eyes were wide with too much white. She offered her hand to him, which he accepted briefly, noticing it was very cold.

'Will we be seeing you at church on Sunday?' she asked.

'Ah, I doubt it,' Lex said. 'I'm expecting visitors.'

It was amazing how easily the lie came. He slipped out the door.

Back at the Point, Lex went onto the beach, trying to lose the tension that had been wriggling under his skin since the visit to town. He'd just settled on a rock ledge to watch the waves when he saw a child skitter onto the sand and walk to the water's edge, scuffing her feet in the waves. She was thin and lanky, maybe five or six years old, and her hair was red and blowing across her face. Behind her dashed a boy. He flung a ball into the shallows, which was fetched immediately by a chunky blue heeler, yapping shrilly. The mother came slowly—a large-framed woman labouring through the sand on flattish feet. She dumped a bag above the high tide mark and followed the children down to the shallow waves. Even from a distance the air was filled with dog-yap and kids' voices and Lex was annoyed at the invasion.

The intruders played for a while, jumping waves and throwing the ball for the dog, then wandered away along the beach towards the lagoon. Their noise flushed the sea eagle from its roosting tree. It took off with heavy wing beats, gradually gaining height above Lex's head. He watched as the bird cruised above the cliffs, circling for several minutes, then drifted out of sight.

Time to go back.

As he stood to hop down off the rock ledge, Lex saw the girl had turned back and was purposefully walking towards him across the beach. He sat down. Two sooty oystercatchers that had been working through the rocks shrilled and flapped into the air, beating off low over the water as the girl began to clamber up towards him. Her face was sharp with concentration and her hair had been stuffed under a soft broad-brimmed hat. Over her blue bathers she wore a loose white shirt that flapped about in the breeze. She had the sort of pale skin that burned, peeled and freckled.

About five metres away from him, she settled on a rock, hands on knees, and stared out to sea. Lex could hear her breathing and see her shoulders hiking slightly from the effort of climbing. She sat still and straight and quiet, watching the waves roll in. Lex wondered when she would move. It seemed unusual for a child to sit still for so long. He looked down to where the sooty oystercatchers had returned to their fossicking.

After a while, the girl stood up without looking at him, climbed back down the rocks and ran along the beach to catch up with her family. Lex watched her go, then stepped down the rocks to the sand and headed home, strangely warmed by those quiet moments of unexpected company.

FOUR

Market day, Callista parked the Kombi along the edge of the grounds where her designated stall number was sprayed on the grass in white paint. Setting up was the bit she hated most—all that bending and lifting and all the other stallholders trying to get a glimpse of her cleavage. Of course they never offered to help, so each week she came early and organised herself before they appeared with their market clutter and their probing eyes.

She was already composedly perched behind her layout of paintings when they arrived, keeping herself preoccupied with a book. Out of the corner of her eye she watched them huff-puffing around and unpacking their wares. As they talked and smoked and bent and lifted, they cast glances her way when they thought she wasn't looking.

She watched the Greeks gesticulating over their second-hand tools. They did all the markets up and down the coast, travelling ridiculous distances to make a dollar. Callista was either too lazy or never that desperate. Sometimes she went to another market half an hour south of Merrigan, but usually she managed to earn enough locally. Merrigan might not be a tourist town, but plenty of passers-by stopped for a look when they saw the market crowd bustling over the oval.

Beside the Greeks, the electrical knick-knack guy was laying out rolls of insulated wire with his sleazy mate, the guitar goof, who strummed endlessly on his guitar as if he'd forgotten how to put it down. It had become his habit to ogle Callista and smile at her flirtatiously. She hated it.

As usual, the church ladies set up their stall at a wary distance from Callista. Mrs Jensen might talk to Callista in her own yard, but she was careful not to associate with her in public. The church crowd knew Callista was an atheist and they disdained her parents' alternative lifestyle. At least they were polite enough to keep their distance rather than talking about her within earshot. As Callista watched them fussing over the ordering of tablecloths and home-baked goods, she saw Helen Beck wave at her over their heads. Of all of them, Helen was the only one who ever took the time to acknowledge her. She was a strange, nervous woman, not particularly adept at making friends but never considered anyone a lost cause when it came to the church. That was why she was always shyly friendly with Callista, ever hopeful that she might save her suffering soul.

It was a shame about her husband, Callista thought. Henry Beck might be a stalwart of the church, but there wasn't much to respect in the way he treated his wife. Nobody commented on it, of course. It wasn't something you could do in a small town. Those who didn't like Henry Beck's condescending way of treating his wife simply kept away from him. Being vegetarian made this easy for Callista, but she figured the church crowd didn't have much choice. Henry Beck was generous with his fundraising barbeques, and even though the locals might be uncomfortable about the way Helen fluttered anxiously around her husband, they accepted him. After all, Callista told herself, smiling, wasn't that the way of the Lord? To love and accept all people?

Callista savoured the right to keep her own company, and at times like this, watching the subtle underlying friction among the church ladies as they shifted and rearranged plates and knitwear on their tables, she was glad she could retreat to her gully to listen to the birds or to distract herself painting. Coming to town was something she saved for necessity.

Painting had long been Callista's main focus in life. She used it as a way of expressing herself, a way of releasing her passion. But over the past year or so she had veered away from serious work, letting the vast landscapes that used to inflame her slip sideways into the sky. Instead, she had kept her hands busy with beach art. Cheap, quick works that she dashed off without engaging her mind. She found it easy to do, using bright colour to please people rather than to challenge them.

She used to produce paintings that stopped people; that made them pause and step back. That made them linger, feeling the play of colour and light. She'd make more money if she worked like that now, but she just couldn't. There was a space inside her that was too dark, and if she went there looking she knew there was no guarantee of coming back. For now, it was best to keep churning out the beach art. It paid the rent and kept her in touch with paints, even if her talent was dormant. And, in truth, it was good for her to spend every second Saturday here, dodging the probing eyes of the guitar goof. The markets were as much about people-watching and socialising as they were about selling goods. And later she might stroll over to the church stall and buy a cake, just to stir things up a bit. At least she still had a sense of humour, even if Mrs Jensen didn't.

Lex woke in the morning to a knock at the door. He must have fallen asleep on the couch, drunk again. Pushing himself up blearily, he saw two small people peering in through the door—the children he had seen on the beach—a boy and a girl, their faces serious and slightly afraid. He swung himself off the couch and pushed open the flywire door.

'Hello,' he said, looking down at them. They were two peas in a pod. The boy was older, maybe about ten. The girl looked thin and frail. They were each clutching a box.

'Would you like to buy some chocolate?' the girl asked.

'It's for our school,' the boy said. 'They're going to use the money to buy more books for the library.'

'Sounds like a good cause. I'll just get some money.'

Lex fetched his wallet and came back to the door.

'Are you a hermit?' the girl asked.

The boy elbowed her. 'Shhh. You're not supposed to ask things like that.'

They stood a moment in awkward silence.

'How much is the chocolate?' Lex asked.

'Three dollars a block,' the boy said. 'You can buy as many as you like.'

'What would I do with all that chocolate?'

The kids looked at him as if he were crazy.

'Eat it,' said the boy.

Lex looked inside his wallet.

'What about the lady next door?' the girl asked.

'What about her? I've never seen her.'

'She's a hermit, for sure.'

'You're a bit hooked on hermits, aren't you?' Lex said.

'We're scared of her,' the girl said. 'We can't go there.'

'How about I buy some chocolate for her as well? Then you won't need to.'

The children looked relieved.

Lex bought four blocks of chocolate. He gave one to each of the children and kept two for himself.

'How did you get here?' he asked. 'I don't see your car.'

'We live up the road,' the girl said. 'We've been watching you on the beach and standing on the cliffs. Mum's worried you're going to jump.'

The boy looked horrified. 'We'd better go,' he said. 'Thanks, mister.'

'My name's Lex.'

'I'm Evan and her name's Sash. She's my sister.'

'Pleased to meet you,' Lex said.

After they'd gone, running barefoot along the grass verge, Lex went into the bathroom and examined himself in the mirror. He was a tall man, broad-shouldered, blue-eyed and a little overweight, although he carried it well for his thirty-eight years. Most men his age were in worse condition. He scuffed his hands over the whiskers on his cheeks. It had been days since he'd shaved and this would definitely be a two-razor job.

He stripped off, tucked a towel around his middle and lathered up. Tensing his lower lip, he took the first careful swipe with the razor just as an unearthly shriek blasted through the bathroom window. The razor jagged his chin and blood trickled. What the hell was that?

Pushing open the window, he saw a peacock strutting along his back porch. Furious, he raced into the kitchen, pulled open a kitchen drawer, scooped up two handfuls of utensils and burst out the back door. The bird flounced across the yard, trailing its tail like a bridal skirt. He flung a handful of serving spoons and a can-opener at it, striking the fence as the bird swept up on top of the palings and looked back at him. As he ran towards the fence where the hedge was lowest, his towel caught under his foot and flipped off. Before he could reach down to grab it, a white-haired craggy face peered over the fence with a frown. It was his neighbour, Mrs Brocklehurst. The hermit.

Her eyebrows shot upwards as she took in his nakedness. For a long moment, he stood there stupidly, unable to speak. Then he whisked up his towel and raced inside.

Back in the bathroom, he finished shaving and cursed. That was just marvellous—getting caught out streaking naked across the back-yard trying to kill his neighbour's peacock. What would she think of him? Still cursing, he pulled on the camouflage pants and green army jumper he'd bought from Beryl. He'd have to come up with a plan, find a way to charm the old dear, get them off on a better footing. He could be living here for a while, and in a place like this Lex didn't fancy an awkward relationship with his neighbour.

Just before he walked out the door, he checked himself once more in the mirror and shook his head. He'd have to drive up the coast soon and get some decent clothes. This army get-up wasn't the best way to make a first impression. Then again, it was more respectable than his birthday suit.

It was late morning when Lex arrived at the markets. He lost himself immediately in the maze of stalls scattered across the oval. At first, he figured there was supposed to be some order to it all, but once he was among the clutter of trestles and tents it was hard to work out where he'd already been.

Most of it was junk. It amazed him that people could scrape a living selling this stuff. Greeks with heavy moustaches stood behind boxes of home-grown vegetables, puffing on their cigars and haggling with their hands. Other stallholders were trying to sell off all sorts of old gear: tools, second-hand mowers, spare parts, hub caps. Some vendors were hidden behind unruly pot plants and buckets of flowers, while other stalls held neatly lined up jams and chutneys and jars of skin-care products on white tablecloths. Among the clutter, there were tables of old books and magazines, second-hand kids' toys and CDs.

Overwhelmed by bodies and jumble, Lex stopped at a poster stall and browsed through the pages of the flick-stand. Nearby, a tarot queen was sitting beneath a tattered purple sunshade, shuffling a worn pack of cards. Just beyond her, two farmers were leaning against a ute, deep in conversation. Passing silver-haired biddies moaned about their aches. Children of all sizes threaded through the crowd, jostling against legs, dragging on prams, whining.

Lex resumed his aimless wandering among the stalls. He bought fairy floss from a hotdog stand, but was disappointed. It wasn't like the stuff he'd bought at the local show when he was a kid. That had been the real thing: pink spidery fly-away stuff, spun like magic onto a wooden stick. He munched through his bag of floss and watched Asian Charlie churning music out of a machine made from an impossible mash of welded pipes that jerked up and down. People were lining up to buy his CDs.

Further into the throng, Lex passed yet another stall of home-baked cakes and knitwear. On one of the trestles he noticed a plate of Anzac biscuits, just like his mother used to make, thin and crispy brown. He jiggled his pocket to find some change and looked up straight into the intense white face of Helen Beck. He must have stumbled onto the church stall.

Helen stared at him without speaking, stared right into him. It was like being X-rayed.

'Hello,' Lex said at last. 'I met you the other day . . . at your husband's butchery . . . remember?'

'Yes,' she said, with a faint shadow of a smile.

'I thought I might buy some of the Anzac biscuits.'

'They're four dollars a bag, and the money goes to the church.'

'Oh . . . good.' What a pathetic response. Lex was annoyed with himself. This woman made him feel so ridiculously nervous.

'Why don't you come up and join our service tomorrow?' Helen said, still holding the bag of biscuits. It seemed she was unwilling to hand them over until she had pressed her invitation on him.

'I'm not much of a church person,' Lex said.

'That doesn't have to matter. We'd make you very welcome.'

Lex shuffled his feet, trying to think of a good excuse.

'The church is good at caring for people,' Helen said. 'You seem sad.'

Lex stepped back. His eyes were fixed on her pale hands, still clutching the biscuits. He remembered how cold they'd been when he first met her.

'Helen.'

The imperious voice came from an adjacent table. Lex turned and saw an old woman with a hook nose glaring at them.

'There are other people over here who need to be served,' the old lady said.

Helen glanced at her, then back at Lex.

'That's Mrs Jensen,' she said quietly. 'She runs our stall.'

Lex handed her some money.

'Helen!' Mrs Jensen again.

'Thanks,' Lex said, taking the bag of biscuits.

'But your change . . .'

'Keep it.'

It was a good opportunity to escape. Helen's eyes made him uncomfortable. He didn't like the feel of them crawling beneath his skin.

She called after him, but he didn't stop. He saw her come out from behind the stall, weaving through the crowd towards him. It'd be best if he just disappeared. Swiftly, he dodged across a few rows of stalls, then slid behind a vegetable stand and a few tents and stopped by a stall crammed with bright beach paintings—starfish, shells, beach sheds, boats, fish. They were racked up on stands and easels and offered protection from view of the market crowd. He'd be safe here for a while. Then he could slip back through the stalls and go home, where Helen Beck couldn't hassle him about coming to church.

Trying to appear like a genuine browser, he looked more closely at the paintings. They were fun. He liked the loud colours, the boldness, the intense blues and yellows and reds. A few times he peered out of the stall to check for Helen Beck, then hid himself again in the small protected gallery created by the paintings. Behind the trestle, the stallholder was watching him closely. She was brown-eyed and brown-haired, with a purple tie-dyed scarf twisted over her head. Her face was round and dimpled, and there was a hint of a smile about her mouth.

'I like your stuff,' Lex said, buying time.

'People seem to like it in their beach houses,' she said. 'But it's bread and butter. Not what you'd call real art.'

'I like it,' Lex said. 'The colours are great.'

The girl shrugged. 'It keeps me off welfare.'

'Is it that bad making a living around here?'

'It's not very lucrative being an artist.'

'You could move to the city. You'd make a fortune in Sydney.'

The girl smiled. 'Why would I want to move to the city when I can live here?'

She was observing him with interest. He could see it in her eyes—gently assessing without being intrusive. It was nice to talk to someone.

'How often do you do these markets?' he asked, wondering if he might see her again.

'Every couple of weeks. Sometimes I take a stall at some other markets further south, on the off week, when there's nothing doing in Merrigan.'

Lex glanced over her paintings again, not sure what to say next. He liked her brown eyes, the warmth about her. There was something appealing about her lack of ambition. He was accustomed to a world where everyone was striving to be something else, to make more money, to accumulate things. Her attitude was different. Simpler.

He flashed a look down the walkway of stalls. And there was Helen Beck. She had seen him and was headed his way. She probably wanted to issue him with another invitation to church. God forbid. Lex didn't want to face it. He tried to squeeze between the girl's table and an easel.

'Excuse me,' he said. 'Do you mind? I need to get through.'

'What?' She looked alarmed, trying to hold the table steady.

'I need to get through,' Lex said.

Glancing behind, he saw that Helen was almost upon them. He pressed past the trestle, catching his foot on the easel and bringing it down. Paintings tumbled everywhere. He should have stopped to help pick them up. But he lurched through the stall, past the girl's orange Kombi parked at the back of the stand, and slipped into the next row.

Immediately he was angry at himself. What an overreaction! What was this paranoia he had about Helen Beck? Was he really so scared of her that he had to create a disaster trying to escape? Embarrassed, he wandered up the row of stalls and threaded his way back around to where he could see Helen and the girl talking. They had already picked up the paintings and placed them in a couple of piles on the table. Lex noticed that the two women were standing some distance apart. It was obvious they weren't completely comfortable with each other. Being local didn't necessarily mean they were friends. He watched them inspect a broken frame together. The girl shook her head and waved Helen's outstretched hand away. Helen must have offered to fix it for her. That ought to be *his* job, given that he'd caused all the damage.

Lex waited until Helen had left then slunk back to the girl's stall. He saw her start when he appeared again and she frowned at him.

'I'm sorry,' he said.

'You could have stopped to help.'

'Yes. I'm really sorry.'

She was fiddling with the broken frame, trying to shove the corners back into position around the painting.

'I could fix that for you,' he offered.

'No, it's okay. I make the frames myself.'

'I can pay for it. I don't mind.'

'Don't worry about it. I'll fix it up at home.' She gave a small smile. 'That was some desperate escape effort,' she said. 'Do you have a problem with Helen Beck?'

Lex shifted uncomfortably and said nothing.

'She gives me the creeps too,' the girl said.

'I should introduce myself,' he said. 'My name's Lex.'

The girl laid the pieces of broken frame aside and was about to introduce herself too when someone else came into the stall and started browsing, a middle-aged woman who asked Lex to move aside so she could see the paintings better.

'I'd better go,' Lex said. 'Are you sure you won't sell me the painting?'

'I'll fix it first. You can pick it up next time.'

'Here's fifty dollars.' Lex put the note on the table.

'That's too much.'

'Call it a damage payment. I've caused you enough trouble today.'

She smiled slightly and turned away as the woman asked to see the other paintings, the ones that had fallen off the easel.

Lex turned and walked away. It was the most alive he had felt in weeks.

FIVE

After the markets, Callista usually went up to Jordi's for a quiet smoke. There was something therapeutic about going bush after the clutter of town and the market crowds. Jordi's place was barely a step above camping, but his hut was dry and he had a warm swag, so it was vaguely liveable even in winter. In spring, he moved outdoors and, instead of cooking over the fire within the old stone chimney that sucked up all the heat in winter, he shifted to a campfire. He had a good camp oven their parents had given him, and a sturdy iron tripod, which he set over the fire to hang the billy on. There was nothing better than tea brewed in Jordi's blackened billy. He had it down to a fine art, knowing exactly when to fling in the handful of tea and remove the billy from the coals.

Callista parked the Kombi just short of the camp and clambered out to the sweet smell of slowly burning wood. A thread of smoke lingered over the camp. Jordi was nowhere to be seen. His clapped-out rusty Landcruiser was just visible further up the hill where the track wound into the higher forest. He might be up there collecting wood. Callista sat down on a sawn log stump away from the drift of the smoke and watched the coals. A lyrebird clacked and chortled across the slope in the tree fern gully. It was higher and wetter here than Callista's coastal gully, so Jordi had birds that she rarely heard.

No wonder he liked it up here. It was all bush except for the patch where the hut stood.

Callista waited a while watching the smoke waft among the eucalypt trunks and up into the crowns, then she gave a loud whistle and flung a coo-ee upslope. There was a sharp whistle in reply. Jordi must be on his way down. Eventually she heard him sniff and spit, and he appeared from behind the hut, his usual raggy, tatty self.

'Hey there.'

He sat down beside her on a log.

'Where have you been?' she asked.

He looked gaunt. She wondered if he'd been eating properly.

'Looking for bower birds. Heard some calling up there this morning.'

When they were kids, the two of them used to search the bush for bowers, crawling on hands and knees through the scrub, following the distinctive calls of the birds until they stumbled across the tiny courtship stage of woven twigs decorated with anything blue the birds could find: bottle tops, drink straws, rosella feathers.

'They'll be fancying up their bower soon,' Jordi was saying. He had already hooked the billy off the fire and tossed in the tea leaves. 'I reckon they'll probably use the old one from last year.'

He poured her a tea in a battered tin mug and they sat quiet for a while. That had been a lot of talk for them. Talk was for town. Up here, they usually just sat together, drinking tea and watching the fire.

Eventually Jordi stood up to fetch his guitar from the hut. Music was always better than talk. It was a comfortable way of just being together, not needing to say anything. He sat down again and picked out a few notes. Callista leaned forward towards the fire and listened, elbows on knees. She loved hearing him play. He came alive, lost his prickliness and that sour look, the disillusionment that alienated him.

Maybe half an hour passed, maybe longer. He stopped playing.

'I met an interesting man today,' she said. 'And I don't know if I'll ever see him again.'

He looked at her, played a few notes quietly.

'Doesn't matter,' he said.

'Yes, it does. I hardly ever meet anyone. I should've asked him out.'

'Was he from 'round here?' Jordi asked.

'Doubt it. There's no one interesting around here. Probably on his way through.'

'City slicker?'

'Maybe.'

'You don't need a city slicker.' His smile was sudden and wry. 'Anyway, you've got me.'

'God help me.'

They laughed.

'What'd he look like?'

Callista was surprised he'd asked. 'What's it to you?'

'Just wondering.'

'Do you think you might have seen him?'

'Dunno, do I . . . if you don't tell me.'

'He was a big guy. Broad shoulders. Smooth face. Walks like a cat.'

Jordi laughed. 'How does a cat walk?'

'I don't know. Smooth, but stealthy, like they're on guard, like they're watching out for something.'

'There's been a big guy coming to the servo.' Jordi stood up and tossed another log on the fire, poked at it with a stick. 'Drives a silver Volvo. Station wagon. Nobody knows anything about him. But he's been a couple of times now. Quiet guy. Hardly says a thing.'

'It might be someone just staying down here.'

'Maybe staying at the Point.'

Callista was annoyed at Jordi for getting her hopes up. 'You don't have enough to think about,' she said. 'What are the chances it'd be the guy Beryl sold the house to?'

'Pretty good, I reckon. He was wearing cams the other day. Looked to me like he'd been shopping at Beryl's. Why would you do that unless you were living 'round here?'

'Do what?'

'Shop at Beryl's. She sells nothing but rubbish.'

'Since when did you care about clothes?'

'Was he wearing cams today? At the market?'

'He was, actually. I watched him for a while. He was hiding in my stall. Hiding from Helen Beck.'

'I'd hide from her too.' Jordi flashed a quick grin. 'Maybe he's not such an idiot after all.'

'He knocked over half my stall trying to escape from her.'

Jordi laughed. 'I like him already.'

Callista sat quiet for a moment, staring into the fire.

'I liked him,' she said. 'I want to see him again . . . What if it *is* him? The guy you've seen at the servo?'

Jordi's beard spread with his smile. 'Then you've gotta think about how to play it. He'll show again. But you have to take it slow. You can't drag a big fish in on a small line. You have to wear him down, so he swims right in to you without knowing.'

Callista looked at him. 'For once that might be good advice.'

Jordi smiled again. 'Just think of the death adder. You need patience for an ambush.'

Callista drove down the mountain, dipping and winding in the shadows of the forest. Down low the vegetation was different again—greener with a thick understorey, and tall eucalypts strung with streamers of bark. The driveway to her parents' house was marked by a cut-off wine barrel full of yellow and purple pansies. She stopped to open the gate and collect the mail.

The driveway was long, and ran through a gully and along a creek before swinging uphill to where the house was nestled in an unexpected splurge of lawn. Her father insisted the green grass was his bushfire insurance. But with the bush hulking right down to the chook pen just behind the house, Callista wondered why he bothered. The house was made of rough wood and corrugated iron, and in a fire it'd go up like a pile of twigs.

She clambered out of the Kombi and slammed the door. There were no cars around, but somebody must be home because all the windows were hooked open. She walked through the cool shadows of the house, tossing the mail onto the table as she passed through the kitchen. Her mother, Cynthia, was out the back digging in the vegie garden, her face shaded beneath a wide straw hat. The slow way she straightened, with her hand propped in the small of her back, reminded Callista that her mother was getting older. These days she couldn't help noticing the deepening creases in her mother's face and the loose skin beginning to fold around her neck.

'Callie, I didn't hear you come in.'

'Are you serious, Mum? The Kombi isn't exactly a stealth machine.'

Cynthia dug her shovel into the dirt and stepped stiffly over the clods of earth. 'I'm turning this patch over and mulching it ready for autumn,' she said, waving an arm over the lumpy brown soil. 'We had tomato worm in this section last year, so I'm letting it lie fallow for a season. But the weeds just keep popping up.'

'Just spray them,' Callista said.

'Poisons! Didn't we teach you anything?' She slung a kind arm around Callista's neck and hugged her. 'How are you?'

'I'm good. Being industrious. You'd like that. I'm doing lots of painting.'

Cynthia raised her eyebrows. 'You're inspired?'

'Just market stuff. But I'll be able to pay you back soon.'

'No hurry. Let's get a cup of tea.'

They sat on the back deck, looking up beyond the chook pen into the forest. The chooks were out pecking and scraping in the garden with their scaly oversize feet. Cynthia poured the tea. It annoyed Callista that she didn't use a strainer, but the tea always tasted fine once you sieved out the bits between your teeth. Her parents had been using this teapot for as long as she could remember.

Callista knew well her parents' beginnings—history was an important thing in their family. It was how you learned not to make the mistakes of the past, and how to walk a better path. Her parents had been big on that: finding ways to erase the wrongdoings of previous generations. Sometimes it was as if they were taking the troubles of the entire world on their shoulders.

Her father had grown up at the Point, going to school in Merrigan and learning in the traditional country way. He went on to study accounting by correspondence so he could have the career his father never had. But there weren't many opportunities locally. He left in his early twenties and moved to a commune just out of Melbourne—turned vegetarian, grew his hair, tended vegetables, did odd jobs on the commune. He liked the cooperative way, working with people towards greater causes, a less intrusive way of living. It was a relief for him to be among people that challenged the old ways, people with new ways of thinking—conservation, living lightly, equality for all.

He met Cynthia in Tasmania, at a demonstration against the flooding of Lake Pedder, and they bonded over a campfire, united by passion and common thinking. When they got married, they did it in the bush, with a small group of friends from the commune, no family. Cynthia was already pregnant with Callista. By then, they'd become convinced the only way to make a difference was at home in your own community. So, after a year, they came to Merrigan and bought a cheap block of land. Cleared country was worth something, but no one wanted bush. They bought the place on the mountain for a song—which was lucky, because that was all they had. Then they got on having their family, living what they believed, touching the earth lightly.

Cynthia passed a mug of tea to Callista. 'How's Jordi?' she asked.

'He's going okay.'

'Do you think so? I often wonder if he's anorexic, he's so thin.'

'He's just wiry,' Callista said. But Cynthia's crumpled brow worried her. Perhaps Jordi was too thin.

'He's had such a hard time,' Cynthia said. She sagged sadly in her chair. 'I've never found it easy to talk to him. It's hard for a mother sometimes, sitting on the outside watching your kids suffer, but not knowing how to find a way in.'

She sat silent for a long time, staring into the bush. Then she turned to Callista.

'He'd talk to you,' she said. 'He trusts you.'

'I can't force him to talk about it, Mum.'

Cynthia said nothing.

'A positive break might help him,' Callista said. 'When's Dad going to start including him in the business?'

Cynthia sighed. 'When Jordi starts showing an interest.'

'Jordi would never ask Dad for support. You know it.'

'And your father won't try to push it on him unless he seems interested.'

'So that's a dead-end idea of mine then.'

'Maybe not. I'll talk to your father about it.'

Cynthia topped up their cups of tea.

'Did you hear about Beryl selling the house?' Callista asked.

Cynthia set down the teapot. 'Is that so?'

'You hadn't heard?'

'No.'

'Everyone in town is talking about it. Everyone's furious.'

'It's what they'd expect of Beryl, isn't it? Has she made any grand donations to the church?'

'Of course not. She'll keep all the money for herself.'

Cynthia sat back in her chair and sipped her tea.

'Aren't you angry?' Callista asked.

'What's the point?'

'The injustice infuriates me.'

'Everyone will learn to live with it in time.'

Callista poured the dregs of her tea on the ground. 'I wish you weren't such a pacifist, Mum. It's no wonder you and Dad never get ahead.' She shook her mug violently to dislodge the last of the tea-leaves. 'And I wish you'd get a tea strainer.'

Cynthia smiled serenely. 'You've been saying that for years.'

In the morning, Callista got on with her work. Mrs Jensen's palings were working out well. Joe Denton from the hardware had let her cut them up with the bandsaw at the store, and she had painted them up and banged them together into frames at home. It all helped to save her a few precious dollars here and there. And she was whizzing off paintings like crazy. There was nothing to it. In fact, it was a bit embarrassing. There was more work in making the frames.

Ridiculously, she was excited about crossing tracks with Lex again. As she worked on the verandah in the dewy damp of morning, she kept thinking about his big shoulders and light-footed walk. There was something about him she liked. There was humour in him, she was sure, yet he seemed so flagged by sadness.

She reckoned there was a good chance he'd come back to collect that painting he'd paid for, and she had to be ready for him next time. What she needed was a way to break through that careful blankness and get his attention. Humming, she propped a board on her easel and started squeezing bright colours onto her palette. Surely the best way for her to reach him was through a painting, something loud and different, something that would leap out at him when he stopped by her stand again.

She began with a slap of blue summer sky and the brilliant yellow-white of sand. Still humming, she stepped back, paintbrush waving like a long finger. She was thinking ahead. Couldn't help herself. Once she got to know him a bit she'd take him to Long Beach. It was her favourite—wild, desolate, remote, windswept. Not a beach for the faint-hearted. That's why she liked it. The loneliness. The wind blasting the sand along and the waves raking angrily at the shore. No one there. The blissful emptiness.

She drifted across to the gully where two restless flycatchers were flitting and skittering high in the trees. It must have been their scissor-grinding call that had distracted her, and the cheeky way they swung their tails about. Callista sighed. Tangents. She was always being kidnapped by them. She looked back to the painting and the idea came to her.

Quickly, she mixed blue-black and whisked the outline of a sooty oystercatcher in flight—solid, chunky, very definite. She painted the bold orange-red eye and the long shanks of its legs tucked backwards beneath its body. The beak she painted agape, like the bird was in mid-call as it flew low over the waves. Time drifted away while she concentrated on bringing the painting to life. More effort than her usual market pieces.

Standing back, she examined the painting, and liked it. It was hardly a masterpiece, dashed off like that in an hour or so, but it was fitting. She liked those thick-kneed legs. The oystercatcher's clunky shape cut through the stereotypic beach colours like a loud clap. If Lex didn't notice it, he'd be half-asleep. Well, no match for an artist anyway.

She left it to dry on the easel and went inside to wash the breakfast dishes.

SIX

In town, having a coffee at Sue's, Lex opened the paper to catch up on the news. It had become a bit of a habit to drop in for a cuppa when he came in to collect the newspapers every few days. Today, whaling was all over the headlines again—it had become a regular issue lately. At home, he'd been reading some of Vic Wallace's old books, and it was an interesting contrast—reading about historic whaling at home and then, in the newspapers, reading about modern whaling and the upcoming annual meeting of the International Whaling Commission.

One of Vic Wallace's books was called *Killers of Eden*. When Lex had first taken it from the shelf, he'd thought it was a murder-mystery, but it was about shore-based whaling in Twofold Bay out from Eden in the late 1800s. The story was about a pod of killer whales that assisted the local whalers over the years. He had been particularly interested in the old black and white photo of George Davidson, the most famous of the Twofold Bay whalers. He looked like a dour and hard old man, tough as nails, as if nothing could scare him. But his wife's face was a tired mask of resignation. The book made the lives of whalers seem heroic, but the wife's face showed there was a cost. It was a hard life, and not a pretty one.

Lex had lingered over a photo of an old whale boat. It was little more than a wooden tub manned by six oarsmen and seemed a meagre weapon against a whale. Yet, according to the book, the whalers slaughtered plenty in a good year, and the killer whales helped them. Old Tom was the best known of the killers. He and his pod assisted the whalers by leading them to a group of whales and then preventing the whales from escaping out to sea. Once the whalers had harpooned and lanced a whale, the killers ate the tongue. Lex had never considered the size of a whale's tongue before, but apparently it was a gourmet meal for a killer.

In another of Vic's books, Lex had read about the Faeroe Islanders of the northern Atlantic. These people held an annual event in which whales were herded into a bay and killed. Sometimes more than a hundred whales were killed at a time, and the photos were disturbing—dozens of row boats in the small bay with speared whales rolling in the water, others trying to escape and hundreds of spectators lining the shores watching the slaughter. These people traditionally killed whales for food and Lex thought he should have found that acceptable. But it made him think of modern whaling, and of the Japanese making excuses to take whales for their so-called research.

Twentieth-century whaling had developed the grenade-tipped harpoon, which was designed to explode once it was fired into a whale's back. The whale was supposed to bleed out internally and die quickly, but the time to death depended on where the harpoon had embedded, and it could still take up to forty-five minutes for a whale to die. This was what Lex disliked about whaling. The killing wasn't humane. And for some reason, this seemed worse in whales than any other animal. Lex wasn't sure why he felt this way.

In the newspapers, there was endless outrage about the Japanese proposal to end the moratorium on commercial whaling. Lex knew, from covering this story on radio in previous years, that the Japanese and other pro-whaling nations would need a two-thirds majority to overturn the moratorium. Over the past few years the Japanese had been buying the votes of other nations, even those that had never attended the meetings before. And each year the vote had been getting closer. As usual, the Japanese were asking to increase their annual research quota of minke whales, and this year they also wanted to add humpbacks.

Once a week on his radio program, Lex used to chat with a zoologist from the University of Sydney. Not your usual kind of academic, this guy had been quite eloquent and had a knack of picking up on issues that concerned the public. Each year, when whaling was in the papers again, they'd talk about whales and the talkback lines would be full of callers. People wanted to vent their anger at the Japanese, and many of them passionately described their encounters with humpbacks migrating along the coast. It seemed everybody who had seen a humpback had been moved by the experience. Everybody, that is, except the Japanese, who still wanted to exercise their right to eat whale meat. Lex discovered, over time, that he was as vehemently anti-whaling as the rest of the Australian public. And so buying the home of an old whaler did not sit well with him and daily he found himself trying to come to terms with it.

'What do you think about whaling?' he asked, when Sue set his coffee on the table. He pointed to the headline in the paper: *Japanese to Take Humpbacks*.

'I don't like it,' she said. 'Whale-watching's an important industry around here.'

'Apparently humpbacks make good steaks.' Lex snorted.

'No, thanks,' Sue said. 'That'd be enough to make me turn vegetarian.'

She turned away to wipe the table beside him.

'Tell me about the whale-watching,' Lex said. 'Who runs the tours around here?'

'Jimmy Wallace.'

'Wallace, did you say? The son of?'

Sue nodded.

Lex shook his head. 'Another Wallace into whales.'

'It's a bit different,' Sue said. 'Jimmy doesn't kill them.'

'Do you think I should go on a trip?'

'That's up to you.' Sue finished wiping the table and was heading back to the kitchen.

'What about my neighbour?' Lex asked. 'Do you think she'd be into it?'

'Mrs Brocklehurst?' Sue shrugged. 'I don't know. You'll have to ask her.'

'I hardly ever see her.'

'No, she keeps pretty much to herself. But you might see her son Frank around. He comes up every week or so to mow the lawns for her.'

'I hope I didn't scare her off,' Lex said, half to himself.

Sue raised her eyebrows. 'Trying to kill the peacock?'

Her eyes twinkled and she disappeared into the kitchen. So the locals were talking about him. He ought to have known.

When Sue came back to set the table she'd just cleaned, he resumed the conversation.

'Why is Mrs Brocklehurst so antisocial?'

'Did I say she was antisocial?'

'Not exactly. But Beryl said she was a bit prickly too.'

'Ah, but that's a different issue.' Sue laid out knives, forks and napkins. 'Mrs B and Beryl don't see eye to eye.'

'Why's that?'

Sue hesitated. 'I don't suppose there's any harm telling you . . . I guess you'll find out sooner or later anyway . . .'

Lex nodded to encourage her.

'Mrs B wasn't very happy about it when Beryl got together with the old man. It wasn't Beryl's place elbowing in on Vic like that. It disturbed the natural order of things.'

Lex wondered about the natural order. Was Sue saying that Mrs B had some right over Vic Wallace? He decided to change the subject. Sue was obviously uncomfortable.

'Do you go to church?' he asked.

'No. Not me.'

'That's a relief. I was thinking everyone was into the church around here.'

Sue gave a small smile.

'Helen Beck's been on to me at every opportunity. I can't seem to convince her that my soul's past saving.'

Sue's face widened into a real smile. 'Either you're with them or you're not,' she said. 'Town's pretty much divided down the middle into those who go to church and those who don't.'

'Her husband's a strange man.'

'Yes.' Sue was short. 'But he's a good butcher.'

Lex finished his coffee and pushed out his chair, scooping up his newspapers as he stood.

'I should get out of your way,' he said. 'Let you clean up. I'll see you next time.'

Lex hadn't been home long when he heard voices outside. It was Sash and Evan, and their mum, and the dog. He didn't really feel like company, but they were all smiles, with a cake on a plate, and there was no choice other than to invite them in.

Sash and Evan bounded in and sat on the couch while their mother placed the cake on the coffee table.

'I'm Sally,' she said, shy and uncertain. She was sweating from the effort of walking.

'Lex.'

'It's nice to meet you. Sash said you wouldn't mind visitors. She's been at me to bake a cake for days. And thank you so much for donating to their library fundraiser. That was so kind of you.'

Lex arranged a polite smile on his face. His space felt severely invaded with all three of them sitting there looking at him so expectantly. He retreated to the kitchen to fill the kettle.

'We don't get many invitations to afternoon tea,' Sally was saying. 'In fact, we don't get out that much, what with me being a single mother and all, with two kids.'

There, the cards were on the table. She looked at him, appallingly hopeful.

'Tea or coffee?' Lex mumbled, dodging her eyes.

'Do you have any juice?' Sash asked, standing up on the couch then diving down again out of sight as her mother frowned at her.

'There's plenty of milk,' Lex said. 'Would you mind giving me a hand, Sash?'

Sash skipped into the kitchen and Lex thought of Isabel. He felt his heart twist.

Together, they poured milk into two plastic cups, which Sash carried carefully to the coffee table. She cantered back to fetch the plates. While Evan studied the whale-boat photos on the wall, Sally rocked herself out of her chair to bend over the cake and slice it with the knife Lex had laid on the table. She passed a plate to Lex, then to Sash and Evan, and sat down breathlessly. With her in it, the room felt small and awkward.

The children devoured their cake and then bounced out of their chairs to explore the room and the rest of the house.

'Lex,' called Evan, 'you've got a double bed in your room.'

As if he didn't know it.

'Lex.' This time it was Sash. 'There's a peacock in your backyard.'

'Run outside and chase it away,' he yelled back. 'It belongs next door.'

Better the child chase the bird than him, after last time.

'There's a map of the world in your toilet, Lex.' Evan again.

'And ten toilet rolls. I counted them. That's a lot of toilet rolls.' Sash, sounding very excited.

Sally smiled apologetically between sips of tea. 'They're very young and enthusiastic. I can't remember when I had that much energy. Can you?'

Time had never moved so slowly. Sally smiled brightly at him, saying little, while the kids dashed around the house on a discovery mission. Eventually Sash came back and seated herself on his lap, as if she had always sat there. She didn't seem to notice Lex stiffen with discomfort.

'I like it here,' she said. 'It feels nice, and you have good things. Can we come again?'

'It *is* a nice house,' Sally said, hitching a ride on Sash's conversation. 'How do you feel about living here?'

'I'm not sure what you mean,' Lex said.

'Oh, don't you know about all the trouble this house caused?' Sally looked uneasy. 'There was quite an uproar over this place when the old man died. He left it to Beryl, but it should have gone to his family. Split the town, it did, Beryl getting the house.'

Lex was quiet a moment. The real estate agent had told him nothing, and perhaps that was just as well. It wasn't a comfortable feeling, knowing he was sitting on a disputed estate. The atmosphere in the room was awkward: Lex contemplating Sally's revelation and Sally wishing she hadn't told him.

'Let's go for a run on the beach,' Lex suggested. Anything to get them out of the house.

The kids rushed out the door.

'Can Rusty come too?' Sash looked up at him.

'I assume that's the dog,' Lex said.

As they walked down through the heath, Lex noticed Sally smiling with relief, as if some invisible hurdle of acceptance had been passed.

He wished she had also noticed that he was cornered.

Lex wasn't sure whether she forgot the platter on purpose, but the next day Sally was on his doorstep to collect it. She surprised him in his board shorts, bare-chested with a towel slung across his shoulders, about to head to the beach. There was interest and approval in her eyes, and here he was again, trying to find a way to escape.

'I'm going for a swim,' he said, handing over the platter and trying to encourage her back out the door.

She was uncomfortably close and he was uncomfortably exposed.

Her eyes were licking at his shoulders and the sprinkle of hairs on his chest.

'I think I'll come down with you. The kids are at school and I have a bit of spare time on my hands.'

On the way out the door, Lex grabbed the camouflage pants and a T-shirt from off the floor and slung them over his arm. He would put them on when he got out of the surf to keep those prying eyes away from his skin. He almost expected her to reach for his hand while they were walking down through the heath where New Holland honeyeaters were darting low and skittish among the banksia cones. He opened the towel out and hugged it defensively around his shoulders like a robe.

'Sorry if the kids took over a bit yesterday,' Sally said. 'They're so excited about having someone new living in the street. And you've been so kind to them.'

And now I want to run, Lex thought, but he nodded quietly and upped the pace. He couldn't wait to escape into the waves. 'I like kids,' he said.

Before Isabel, he hadn't had time or tolerance for children. But after Isabel was born and then lost, he learned how precious children were. He learned how fragile the thread is that binds them to the earth. How they can stop breathing and disappear like vapour.

'They really miss their father,' Sally said. 'It's hard for them not having a man in their lives.'

'Yes, it must be.'

Sally looked at him. She opened her mouth to say something, but Lex cut her short, before she led them into trouble.

'I've gotta run. Getting cold. Better plunge in quick or I'll change my mind—about the swim.'

He sprinted off barefoot over the grass.

Down on the beach, he spiked straight into the water and dived beneath the peaking waves. Luckily it was a calm day and just beyond the breakers he bobbed up and down in the chill water for as long as he could, periodically checking the shore, hoping Sally would leave. But she stayed there, sitting on his towel on the sand, hunched over and hugging her wide knees. She was in for the long haul and soon he'd have to go back. He swam until the cold started to seep into his bones and dull his muscles then went slowly ashore.

She watched him come up the beach, and there was nothing for him to cover himself with until she shifted her bulk off his towel and tossed it up to him. He quickly whisked the towel across his shoulders and wrapped it snugly around him. She never shifted her eyes from him. He figured it was a long time since she had seen a man's body so revealed and she was unembarrassed about studying him. He was glad he wasn't wearing Speedos.

'You're a good-looking man,' she said, unabashed. 'They're a rarity around here. You must be from the city.'

Lex wiped the dripping salt water from his nose and frisked a hand over his head, flicking more water to the sand.

'Yes,' he said. 'City born and bred.'

'Making a sea change, eh? It never lasts for long. There's not enough to keep city folk entertained here in the country. People come here and rot, it's so quiet.'

Lex frowned.

'The only way you'll stay is if you marry a local. And then you'll be trapped. You can't take country folk into the city either, you see. They can't stand the fakeness—it's a pretender's way of life. So you'll have to stay here . . . if you marry a local.'

'I wasn't planning on getting married.'

'No,' she said. 'Men never do.'

He glanced away and she pushed herself awkwardly to her feet.

'I'd best be getting back,' she said. 'I'll go and wash that plate.'

She looked at him sadly for a long moment then lumbered away across the sand.

SEVEN

As Lex came up from the beach he saw a small white car angled on the grass outside his house. He also saw the shape of a woman, hands on hips, legs firmly astride, standing on the deck. He kept walking along the grass track to the road, curious and surprised, until he recognised the woman and saw the defiance in her stance. His stride strangled and his heart knocked and emotion swamped him so suddenly he was bruised by it.

Jilly. What was she doing here? He didn't need this. But his heart rolled with hope.

As he walked across the heath to meet her he noticed she had about her the sharpness and rush of a city person. There was an efficiency and tautness in her stance that he had forgotten. By the primping of her left hand, he could tell she was annoyed by the energetic lick of the wind at her tightly constrained hair. There was a wild moment when his feet tingled to spin and flee through the grass back to the beach. If he did, he knew he would rabbit into the waves and swim out as far as he could go. Straight into the blue and the beginning whitecaps ticked up by the afternoon breeze. But he went on.

At first there was a thick silence as he stood at the base of the steps with the yellow grasses tickling his ankles, looking up at her and feeling nothing but emptiness. He realised he was looking for something in her face that wasn't there. She didn't connect with him at all. Her whole body was wired tight with nerves and anger, and it was hard for him not to cry. The hope he had summoned as he walked back up the path to the house slumped to vague curiosity. On recent form, he expected her to blast him, hammer him to a pulp. He braced himself for it. But she stood taut on the deck, saying nothing.

Not knowing what else to do, Lex stepped up and hugged her, wrapping his arms around the thin entirety of her, holding her close, waiting for a response. In the space between them there was nothing that he could grip on to. He was expecting emotion and familiarity, but her body and smell seemed foreign, like she was a stranger. Yet somewhere in the tight space of angles and awkwardness, history invaded the hug, but it brought no warmth. It was heavy and immensely sad. Lex held on to her as if he were sinking, then she pulled away and he opened the door for her. While he made tea in the kitchen, she stayed near the windows, stiffly watching him.

She was dressed in smart beige shorts and a burnt-orange singlet top that sank low at the neckline and hugged her breasts so that he could see the faint crease between them. So, she wanted to scarify him and raise blood from the past. Lex's hands shook so much the cup clattered as he placed it on the coffee table. He retreated to the couch on the other side of the room, his back to the wall.

The way Jilly scanned the room Lex knew she was searching for evidence of another woman—perhaps a sunhat, sunglasses, a pair of thongs, a T-shirt thrown over the back of a chair. She'd be disappointed that everything was so male and solitary. A half-empty cup of coffee was sitting on the table. A pair of shorts was discarded in the middle of the floor, and a towel slung on a chair. He'd left a paperback forked open on the couch, a stack of playing cards on the table, and a pile of dirty dishes in the sink. There was nothing that she could accuse him of.

Seeing her close, he was surprised by the pointiness of her nose. He had forgotten how she plucked her eyebrows too thin so that they seemed like startled birds in flight. There was an austere severity in the way she had dragged her hair back into a ponytail. Growing her fringe out had also given her a sharper look.

'What *is* this place?' she asked finally.

'It's my retreat,' Lex said.

'I mean, what *sort* of place is this? Who would live out here? There's nothing to do.'

'There's plenty to do. It's very cleansing.'

'You're fooling yourself, Lex.'

'I've been doing lots of reading. See here,' he said, moving to the bookshelves. 'There are all these books on whaling.'

'Since when have you been interested in whaling?'

'I used to cover it on radio every year. Don't you remember?'

'No. I didn't listen to all your programs, Lex.'

'I've been getting up to speed on the history of the industry. And I can't see any rationale in the whole thing. Have you been following the arguments between the Japanese and the anti-whaling nations going to the IWC?'

'What the fuck is the IWC?'

Jilly looked incredulous. This was not going well.

'The International Whaling Commission,' he explained. God, he sounded so pathetic.

'Lex, I didn't come here for a lecture on whaling.'

Jilly started pacing around the room. She was waving her hands now and Lex knew it was over before it had even started.

'Why are you here then?' he asked.

'Your mother told me where you were. She said you wanted to see me. Though God knows why. I can't see there's anything we can achieve by this. Other than to get proceedings started.'

Lex crumpled. She hadn't come of her own volition after all. 'Mum set this up then,' he said. 'She wants us to get back together.'

Jilly looked at him without affection.

'We could at least talk,' he suggested.

'There's nothing to talk about.'

She was looking around the house again, walking down the hallway to peer into the bedrooms. Lex didn't follow her.

'This house, Lex. What is it? A holiday house? I mean, it's not even your style.'

'What is my style, Jilly?'

She laughed flippantly. 'Not this anyway. This is hick. You're more sophisticated than this.' She laughed again. 'Come on then. Talk. What is it you want to say to me?'

Lex was tongue-tied. How did he start in on all of that?

'Oh God.' Jilly was impatient. 'Don't be pathetic. Your job is words. You're good at them.'

She opened the pantry and looked down at the bottles of wine and whisky.

'So, you're drinking.' Her voice was a sneer.

'From time to time.'

She was going to hook right in, telling him what to do again. He'd already forgotten what it had been like . . . Jilly turning into a shrew after Isabel died . . . the endless barrage of complaints about his faults. Her nagging was part of what had driven him down here.

'This doesn't look like the stash of a casual drinker.' She shut the pantry door.

'You don't have to be the moral police.'

The look she cast over him was derogatory. 'You're my husband, for Christ's sake. And you're falling apart. No wonder I couldn't live with this.'

She sat down on the couch and pulled a packet of cigarettes out of her handbag.

'What's this?' Lex asked. 'You don't smoke.'

'You weren't an alcoholic either.'

'I'm not an alcoholic.'

'Borderline, if you ask me.'

'I'm not asking you.'

'What *are* you asking me then?'

'To try again. Let's get some counselling. Try to work it through. There's got to be something left.'

She stood up and exhaled. Lex watched the smoke snaking up from her mouth. It looked so foreign. She turned to him and her eyes were empty.

'Aren't we a bit past that?' she said.

'We have nearly five years of history. Surely that's worth something.'

Jilly considered for a moment. 'I think it's best we leave ourselves some dignity,' she said. 'Leave our past undissected. We'll only pull apart what we had.'

'Haven't we already pulled it apart?'

'At least we still have some good memories from before Isabel died.' Jilly put the cigarette to her lips and sucked in deeply. 'That's when we were our best.'

'We could try to build on that.'

'I don't think so.'

She paused and watched the sea rolling in. Lex felt despair congeal in his chest.

'I think we should talk about a settlement,' she said.

'I'm not ready for that.'

'Think about when you will be. We need to get this over and get on with our lives.'

'What if I still love you?' he asked.

Jilly stared at him briefly then went into the kitchen and stubbed out her cigarette in the sink. She came back and sat down. Then she spoke without looking at him.

'Every time I look at you, I see Isabel,' she said. 'I can't live with that.'

'You could use that to remember her.'

'No,' she said. 'I need to forget. I fall apart remembering. Don't you see? I can't remember her until later, when I'm stronger.'

'I can wait till then.'

'Lex, it's going to take years.'

'Isn't marriage supposed to be for life?'

'Well, I'm sorry. I can't live each day beside you wondering if it might have been different if you'd checked her just a little bit earlier, before I woke up.'

'We couldn't have known she was going to die.'

Jilly was crying now and her voice became louder. 'It can happen to anyone, anytime. We should have been more vigilant.'

'The paramedics said we couldn't have done anything more.'

'They were just being nice,' Jilly yelled. 'Can't you see that? We should have checked her more often. We should have had a baby monitor.'

Lex was ragged with grief. 'We couldn't listen to her every breath.'

Jilly's breathing was loud and she stood up slowly. 'I'm sorry, Lex.'

She opened the door and stepped out on the deck, pausing a moment to look out, as Lex did every time he left the house.

'I dropped some papers in your letterbox,' she said. 'Try to be reasonable. I know it's going to be hard for you.'

Then she walked down the steps and went to the car without looking back.

'It wasn't my fault,' he breathed. But even as he said it, he wasn't quite sure he believed it.

He watched her reverse out, swing the car in the gravel and drive away. As he turned back to the house, he thought he saw something move on his neighbour's verandah. A shadow shifting in the dark. Then nothing. Perhaps Mrs Brocklehurst had been listening. Perhaps she was watching him. Perhaps she'd heard everything Jilly had to say. Not caring, he went inside to pour his first big whisky for the day. It wouldn't be his last.

Lex had met Jilly five years ago, at a quiz night where he was the visiting media personality. Those sorts of affairs bored him, but being a drawcard and entertainer at community fundraisers was part of his job as a radio presenter. They always asked for him because he was good at making people laugh and feel comfortable. He'd learned it from the studio, teasing stories out of people, shuffling time through pleasantly, keeping listeners tuned in.

That night at the quiz, Jilly was on the same table as some friends of his. He noticed her straightaway. She seemed bored, as if she'd come against her will to make up team numbers. While everyone talked and drank, Jilly sat preoccupied with her mobile phone and a work document, emerging every now and then to contribute the odd answer.

Lex tried to talk to her, but she managed only a faint smile in response and pointedly continued talking to the woman beside her, closing him out with body language. He was miffed, being unfamiliar with rejection. In between short stints at the microphone, he sat and studied her—the sharp lines of her face, the blunt cut of her short hair, the paleness of her skin, her erect poise. She looked back at him with round eyes that showed her annoyance. Her lips were tight and her eyebrows arched upwards.

'Why are you watching me?' she asked him, when they were alone.

'I'd like to take you to dinner,' he said, watching her eyebrows skate higher on her white forehead up beneath her straight fringe.

'And ravish me no doubt.' She sounded bored. 'I've heard about you and your attitude to women.'

He laughed to hide his shock. He cut his voice low and deep and gave it his best shot. 'Why don't you give it a go?'

'What would make *me* any different?'

'Take a chance.'

'Sorry. I'm very busy at the moment.'

'Do you have a boyfriend?'

'Persistent, aren't you?'

'Well, do you?'

'No. And I'm not looking for one.'

'I can be nice.'

'Look, I'm sorry, but I don't think so.'

Lex was called to the microphone then, and she left shortly after. He saw her scoop up her tiny sequined handbag and stride away, neatly tucked into her fitted black suit, her legs flashing at him, long and slender on elegant black shoes.

That was it. He had to have her after that. The challenge was too great to walk away from. And she entranced him. She was different. All the other women were like autumn leaves in comparison. Jilly was strong, sharp and shrewd. She wasn't going to be hoodwinked by charm. He was going to have to fight to win her. He was going to have to change.

And he did. It took months. He cut all the other women from his life, cleaned up his drinking, and followed her doggedly, asking her out time and again. She magnetised him with her indifference and aloofness, evading him, side-stepping politely around him. Until, finally, she allowed him to love her—and the relief was so immense that he lost himself in her completely.

And then there had been Isabel.

The next day was piercingly bright and sunny. Lex sat hunched over his coffee cup counting off the days since he had arrived here. Seven weeks at Wallaces Point and his recovery was going nowhere. He stared out, unable to peel his eyes from the glittering face of the sea. Jilly's visit had stripped him again, and he was having one of those days when he could only contact the dark side of himself—black memories stretching all the way back to boyhood, with no sunlight in between. There was only emptiness yawning from within him, rising like a black swamp, sucking at him. Everything was too hard alone.

His mother was right. He couldn't do life without Jilly. He needed her to lead him back home. But that wouldn't happen now, no matter how much he wanted it. He had read the letter she'd left for him, and the list of their possessions. She was asking him to mark what he wanted, requesting that he try to be fair and only ask for half in value. She had even included a list of estimated prices alongside all the objects in their life. It had shocked him. Was this how it had to end? With a list of their accumulated belongings? Was that the sum total of their lives together? If that was it, she could keep the lot. He didn't want any of it.

He stood up to fetch a bottle of wine and paused to look out the window at the steady roll of waves. The sun flashed blindingly silver off the surface of the sea, making him squint. It was too bright inside, too light, too warm. This place was too much of everything.

He went to turn away then stopped. There was something out there. He shielded his eyes with a hand and squinted again, trying to see through the glare.

As he leaned forward to the light, peering through the smeary windows smudged by salt and spring storms, a long white knobbled flipper lurched above the swell about two hundred metres off the Point. His heart jolted. Out there in the blue the flipper flashed again, black and white, glinting silver. It waved lazily from the water then slapped down with a splash that was visible even from this distance. Lex couldn't believe it. There was a whale out there.

The flipper raised and waved, crashed into the water and lofted up again. Lex found himself straining to hear the splashes, ridiculous though it was with the space of busy sea between them. He snatched his hat off the chair by the door, took the steps off the deck by threes, and ran barefoot through the slip of grasses and across the warm tarmac to the cliff edge.

Straining against the light, he waited for the flipper to sail again, and was crazily excited that it seemed closer, close enough to clearly see the knobbles along its rim and the flash of white beneath, to almost feel the slap of it smashing the water, the spray flying into the air. He found he was holding his breath, waiting for the whale to appear again, waiting for some other sign.

When the whale rolled, raised its tail fluke from the glistening waters and slapped it down with a tremendous splash, Lex was gasping and nattering aloud like a boy. He laughed and sang into the warm up-breeze, a surprised surge of excitement tingling through him. When a puff of spray shot into the air amidst the waves, he whooped and hooted.

A whale's exhaled breath.

He didn't drink any wine that day.

EIGHT

A week after Jilly's visit, Lex's mother, Margaret, arrived at the Point. It was late afternoon, and he was down on the beach when he saw her car up near the house. Occasional whale sightings over the past few days had interrupted his melancholy over Jilly, but today had been a bad day and he was on his third bottle of wine and in no state to entertain. He hadn't even showered.

He tossed the bottle up above the high tide mark, to collect later, and splashed into the water to wash his face. Margaret was on the deck when he came up from the heath.

'So, is this it?' she called. 'Am I at the right house?'

'This is it,' he said. 'Go on in out of the wind. I'll bring your bags in.'

By the look on her face he knew it was going to be a difficult visit. She had obviously come with an agenda. He could depend on his mother for that much. She never did anything without a self-fulfilling purpose.

Inside, she gave him a crisp motherly hug. She was a tall woman, quite robust of build, but she was shrinking as she aged and didn't look nearly as formidable as she had when he was a boy. There was that brusque way she had of appearing to judge everything around her all the time. Lex could tell immediately that she didn't like the place. She pulled her sunglasses off her nose and put them on the coffee table.

'Quite a location, darling,' she said, peering around the lounge room. 'But it's a dreadful road. You'll have to get the local council to do something about that. I thought my car was going to shake to pieces.'

'Welcome, Mum. I'm glad you've come. Cup of tea first, or would you like to see your bedroom?' He was amazed how sober he felt.

'I suppose you'd better show me around the house. You can't really be thinking of staying here for long though, darling. I mean, this really *is* the end of the road. The house is so hot, and it's only spring. Don't you have any fans?'

'The onshore breeze is my fan, Mum. It comes most nights.'

'Let's hope it comes soon.'

Lex led her down the corridor. 'You can have this room next to mine. It's got a great view. You might even consider sleeping with the curtains open. There'll be a moon tonight and you'll be able to see the waves rolling in.'

'I wouldn't dream of it,' she said. 'Some Peeping Tom might look in on me.'

Lex put her suitcase on the bed. 'As you said, Mum, this is the end of the road. No one comes here.'

He made a pot of tea and sat down on the couch while his mother settled into her room and rearranged her image in the bathroom. It seemed to take forever. He had forgotten her mortgage on the bathroom in the mornings at home, and how the rest of the family had to organise themselves around her and shower at night when the bathroom was free. Except for those nights when she had been out with a lover and had to 'refresh' before she slipped into bed with their father, both of them pretending nothing had happened.

'Mum, you don't have to go to any trouble,' he called out. 'It's only me.'

'Darling, I couldn't live with myself if I looked like a hag.' She came into the room carrying a *Vogue Living* magazine.

'Old age is going to hit you hard.'

'I intend to age gracefully. There are plenty of plastic surgeons around these days.'

'Don't tell me, you've booked in for a facelift.'

'Not yet, but I'm considering it.' She looked down on him with distaste. 'You look like you could use a shower, darling. Or are you saving water? I saw the signs about the water restrictions as I was driving down here.'

'I'll have a shower. Just for you.'

She sat on the couch against the side wall, back to the sea, and flicked through her magazine. 'I brought this with me because I figured they wouldn't sell any worthwhile magazines in the local newsagency.'

'You'd be surprised.'

'Yes, I would be. I can't believe you're living here, Lex. This is so out of character for you. So below you. I mean, really, this place is just a holiday shack. Surely you miss your lovely house back home. You and Jilly did such a good job on it.'

'It was all Jilly. She was the one with taste.'

'Men always rely on women for taste. It's only natural.'

'Thanks.'

'Oh darling, don't take offence. Of course you have good taste. It's just that there's something about a woman's touch, isn't there, in making a house feel like a home.' She was looking at him over her bifocals. 'Darling, you really should take that shower. You look a wreck. The rural life is not treating you well. Looks like you've been drinking too.'

'Can we get into this later?' Lex ran a hand through his greasy hair. 'You've barely walked through the door.'

He heard running feet on the stairs and Sash burst in.

'I knew you had a visitor,' she said, puffing. 'I ran all the way from the house.' She stared at his mother.

'Sash, this is my mother. She's come down from Sydney to see me.'

He saw his mother frowning down her nose at Sash. Her eyebrows were question marks.

'Shouldn't you be home helping your mother?' Margaret asked.

'Mum told us to get out of the house.'

'Well, there isn't room for you here.' Margaret set her magazine down. 'I've just arrived and I haven't seen my son for weeks. Lex can play with you another time.'

Sash nodded and turned quietly out the door.

'Thank goodness for that,' Margaret said when she was gone.

'You could have been a bit kinder,' Lex said.

'I haven't the patience for children any more . . . Although, if you had another one, of course that would be different.'

His mother had never been good with children. God knows, she had been a shocking mother. He and his sister had brought themselves up, with his father being barely functional most of the time. It wasn't until Lex was a teenager that he understood why his father sat alone with a bottle so much and hardly engaged. The only time he lit up was when Margaret was around, and then he was like a clown show, stumbling over himself to be interesting. Of course, he was always in competition with the latest lover. Always the boring husband. Never quite good enough. He was such a small, weak man. Later Lex understood that Margaret had made him that way. Before Margaret, his father might have been different.

Lex grew up determined not to be like his father. But then for many years he was just like his mother—womanising, juggling multiple partners secretly. It was the trap of his childhood: a fear of attachment, a fear of giving in, lest he became his father. Trying to stay above it, he focused on the challenge of the conquest, gathering about him a treasure chest of charms. But when a woman got that look in her eye, that gleam of devotion, it struck a chill in him and he would run again, chasing himself into another relationship, another bed, another body. His life was going to be like that over and over, until Jilly stopped him.

Margaret adored Jilly, of course. She was a fine match for his mother—someone Margaret couldn't stomp on. Jilly was too assertive for that. And Margaret admired Jilly's flair, her eye for fashion and design. Jilly kept Lex in smart clothes and made sure his image lived up to his public persona. It wasn't something Lex cared about all that much, although he'd been happy to finance it if it kept Jilly happy. Yes, Margaret must miss Jilly and her strong, decisive ways.

It wasn't until they were well into their second bottle of wine that evening that Margaret started in on him.

'Darling, you really must tell all. I just can't bear not knowing what you've been up to.'

The face she turned on him was demure and persuasive. It could have been the expression she used for her lovers when she wanted to know something. It sickened him.

'There's so little to tell.' Lex evaded her by filling their wine glasses.

'There must be plenty to tell. You've been here nearly two months now.'

She smiled and patted his hand. He should have guessed that she had planned out her tactics.

'What's going on?' she asked. Her tone had shifted to the inquisitive.

'Nothing.'

'Well then, how long are you going to stay here?'

'I don't know.'

'Darling, I understand you need a break from all that went on. But when you get it out of your system, you could try again with Jilly. Perhaps you could have another child. I know Jilly wants you back.'

'Mum, when you sent Jilly down here, she made it very clear she wanted nothing more to do with me. She talked about settlements, not second chances.'

His mother's face hardened. 'She's lost respect for you, has she?'

Lex topped up his glass so he wouldn't have to keep looking at her. His mother could be so cruel.

'Well,' she huffed. 'All I can say is it's a shame you didn't make better use of her visit. It took me a lot of effort to persuade her to come down here to see you. It looks like I wasted my time.'

'I'm not coming back yet, Mum.'

Margaret raised her eyebrows. 'You've more to do down here, have you? More drinking? More playing with other people's children?'

Lex attempted to ignore the dig. 'I thought I might get a job.'

'A job!' Her voice was shrill. 'I didn't know they had any openings down here for journalists.'

'I'm sure they don't. I'll do something else.'

'Like what?'

'I don't know. I might work on a farm or something.'

'What!' Margaret stood up, furious, and then sat down. 'Oh, just pour me another glass of wine. I'm too drunk to drive home so I might as well get smashed. My highly educated son's going to get a hick job on a farm.'

Lex topped up her glass. 'It'll be okay, Mum. I just need a bit more time.'

In the morning, he packed her into her car and watched her drive away. There was more than the usual distance between them and they both knew she wouldn't be visiting again soon.

In Merrigan the next morning, collecting his newspapers, Lex asked the newsagent, John Watson, where he could buy binoculars. It was a long shot. He would probably have to drive up the coast to a larger town.

'Sam Black might have some down at his tackle shop,' the newsagent grunted.

'There's a tackle shop in town?'

'You're obviously not a fisherman.'

'Not yet.'

John Watson didn't smile. 'It's behind the supermarket, 'round the back near the loading bay. If he can't help you, he'll know where to send you.'

Lex walked down the street, around the dog-leg corner and skirted the car park to the west of the supermarket. The tackle shop was a ramshackle old store tucked behind the garbage hoppers. No wonder he hadn't seen it before. As he opened the door and let himself in, a plastic frog at floor level croaked.

It was dingy inside. Fishing rods of varying sizes poked out of a wooden rack along one wall and a long wooden counter ran along the other. A big white freezer by the window was crammed with packets of frozen bait. Leaning up against the counter, a young bearded shaggy-looking man was examining a fishing reel with a short wizened fellow that Lex assumed must be Sam Black. Both men turned to look at him briefly without smiling then turned back to the reel. Lex pretended to examine the fishing rods for a while before approaching the counter.

'What can I do for you?' Sam Black asked. His voice was raspy and his glance was aimed at Lex without quite connecting, so it seemed like he was talking to someone else in the room. Lex hesitated.

The other guy sniffed loudly and hawked to clear his throat. 'You deaf or something? Sam asked you what he could do for you.'

'Sorry,' Lex said. He tried not to flush with annoyance. 'I'm looking for some binoculars.'

Sam pushed his glasses up the bridge of his nose, mumbled something and doddered towards the back of the store.

'He's just seeing if he's got some,' the young man said, fiddling with the reel.

His skinny bum was half hanging out of an old pair of loose faded jeans and his back was thin and slabby. Lex could see the bones of his shoulder blades poking through the thin material of his faded shirt. His hair was long and scraggly and he smelled smoky and unwashed.

'You new round here?' the guy asked, squinting at him. He leaned forward to get a closer look at Lex's face. 'I've seen you before. You drive a Volvo, don't you? I've seen you down at the servo. Pumped your petrol for you.'

Lex remembered now the young barefooted man at the local service station grimly pumping the petrol without saying a word. Lex had tried to nod and smile at him, but the guy had avoided eye contact.

'I've just bought the house at the Point,' Lex said.

'Ah,' the scrawny guy said, scratching at his leg. 'The Wallaces place.'

There it was again. The implication that the house shouldn't be his. Lex was beginning to feel irritated by it. Pity he hadn't met any of these Wallaces so he could set them straight. The house had been fairly purchased. He shouldn't have to feel guilty about it. Lex shifted his weight, hoping Sam Black would return soon from the depths of his storeroom. This guy was smelly and kept examining him like he was a flea. The less time he had to spend standing near him, the better.

'Sam, I'll come back tomorrow,' the scraggly guy yelled. He coughed up a glob of spit and swallowed it back down again. 'Gotta get back to work.' Scooping his reel off the counter, he took a wide berth around Lex and sloped out the door.

Sam Black scuffed back to the counter carrying three cardboard boxes.

'Who was that?' Lex asked. 'Looks like he could use a good wash.'

Sam grunted. 'That's Jordi. Don't mind him. He's not too bad. Just lives a bit rough.'

Sam squinted down at the three boxes he had placed on the counter and Lex felt dismay thicken. He'd hoped this old man might chat with him, but that appeared to be the end of it.

'I'm new around here,' Lex said, clearing his throat.

Sam Black squinted at him, not quite focusing on his face. 'Yes,' he said. 'We're not much used to strangers.' He looked back down at the boxes under his gnarly old hands. 'But we'll get used to yer. I hear yer've bought the place out at Wallaces.'

'Yes, from Beryl Harden. Although I gather that's a crime too.'

Sam Black nodded. 'Split the town it did, her gettin' that place. Church against the Wallaces.'

Lex frowned and shrugged while the old man stared at him like he expected something extra of him.

'Anyway,' Sam said, in his scratchy voice. 'Got some binoculars for yer to look at. See if any of them's any use to yer.'

Lex chose some 10 x 40s and paid for them with cash.

'Thanks, Sam,' he said on his way out. 'I appreciate your help.'

Wandering back by the newsagency, Lex scanned the noticeboard to see what was going on in town. Among the usual ads for old cars and used furniture, there was a phone number for somebody trying to sell a surfboard, an old Malibu. He wrote the number down on his hand and dialled it from the phone booth across the road.

The woman on the end of the line told him she had given the board to John Watson to handle the sale. It had been her husband's, but he hadn't used it for years. Her son had played around on it a bit when he was learning to surf in his teens, until he bought himself something smaller and zippier. He had wasted too much time surfing when he should have been helping out on the farm. Now the son had shot through to the city for a more exciting life. He was supposed to take over the farm, and yet here they were in their sixties, still doing all the work. It was too much for them. She had to get rid of the old board, she said, because every time she looked at it she was angry. The kids say there's nothing to do here, she told him bitterly, but the young people of today don't want to work. They're lazy. They only think of themselves. She told Lex the price, and he accepted it without discussion. One hundred and fifty dollars seemed a bargain to end a conversation he didn't want to have.

He left a cheque at the newsagency and shoved the board in the back of the Volvo. He could see John Watson wondering why he didn't grow up and get a job. But he didn't wait to explain that he hadn't bought the board to surf. What he needed was a paddle-board to take him out to the whales.

Friday morning was clear and quiet, and Lex could feel the building warmth of summer in the air. There were whales about. He tugged on the wetsuit from the laundry cupboard and dug out a set of old goggles and a snorkel. With the board under the crook of his arm, he headed down to the beach.

Owning a surfboard felt alien to him. Surfing was something all the other boys at school had done—the trendy ones, whose parents owned houses at the coast. Not him. At school he used to hear them talking about hanging out on headlands, listening to music and waiting for the surf to come up. It had always sounded boring to him. Now, on the beach, it was different. He set the board on the sand and ran his hand over the clumps of old wax that still clung to the surface. There was something reassuring about owning a board with history, a life before him. At least the board was experienced, even if he wasn't.

In the shallows, he strapped the leg-rope around his ankle. He was pleased that the board couldn't escape him if he was flicked off in the surf. He carried it out into the waves, pushing through the breakers. When he was far enough out, about chest deep, he slid onto the board in a lull between waves, on his stomach, and started paddling, dipping his arms in up to his elbows and pulling strongly. It felt good, free, and the board was surprisingly eager to move. A large wave crested in front of him and he paddled madly to thrust over it before it broke. The Malibu responded and slid up over the wave. Lex smiled. He could get used to this.

About fifty metres out, he stopped and looked around. Lying on his stomach he couldn't see much, so he swivelled to sit and search the waves. There had been a pod of whales out here earlier, maybe four of five of them, travelling slowly. He had seen them from the cliffs before he came down to the beach. They had been a few hundred metres out, cruising slowly towards the Point. There was no sign of them now.

Sitting on the board he felt the tide tugging him shorewards. He shifted back onto his stomach and paddled further out, another fifty metres or so, then sat up and scanned the waves again. Five minutes passed, maybe ten, then he saw a spout rise further out. He was in luck. The whales were still short of the Point, moving slowly. Dropping to his belly again he paddled on, heading towards the whales. It was a reflex reaction. He really had no idea what he planned to do. He had only thought as far as buying the board and paddling out here.

Another fifty metres and he stopped again, pulled the goggles on and slipped into the water. He wasn't sure how close he was, whether he'd see anything, and his heart was pounding with excitement. The water was a deep green-blue, light at the surface, with sunrays shafting through. It was like being in another world.

He looked around. At first, he heard little except the hollow sound of his breathing in the snorkel and the swish of the water, and each time the board bumped against his head it made a dull clunking sound. Then came a sound, a hollow moan that descended deeply before rising again and then trilling downwards. Several notes followed, one sliding into the other, up and down a rolling scale. Whale song. Stunned, Lex clung to the surfboard, shivers running through him in waves. He had company close by. The moment was enormous, humbling, overwhelming.

Lifting his head out of the water he tried to see how close they were. Two or three minutes passed before a spout rose skywards, about a hundred metres off, vapour rising over the surface of the water in a bushy V. Pulsing with excitement, Lex hauled himself onto the board and paddled in the direction of the spout, slowly now, dipping his hands in quietly. After a while he stopped. It was hard to gauge distance over water and he had no real idea where the whales were. Then below, right beneath the board, he saw a massive dark shadow slip through the deep. A moan ascended through the water and, forty metres off, a slick black back rode to the surface and exhaled a puff of spume with an explosive snort.

Lex whimpered, and his heart escalated somewhere between exhilaration and fear. But he couldn't stop now. He paddled close again, then quickly slipped off the board and dipped his face under. Beneath him in the green watery light he could see the slowly moving shapes of three humpback whales gently riding through the haze. They were massive and fluidly buoyant. It was as if they were gliding rather than swimming. Beside one was a smaller shadow, a calf clinging closely to the flank of its mother. They cruised below him, rolling languidly, turning slowly, cruising back. He could see the pointed shapes of their heads, the slow waft of their long pectoral fins, the knobbles that studded their heads and fins, the startling white of their bellies, the long grooves that marked their throats.

He wondered if they knew he was there, if they were watching him. But of course they knew. This was their world and he was an intruder. With pounding heart, he realised he may have done a silly thing following them out here and moving in so close. They could easily knock him off his board. They could kill him with one swish of an enormous tail. Yet he couldn't pull out. He was riveted by the incredible sight of them, the grace of their immense bodies suspended in blue, dappled by the shifting shafts of sunlight.

Suddenly his heart froze and he focused on one whale. It had separated from the pod and came slowly swimming towards him about twenty metres below. The great animal rolled on its side, flashing its white throat and belly, and Lex was startled to see an eye staring at him, surprisingly small. Then the whale rolled again, sliding deeper, and curved away back to the pod. A string of low moans ensued, reverberating through the water. Lex was transfixed, but knew he should leave. The whales had given him time, and perhaps he was too close to the calf.

Trying not to thrash his fins, he dragged himself back on the board and paddled slowly away.

On the beach, he collapsed on the sand, overwhelmed by a sudden rush of emotion. Tears came, and he lay on the Malibu, crying as if he would never stop. He was engulfed by conflicting feelings—joy, grief, fear, hysteria—and he allowed it all to wash over and through him, until eventually, exhausted, he rolled onto his back on the unforgiving hardness of the board and stared up into the sky. That had been one of the peak moments of his life. How could that happen, he asked himself, when so recently he had seen the bottom of low?

When he stood up, he noticed Sash sitting on the rocks watching him, and above the cliffs he saw the shape of Sally, looking down. Sash saw him glance at her and came running across the sand. She was small, pale, alarmed.

'I saw you,' she said.

Lex felt drained and unable to engage. 'What did you see?' he managed.

'I saw you swimming with the whales.'

She looked at him with wonder, like he had performed a miracle.

'Yes,' he said.

'Then you came back, and I saw you lying there on the surfboard for a long time.'

'Yes.'

'Were you crying?'

'Yes.'

Sash regarded him with eyes that seemed much older than her years. She took his hand. 'You're special,' she said. 'I've never seen anyone swim with the whales.'

Lex looked out to where he could still see the vapour spouts of the pod, just rounding the Point.

'They let you, didn't they?' Sash said. 'I mean, they didn't have to, did they?'

'No.'

Her smile was like a flash of sunlight.

'They like you. Like I do.'

Lex smoothed his hand over her head. Her hair was warm and soft. She smiled again and they walked together up the path from the beach.

NINE

Saturday, market day again. Callista sat at her stall feeling shaky and off-balance. She was nervous about the oystercatcher painting, and whether Lex would show up. Fortunately, the morning had been busy, but it was tricky for her to scan the crowd for him, in between closing sales and sorting change. By late morning she started to think he wouldn't come.

Searching for his face yet again among the passers-by, she clashed eyes with the guitar freak and was shocked by the boldness rising in his gaze. He was gyrating his hips while he played, smirking and leering at her. There was no subtlety about him at all. Keeping her face blank, she looked away, annoyed. With her arms folded protectively across her chest, she kept watching out for Lex.

Then, finally, she caught sight of him in the crowd. Damn. He must have seen her first. She saw him disappear behind a stall and then there he was, passing the church stand. Callista watched him heading towards her, pausing at various stalls. They almost eye-contacted but he slid his eyes away. Good. Her heart galloped. She knew he had been looking for her. She had a few quick moments to rearrange some umbrella paintings and slip the oystercatcher painting onto the display before he swung back her way. When she saw the shape of his shoulders easing along the stalls towards her stand, her hands and heart tingled.

'Busy today, aren't we?' he said.

His voice was rich, quiet and mellow, and meant for only her to hear.

'Have you been watching me?'

His slow smile made her breathless.

'It pays to check the lay of the land before you move in.'

'I don't like being watched.'

'You've been doing well today.' He stepped back a little and scanned her works. 'This is different,' he said, closing immediately on the oystercatcher. He lifted it and glanced at her. 'Is it for me?'

She hadn't expected him to be so direct. It caught her out.

'It *is* for me, isn't it?' he insisted.

She was disarmed by the smile that tweaked his lips.

'I haven't decided to sell it to you yet,' she said, feeling cheeky.

'Yes, you have,' he said. 'I want it.'

She raised her eyebrows at him. 'It's not as simple as that.'

His face clouded. 'No, I didn't think so,' he said, turning away. 'I'll give it some thought.'

He was already gone, unreadable, soaked into the restless crowd. Callista sat down with her heart thudding. She was worried and uncertain. What if he didn't come back? She'd have blown her chance.

A lengthy half-hour dragged by. She made a few sales, checked her watch a few times, fobbed off an attempted approach from the sleaze with the guitar grafted to his chest, sorted her change, sipped from her water bottle. The flutter was gone. She was swapping notes and coins with an old lady in a blue cardigan when a hot dog appeared by her hand. It was hanging limply out both ends of its bread roll, bathed in too much tomato sauce.

'Thank you, but I'm vegetarian,' she said.

'There's not much meat in this.'

Lex's laugh was straight up from his feet. It rocked them both and turned heads nearby. Callista tried to withhold eye contact, but she could feel him too close, watching her as he bit into the hot dog.

He was wearing Levi's today. They looked good on him, snug around his waist. A loose shirt masked the belly he was carrying underneath.

'How much for the oystercatcher?' he asked, leaning against the easel at the side of her stall.

'It's not for sale.'

His face closed and he withdrew a little from the stand. Callista's heart galloped as his arms folded over his chest.

'It's a gift,' she said. 'Take it. And I have the other one here for you too. I fixed the frame.' She pulled the painting from under the trestle.

His eyes were more intense than she remembered, very direct, not shy. He had opened towards her again. Callista saw it in the easing of his shoulders and the relaxed shift of his hand to grasp the wraparound sunglasses nestled in his fine hair. She would have to be careful with him—he was more fragile than she thought. The smile that shot across his face reached through to her toes, until he closed it off by lowering his sunglasses.

'Can I buy you a coffee after this?' she asked.

'You mean after I finish eating your hot dog? Or after the rabble departs?'

'Either. Or.'

'Do you want me to hang around and entertain you?'

Was it cheek or arrogance? Callista wasn't sure. This was a risk, but she was committed to taking it.

'I'll pack up now,' she said and started to collect the paintings off the stand. 'I'm finished with being polite to the public today.'

'You weren't very polite about the hot dog.' He was already assisting with shifting paintings into boxes. 'It was a very good hot dog.'

'It looked like something dead,' she returned, as she hoicked a box into the back of the Kombi.

Lex was already there with another box. He dismantled the trestle table while she was folding the tablecloths. It was as if they had done this together before. When they were finished, she dragged the side doors of the Kombi shut. Lex had already let himself into the passenger seat uninvited. It was an intrusion, but she let it go. She climbed into the driver's seat beside him, her heart somersaulting.

'You'd better tell me who you are before we drive off into the sunset,' he said. 'Then I can be sure I'm not being kidnapped.'

'I'm Callista,' she said. 'Callista Bennett.'

Something changed when they drove down the main street, and Callista wasn't quite sure what it was. But the easiness in him dissolved into quiet tension.

'I'm not sure I want to go to the café,' he said.

His eyes were flat and Callista knew he was closing her out and running scared. She'd have to make sure she didn't pressure him.

'I still have some coffee in my thermos,' she said. 'We could go and sit down by the river.'

'All right then.'

He wound down the window and sat with his elbow hooked outside, about as far away from her as he could get. Callista swung the Kombi down a side street and stopped in a small car park overlooking the river. Today the water was running wide and blue, reflecting the clear spring sky. They sat on a bench chair with the thermos between them, and Callista poured coffee into plastic mugs.

'It's black, I'm afraid. I don't have any milk.'

'Black's fine.'

She watched him lift the mug to his lips and sip his coffee.

'Are you staying around here?' she asked.

He held the mug in both hands and stared at the moving water. 'For a while.'

'It's a nice area. I hope you like it. Lots to see. Not too many tourists. It's peaceful.'

'Yes. I like things quiet.'

Callista laughed and was surprised at the sound of it—light like a bell. 'You look like a man who's had a bit of fun in his time.'

He smiled briefly, but his face clouded over. 'Not recently. But I'll get over it.'

He looked so forlorn. She watched him sip his coffee. He didn't speak.

After a while he shook his head. 'I shouldn't have dragged you away from the markets. You'll be losing money doing this.'

'I'm fine. It was my choice to close up shop.'

They sat awkwardly for a moment while the water flowed impassively by.

'It's a strange place to settle into.' Callista tried again. 'Small-town mentality. But you'll get to know people.'

'I'm not sure how long I'll be staying.'

'Are you renting a house down here?' she asked.

'I've bought an investment property. Just thought I'd stay in it for a while. Get a feel for the place.'

'Well, I'm a local through and through,' Callista said. 'If you like I can show you around sometime. There are some great spots along the coast that are hard to find without a bit of local knowledge.'

He looked at her for the first time since they'd sat down. 'What do you do around here?' he asked.

'You've seen it. I paint. The beach art keeps me alive. I make enough money over summer to pay rent for the year.'

'What about the rest of the year?'

'I paint other stuff. If the mood takes me. Or I do nothing—just waiting for inspiration to strike.'

'Nothing?'

She shrugged. It was hard to explain. Nobody except Jordi ever understood it. 'I walk the beaches. Feel the air. Watch the light. If there's something special, I paint it.'

Lex was listening with interest. 'I don't have an artistic bone in my body.'

Callista laughed. 'Art doesn't always come from your bones. It comes from your heart. And your mind. You feel it.'

'You've lost me then. I don't have a heart either.'

He stopped as if he had run out of puff. Callista watched him drain his coffee.

'I have to get going,' he said, standing up. 'Thanks for the coffee.'

She waved up at him without standing. 'I'll see you 'round then.'

He walked back towards the markets with his hands dug in his pockets. It hadn't exactly been a dream conversation, but it was a start. He was interested in her. And Jordi was right. She'd have to have the patience of a death adder.

Callista couldn't stop thinking about Lex. It was as if he had invaded her mind. She drove home from the markets wildly happy, singing loudly and tunelessly, enjoying the blast of air riding in through the open window. At night, she woke thinking of him, trying to recall the blue of his eyes, and shivering each time she remembered the way his smile made her toes tingle. She'd have to be careful or he could become an obsession. And obsession was not a healthy thing for her, unless she was focusing on a challenging piece of work, something that required constant determination and inspiration.

The fact was, she had developed a crush on him. Very girlish and pathetic, but madly exciting. And she figured that a little bit of obsession couldn't be too harmful. Not if she kept a check on it, and reminded herself frequently that reality rarely delivered what dreams promised. What was there in life if she couldn't indulge in a little bit of fantasy and excitement? She wafted around her house in the gully humming, singing and painting, and started planning how she might possibly meet up with him again.

The problem was trying to find a way to cross tracks with him without seeming too obvious. For instance, she couldn't just drive out to the Point and drop in on him, because she wasn't even supposed to know where he lived. Sue had said he didn't come into town very often, so there wasn't much chance of running into him down the street, and she couldn't waste a lifetime hanging out in town anyway. In the end, the only pathetic strategy she could come up with was to organise for Jordi to ring her from the servo if he saw the Volvo heading into town.

He didn't ring for days. Then the call came. She was midway through painting a boatshed when the phone rang. She knew, even before she lifted the receiver, that it would be Jordi.

Callista tossed her paints into the sink and ran for the Kombi. She was halfway into town before she realised she'd forgotten her sandals. Oh well, he'd have to see her as she was—paint-spattered and barefoot.

Slowing down in the main street, Callista knew this was a good day. On Saturdays when the markets weren't on, there was always a sausage sizzle in town. It was a fundraiser for the church, subsidised by Henry Beck. He and Helen would be outside the butchery turning sausages on a portable barbeque, and Mrs Jensen would be collecting the money. Of course, Lex may try to dodge all that. But if he wanted to stop by Sue's for a coffee, he'd have no choice but to get caught up in it.

Callista parked the Kombi in a side street and wandered past the newsagency. John Watson always had a stand of cheap books set up in the street, and she used this as an excuse to stop outside the shop. There were quite a few people on the footpath by the sausage sizzle. Mrs Dowling was buttering bread. Mrs Jensen was collecting the money. Helen Beck was working at the barbeque. Henry was grandly handing out sausages like he was the Lord Jesus dividing the loaves. Inside the butchery Callista could see Henry's assistant, Jake Melling, serving a customer.

While she pretended to peruse the books, Callista heard Henry carping on at Helen not to turn the sausages too frequently. It was a woman thing, he was saying, to meddle with meat too often. Why couldn't women just leave things alone? Mrs Jensen was keeping stiffly quiet—not an easy task for someone usually so outspoken—and Helen was looking teary and fragile with Henry glaring over her shoulder. Poor woman. Didn't he ever get off her back?

Callista had just picked up another book and was flicking

absently through the pages when Rick Molloy, Jordi's mate, came around the corner and spotted her at the bookstand.

'Hey, Callista. What are you doing in town?'

'I *do* come in sometimes,' she said.

'Watcha doing here?'

'Browsing.'

Rick smirked. 'C'm on, Callie. *You* don't browse.'

'Well, I am today.'

She saw Lex step out of Sue's café.

'Quick.' She dragged Rick into the newsagency and pulled him down the magazine aisle. 'Choose a magazine,' she whispered. 'I'll buy it for you.'

'Callie, you're losin' it. You can't afford to buy me a magazine.'

'Just do it and shut up. Look normal.' She shoved five dollars into his hand.

'What's this?'

'Bribery to shut you up.'

Rick took the money and smiled. 'Who you lookin' for?'

'Nobody you know. Now stop talking and pick a magazine. I've got to go.'

She swished out of the newsagency just in time. Lex was just leaving the sausage stall with a sausage sandwich in his hand. His head was ducked low and Callista noticed Helen Beck staring at him. Callista wondered what had happened. Behind her, John Watson had come to the door of the newsagency and was watching her. Oh well. What the heck. She could cope with making a spectacle of herself.

'Lex,' she said, cutting in front of him. 'How are you?'

He looked up, surprised. 'Mmm. You've caught me with a sausage sandwich again.' He paused. 'Do you want one?' Then shook his head. 'No, no. You're a vego, aren't you? No meat.'

Callista started walking beside him, away from the church stall and the newsagency. She glanced back. Helen was still watching them.

'Did Helen invite you to church?' she said.

'How did you guess?'

'I hope you had an answer ready.'

'I'm running out of excuses,' he said.

'Just tell her you're an atheist. It works every time.'

Lex looked at her, interested, while he bit into his sausage.

'Hey,' she said. 'You forgot your paintings the other day. The oystercatcher was a gift. You're not supposed to leave gifts behind.'

His face was blank for a moment then he clicked. 'Yes, I did forget, didn't I?'

She laughed. 'I see I've made a big impression on you. Can you even remember my name?'

'I remember that it's unusual.'

'It's Callista.'

'That's right.'

'So what have you been up to?'

He looked healthier than the last time she had seen him. His face was browner, more relaxed.

'The whales have been going through,' he said. 'It's been amazing.'

'They're great, aren't they? We see lots of them these days. They're really making a comeback.'

'I heard them singing once. Off the Point. Incredible. I didn't know they sang.'

'Only the males sing. Mostly in the breeding grounds. Only some of them sing when they're migrating. It's not usual.'

She had his attention.

'You seem to know a bit about whales.'

'This is the south coast,' she said. 'You can't live here without knowing about whales.'

She stopped and he noticed her bare feet.

'Lost your shoes?' he asked.

'Forgot them. I hardly wear them. It keeps me in touch with the earth.'

He smiled. 'You certainly look earthy.'

Callista was dismayed. She noticed the dirt between her toes, and he had just about finished his sausage. She didn't have much time.

'Where did you say you were staying?' she asked.

'Out at Wallaces Point.'

'Ah. No wonder you're seeing whales.'

Lex nodded and seemed lost for a moment. He had the forlorn look of a small boy that can't find his mother.

'You'll have to come over to lunch and pick up your paintings,' Callista said. 'I live out of town, but it's a nice place. A bit different from what you're used to. I live in the bush.'

'I'm not sure when I could come.'

'How about tomorrow. Unless you're going to church, of course.' She smiled her fullest, most mirthful smile, and it got him.

PART II

Turbulence

TEN

Twenty minutes south of the Point road, Lex turned west off the highway onto a dirt road that wound down across a gully and then climbed swiftly along a dusty ridgeline, passing trees coated with brown dust. Callista's gate was half-hidden in scrub, and the driveway was little more than a rough track. He followed it along the ridge among gangly eucalypts before it turned sharply downhill, diving through dense acacia thickets and ti-tree scrub.

Keeping his foot flat on the groaning brakes, Lex eased the Volvo down the hill, jolting over drainage gutters every twenty metres or so. The two bottles of wine on the floor rolled and clinked, and he stopped to lift them onto the passenger seat.

At the bottom of the hill, the track emerged from the bush onto a grassy area. Callista's Kombi was parked just off to the right beside the dam, and Lex pulled up beside it, his hands wet on the steering wheel. He was nervous. The bottles of wine smiled at him from the passenger seat. He'd have to be careful not to drink too quickly.

As he walked across the dam wall, a bottle of wine in each hand, he saw Callista wave from the front verandah. She met him on the cut grass that surrounded the house and glanced at the wine.

'Feeling thirsty?'

'I wasn't sure what to bring.'

'You can never go wrong with wine. Especially if it's in a bottle. It's generally only the cardboard variety here. Artist's budget.'

She reached for the bottles and took them just below his hands, without touching him, thank God. Looking up at the house, Lex absorbed its simple lines and large uncurtained windows. Wind chimes of varying sizes tinkled in the breeze. He glanced down into the gully, felt the hugging warmth of the damp air, the humidity.

'It's humble,' Callista said. 'But I like it here.'

'It's quiet.'

'You're used to the sea.'

She smiled, and her eyes were encouraging, warm and brown in her round face. Lex noticed a dimple flickering high up on her left cheek.

'It's not quiet when the cicadas get going in summer,' she said. 'They make the whole place throb.' She stepped up onto the deck and waved him towards a battered armchair. 'Take a seat. It's comfortable, even though it's old. Shall we open some wine?'

Lex nodded and lowered himself into the chair, happy to let her lead the conversation. With his heart skipping and the sweat prickling uncomfortably in his armpits, he couldn't think of anything to say. It was years since he had been this nervous around a woman. He looked along the porch and down to the gully where small birds flitted. Deep in the hummocks of vegetation another bird commenced a steady whoop-whoop-whoop.

Callista came out with two glasses of wine and a broad smile that sent his heart knocking. She handed him a glass and put hers on a small table between the two chairs, then went back inside. He watched her purple skirt flick around her legs and took in the curve of her waist. She had bare feet, of course. With a dry mouth, he reached for the wine, savoured the cool relief of it slipping down his throat.

She brought out a plate with some cheese, crackers and a bowl of hummus, then sat down with him and gazed out at the scrub.

'You know, I never get tired of looking at this view,' she said.

'I love the way the light changes over the trees during the day. The shadows and the dapples and the greens, they're always different.'

Her laugh was tinkly, like the wind chimes. Lex sat breathless, still trying to think of something to say. He raised his glass and noticed the moisture sweating off the cold wine, licked it without thinking. Then he felt her eyes on him.

'What do you do for a living?' she asked him.

'Nothing right now. I'm taking a bit of a break.'

'From life?'

'You could say that.'

Her face was very kind. Lex drank more wine and shucked his eyes out of hers.

'Are you going to be here for long?'

'I don't know,' he said, evading her gaze. A positive answer could be some sort of commitment. She was watching him closely, as if from observing his face she might work him out. 'Guess I'll have to find some work soon. If I'm staying. Any suggestions?'

'There's never much going around here. You know . . . it's a rural economy. Look at me and Jordi.'

'Jordi?' Lex remembered the shaggy guy at Sam Black's tackle shop.

'My brother.'

'I think we may have met. Down at the servo.'

Callista frowned. 'Jordi's a complex guy. He's a bushie. It's where he belongs. He hates the servo.'

She refilled his empty glass and topped up her own. They sat in silence for a while, watching the bush shift occasionally in the breeze. Fairy wrens hopped and twittered around a clump of lantana near the edge of the gully. The wind chimes tinkled intermittently.

'Oh.' Callista started as if she had almost fallen asleep. Was he that boring? 'I'd better check the lunch. I hope it hasn't burned.'

He stood up and followed her through the glass sliding door. It was cool and shadowy inside. The moodiness of the bush penetrated even in here. A small square table crowded the doorway and the kitchen was a makeshift affair with a small sink and rough wooden benches. Beneath the benches, mismatched crockery was stacked on shelves in uneven piles. Lex eased carefully past the table and into the narrow lounge area where two large worn armchairs turned their faded backs on the windows. An old stereo was crammed beneath the stairs. There were several paintings leaning against it.

'Mind if I have a look?' he asked.

Callista shrugged. 'I suppose not.'

He squatted to see the paintings in the dim light. The first was a chaos of trees and bark, blue and brown, a tangled forest. He liked the crazy thrust of the branches and the shards of bark ripped ragged by the wind.

'This isn't the local bush, is it?'

'No,' Callista said. 'That's up in the mountains. It's dry up there, and wild.' She came forward from the stove, oven mitt in her left hand. 'I'll take you there sometime.'

Lex carefully shifted the canvas aside. The next painting was black and bold, a distorted face, teeth, weeping eyes, all twisted and irregular.

'What's this?' he asked.

She quickly removed it. 'Self-portrait on a bad day.'

She shuffled the other paintings quickly in front of him: a wild frothy beach scene, a cloudy sky cut by an arc of birds, more trees, all different, some madly exciting spatter-grams of vibrant colour, a portrait of Jordi. It was a potent picture.

'He's not a happy man, is he?' Lex commented.

Callista examined the painting for a long moment, and she looked so sad that Lex wished he hadn't mentioned it.

'He's had some hard times,' she said.

He watched her face twisting with pain in the shadows.

'It was when he was quite young,' she continued, half to herself. 'He was about twenty. Things happened to him that shouldn't happen to anybody.'

She put the painting away then paused, lost, before she remembered what she was doing. 'I think I'll serve up now. The quiche is ready.'

While Callista fiddled in the kitchen, Lex stood awkwardly near the stereo. He saw another painting leaning against the wall under the stairs. Without thinking, he leaned over and lifted it out and sat it across the arms of one of the chairs where a shaft of light was cast through the window.

It was a beach scene—a long view from the sands across still waters to an early evening sky with the light fading from it. The sky was lit in subtle hues of pink, fading to mauve, purple and then night-blue right down on the silvery water. A flat white disc of moon sat off-centre above the quiet sea. It was a peaceful painting. Lex sipped his wine and sank into its tranquillity.

'You should hang this one,' he said. 'Why is it tucked away?'

In the kitchen, Callista's face crinkled with dismay and then washed over with carefully arranged calm.

'I didn't realise you'd found that one,' she said.

'I'm sorry.'

'That's okay. Do you mind putting it back? Lunch is ready.'

She took the food outside.

They ate quietly, cutlery clinking on their plates.

'I had a difficult time just after I finished that painting,' Callista said eventually, laying down her fork and looking at him. 'I sell or give away most of my work, but I can't seem to separate from that one. Silly really. I'd sell it easily. But you see . . . giving it up would be like giving away part of myself, and I'm not quite ready to let it go.'

'You don't have to explain.'

'No, but I want to.'

The wind stirred in the chimes.

Midday stretched to afternoon. They talked a little, sat, drank, contemplated the gully, talked a little more. Lex couldn't work her out. It seemed they were both watching each other, both unsure, both a little nervous. He remained guarded, swinging between attraction and fear. He held himself a pace behind her, controlling the wine, choosing his words. He had changed. He used to be bold and assertive with women.

The second bottle slid down smoothly, warm and red and with a new touch of intimacy. There was a lull in their conversation, a lengthy silence, and between them the air that had been flowing so pleasantly suddenly charged itself electrically. It came from nowhere and they looked at each other, looked away. Lex's heart was tumbling again and his legs yelled at him to run, or in a minute he'd be kissing this woman.

'It's getting late,' he said. 'I'd better go home.'

Callista's hand was only a short distance away on the arm of her chair. It wouldn't be so hard to lift his hand and close it over hers. But he'd lose himself again, so ready to tumble. Fear strapped him.

'Are you okay to drive?'

'I'm fine.'

Lex knew he had to leave soon. Too quickly he stood, and staggered a little.

'Are you sure you're okay to drive? I don't mind cooking some dinner, and there's a spare bed here you can use.'

Those brown eyes were looking into him, those full lips. He had to be careful. She could reach inside and snatch him out.

'No, I'm fine. Thank you.'

He was off the deck and ready to head to the car.

'Your keys are on the table inside,' she said, smiling quietly at him. 'And you have to come upstairs and see the view from the balcony before you go. It's the highlight of this place.'

She was holding the door open for him, so he had no choice but to follow her inside. He moved up the stairs behind her into the calm late afternoon light flooding the loft. It was a large airy room, with a queen-size bed covered by a white quilt. Two cane chairs were arranged around a low wooden coffee table. The balcony was just past the chairs with a glass sliding door leading onto it.

Callista stepped out there, the light touching copper in her hair as she leaned out on her elbows. From the balcony, the gully and its crowded heaped canopy seemed closer. Lex gripped the railing and tried to focus on the view, but he was achingly aware of the fine brown hairs on Callista's arm, the fluid curl of her brown hair across her cheek, and of his own catchy breath.

'What do you think?' she asked, all smiling brown eyes and smooth cheeks.

'About the view?'

How obvious was it that he was thinking about her lips and her thighs and the texture of her skin? She looked down, and Lex was aware of the slight lift of her shoulders with each breath. Then she shifted her left hand and closed it gently over his. It was warm and smooth and full of light. His own sweaty hand swivelled to grasp hers as he gave in and tugged her towards him, grazed his lips on hers, sighed.

They grasped each other, crushed into each other, tasted each other. Lex was so tangled with fear, but his body couldn't get enough of her. His hands stroked over her shape, pulled her to him, slipped and tangled in her long brown hair. She was looking straight into his eyes as she touched him.

They went back into the loft. Holding him with eyes that were now strong and black, she flicked off her top, dropped her skirt on the floor and hooked off her underwear. Now he could see all that smooth brown skin.

He stripped, struggling with the zip of his jeans. His body was shaky, unpractised, tentative. He crouched at her feet, her calves in his hands, head down, trying to slow his breathing. He had to pull out of this. Panic in his chest. He hadn't touched a woman other than Jilly in years. The need erupting in his chest terrified him.

Callista tugged on his arms, drew him up. She pressed against him, kissed him, flicked her tongue lightly along his eyelashes.

On the bed she was powerful, even on her back, arched up against him, so much in control. Her moan slid through him deliciously, and then the contraction of her orgasm as he caved into her, unable to hold back.

They lay damp with sweat and lovemaking, spooned against each other, angled across the bed where they had fallen. Lex's cheek was in her hair, his hand soft on her belly, their legs enmeshed. Time slid over them, late and mellow and threaded with the early evening calls of the bush; the slow piping of the eastern yellow robin, the last late whooping of the wonga pigeon, the cackle of a kookaburra.

Lex breathed the sweet apple smell of her hair. His fingers drew tiny circles on her belly. He had forgotten that silken smoothness of a woman's skin, that particular feel of it against the hairiness of his own body. Losing Jilly, he had blanked out everything, even the memory of this drunken post-coital euphoria.

Then he remembered. The thought passed through him like a shock. Even as he fought against it, his body tensed. In his delirium he hadn't thought of protection. What if he got this woman pregnant? He didn't even know her. What was he doing? One afternoon of conversation and here he was, out of control and forgetting all the rules.

Callista must have felt him tense. She lay against him a little longer then moved away, pulling the sheet up around her and hugging her knees to her chest. There were tears in her eyes.

'It's okay,' she said, walling him out. 'It's just fine. You don't have to worry. I can't get pregnant.'

They looked at each other. Lex felt his nakedness. All that smooth air between them had gone.

'You'd better go,' she said, as he pulled on his clothes.

Callista lay curled up in the bed as the dark seeped in. She heard the Volvo start, saw the glow of the headlights in the trees, heard the familiar crackling bush silence resume after the car ground up the steep hill. The sheet was damp from her tears and from their lovemaking. She could smell the sweet-sour muskiness of it.

That black hole was opening up in her again. She had fought so hard to hold it back over the past year. Why did it have to come now, with Lex wrapped warm around her? Was it just because he'd tensed? Was she still so brittle about it all?

It was that painting. She knew she should have put it away.

In the blue of dusk, she rolled off the bed, went downstairs naked and blasted some cask wine into a tumbler. Placing the painting on the chair as Lex had done, she sat down in front of it and drank the wine like water. Even now it was difficult for her to look at this painting, still so hard to go back there. Ah, the vault of memory—it had a habit of cracking open.

She remembered sitting on the beach on a still evening, Luke Bennett holding her hand. He was her husband. Earlier that week they had found out she was pregnant, and Luke had been overwhelmed by it. He'd insisted they get married straightaway. So they had. He said he wanted to be a *real* father. And he'd been so serious and intense about it, he'd even asked her to change her name. Why not, she'd thought. What's a name if it's not a gift to give away? If it was important to Luke that she was Callista Bennett, then she was happy to do it.

They had been married in a registry office, so excited, aflame with it. The celebrant had been dry and bored, annoyed by their joy and spontaneity. But it hadn't mattered. They had four blissful weeks. Callista sang and dreamed and painted. She had been so serene. Doped on progesterone. She had been floaty and doughy and beautiful. The beach scene just poured itself out onto canvas. She was so full, so optimistic.

Luke drifted in and out of her harmony. He left each morning, clean and shower-damp, hooking his tool belt off the kitchen chair as he waved out the door. He came home sweetly sawdusty and amorous. They made love each evening in the shower, with the dust running off him in rivulets, and then made love again on the bed or on the kitchen table after dinner.

Later Callista wondered if they had done it too much—if you could cause a miscarriage by having too much sex.

The night she miscarried, Luke wanted to make her have multiple orgasms. He had teased her into a frenzy till she was begging for him. Then he went on, after she thought she was spent. He went on till she screamed at the ecstatic agony of an orgasm that wouldn't end. They both listened to the echo of her voice in the gully.

Luke released her gently after that. The smile on his face was contented triumph. He rolled over with her hand in his and fell asleep. Until her spasms woke them in the night. And she started to bleed.

Callista couldn't remember how long Luke stayed. She had been in such a fog, so sick and so weak after all the bleeding. The blood had soaked the bed and Luke had taken her to the hospital. She could barely remember the drive. There was pain and more blood and weakness and a sinking blackness she had never known before. They both came home from the hospital hollow and pale, shocked by the loss. One minute there was a child and a whole future between them, the next minute there was a vacant space echoing with betrayed hopes.

It seemed to Callista that they were both ghosts, not of substance. In that time after they came home from the hospital, she couldn't remember any conversations—although they must have said something to each other. What she did recall was Luke's dejection, his patent disappointment—not through words, but by the long sad look on his face. During the preceding weeks he had imagined his future around this child. He had married Callista for it. And now there was nothing. No baby. No child. No future. After a couple of weeks he went away for a while. He said he needed to mourn alone.

But he came back after a month. At least, the shadow of him came back. He was as empty as she was. When Callista was well enough, they tried to get pregnant again. They weren't sure if it was what they wanted, but they did it to fill the emptiness, to see if they could replace what they had lost. But time went by and Callista did not fall pregnant.

They tried again and again, Luke's anger escalating with each month slipping away. Six, twelve, eighteen months of it. She couldn't fall pregnant. They had lost their chance. And, with time, Luke's lovemaking became rougher. The tickles became slaps became hits. Until he pushed her down the stairs one night, then snatched his bags that were already packed. He went out into the night, and never came back.

That was when Callista painted the black and white self-portrait.

ELEVEN

Lex nursed a wicked hangover with a strong coffee at Sue's. He had driven home from Callista's like a maniac and crashed in on his whisky stash. She had cleaved him open like a watermelon and now he couldn't control the leak of his emotions. Even the whisky didn't help. He knew it had been stupidity to go over there, knew he wasn't strong enough to stay in control. And he had lost it. He had fallen into the magic of her, and it had left him bruised and shaken. He wasn't ready for a relationship. The healing had barely begun. But the memory of her was still strong in his hands.

Sue came to top up his cup. She looked down at him with a careful blank face.

'Hungover?'

Lex stared into his cup. 'I've had a tough week.'

'I heard you had some visitors out at the Point recently.'

He set down his cup. 'I didn't realise my life was public property.' Somewhere in his chest, anger simmered.

'You didn't expect privacy in a country town, did you?'

'How silly of me.' Lex's anger was popping to the surface. 'I thought I could come here and hide away for a while.'

Sue smiled knowingly. 'Life has a habit of dragging you in, doesn't it? There's no hiding away.'

He forced the anger down and hunched over his cup again. 'My wife visited,' he said. '*Ex*-wife, by now. And then my mother dropped 'round for a chat.'

'You don't have to tell me anything.'

'Everyone knows everything anyway. Isn't that what you're telling me?' Irritation fizzed under his skin.

'No,' Sue said. 'The details are yours to keep. But you can't hide in a small community like this. Better to be honest up-front.'

'I'm not hiding anything.'

Sue raised her eyebrows. 'Just being selective about who you tell.'

'I'm not here to tell. I'm here to forget.'

'Sure.'

Lex shoved some money on the table and walked out. He strode angrily down the street, past the butchery, past Beryl's and all the way to the supermarket before he started to calm down. Then he turned around and walked back. He had to be quick before it was too late.

Beryl leaned out the door of her shop. 'You okay, honey?' she asked.

He waved and walked by fast. 'Fine, thanks.'

With a crack, he opened Sue's door, startling her from the kitchen.

'I'm sorry,' he said.

She wiped her hands on her tea towel, looking at him seriously. 'That's all right. I'm pretty thick-skinned.' She nodded towards a table. 'Do you want another cup? I think you could use one.'

Lex sat down and the hangover returned with great intensity. When Sue came back, she set a fresh cup of coffee in front of him and joined him at the table.

'How are you going in that house out there?'

'The house I'm not supposed to own?'

'People been giving you a hard time about it, have they?'

'Nothing direct.'

'You know how these things are,' Sue said. 'It's always awkward when someone changes their will and leaves their property to someone else. Especially in a small town.'

Lex shrugged.

'Have you been over to introduce yourself to your neighbour yet?' she asked.

'Other than the run-in with the peacock, no.'

Sue grinned. 'Perhaps you should. Mrs B's not a bad old stick. And it'd be nice for you to have someone to talk to out there.'

'I see Sally and her kids from time to time.'

'Sure, but I think you'd like Mrs B. What about that whale-watching tour you were asking me about one time?'

'What about it?'

'You said you might invite Mrs B.'

'You think I should?'

'Why not. She can only say no.'

'But it's a Wallace thing, isn't it? Wallaces and whales again.'

'We've been through this. You go and see. Jimmy's a very good operator. You'll have a good time.'

'I suppose I should reserve judgment until I've been on one of these cruises.'

'Perhaps you could try to enjoy yourself instead,' Sue said. 'That'd be healthier for you.'

When Lex got home, he found Evan sitting on the steps. He hadn't seen Evan in a while. It was mainly Sash who dropped in for visits, or occasionally the three of them—Sally and the two kids—asking Lex if he wanted to come for a walk on the beach. Today, the boy looked miserable, hugging his knees and rocking back and forth. Lex sat down beside him.

'You got some stuff going down at home?' he asked.

The kid nodded without looking up. He was struggling not to cry.

'There's a man in our house,' he said. 'He's in Mum's bed.'

Lex tried to look suitably concerned. 'That's full on.'

'Me and Sash usually hop in bed with her on the weekends. Now this big fat bloke is there all the time.'

'Where'd she find him?'

'At Sue's. He was there for some tucker.'

'At the café?'

'Yeah, Mum helps out down there sometimes. For extra money.'

'But this is a bit too much extra, hey?'

'Why can't he just leave us alone?'

'Maybe he likes your mum.'

'Course he does. She's nice.'

'Sure, and maybe she's a bit lonely.'

'How could she be lonely? She's got us.'

'It's a bit different, don't you think? Giving you guys a hug or snuggling up with a fella?'

Evan gestured back up the street. 'His truck's up there. Did you see it? Parked outside our place? Everyone'll know.'

'Lucky hardly anyone comes down here.'

Evan looked at him incredulously. 'People will know about it. I'll be dead at school.'

Lex tried to find a constructive angle. 'What sort of truck does he drive?'

'Big Mack.'

'I thought a kid like you'd be impressed by that. A big truck.'

'He's in bed with my mum. And it's not his house.'

Lex backed off and they both watched the sea. There were gannets fishing out there.

'What's "chemistry"?' Evan asked. 'I heard Mum say something to Sue about chemistry. What is it?'

Oh God, Lex thought. Do we have to do this? He drew a deep breath and tried to explain. 'It's this thing where a man and a woman look at each other and they just know something's going to happen.' He thought of Callista and his stomach shrivelled. Despite the lack of wisdom of their lovemaking, he was still wishing he could see her again, yet he was afraid to contact her.

'Like what? Like a car crash?' Evan asked.

'A bit like that. They know they're going to kiss.'

Evan looked appalled. 'That's disgusting,' he said. 'Has that ever happened to you?'

'I'm afraid so.' Lex could see he had gone down in the kid's estimation. 'Where's Sash?' he asked.

'Shut in her room. With her dolls and Rusty. Rusty *hates* him. I wish he'd bite him.'

'So this isn't the first time.'

'No. He's been coming every week.'

'It's a happening thing then.'

'What am I going to do?' Evan's voice wobbled.

'Can you find a way to like him?' Lex asked.

'Why should I?'

'Because you might have to live with it.'

'But I don't want to.'

Lex contemplated another tack. 'How's your mum?' he asked.

Evan looked suspicious. 'What do you mean?'

'Well, does he make her happy?'

Evan considered a moment and his face fell. 'She sings,' he admitted. 'And smiles to herself.'

'So he's making her feel better.'

'Maybe.'

'Well then. What's he like? I mean, is he okay?'

'He doesn't even talk to me.'

'What about talking to your mum? Could you do that?'

'Like tell her not to let him come back?'

'I don't think that'd work, do you? Maybe you could ask her to keep the cuddles for the bedroom.'

The boy suddenly looked like he might cry. 'He's not my dad.'

'No,' said Lex. 'You've got your own dad.' So that was the issue. The kid didn't want his dad replaced.

Evan leaned back against the steps.

'Have you been for a ride in the truck?' Lex asked.

The kid shook his head.

'Maybe you could ask him to take you for a spin.'

'Do you reckon he would? I don't speak to him.'

'You could try. He might be all right when you get him away from your mum. He might notice you're a cool kid.'

Evan looked a little less worried. They sat for a while. Then he jumped up and put his hands in his pockets.

'Think I'll go and ask him,' he said, glancing up the road.

Fifteen minutes later, Lex heard the truck start up.

The peacock was on Mrs Brocklehurst's porch when Lex went next door to invite her out whale-watching. The house was such a contrast with his that the fence seemed to mark the boundary with another world. Lex's place was all straight lines and simplicity, whereas Mrs B's was shadows, verandahs, tacked-on rooms and junk. From the rusted bus down the back to the old green Peugeot parked on the front lawn, everything spelled decay and disorder.

As Lex mounted the front steps, the peacock inspected him from the railing, then flounced down at his feet and dragged its tail in front of him. He stepped around it and knocked, rattling the flywire door.

'Who is it?' a raspy voice called from within.

'It's your neighbour. Lex Henderson.'

Lex heard some banging and shuffling, and a white head loomed out of the dark. She looked up at him piercingly with washed-out blue eyes.

'Lex, did you say?'

'Yes. Lex Henderson.'

'What do you want then?' She frowned at him and then a smile tickled the thin straight line of her mouth. 'I hope you're not after my bird.'

'No,' said Lex. 'The bird wins.'

'At least you're better dressed today than the last time I met you,' she said, looking him up and down.

The peacock tapped along the porch and slid past Lex's legs into the house.

'Actually, I wondered if you'd like to come whale-watching with me. I was thinking of going on a tour.'

'Now why would I want to do that?'

Mrs B's eyes narrowed and her brow furrowed deeper.

Lex shifted his weight, unsure. 'I thought it might get us off on a better footing than our last meeting . . . in the backyard.'

'Yes, I haven't forgotten it.' A real smile stretched her face. 'More excitement than an old woman like me has had in a long while. Old Percy here was none too happy about it though.' The peacock strutted and threaded between her legs. 'Why do you want to go on a whale-watching tour?' she asked. 'Don't you get a good enough view of them from here?'

'I do get a good view here,' Lex said. 'I just thought it might be different out on a boat.'

'Jimmy Wallace runs those tours, doesn't he?'

'Yes. That's what they tell me.'

'Who tells you?'

'Sue from the café.'

'Jimmy's been doing those tours a few years now,' she said. 'I wouldn't mind seeing if he's any good at it.'

Lex smiled and Mrs B reached down to run her hand along the peacock's back like she was stroking a cat.

'When do you want to go?'

'I was thinking of Tuesday.'

She nodded. 'The Wallaces owned that house, you know,' she said. 'The one you live in.'

'Yes, I know.'

'You want to know about them, don't you?'

Lex shifted. 'I'm not sure.'

'Sue didn't tell you? That I know about the Wallaces?'

'No.'

'She's clever then, isn't she? Set this up so I could fill you in.'

'It was my idea,' Lex said.

Mrs B nodded without smiling. 'All right, I'll come.'

'I'll pick you up at eight then.'

Mrs B's pale eyes twinkled. 'How about I come over? I think I can still walk that far.'

TWELVE

Callista lay heavy on the bed, legs leaden, her eyes flitting with the shadows skittering on the ceiling. It seemed she had been lying there forever, bearing the weight of darkness.

The phone rang out and stopped. Rang out and stopped.

Time melted.

Jordi appeared. His face swam in and out, intruded on the shadows.

'I called you from the servo,' he said. 'I thought you needed help.'

'Is that you, Jordi?' Her voice sounded stiff and strange.

'How long have you been here? When did you last eat?'

'I don't know.'

Like a dream, she felt Jordi's gentle hands undress her and lift her into the bath, swishing warm water over her. Then he wrapped her in a dressing gown and carried her to a lounge chair, combed out her hair. He gave her water and fed her. Put her back to bed. Asked no questions.

Each day he came in the morning. On the porch he set her up with food and water and a book to read. She stared into the bush and read a few sentences at a time. She was so weary. At dusk Jordi came back. He fed her and helped her back to bed. Each evening he smoked a joint on her balcony and the sweet tangy smoke wafted back into her room.

One evening, he brought his guitar and sat with her in the warm sun on the verandah. He played for himself, bent over the instrument, his eyes closed. Then he put down the guitar and looked at her.

'It's enough, Callie. You have to stop.'

Callista barely heard him through the fog.

'Listen to me,' he said, louder this time. 'This has to stop. I'm not watching you go through this again.'

Tears squeezed out and ran down alongside her nose, dripped off her lip.

'No,' he said. 'We're not doing this again. I know it's hard, but sometimes you've just gotta pick up the load and move on.'

Callista was so tired she couldn't even think of moving. But Jordi was watching her. Delving into her. She tried to wade out of the fog.

'You've got to keep moving,' he said, voice low. 'I know about these things.'

He was right. He did know. Jordi knew, more than anyone. Callista stared at him, feeling a question take shape slowly within her. It was a question that would take them to a place they hadn't been before. But today she needed Jordi's strength. She needed to know how he had picked up his pieces when everything in his life had collapsed. It must be nearly eight years since Jordi's girlfriend had suicided. He'd found her hanging in the shed behind the house they were renting. He had only gone down the street to buy some bread. But it was all the time she needed. She had it planned. She wanted to go. Even Jordi wasn't enough to hold her here.

'How did you manage?' Callista asked. 'After Kate?'

Jordi looked out into the gully for a long time before he answered.

'There's no secret,' he said, turning to her at last, eyes intense. 'There's no easy way.'

He knew as well as Callista how a person could get lost in the mist. She watched him as her chest hollowed and fresh tears seeped.

'You just have to hook a line into life and go with the tide,' he said. 'Otherwise you'll drown.'

Callista wiped tears on her sleeve.

'The way opens up after a while,' he said.

She felt herself floating out towards the sky with the breeze. She watched the light playing in the canopy, dapples rippling over the grass as the trees moved.

'What brought it on this time?' he asked.

She couldn't answer.

'It was that man, wasn't it?'

'It wasn't his fault,' she said, with effort. 'He was here, and I sent him away.'

'So what are you going to do about it?'

Tears oozed again.

Jordi rolled a joint and dragged deeply on it several times. 'Here.' He passed it to her. 'Have some.'

'No.'

'You need it.'

She took the joint reluctantly. She didn't want to partake in this, didn't have the energy for it. But he was watching her, waiting for her. So she took a few drags. Just for him. Then he sat back and sucked on the joint pensively.

'What are you going to do about him then?' he asked again, slowly releasing a puff of smoke.

'I don't know.' Her head spun with the dope and she still felt as heavy as mud.

'Yes, you do. You're gonna go out there.'

'What?'

'To the Point,' he said, a smile twisting within his beard. 'Give it another week and he'll be waiting for you.'

At the wharf, Lex and Mrs B joined a small knot of people waiting for Jimmy Wallace to bring his boat in from its mooring. They could see the boat not far out, chugging slowly towards them, rolling lazily from side to side. The weather had been calm and warm early, but now a light wind had sprung up and Lex could see the occasional whitecap licking on the sea. He tugged a box of seasickness tablets out of his hip pocket.

'There's a bit of a swell out today,' Mrs B said, eyes dancing in her crinkly face. 'See how she's rocking already?'

Lex groaned. 'I'm going to die.'

The old lady was lively. She seemed pleased to be out, different from her sharp manner when Lex had introduced himself to her just a few days ago.

They watched as the boat bumped up against the wharf and a wiry bearded man in shorts leapt off and tied her up. He skipped quickly back on board and lifted out another rope at the stern while the engines revved slightly to swing the rear of the boat in. The man tied the stern up as well, then he hooked a set of aluminium steps to the side of the boat so the passengers could climb aboard.

'Hello, Jimmy,' Mrs B called, waving a bony hand.

Jimmy Wallace helped her up the steps. He was short but sprightly and a wide white grin flashed out of his grey beard.

'Good to have you here, Mrs B,' he said. 'Welcome aboard. I'm surprised you haven't come out with us before.'

'I don't get out much these days,' she said, taking Jimmy's hand and stepping carefully onto the boat. 'I needed Lex here to invite me.'

Jimmy's eyes crinkled in the sun as he reached out a friendly hand to Lex. 'Thanks for bringing her along.'

'Lex is my new neighbour,' Mrs B said. 'He's bought your father's house at the Point. But he seems like a reasonable fellow.'

'Pleased to meet you,' Jimmy said, without missing a beat.

Mrs B had eased them through the introduction so tactfully there had been no opportunity for hesitation. She was a clever old woman.

'Just take a seat over there,' Jimmy said, pointing to a couple of seats near the stern. 'All the punters tend to head up to the bow, but it gets cold and wet up there. You'll get a good enough view from here till we get ourselves out a bit.'

Padding barefoot around the deck, Jimmy checked his passengers and made a few adjustments to the controls. Then he sat down behind the wheel, pulled down a microphone from above his head and winked at Mrs B. 'Just have to give everyone a bit of a commentary. Fill them in a bit.'

Lex watched him set the revs up and spin the wheel to head them directly out to sea, angled slightly across the swell. He hadn't expected Jimmy to be so affable. He didn't know what he had expected really, but not this openly friendly man with wavy grey hair.

'Hello, folks,' Jimmy said, as they gradually gained speed, bobbing slowly across the waves. 'Glad to have you on board. We've picked a fine day to be heading out, although unfortunately we're going to roll a bit once we get out beyond the heads. We've got about three hours' sailing time ahead of us, and there's a good chance we'll get to see whales. It's the best time of year for sightings.'

Lex watched Jimmy's face as he spoke. He'd have been through this spiel dozens of times before, but it still didn't sound rehearsed. He had a warm and natural way of speaking. A comfortable way of imparting information. He didn't look like the son of a whaler; the son of a man who had shifted west to hunt whales even when the industry was dying. How did Jimmy live with that, Lex wondered. How did he feel about taking people out on joy-trips to observe the very animals his father had killed? It was ironic the way life switched things upside down.

'What we're most likely to see is humpbacks,' Jimmy was saying. 'They're the most common species along the east coast. And right now they're heading south to Antarctica. They breed up north off the coast of Queensland over the winter. And then this time of year they're heading south on what's called the southern migration. It's absolutely the best time for seeing whales because they're cruising slowly down the coast with their little ones.'

Jimmy pushed the microphone away and let people settle into the rhythm of the sea for a while. The boat rode steadily over the swell and swayed as the waves rose and fell beneath them. Lex wasn't sure whether he felt well or not, and tried not to think about it.

As they moved further out, the air grew colder and the boat seemed to move faster. Everyone nestled into snug hollows around the boat and donned extra layers of clothing to protect them from the breeze pouring over the bow. Lex began to be certain about the beginnings of queasiness churning in his stomach. It was going to be hard for him to hold on in these conditions. He was glad when Jimmy started talking again to give him something else to think about.

'Fifteen or twenty years ago you'd hardly see a whale along this coast,' Jimmy said. 'They were thumped pretty hard by the whaling industry and it's taken a long time for them to recover. Most of the serious whaling was done offshore from factory boats in the Antarctic. But at one stage, there used to be a series of whaling stations up and down the Australian coasts as well. The closest one to here was down at Eden, further south. There's a good whaling museum down there too. I'd definitely recommend a visit, if you happen to be passing through. Whaling finished up down there sometime in the 1920s, but they were still whaling at Albany over in Western Australia up till the late seventies. By then whale numbers had dropped right off . . .'

Lex wondered if Jimmy would mention his family's involvement in whaling. This might be a good opportunity to denounce it. But the commentary ended and Lex hunched in his seat, trying to ignore the foul sensation of seasickness throbbing in his guts. The wind had kicked up from the north-east and the boat was rolling in the increasing chop. He was past the stage of caring and knew he was going down fast. Watching the horizon only added to his nausea. The end was nigh.

'Look up, sonny.' Mrs B leaned towards him. 'If you don't look up, you'll be sick.'

Lex wallowed miserably in queasiness for an interminable length of time. Then Mrs B jolted to her feet.

'Jimmy. Is that something out there?'

Lex could barely lift his head. He tried to focus where Mrs B was pointing, but the sea was a sickening mishmash of whitecaps. He heard everyone yell and noticed a blast of spray a few hundred metres out. Jimmy spun the boat and it suddenly ran much smoother. But it was too late. Lex hurled over the side.

'Fish bait.' Jimmy laughed. 'What are you trying to catch?' He slapped Lex on the shoulder. 'You'll be right now. It helps to throw up. Now get up and look for signs. It helps to think about something else.'

Lex staggered to the railing and clutched it. He did feel mildly better after vomiting.

'There's another spout,' someone called, down at the bow.

He could see the whales now, a pod of three or four, travelling. He could see their black backs sliding sleekly through the water and the small dorsal fin rising before they up-tailed, showing their flukes. Jimmy slowed the boat.

'We could be following too fast, too close,' he explained. 'They've dived now and they may not show again for a few minutes. We'll let them be, see what they do.'

Time stretched slowly. Lex was surprised to find himself excited, full of anticipation. He thought his experience swimming with the whales off the Point might have dulled him to this. But he was right into it. And Mrs B was flushed pink, scanning the waves with her sharp blue eyes. She smiled at him and gripped his hand suddenly.

'Over there!'

There they were, not far off. Maybe a hundred metres. Jimmy had done the right thing cutting the motors. It must be noisy for the whales down there, with the amplified thrum of the engines buzzing in the water. Lex realised he was holding his breath, waiting.

'Flipper,' Jimmy called.

They saw the white underside of a pectoral flipper raised above the waters like it was waving at them. There was a smashing spray as it slapped back down.

Then it was calm for a while. The boat shifted with the swell. Lex noticed Jimmy keeping a steady hand on the wheel to hold the boat angled into the waves so the rocking wouldn't get too fierce. Some of the passengers started grumbling and making snide comments to each other but Jimmy ignored them. He must be used to this.

Minutes crept by slowly. The sea rolled blankly around them, slapping against the side of the boat. Then an airy blast shattered the waiting. A spout shot up just fifty metres off the port side of the boat. They could smell the fishiness of the whale's breath and see the curve of its back breaking the water. Lex's heart thrilled. He shouted with Mrs B as the tail flukes lifted, water streaming from them, then glided back under the swell. Mrs B was hanging on to his arm, her face pale, eyes wide.

They waited, scanning the waves.

A little further off, a knobbled flipper wafted out of the water. It waved and wobbled, then dashed down.

'Hey,' Lex yelled. 'What's that?'

Just near the boat, about fifteen metres off, a slabby black head mottled with white slowly lifted out of the water. The head emerged vertically, water running down the parallel pleats of the whale's throat and dripping from the lumps along its jaw. Lex stopped breathing, took in the cluster of barnacles adhered to the whale's throat, the white eye peering at them. Then the whale sank slowly out of sight again.

'Spy-hopping,' Jimmy said. 'It's called spy-hopping. You're lucky. We don't see that very often.'

The head broke the surface again. This time Lex saw the downward-turning angle of the whale's mouth, several small rings of white marking the top of its head. He wondered how the whale did it, how it lifted its head out of the water like that, whether it used those massive tail flukes to hold itself vertical. And yet the movement seemed so delicate, so controlled. Spy-hopping. What a wonderful way to describe an encounter with a whale. A whale's way of watching humans. Lex smiled and the whale sank away slowly beneath the rolling swell once more.

Beside him, Mrs B was shaking with excitement, so Lex sat down with her on a bench along the railing. She grasped his hand, wordless for long moments, and then she was laughing and crying, dashing the back of her hand against her eyes to brush the tears away.

For twenty minutes or more, Jimmy guided his boat along at low revs, following the whales as they moved south, travelling slowly. From time to time, he cut the engines and they watched the whales wallowing not far off the boat. There were more spouts with showering drops, and a few more flipper flags. Then, eventually, the whales slipped beneath the waves.

The whales broke the ice for Lex with Mrs B. Over the days that followed, he stood with her often above the cliffs at Wallaces Point watching whales round the headland. They didn't talk much, but in snippets she told him about the Wallaces. She told him how the first house at the Point had been built by Vic's father, who had brought his family from Eden hoping for a better future than felling logs in the wet forest. Vic had been just a boy then, and for a while he had attended the same school as Mrs B, before he joined the logging gangs and disappeared for lengths of time cutting wood in the hills. By adulthood he tired of it and took his family west to Albany. It was unusual for families to shift long distances back then, but Vic had been lured by the call of the sea and the mysteries of whaling, based on his grandfather's old stories of whaling down by Eden. Vic and his family had returned from the west just before the whaling station near Albany closed down. The old house had been in ruins after years of disuse and Vic had started all over again. He had resumed a normal life until retirement, but after his years at sea he couldn't live away from the water. Hence all the effort to rebuild the house at the Point. There were few whales going by back then, the numbers had collapsed. But Mrs B remembered Vic sitting on the deck for hours, waiting, with his binoculars in his lap.

Lex thought about the old man watching for whales. He understood now why the house was all windows embracing the sea. But he couldn't rationalise the old man's thinking. What went on in Vic Wallace's head when he saw a sleek black back rolling through the swell? Was it a celebration of his past? Did it remind him of the thrill of hunting down a whale, the excitement of firing a harpoon? Or was he thinking of something else? Was he responding to a glimmer of regret, a sense of guilt, of waste, of loss? How could anyone not be moved by the majesty of seeing one of those great animals cruising down the coast? Within his own joyful observation of the whales, Lex couldn't find any empathy for the old man. He felt only anger at a man who refused to see the imminent death of an irrelevant industry until its very end. What kind of passion for whales did that reflect? At best, Lex could only see it as a passion for killing.

THIRTEEN

Lex was standing alone on the Point one balmy afternoon, looking for whales and watching Sash and Evan on the beach, when he heard a throaty engine roar. It was the orange Kombi clacking up in a spray of dust. It reversed onto his grass and Callista leaned out the driver's window, hair flowing over her brown shoulders.

'Get in,' she said. 'I'm taking you for a drive.'

Lex's heart rate ratcheted up quickly, but he held his face steady. He wasn't sure he wanted her to know just how much he'd been thinking of her. In fact, now that he was near her again, he wasn't sure about anything. The way she had reacted last time had been enough to terrify anyone. Especially him, wallowing in uncertainty as he was.

Today there was a wildness about her that Lex hadn't seen before, a do-or-die recklessness that made him nervous. Even so, he was pleased to see her. He hadn't really known what to do after that afternoon of passion in the gully. So he had hidden away here at the Point, pretending nothing had happened. He kept telling himself that it was better this way, and that it was too soon for him. But he had been thinking of her often, dreaming of her.

'I'll just get some shoes,' he said.

'You'll need boots where I'm taking you.'

Callista turned the Kombi around and kept it idling on the

roadside while Lex fetched some boots and socks. He tossed them on the floor of the Kombi, hauled himself inside and watched her as she revved the reluctant beast onto the road. She was thinner and her brightness seemed fragile.

'You're a surprise,' he said. 'Where are we going?' He hung on to the dangle-strap above the window as the van lurched and jolted over the potholes.

'Up to the mountains. I want to show you a bit of local scenery.'

'You don't have a gun in the back, do you?'

She didn't laugh. And tension remained thick between them. This wasn't going to be an easy trip. They were both trapped in the memory of last time: the feel of each other's skin, the awkwardness of Callista's outburst and the abruptness of Lex's departure.

He watched her hands white-tight on the wheel and let the silence spin out. This was her game. He would sit back and let her play it.

On the highway, they headed through Merrigan and just north of town Callista bounced the Kombi onto a dusty dirt road running west. They jolted up and over a wooden bridge spanning the river, where the water ran dark and black beneath them and casuarinas drooped their branches low over the banks.

'There's a good swimming hole down there.' Callista pointed and yelled over the whine of the engine. 'We can stop for a dip on the way back, if you like. It's going to be pretty warm up there today.'

Lex nodded and tried not to think of being naked with her in the water. He should be distant with her, careful. Who knew what she wanted from him today.

For a while the road ran along the river, across the green irrigated dairy flats. Lex could smell the grass and the sweet aroma of fresh dung and cows. Beyond the farms he could see the dry creases of the foothills slowly folding away up towards the rugged tops of the mountains with their purple cloaks of distant eucalypts.

Eventually, they turned towards the mountains. Lex held on tight as the Kombi swerved and swayed in the gravel, dust oozing through every crack. The road was roughly corrugated and Callista had to concentrate on holding the Kombi on track as they started to climb. Soon she had to drop into a lower gear and the high-pitched engine roared with effort. There was no space for conversation and Lex was thankful. The air between them was tight and awkward, and anything he said could be wrong. Instead, he studied the landscape, keeping himself focused away from Callista.

The foothills rose and fell and then surged up steadily to a ridge-line. As the road steepened, Lex glanced down the slope falling away beside the van. Spindly eucalypts with streaky rough bark clung to the hillside and the understorey was sparse and straggly. He wondered if there was water anywhere in this dry country.

They swung around a corner. Across the steep valley raw heads of granite jutted. It was surprisingly rugged. Sometimes the drop-off on both sides of the road seemed bottomless. Lex stared out over the craggy mountain tops and tried not to look down. The Kombi's shaky hold on the road made him nervous, but the surface was mostly good and Callista drove confidently. She knew where she was going.

'They use these roads to access logging areas,' she yelled over the engine-shriek. 'They're pretty well maintained. That's the only reason we can get up here in this rust-bucket.'

He nodded. He was watching her knee vibrating in time with the roughly labouring motor.

Eventually the road levelled out, bringing them onto a plateau with logging roads running off periodically to the south and the mountains rearing off to the north-west. Callista parked the Kombi at the head of one of the logging roads. The silence when the engine stopped was immense. Cumulus thunderheads were building west-ward beyond the peaks, but the sun was still strong. Lex allowed the silence to swell. Taking the lead was her responsibility. He didn't feel like making it easy for her.

'There's a track goes off from here.' She pointed into the scrub. 'It leads to that knoll over there. We have to go down and then it's a bit of a climb. But the view's great.'

Bush flies buzzed into Lex's eyes and the corners of his mouth as he tied his laces. Callista was waiting for him at the side of the road, watching him. He followed her over the lip of the verge.

The slope was steep and dry and the track very rudimentary. It was more of a scramble than a walk, but they scraped quickly down to a gully line. From there it was a hard slog uphill to the knoll. Lex had to concentrate on his footing so he wouldn't slip. His feet scrabbled in the gravel, but Callista seemed to walk like a mountain goat.

They paused for a breather.

'I grew up in this country,' she said. 'It's a tough landscape, but beautiful. Not many walkers come here. This park is for scrub-bashers.'

The climb to the top was strenuous and committing. It was far rockier and more precarious than Lex had anticipated. They had to scrabble up over boulders and slabs, and use trees for handholds to pull up on.

At the top, a dome of large rock slabs perched high above a delirious plunge down to the valley floor. Lex was wet with sweat. His heart thumped with exhilaration. They were so high. The building clouds in the distance appeared three-dimensional. Over to the east, the sea was royal blue. The air was fragrant with the pungent tang of warm eucalypts. A light breeze licked deliciously at his damp skin. He was very aware of Callista standing puffing beside him, smiling at the view. Hands on her hips, eyes closed in the sun, she looked less translucent than she had in the car when she picked him up at the Point.

'Let's sit in the shade,' she said, bobbing over the rocks to the loose shade of two sprawly eucalypts.

From there the earth fell away, tumbling down into the valley, and the view rolled across the rugged mountains peeling away like torn pages in a book. Callista dumped her daypack and slung the water bottle to him.

'Thanks,' Lex said. 'I'm hot.'

'You smell good,'

He snorted.

'No, I mean it. I like the smell of male sweat.'

He used the front of his T-shirt to wipe his forehead. 'I wasn't sure if I was going to see you again.'

'Merrigan's a small town. There's no escape.'

'Who's running?' Lex was annoyed at himself for being attracted to her again.

'If anyone's been running, it's been me,' Callista said. She was suddenly pale again. 'I'm sorry I threw you out the other day.'

'I'll get over it,' he said.

'It was that painting,' she admitted. 'You shouldn't have pulled it out.'

'Maybe you should get rid of it.'

'I'm working up to it. It takes time to let go of some things.'

'Yes,' he said quietly.

She looked at him with very clear eyes. 'Aren't there things in *your* life that upset you like that?'

Lex thought of Jilly. And that photo of Isabel. But he didn't want to talk to this woman about that. He hardly knew her.

'Everyone has baggage,' he said. 'Unfortunately you can't get far in life without picking some up.'

Callista hugged her arms around her knees. 'My family gave me history. And not all of it's pretty.' She looked at him. 'History can be a burden, you know.'

'My family history is boring.'

'Boring or buried. Families have a tendency to bury the interesting parts. They want to escape the legacy of the previous generations. Sometimes it's better not to know.'

They looked out across the folds and hummocks of the mountains. Lex let the wind flow through his soul. It was glorious up here with the smell of the dry bush rising up to them and the clouds building in massive piles above the mountains. But he was too aware of Callista beside him to lose himself in the landscape. She made him self-conscious and hyper-alert.

'Why did you come to Merrigan?' she asked. 'It seems like a strange place to choose.'

'The place chose me. The house. It was a great find.'

He noticed her tense.

'And I needed to get away,' he continued, watching her. 'Try something new. I've always wanted to live at the coast.'

'Don't you find it quiet, after the city?' She let the tension drop out of her shoulders again.

'The quiet is good. You can get fenced in by city life. Carried along by the rush of it. I'm glad to stop.'

She smiled and Lex felt his toes curl.

'Don't stop completely,' she said. 'It'd be nice if your heart kept beating. How else will I get to know you?'

She leaned back on the heels of her hands and looked away from him, gazing across the mountains. Then she continued talking, as if she were thinking out loud.

'I don't blame you for running down here,' she said. 'It seems like such a fresh place. It looks uncomplicated on the surface. But we have our foibles too. I've lived here all my life, and sometimes I wish I could run away. Life gets complex, even down here.' She sighed. 'But there's no such thing as a fresh start, is there? I mean, you take it all with you, whether you like it or not. The things I want to escape are in my heart.'

'*Bury My Heart at Wounded Knee*,' Lex murmured.

'What's that?'

'A book I read years ago, about massacres of American Indians.'

'There must be massacres in every white family history somewhere.'

Lex stared at her. It seemed a strange thing to say. 'We never hear about them.'

'No,' she said. 'Boring or buried, as I said. Mostly buried, I'd say. Nobody wants that sort of thing linked to their past.

That's why white men write history. So they can write things out of it.'

Lex was silent, feeling uncomfortable.

'Was your family involved in killings?' he asked eventually.

'God, no! Not of people.'

'Of animals then? That's not so bad. Everybody has to eat.'

'I guess so,' she said quietly.

He turned to look at her, and noticed her face had become pinched and pale.

'You don't look well,' he said. 'Should we head back?'

'In a minute,' she said. 'I want to look at the view a bit longer.'

They sat in silence together, letting their thoughts drift away. The clouds were thickening over the mountains and a cooler wind had sprung up. Lex felt somehow cleansed. But now he was physically aware of Callista, and he felt the air between them condensing as the sky greyed over.

She leaned back and looked at him, and Lex's heart battered in his chest. They were both thinking of being naked on her bed together. He swept his eyes away, nervous and unsure after last time. The silence hung for a moment then she swung over onto her knees, clasped his chin with a firm hand and kissed him. Her mouth tasted salty and enticing.

They made love on the rock slab, with the clouds riding above them and the wind whipping in the trees.

'How did this happen again?' he said afterwards, reaching a hand up to shift her hair back from her cheek.

Callista's laugh rang across the cooling mountain air as the wind-change gushed in.

'We didn't even take off our boots.'

At the Point, Callista sat uncertainly in the Kombi, not wanting Lex to shift his hand from where it sat on her thigh. If he disconnected it might be all over. And she didn't want to imagine driving home alone.

'Is it okay if I come in?' she asked. It was hard to sound casual. She found it difficult to read him.

His hand tightened on her leg. 'I was hoping you might stay the night.'

'That'd be great.'

Despite her show of confidence this afternoon, she really wasn't sure how to handle him. She'd have to take each opening he offered her. Find a way to inch under his skin. As she stepped up onto the deck, she noticed neat rows of shells and other sea-litter lined up along the wooden planks.

'Some shell collection,' she said.

'It's just bits and pieces.'

She knew he was fobbing her off. 'Do they mean anything to you, all lined up like that?'

Lex looked at the shells for a moment, like they were foreign objects. 'The passing of time,' he said. 'Days passing. Hours. Minutes sometimes.'

'You want time to pass?' Most people wanted to slow life down.

He was still staring at the shells. 'It helps me.'

His eyes shuttered and he opened the door.

'It's a great house, isn't it?' Callista said, stepping inside.

'You're not going to give me a hard time about it too, are you?' Lex dumped his boots near the door.

'About what?'

'About this house. And how it should have gone to the Wallaces, and all that.'

Callista watched his face carefully. 'Have people been hassling you about it?'

'Not exactly. But they never fail to mention it and make me feel like some sort of traitor for buying it. Do you know the Wallaces?'

'Of course.'

'Well, tell them I didn't mean to buy their house, and I'm sorry. I just want to live here in peace for a while. That shouldn't be a sin.'

'It is a nice house,' Callista said. 'No wonder the Wallaces were upset about losing it.'

'It is, except for its history.'

He came up to her and pressed her against the wall. He kissed her, his hands travelling over her body.

'Old man Wallace was a whaler,' he said. 'But you probably know all that, so let's not talk about it now.'

She held him off gently. 'You have something against whaling?' she asked.

Lex paused and stroked her cheek with a finger. 'Don't you?'

She shrugged. 'I don't like it,' she said. 'But the humpbacks are recovering . . .'

He picked up both her hands and held them against his cheeks.

'It'd be nice if we humans could leave something alone,' he said.

'You're an idealist,' she said.

He kissed the words out of her mouth.

'Aren't you an idealist?' he asked, trying to unbutton her top. 'Being an artist?'

'I'm a country girl,' she said. 'I'm practical.'

'Let's be practical now,' he said. 'We can argue later.'

Callista dodged him. 'I brought champagne. It's in an esky in the back of the Kombi.'

He laughed. 'It won't have survived the trip.'

'I'll get it and see.'

She fished the bottle out of the Kombi. She had spent the money on the champagne so they might as well drink it.

'Bring it here,' Lex said, from the deck.

'No. I'll wait for you near the cliffs.'

'While I get the glasses.'

She smiled. 'You're already reading my mind.'

'God forbid. It's a bit early for that.'

He went inside.

Callista crossed the road and found a soft spot in the grass where the bank rolled down to the sandstone rocks and dropped off steeply into the water. She sat and watched the sea, the clouds building out over the horizon. She heard Lex come up behind her. Then his hand touched her hair and he sat down close beside her.

'Here, let me open that.'

She handed him the bottle and watched him ease the cork out.

'You've done that before,' she observed.

'Maybe once or twice.'

'Have you had a lot to celebrate in your life?'

'No,' he said, eyes flattening. 'I just like champagne.'

'Let's have some then.' She watched the bubbles whizzing upwards in her glass and tried brightly to hook back the part of him she had just lost. 'What do you think you'll do when you grow up?'

Lex sipped his champagne and twirled the stem of his glass between his fingers. 'I don't know,' he said, flippant. 'Buy a yacht and sail around Australia.'

Callista felt the stirrings of frustration. He was holding her at arm's length, letting her know he didn't want her to get too close. But she let it go.

'I hear you're no good at sailing,' she said.

He raised his eyebrows. 'Who told you that? Mrs B?'

'Country grapevine.'

He grunted. 'What about you?' he said. 'What do *you* want to do?'

'Create great paintings and exhibit in big-time galleries where people will pay a fortune for my work.'

He smiled.

'Yes,' she admitted. 'Dreams. But you have to have them. Otherwise what is there in life?'

'There's sex,' Lex said.

He kissed her, and Callista kissed him back.

It was okay, she thought, playing along with this lust game. She wanted him too. For now she was happy to tangle in the romance of it all. That was part of the falling. But he'd have to give more than that eventually, because she was in this for more than the physical side of things. She wanted to know the man inside.

In the morning, Callista pulled an easel from the back of the Kombi and set it up across the road on the grass. She started to sketch the lines of the coast on a canvas, varying the curves of the beaches and the humps of the headlands to make them more interesting, raising the rock walls more dramatically. You could do that with art—change the rules, shift the skylines, embellish the colours. Pity it wasn't so easy to change the rules of life.

She applied a wash to outline the tones and then started squeezing out paints.

Lex came across the road with a newspaper and can of lemonade and sat on the grass beside her.

'What are you doing?' he asked.

'Trying to put some life into that headland over there.'

He looked up, shading his eyes. 'The colours are interesting.'

'Different from what you'd expect. But they'll work. You have to stand back to get the effect. And it's too soon anyway. I'm just getting started.'

He put his hand around her ankle and stroked her calf for a while.

'I'm concentrating,' she said. 'Find something else to do.'

'I like watching you.'

'Good,' she said. 'But you're distracting me.'

'What paints are you using?'

'Cheap acrylics. Same as I use for my beach art. I'm just mucking around.'

'When do you paint real things?'

'What do you mean?'

'Things you want to exhibit and sell for a decent price.'

'When the mood takes me.'

'And what do you use then?'

'Mostly oils. Sometimes better quality acrylics. Depends on how quickly I want it to dry.' She gazed out at the frothing manes of the incoming waves. It had been a while since she last pulled out her good paints.

'So you're a versatile woman,' he teased.

'I'm a normal woman.'

'There's no such thing.' He pulled out some grass and threw it at her.

'What's in the newspaper?' she asked, trying to concentrate on working the headland. She needed to focus on creating an impression of the columnar rocks and the clutter of boulders at the base of the cliffs.

'The Japanese again,' he said, spreading the paper out on the grass. 'They're sailing south to start their annual whale research mission.'

'Research mission? I thought they were harvesting for restaurants.'

'Yes, but they call it research.'

Callista looked down at the thin fair hair on his crown while he frowned into the paper.

'There's a Greenpeace ship heading down too,' he said. 'To disrupt things.'

She watched him lift his head to look out towards the horizon.

'That's something I wouldn't have minded doing when I was younger,' he said. 'It's good to feel strongly about something. To have passion.'

'Don't you think it's all a bit irrational?' Callista asked. She wasn't sure she understood his way of seeing things. 'It must cost Greenpeace a fortune to chase them down there.'

'That's what donations are for,' Lex said. 'That's why they have members. So people can believe in things from home, knowing someone else will risk their lives to take action on their behalf.'

'But what does it all mean in the end? The Japanese still get their quota of whales.'

'Having Greenpeace down there keeps the issue on the front pages of the paper. That's what it's all about.'

'Not about stopping the catch.'

Lex smiled up at her. 'It's nice if they can do that too.'

Callista dipped her brush in some paint and mixed a grey-brown.

'Why does it have to be an issue?' she asked, to be provocative. 'Why can't they have a limited catch?'

'The Japanese don't need to eat whales.'

'Isn't it supposed to be cultural?'

'Only since the Second World War. I'd hardly call that entrenched culture.'

'They probably think it's inhumane to eat kangaroos.'

Lex snorted. 'Whales aren't doing quite as well as kangaroos.'

'Humpbacks are recovering.'

'That's what the Japanese say here.' He flicked the newspaper with the back of his hand. 'They say humpbacks can sustain a controlled harvest. But who's ever been able to control the Japanese?'

'Better to work with them on this, than have them go off and do what they want anyhow.'

'They shouldn't eat whales at all.'

'That's a value judgment if I ever heard one.'

Lex looked at her as if he didn't quite believe what she was saying. 'Whose side are you on?' he asked.

'Nobody's,' she said.

'You ought to have an opinion one way or the other.'

Callista set down her palette. 'I don't like whaling either,' she said. 'But where's the argument in it if the populations are recovering? We harvest everything else.'

'They'll kill too many.'

'That's why you have to work with them. So you can police them.'

'We can't even police them *now*, when they're only supposed to be whaling for research. Research, my arse.'

He stood up with the paper and then tossed it to the ground. The pages fluttered in the breeze. 'I'm going for a walk,' he said.

Callista watched him stride down the grassy bank and along the sands towards the lagoon. She'd paint him in later. A black daub on the sand. It'd give the painting scale, and create a sense of solitude and loneliness—a single figure far down the beach. She wished she felt confident enough to paint herself in too, by his side.

FOURTEEN

Callista drove up to Jordi's shack. It was a clear cool summer evening and Jordi was outside as usual, sitting by the campfire bent over his guitar. The gas lamp he'd rigged up was hissing quietly and the fire was a muted glow. As she dragged up a stump, Callista saw him lift the lid of the billy to check there was enough water for two. He set his guitar aside.

'Hey, Jordi.'

'Yeah, how's it going?'

He shook some tea-leaves out of a jar, tossed them into the billy and hooked it off the fire.

'I love the way you do that.' Callista wasn't sure how to say that it felt familiar and comfortable, that it was part of the ritual of seeing him.

'There's nothing to it.' He examined a couple of old tin cups and screwed up his nose. 'Bit dirty,' he said.

She watched him dash some water into the cups from a plastic jerry can, then swirl his fingers around inside to loosen the dregs. He chucked the water onto the dirt at his feet.

'What you been up to?' he asked, filling the cups with tea.

'I've been busy.'

'Doing what?'

'Bit of painting. The markets. This and that.'

'It's that fella, isn't it?'

Callista grimaced. 'The news isn't out yet, is it?'

'Nah. But it can't be far away. I just know you.' He spat into the fire. 'You're gone. I can see it.'

'Is that such a bad thing? You encouraged me to go up there. And I think he'll be good for me.'

'More like you'll be good for him.'

'I'd like you to meet him. Properly,' she said. 'He's nice, Jordi.'

'Nice!' He spat into the fire again. 'Try again. What's he really like? And I don't mean in bed.'

She thought a moment, stirring her tea with a tarnished spoon.

'He's cautious,' she said. 'Doesn't want to give anything away.'

'Reckon he's hiding something?'

'He must have some reason for being here.'

'Can't crack it?'

'He's seamless as an egg. He doesn't want to talk.'

Jordi poked the fire with a stick and threw another log on.

'What's gonna keep him here then?'

'What do you mean?'

'He'll leave when he gets over whatever's eating at him. They all do.'

'You think I'm wasting my time.'

He shrugged and poured himself more tea. 'He needs an anchor,' he said. 'Something to hold him down.'

'What? Like a relationship?'

'Nah. That's not enough. He needs something more routine and less threatening. He needs a job.'

'Why would a job do it?'

'It's called investment. Once you get to know people, it's harder to leave. When a relationship gets sticky, you can just walk out the door. Once you've got other friends, it's harder to go.'

'That's cynical.' Callista tipped the dregs of her tea out on the ground.

Jordi sniffed. 'Much as I love you, sis, I can tell you this. He ain't gonna stay just for you.'

'Well, thanks.'

'You're complex and emotionally untidy. He needs a broader focus than you.'

She struggled not to be offended. Sometimes Jordi could be so frank it hurt.

'So how do you know all this?' she asked. 'Not from life experience.'

He stared at her, face hollow and thin in the firelight. 'I watch people,' he said.

He poured the remnants of tea inside the billy onto the fire and doused the flames.

'So, can we do dinner?' she asked tentatively.

'Nah, if I have to meet him, we'll go fishing.'

Jordi took them to a rock platform near the mouth of the Merrigan River. Standing up on the cliffs above the foaming sea, Lex looked down with dismay at the tiny eroded access track that Jordi pointed to. It slid down a steep gully between coarse prickly bushes, and then they had to climb down a sandstone crack to reach the platform. This wasn't quite the peaceful fishing expedition Lex had had in mind.

On the rocks, he looked back up and tried to slow the excited batting of his heart. It had felt risky coming down, and if Jordi hadn't been with them there was no way Lex would have done it. Too scary, too dangerous. He tried to concentrate while Jordi showed him how to set up the rod and bait the hook. They were fishing for blackfish today, using shrimp for bait. Lex wasn't sure whether the strong odour he could smell was coming from the bait bag or from Jordi's hair. But the guy sure knew what he was doing. While Lex shuffled tentatively around the rock shelf in his boots, Jordi bounded here and there in bare feet. He must have leather for soles.

Anxiously, Lex followed Jordi out to the edge of the rock shelf and looked down into the heaving sea. Waves smashed and poured over the rocks, and it all felt a bit too close. But Jordi was showing him how to uncock the reel and set himself up for casting. As he whizzed the line out, Jordi made it look like an art form. He indicated to Lex where to stand and went to fetch his own line.

Lex held the rod, feeling like an amateur. He wouldn't have the faintest idea what to do if a fish bit, and wasn't even sure he'd know it was nibbling. The tug and pull of the surf was confusing. And he'd look like a complete idiot if he stood here for half an hour and then pulled the line in with no bait left on it.

Jordi rock-hopped past with a rod in one hand, his fishing basket in the other, and a fag in his mouth. He nodded at Lex and perched himself on another rock further out, even closer to the surf. Lex watched the surf spray sprinkle him as he set up his rod. Jordi looked so at ease, squatting down on the rocks, tying on the hook. And Callista, sitting further behind, nestled on a pile of rocks, looked comfortable too, in some sort of reverie, gazing into the waves.

At first, he couldn't relax. The constant surging of the waves over the rocks just below made his heart tumble. Jordi had said they'd have to retreat up the rock shelf as the tide came in and Lex wasn't sure how he'd know it was time. He'd heard so many stories over the years of rock fishermen being washed away. And they were often experienced too. People who knew what they were doing. There was no way he could judge when a bigger wave was coming in. And he already felt too close to the surf. He didn't want to wait until the sea was licking at his boots.

Eventually though, as time passed, he began to relax and he leaned up against the rock behind him. It was mesmerising to watch the green swell rising up towards the platform and the waves splitting into rivulets of foam, frothing over the rocks and then sliding off with a hiss and a rush. The roar of the sea around them was soothing. It cut everything else out.

After a while, Lex realised he was happy, surprisingly at peace, and somehow alone, even with Jordi and Callista alongside. He glanced around at them and saw their faces, smooth and still, their eyes glazed into distance, their minds pleasantly disengaged, just being there, thinking of nothing, like him. So this was why people fished. Not just to haul in a catch, but for this—this detachment, this solitude. He smiled to himself. It was a revelation.

'Yo!' Jordi called.

But too late. A wave crashed suddenly over Lex's legs, tugging at him, saturating him.

'Pull back,' Jordi yelled.

He indicated to Lex where he wanted him to move to, and Lex galloped there with his heart in his mouth. The line snagged behind him. He dragged at it frantically as another wave foamed over the shelf and swelled around his knees. A larger set of waves must be coming in. He needed to get to higher ground, and he wanted to drop the rod and run, but it was Jordi's rod.

Then Jordi was beside him, fag still in his mouth. He leaned over and grabbed the rod with a firm hand. 'You're right, mate,' he said. 'Leave her to me. Just pop over there and I'll fix her up for you.'

Lex was happy to give the rod over. He scampered up onto the next rock ledge and watched Jordi standing amongst the straining foam, jerking the rod to free the hook. He gave the line three hard pulls and then the hook seemed to twang free or break off. Jordi reeled in the line and leaped up to where Lex was.

He flashed a brief smile out of his beard. 'That one came from nowhere, didn't it?'

'Bit close for me,' Lex said.

'You were all right.' Jordi looked at his trousers. 'Just got a bit wet.'

He examined Lex's line. 'Lost the hook,' he said. 'I'll just fix another one on for you.'

Lex watched him lope across the rocks to fetch his fishing basket. He came back and pulled out another hook and baited it up again.

'Here, you have a go at casting,' he said, handing the rod back to Lex. 'Like this. That's right. Now cast it right out there.'

Lex whipped the rod up and over his shoulders like he'd seen Jordi do earlier. He felt the line paying out from the reel and liked the sound of it.

'If I don't drown, I can see myself learning to like this.'

Jordi flashed another small smile. 'Look after my sister and I'll see to it you don't drown.' He bent to pick up his own rod.

'Oi,' Callista called.

Lex saw her waving from the rock ledge she had retreated to when the bigger set of waves had rolled in. She had a smile on her face like a fresh breeze.

'Are you having fun?' she called over the roar of the waves.

'Great,' he yelled. 'Just marvellous. You'd better say goodbye to me now, in case I get swept away next time.'

'You'll be right. Just keep your eyes open.'

They fished from the rocks for a couple of hours. Jordi pulled in a few fish, Callista caught one, and Lex pulled in some seaweed and lost two more hooks. But he figured he gained more than he lost. The easy companionship was some of the best he'd had here at Merrigan. There was a general feeling of camaraderie and support that went beyond Jordi's aside about taking care of his sister. There was a sense of tolerance and acceptance, even with his bumbling breakage of lines and dodgy casting. And there was a peacefulness and startling proximity to nature that he hadn't expected. It came with the near rush of the waves, and the intensity of the sound of water hammering over the rocks and gurgling among the cracks. There was a strange exhilarating joy in the risk of it and the bonding that arose from sharing the experience.

When they sat higher up to have lunch, tearing apart breadsticks and shaving slices of cheese, Lex felt the comfort of companionship, even with Jordi who he hardly knew. He began to see that perhaps you didn't have to have things in common with people to enjoy their company. There might be friendships he could make here in Merrigan after all.

It was warm that evening, and the sun lingered round and hot over the mountains. The house seemed breathless, waiting for the sea breeze to arrive. Lex took out the fish that Jordi had cleaned and scaled for him, and laid it on the chopping board, not quite sure what to do with it. Fish and chips were usually his limit, except for those occasions when Jilly cooked up some fancy fish recipe for a dinner party. And then his job had been to produce appreciative comments and clear the dishes away. He considered stashing the fish in the back of his freezer and forgetting about it, then decided he might wander next door and see if Mrs B had any suggestions.

There was a car parked beside her green Peugeot on the lawn and Lex almost turned back rather than interrupt, but Mrs B's raspy voice called to him from the shadows of the verandah.

'We're up here having a cup of tea, Lex. Why don't you come and join us.'

He walked hesitantly up the creaky steps onto the verandah and saw Mrs B sitting on a weathered old lounge. There was a man beside her, leaning up against the wall.

'This is my son, Frank,' Mrs B said. 'I've been wanting you to meet him.'

The man stepped forward, reaching out with a friendly hand, and it was like meeting a younger masculine version of Mrs B.

'Bit of a family resemblance,' Lex said.

Mrs B laughed. 'I didn't think anyone could look as cracked and craggy as me.'

Lex and Frank shook hands.

'Frank, get him a cup of tea, would you?'

Frank smiled blandly and went inside to find a cup.

'How are you, lad?' Mrs B asked.

'I'm fine. But I've got a fish I don't know what to do with.'

'So you're not much of a cook.'

'Never had to be. Any suggestions?'

Frank came out and handed a cup to Lex. 'Try wrapping it in foil with a dob of butter and a few herbs,' he said. 'Then pop it on the barbie or stick it in the oven. Good easy bachelor's meal. Tasty, but simple.'

'Sounds good.' Lex nodded. 'I'll give it a try. I've never had to deal with a fresh fish before.'

'You're not a fisherman?' Frank asked, sitting himself down on the couch with a grunt and a sigh.

'Unfortunately, no.'

'You'll get into it if you stay around here for long.'

'Frank's come over to do my lawns,' Mrs B said. 'But I told him to wait until it cools down a little.'

'I could help out,' Lex said. 'I don't mind mowing lawns if Frank can't get up here sometimes. So long as the lawnmower's functional. I'm not much good at fixing things.'

'Like fish,' Mrs B said, and they laughed.

Lex leaned against the railing and sipped his tea.

'Haven't seen any whales lately,' he said.

'The migration's done,' Mrs B said. 'They should be south, feeding up in Antarctica. Anyone who's coming by now isn't where he ought to be.'

Lex thought about the great upwelling of nutrients in the Southern Ocean where the cold Antarctic waters collided with the warmer currents from the north. The Antarctic Convergence, it was called. Massive swarms of krill abounded there, and pelagic creatures of every sort converged there too, for a feast. He thought of humpback whales feeding, taking in great mouthfuls of krill.

'I'd like to see whales feeding,' he said. 'It's supposed to be amazing. They run tours in Alaska.'

'Too cold over there for me, sonny. And too far away.' Mrs B frowned. 'Are you always dreaming about being somewhere else?'

'No. I like it here.'

'I told you he was mad about whales,' she said to Frank.

'Thanks for taking her out whale-watching,' Frank said. 'She had a good time. Didn't stop talking about it for days.'

'You could have taken me,' she said to him. 'You could have taken me years ago.'

'I didn't know you wanted to go.' Frank tried to defend himself.

'You didn't ask.'

'It's a neighbour's job.' Lex swept between them. 'Takes an out-of-towner to think of these things.'

Frank narrowed his eyes at him. 'You from Sydney?'

'Yes.'

'Bet you haven't been to the Opera House in years.'

'Not for a long time.'

'See?' he said to his mother. 'Like he said. You just don't do these things when they're on your doorstep.'

Lex finished his cup of tea and tossed the dregs over the railing. 'Best get back and have a go at that fish,' he said.

'Good luck.' Mrs B's thin lips stretched into a smile. 'Make sure you don't burn it.'

After the fishing trip, Lex didn't see Callista for nearly a week. He rang and left a couple of messages for her, but she didn't return his calls. This left him feeling wrung out and uncertain. The fishing trip had kindled a kind of reckless optimism in him, a surge of enthusiasm to know her better. But then this silence . . . what did it mean? Had he been reading too much into their interactions? Or was he simply being ruled by the physical side of things? By the sex. He ought to have a better grip on himself. She was more complex than he'd thought.

Then one day she arrived at the Point at dusk, restless and irritable, and suggested they make a fire on the beach.

While she fetched wine glasses, he stuffed some driftwood into a sack. He'd been collecting wood from the beach and saving it for winter for the wood heater. But if Callista wanted a fire tonight, she could have one. Anything to avoid conflict—although, watching her mood, it seemed conflict was inevitable. Something was eating at her. It made him wonder if he really needed all this . . . another relationship when he was still healing from the last one. He shouldered the sack and followed her down to the beach.

Above the high tide mark, he scooped a hole in the dry sand and set a small fire in it. Callista was silent and he was unsure of her mood. She watched him with folded arms as he crouched over the wood and touched a match to the crushed newspaper to light it. Then she sat down on the sand and he sat beside her and watched the eager flames licking at the grey wood. Even though it seemed incongruous sitting in shorts by a fire, he was enjoying the leaping crackle of the flames and the smell of smoke. Perhaps this had been a good idea. And the wine wasn't too bad either. He was using it more in moderation these days. Not needing to wipe out any more.

He peered sideways at Callista, wondering if she had tears in her eyes, or if it was just the smoke making her eyes watery.

'How was your day?' he asked.

'Didn't get up to much,' she said. 'Just a bit of painting. Made a few frames.'

They watched the flicker of the flames for a while.

'Feeling better?' he asked eventually.

'Better than what?'

'Than when you got here.'

'I'm feeling fine,' she said. She seemed to be keeping a check on herself. 'When are you going to get a job?'

A job! Lex almost laughed. Was that what was bothering her?

'I suppose I could get a job,' he said. 'But I wouldn't know where to start.'

'You might pick up something on one of the dairy farms around here. There's always someone looking for help.'

'I suppose I could ask around,' he said hesitantly. 'I'm not sure about cows though.'

'You can't work on a dairy farm without working with cows,' she said.

'I've never been near a cow.'

'Not even at your Agricultural Show?'

'Not even then.'

Callista snorted. 'I'm sure it'll be the beginning of a beautiful new relationship for you.'

They lapsed into silence again. Lex felt the cooler night air slipping in off the water.

'What have you been up to today?' she asked.

At least she was trying to be conversational.

'Reading,' he said. 'Reading history books from my shelves. I'm a walking encyclopedia on whaling now. I know so much about it I could do a documentary.'

Callista was silent.

'I spend a lot of time thinking about the Wallaces,' he said. 'There's something in the walls of that house.'

'That's what happens when you buy a house with history,' she said. 'But that's all it is. History. You should let it go.'

'I'm trying to understand what sort of person would hunt whales,' he said. 'Did the old man love the whales? Or did he love to kill them?'

'Both probably. You can love the courage of something that you kill. Killing doesn't mean that you have to hate.'

Lex threw another few pieces of wood onto the fire.

'So tell me, why are the Wallaces still making a living out of whales?' he said.

'What do you mean?'

'Jimmy Wallace's whale tours.'

'It's hardly the same thing.'

'It's still exploiting whales for a living.'

Callista stared at him. 'I think you're becoming paranoid about all this. Whale-watching is a careful tourist industry and Jimmy Wallace respects the whales. Otherwise he wouldn't be there. He wouldn't do it.'

'Then why doesn't he mention his family's history in whaling. It'd be a great opportunity to make up for the past.'

'Would you mention it, if it were you?' Callista's cheeks were flaming. 'Would you drag yourself back through the past every time you went out to watch whales? I don't think you'd have either the courage or the strength. Some things are too big to apologise for in small insignificant ways.'

She was very angry now. Her eyes were flashing in the firelight. He should have known better than to have a go at a local. He should have expected solidarity.

'I suppose it hasn't occurred to you, has it, that Jimmy Wallace might be ashamed of his past,' she said. Her eyes were bright and she held her head high. 'I happen to know that he loves whales. He never could stand the harvest. And he's had to carry his father's history all his life. But at least the industry did stop. So what does it matter if the old man loved his whaling books and stories? It was a job and a way of life for him. We all hang on to things that were exciting for us. Especially when we've moved beyond them. When things finish, memories are all we have left.'

Lex shook his head. She was really prickly and irrational tonight, and he had no idea what he'd said that had set her off. 'I just thought some sort of admission on Jimmy's part might help restore the balance.'

'Balance? There's nothing balanced about any of this.' She was furious.

'I'm sorry.' He backed down, astounded and confused. She was really over the top tonight. 'I'll let it go.'

But she stood up, crying, and stepped away from him around the fire. She paused as if she were about to say something else, but changed her mind and walked away over the sand into the dark.

Lex sat by the fire, wondering exactly where things had gone wrong.

FIFTEEN

Callista watched the sky from her verandah in the gully. It was brown with dust, and clouds were mounting, blotting out the sun. The weather was changing—a summer storm coming in. From late morning the wind had increased, clanging the wind chimes. It had been a dry year and with this early hot spell, dry air was blasting in from the hills, scattering dust with each gust. Not a nice day to be out.

She paced the verandah restlessly. The wind was making her fearful and edgy. What to do in this weather? Should she drive up to Jordi's where the wind would be whipping even more wildly in the trees?

The ringing of the phone made her jump. She shut the door behind her as she went inside to answer it.

'Who is it?' she said.

'It's Lex. I'm sorry about the other night. You're right. I should look for a job.'

She hadn't expected to hear from him after her performance on the beach, and she'd been unsure whether she should contact him. She'd thought he might be angry with her. That he might have written her off as too emotional and too difficult. It was a conclusion she had come to herself—that no decent man could tolerate her mood swings. She should have been more restrained. More measured and controlled.

'Is something else bothering you?' she asked tentatively.

'Yes. There's a storm building out here and it feels lonely.'

She hesitated, on the edge of relieved tears.

'You could come out and have dinner with me,' he said.

'Okay. I'll be there soon.'

Perhaps it would be better than last time. She would try to hold herself together. And it was a positive step if he was willing to consider a job.

When she pulled up in the Kombi, Lex was at the window, watching the whitecaps chopping up the sea. The air was cooler here at the coast, and swirling in a hundred different directions.

'Let's go down to the beach,' she yelled, tugging her coat out of the car. 'It might be calm down there by the lagoon.'

She saw him shake his head, but he appeared at the door with his coat and joined her, hiding from the wind behind the rectangular brick of the Kombi. Wind gusts buffeted it and they could feel it sway with each blast. She hooked arms with him and they crossed the road.

As they walked down through the thrashing heath, the wind whipped the grass and snatched at their coats and roared eerily in the casuarinas. But on the sand it was surprisingly calm. They walked the length of the beach right down to the lagoon. Looking along its choppy brown waters, they could see grey clouds boiling and tumbling from the mountains towards the sea, and the wind was cold. It swung down the lagoon and in a matter of minutes Callista was chilled. She reached for Lex's hand, and for a moment they huddled against the blast then turned back. There was no sense in this.

The wind had shifted around and now the full length of the beach was whipped by spitting sand. They ran down the beach, up through the shelter of the heath and across the road to the house. Callista was relieved to close the door and shut the wind out.

Inside, it was quiet and warm, a stark contrast to the wildness of the beach and the tossing casuarinas, now straining inland with the escalating winds. Callista picked up the weekend paper from the couch and flicked through it while Lex made coffee and started chopping things for dinner. He turned on the radio to listen to the weather forecast on the seven o'clock news and the presenter's voice sounded hollow, like it was somewhere far off underwater. Out to sea, Callista could see the storm congealing in the late afternoon sky and an early dark creeping in. Distant jags of lightning crackled through the radio and Lex turned it off.

'I'm going to have a shower,' he said.

Callista considered joining him, but didn't. She felt too ragged waiting for the storm. Instead, she watched the sky and frowned into the newspaper until Lex returned from his shower, smooth-shaven and freshly combed. Whatever romantic agenda he had planned for tonight, she didn't feel up to it. Out the window, the sky darkened further and the storm's moodiness intensified. She got up to turn on the lights. It was silly to feel as nervous as this. She'd seen plenty of storms before.

Lex opened a bottle of wine. He sat down beside her on the couch and handed her a glass.

'To storms,' he said, clinking glasses.

'I hope we get a good lightning show,' she said. 'There's no better place on the coast to see one than here.'

Time slithered past and dark oozed in, punctuated by wind and distant flashes of lightning. The wind started to moan in the wires and rattle the windows. They played a few mindless hands of rummy at the coffee table, pausing periodically to watch the lightning blinking on the horizon. The storm was blowing closer. Soon rumbles of thunder joined the batter of the wind.

Callista had her glass of wine in one hand and a hand of cards in the other when the lights flickered and blanked out. In the moments of dark that followed, her heart shattered in her chest and sweat broke in her armpits.

'Are you okay?'

Lex's voice was strange and near in the thick dark.

'Yes.'

'Stay put. I'll find the torch and get some candles.'

Callista hoped he'd be quick. She didn't like the blackness pressing in around her. She heard a click as he placed his wine glass on the table. There was a shuffle and whisper of movement as he walked into the kitchen, then the blunt beam of a torch jiggled across the room and flashed in her face.

'Sorry,' he said, then laughed. 'Look at you. Wine in one hand, cards in the other. What a girl.'

'I couldn't see to put them down.'

He clattered around in some kitchen drawers to find the candles and then set them up in empty wine bottles around the room. He disappeared to put one in the bathroom.

'Lucky you have so many empty bottles,' she said.

He smiled over the flickering candle flame. 'I prefer them full. But I'm getting better. You're a good influence on me. Would you like another glass?'

His closeness made her uncomfortable in the candlelit room with the black knocking to get in from outside. He seemed big and shadowy and powerful. Hysteria rattled in her chest, made her withdraw like a prodded snail.

'Perhaps I should go.'

'Don't be ridiculous. I'm not letting you drive home in this weather. Sit down. We'll eat. Dinner's still warm.'

Callista sat and tried to slow her hammering heart. She watched lightning skittering over the water, illuminating the headlands with reliable irregularity. She tried to focus on the plate of curry and rice Lex gave her, the rich smell of fresh coriander and the sweet aroma of basmati rice.

'I've extended myself tonight,' he said. 'I've picked up a few hints from you. Like the coriander. I've never used it before.'

The cuts of lightning shivered nearer, and as they ate, the storm blasted in with darts of white shattering the sky. Thunder cracks shook the house, and wind hurled itself in sharp gusts against the windows, swirling up under the eaves. The house shuddered as if it might take off. Then the rain came smashing in, blasting and drumming against the windows and crashing on the tin roof.

'It's almost enough to make you believe in God,' Callista said.

After dinner, Lex gave her a foot massage, his head bent in concentration so she could see the thinning of the hair on his crown. She found she liked the firm probing touch of his knuckles kneading into the ball of her foot and his fingers circling up into the tension stored high in her arch. The release he triggered washed right up into her neck and shoulders.

He kept topping up her wine glass, so eventually she wasn't sure if it was the snug bigness of him close beside her or the warmth of the wine that gradually made her relax. Slowly, she stopped jolting with each bright flash of lightning and each whip-crack of thunder. Instead, she watched the line of his jaw as he sipped his wine. The soft yellow candlelight flickered on his chin and somehow warmed the room, even with the wind blowing in under the doors.

Was there a lull in the wind or was it the candlelight that suddenly made his eyes thick? The room circled in a slow spin as she closed her eyes and let him kiss into her neck and up along her throat to her chin.

Taking a candle, he led her into the bedroom, sat her on the bed. He undressed in front of her, scooping his shirt from his shoulders with quick hands while holding her eyes firm with his. Then, very gently, he tugged at her clothes, peeled them off delicately like giftwrap, then lifted up the warm doona to cover them.

After Callista fell asleep, Lex got up to blow out the candles. The house was cold and the wind was still tearing at the eaves. It was hard to believe this was summer. Outside was black, and he stood in the kitchen listening to the racket of the storm. Back in bed, he wrapped himself around the sleeping woman beside him and lay awake absorbing the touch of her skin and the smell of apples in her hair. Eventually the teeming regularity of the downpour began to make him doze.

A flash of light jolted him awake. Had it been another flare of lightning, or something else, car headlights perhaps? He sat upright, straining into the dark, listening. There was nothing but the roar of the wind.

'What's wrong?' Callista murmured from beneath the feathery warmth of the doona.

'I saw a flash of light. I'll have to go out.'

'This is a lightning storm, Lex.'

'It might have been a car.'

He turned on his torch and Callista sat up.

'Nobody will be out driving in this,' she said. 'Especially not all the way out here.'

Lex yanked on his clothes in the torchlight. 'I have to check. I didn't see Mrs B come back this afternoon. She was going to visit Frank.'

'So you're really going out there,' Callista said. 'Do you want me to come too?'

'That's up to you.'

'Do you have another torch?'

He fetched one from the kitchen and tossed it onto the bed. He pulled on his Gore-Tex and boots while Callista dressed quickly. He thrust a woollen duffle coat at her.

'Wait here,' he said. 'I'll come and get you if there's anything.'

Outside was wild. He couldn't believe the intensity of the wind and the clamour of the rain battering against his raincoat and needling his face. Within seconds he was drenched. In the feeble torchlight, he navigated to the cliff edge and peered out into the dark. There was nothing—just the roar and pound of the sea tearing at the rocks. He moved further around the lip of the cliff, uneasy, unsure, afraid of being snatched and whipped over the edge.

There! He thought he saw a dim light in the murk. Leaning out, he stared into the rain and wind, cursed and wiped the water from his eyes. He could just make out two beams—maybe headlights—

hard to see through the thrashing salty air. Perhaps a car had gone over. Panic surged in him and he dashed back to the house. There wasn't much time, if any.

'Quick,' he yelled. 'I think there's a car down there. Grab my phone from on top of the fridge.'

God knows why he'd kept it charged all this time. Was he still subconsciously waiting for a call from Jilly?

Callista came out into the dark, waving the torch as she pulled on a hat. Lex didn't pause to look at her face. He hooked her arm and pulled her across the road through the rain and wind, through the hiss of the threshing heath, down towards the beach. Staggering down the wooden slats onto the sand, he could hear the roar of angry, wind-whipped waves smacking and thundering onto the beach. It was so dark. An occasional fork of lightning flickered over the sky. The rain was steady, soaking.

In the torchlight, the sea was alien. The waves were mashing together in confusion—a mess of water and froth and tangled directionless slappers and dumpers. Lex grasped Callista's forearm and guided her fast up the beach towards the cliffs. They neared the rocks, slick and black in the wavering beam of the torch. Staring into the water, Lex could just make out the hump of a car roof with waves smashing over it.

'Stay on the beach,' he yelled to Callista, 'And try to give me some light if you can.'

He shucked off his Gore-Tex and trousers and powered into the churning sea, straining against the shoreward thrust of the waves and the blast of the wind. The water was cold and angry and alive, like a beast. It curled around his thighs, dragged at him, crashed into his chest, clawed him back.

Ten metres out around the rocks and he could see the car more clearly. It had spun in the fall so that its nose was facing the shore. The headlights cut dimly through the wild darkness. The front end was caught up on a rock, keeping the nose out of the water, and waves were engulfing the rear.

He hoofed barefoot over the rocks, feeling the rough surfaces slice his soles. His leg caught in a crack and twisted, but he had to surge through the gouge of pain. The knee had to stay strong.

He reached the car, Mrs B's Peugeot, and leaned himself against it while a wave crashed on him, a vast mass of black heavy water. He felt his way under the water to the handle of the driver's door and clamped his hand on it.

Oh God, let it open, he thought.

It wouldn't budge; it was jammed tight. Perhaps if he used both hands and wrenched it down. Like this. It moved. He leaned into the rise and swell of an oncoming wave and hauled back on the door, heaved against the water. He'd have to be quick. He'd have to find the seatbelt. Snap it open, pull her out. What if she was already dead?

Water gushed into the car with the wave. It rose right to the roof and sucked out again almost as fast. The meagre light from the headlights was useless, he had to navigate with his hands. A body was slumped over the steering wheel. He leaned in across and fumbled for the seatbelt catch. His fingers were slow and thick with cold and he couldn't make out the mechanism.

Another wave cascaded in. Lex took a breath, submerged. He spat out the salt as the water frothed and bubbled out again through the door. There. The belt gave with a jerk. Now he wrapped his arm around Mrs B. It must be her, although he couldn't see in the wet dark. He couldn't be careful dragging her out with the crush of another wave pounding in on them. Speed was what he needed to get her head up out of the water.

With waves battering them, Lex hauled her out and wrapped her across his body, pinning her to his waist. Then slowly he ground in towards shore, propping his legs against the rocks with waves heaving and pounding at his back. Already he was revising CPR in his head.

It was then he heard a terrible roar of wind out to sea, ugly and sinister, like death. He felt the wave coming with it, a swelling mass of water whipped by the gust. If he didn't make it fast into shore, he and Mrs B would both be swamped and then sucked out by it like wisps of paper. He forced his legs through the mishmash of cross-cutting waves. Then the sea started pushing with an urgency that horrified him, lifting up, beginning to sweep his feet away. They were dragged high, tossed into the air, then plummeted through a furious mass of angry water. Under they went, tumbled. And then, incredibly, he was on his feet and pushed ashore by the water at his back, until it licked his heels high up on the beach.

Quick now. It might already be too late.

He dropped to his knees over Mrs B's body, yelled for Callista, and then groped for Mrs B's face to begin CPR. In the dark, his fingers mapped out the structures of her face. He straightened her up, dipped his fingers in the hollow of her neck to check for a pulse. It was there, weak and thready. There was no time to see if she would breathe, she was probably full of water.

He pegged her nose with his left hand, lifted her chin with his right, inhaled, clamped his lips over her cold slack ones and blew air into her chest. Three times. It was too dark to see if her chest rose and fell, but the air had gone somewhere and he felt a whisper of it puff out of her mouth on his own wet cheek.

How was it that he was here doing this again? Hadn't he had his turn for this lifetime?

He had to kill thought. Focus on the rhythm. Feel for the rise of Mrs B's chest. Feel the soft puff of air exiting her lips as he drew breath. Try to shield both their faces from the rain. Where was Callista?

At last he heard her, screaming for him, somewhere up the beach. Between breaths he roared a reply, then he was down again, working on Mrs B. Her pulse was still there—weak, but steady. Maybe they were going to win.

The ambulance came. Callista had called them after the gust. She had yelled into the mobile phone, she said, so they could hear her above the wind. She had called them even though she hadn't believed Lex could pull anyone alive out of there. When she saw the lights piercing the dark near the top of the cliffs, she went to guide the paramedics onto the sand while Lex remained with Mrs B, locked into the pattern of resuscitation.

The paramedics took over with strong torch beams and assertive confident hands. They rolled Mrs B a few times, shifted her into recovery position and gave her a thrust on the back. She vomited the sea out onto the sand and then sputtered into gurgling breaths. Lex was dazed by their competence. It was the same as last time, with Isabel—the same, but different. Mrs B was going to live. He shrivelled into the cold and tiredness that was seeping through him.

The paramedics slipped Mrs B onto a stretcher. Lex felt like he could use one too. Cold was stiffening right through him and his feet were wincingly tender. Thank God for Callista, who hooked his arm and steadied him as they followed the stretcher across the beach and up onto the heath. There was just a spattering of rain now amidst thick sea mist. Lex could see the salt air swirling in the torch-light. The night subsided to an eerie, uncanny peace. On the heath track, the wet grass was like a cushion under his raw feet.

The paramedics slid the stretcher into the ambulance under blinking red lights.

'Jump in,' one of them said. 'The girl's face needs attention, and you look like the walking dead.'

Callista's face had been flayed raw by whipping sand and his own legs and feet were laced with oozing bloody gashes. They climbed into the brightly lit interior of the ambulance and sat, still and numb, while the paramedic strapped a mask to Mrs B's face and started the hissing flow of oxygen. He tossed them a couple of blankets and turned back to Mrs B. The ambulance lurched and swayed down the Wallaces Point road towards Merrigan.

The hospital was all bright lights and clean white linoleum. It seemed surreal after the dark wildness of the beach. Lex was still in shock from the feel of Mrs B's slack mouth beneath his, and the exhaustion of performing CPR. He hobbled into reception behind Callista while the paramedics disappeared through flap doors with Mrs B. The waiting room was empty. Behind the desk, the white-clad nurse looked hard at Callista.

'Have you been here before?'

'Do we look that bad? I'm Callista Bennett. I've certainly been here before. Tonsils when I was a kid. And a few other visits.'

Lex gazed around the starkly lit room, then back at the nurse. He felt strangely absent, like he wasn't really there. He watched the nurse frowning as she punched at the computer keyboard.

'There's nothing under Bennett,' she said, squinting up at Callista. 'Could you be under another name? Aren't you Jimmy Wallace's girl?' She focused back on the computer screen. 'I thought you were in here under Wallace . . . Here you are.'

The nurse sounded pleased with herself, but Callista looked suddenly pasty, and Lex's chest constricted. He felt himself zinging somewhere up near those bright lights, looking down on himself and the girl beside him.

'It's Bennett,' he heard himself say. 'Callista *Bennett*. Didn't you hear her?'

'Here it is,' the nurse said, holding out Callista's file to show him. 'Callista Wallace.' She smiled kindly at Callista. 'Well, honey, you've had a hell of a night. What have you two been up to?'

Lex struggled with dizziness. He felt like he was falling in on himself. Callista Wallace? It must be a mistake. It must be wrong.

'I feel ill,' he said.

The two women turned to him and suddenly he was back in his body. The nurse was hesitant, Callista panicky. There was throbbing in his feet and in his legs. He felt hot, sticky.

The world folded around him into quietness.

In the morning they visited Mrs B in her room. She looked small and frail in the bed, her face as pale and grey as her hair. She was sleeping. She was exhausted, the nurse said, exhausted and weak, but she would be all right, so long as she didn't succumb to pneumonia. It was a risk, she told them, because of all the fluid she'd had in her lungs, but they had her covered with antibiotics just in case.

Lex stood by the bed and watched her breathing. It was reassuring to see the regular rise and fall of her chest. Last night was still heavy in him. Despite the painkillers they had pumped into him after the faint, his feet were agony. He hadn't known pain could do that to you—make you faint. Pain and complete exhaustion.

This morning Callista was hesitant with him and he was too vague from the drugs to engage with her. Each time he considered her name—Callista Wallace—there was a numb buzzing in his brain. Why had she hidden it from him? Why had she hidden who she was? When he flashed back to all the discussions they'd had about whaling, Wallaces, the Japanese . . . if he'd known, then perhaps he'd have understood. Or perhaps he'd have withdrawn. Who knows; he was too hazy to think about it now.

One of the nurses coming off shift drove them back to the Point. Lex sat silent in the back, only half-listening to the women as they discussed the storm. Sheds blown over. Telephone and power lines down. Trees blasted over. Roofs peeled off. Their chat seemed to trivialise everything.

At the end of the Point road, the nurse stopped her car on the gravel in front of the house. She hopped out to look over the cliffs at Mrs B's Peugeot swamped in the licking surf.

'I'm impressed you got her out of there,' she called to Lex.

But Lex was looking at the house, uneasy. 'Something's wrong,' he said.

He stared at the house, curious cartwheels turning in his chest. What was it that was different? He couldn't put his finger on it. Was he still light-headed from the painkillers?

The front of the house looked cleaner somehow. He noticed there was movement inside the windows, a slow flap of curtains. That absent feeling was back as he hobbled across the road. He shuffled painfully across the lawn and looked blankly into the house. The windows were gone. The entire frontal face had been punched in.

Slowly he climbed the steps. The door was an empty frame with shattered glass around its rim. It crunched as he pulled it open, mashing glass fragments. Inside was an explosion of glass and water. Splinters of glass were shot everywhere across the room. Lex stepped inside. He picked his way over glass scattered across the floorboards, careful not to slip in the pools of water on the floor. The couch and armchairs were drenched. His playing cards were strewn across the room. Half the books had tumbled from the bookshelves, and Vic Wallace's whaling-boat photos had crashed to the floor and lay smudged in their broken frames. The back windows were gone too. Spat outwards. Over the sink, the curtains flapped and fluttered in the breeze like prayer flags.

Blankly, he drifted through the ruin of his home, sweeping glass off the table and the kitchen bench with the back of his hand. He picked up a sodden book from the floor and shook the glass off its cover. It was strange, this floating, absent feeling that had come over him again, like it was happening to someone else.

'It's like a bomb blast,' Callista was saying.

Lex hadn't noticed her come to the door. He looked into her shocked face and felt nothing. He was so detached, so floaty. Surely he should be feeling upset.

He placed the book on the kitchen bench and walked down the hall to the bedroom. The wind had smacked the bedroom door shut. He forced it open and stopped. Glass was scattered all over the room. The bed was soaked. The curtains whipped in the wind and the sea seemed to roar in unchecked.

Numb, Lex stood in the doorway and stared out through the wreckage. He watched Callista wrap a towel around her hand and sweep the shattered glass off the bed onto the floor. She kicked some glass out of the way and dragged the chest of drawers aside where it had toppled against the bed. A drawer fell out and with it a framed photograph, the photo of Isabel. Callista bent to pick it up.

'Thanks,' he said, voice hollow. 'I'll have that.'

A strange noise huffed out of her as he pulled the photograph from her hand. Her eyes were hurt and angry. She tried to snatch it back.

'What's this,' she said, eyes snapping. 'A child? *Your* child?' She tugged frantically at the other drawers, tipping the contents onto the floor. 'And what about your wife? Is there a photo of her too? What else are you hiding?'

'Hiding?' Lex was suddenly exploding with outrage. 'Hiding? What about you? You didn't tell me you were a Wallace.'

'Is it such a big deal?' Callista was wild, reckless, struggling with some desperate thing inside her. She felt as if she might throw something.

'Yes it is, given that this is your grandfather's house.' Lex was like granite.

'What are you saying?'

Something unfamiliar was curling over in him, like a wave breaking. He wished Callista would stop before something snapped in him. There was hammering in his head. The rumble of anger boiling deep within him was pressing to the surface. He tried to hold on, but his voice came out hard.

'When were you going to tell me?'

Her eyes flashed. 'Tell you what?'

'Your real name . . . Callista Wallace.'

'I told you my name. My married name. I wasn't hiding anything.'

'Of course you were hiding something. We talked about Wallaces dozens of times and you never mentioned it. Why's that? Were you trying to woo me so you could win back the house?'

Callista thought she would erupt. 'That's a disgusting suggestion. I enjoy your company.'

'What? Like on the beach the other night, when you ripped me to shreds?'

'When you were hooking into my father again! What was I supposed to do? Stand by and watch you annihilate him?'

She was backed into a corner, fighting like a cat. And Lex was hot with seething anger. The room was too small for their emotions.

'I think you should go,' he said.

But Callista stood firm and defiant. 'Not until you tell me.'

'Tell you what?' he asked, incredulous.

'About your wife and your daughter.'

Lex glanced at Isabel's photo and his fury left him. He felt bereft, betrayed, demolished.

'My daughter's dead,' he said, flat and tired. 'She died from cot death. And my wife blames me. So now she's divorcing me. That's about all you need to know.'

He side-stepped past Callista's shocked white face, through the shattered window and out onto the deck.

'Don't go,' she said. 'Please don't go.'

But Lex hobbled down the steps.

The nurse was standing on the grass.

'If the Kombi won't start, make sure you take her home,' he said, as he limped towards the heath. 'I want the house empty when I get back.'

When he returned, the cars were gone and the house was quiet. He was glad of it. He needed solitude, space around him, the cleanliness of empty air. The past twenty-four hours had been too much for him—the storm, resuscitation again, Callista . . .

He went next door to check Mrs B's house. Things had blown over there too. A corner of the roof had lifted. The old bus had toppled over. The front door was hanging loosely on torn hinges. Out the back, he found the peacock crushed under a sheet of tin, its bright feathers already fading. Of everything, that upset him most.

Sitting on the back steps of his neighbour's house, tears came from nowhere. He cried for Isabel, for Mrs B, for the peacock, for his house. Even for Callista. There were parts of all of them gone forever.

PART III

Aftermath

SIXTEEN

After he buried the peacock, Lex drove into town to see how others had fared in the storm and to organise a glazier to replace his windows. At the far end of town, the street was clogged with police cars. Lex was sure they hadn't been there when the nurse drove them home a few hours ago. As he parked the Volvo, he noticed that the front door of the butchery was sealed with yellow tape. He ducked into Sue's, wondering what was going on.

In the café a cluster of dark-suited strangers was hunched around a table against the wall. Sue was nowhere to be seen so Lex slipped into the kitchen looking for her.

'Sue,' he hissed. 'What's happening?'

She looked up from the bench, stressed and white.

'Oh, it's you,' she said. Her face melted into tears. 'It's been a terrible day, Lex. A terrible day.'

'What are all these people doing here?'

'Henry Beck died in the storm. It was an accident.' She sat down on a stool and wept.

'What happened?'

'I found him,' she said, wiping away tears. 'I came in early to check the café after the storm and I noticed lights on in the butchery and the back door open. So I went in, to see if there was anything I could clean up for them. Henry was in there, all curled up on the floor with a knife in his stomach and a huge lump of meat hanging over him dripping blood on his head.' She shivered and wept. 'I'll never forget the sight of it.'

Lex felt useless. He didn't know what to say.

'I rang the police straightaway,' Sue said. 'And they rang Helen.' She started crying again. 'I should have rung her myself, but I wasn't brave enough. I was such a wreck after finding him, you see.'

'What happened then?' Lex asked.

'Helen came down to see him, of course, but they wouldn't let her in, because the forensic crew was still working in there.'

'They made her wait?'

She nodded. 'Poor Helen. They made her wait, and she kept wringing her hands and asking me why they were calling Henry "the body". Kept asking if that meant he wasn't Henry any more. That he wasn't human.'

Lex tried hard not to imagine Helen standing at the door, anxious, terrified.

'Then they let her in,' Sue said. 'And they were all lined up against the wall, you see, because they wanted to watch her reaction so they could tell whether she'd murdered him or not. I knew what they were thinking. Wretched souls. Well, when they let her in, Helen just stood there, holding on to the door. She was so white, Lex, and shaking all over. I don't know how they could even think she'd murdered him. She walked so slowly across to him, and sat down beside him in that pool of blood, and she pushed the hair back from his face, so gently. It breaks me up to think about it.' She oozed fresh tears. 'There was blood all down his face and she sat there picking it off with her fingernails. She was so careful and gentle about it, so as not to hurt him. Lex, it'd tear your heart out to have seen it.'

He patted her arm.

'Those stupid policemen just stood there watching her,' she said. 'They didn't know what to do. So I pushed my way in there past them all and I took her home. I had to whisk her past her poor son

Darren so he wouldn't get a sight of the blood. Poor boy. He was in the hallway, waiting. He didn't know what was going on. So I got her past him and I put her in the shower so she could wash herself clean. Poor thing. Then I got the boy to call Mrs Jensen. There was nothing more I could do after that.'

'What's happening now?' Lex asked. 'Have the forensic crew sorted it out?'

She jerked her head towards the door into the café. 'That's what they're doing in there now. They've got their theories.'

'Like what?'

'No witnesses, you see. They have to work it out.'

'And?'

'They're saying that Henry was probably out the back sharpening knives, with the side of beef out ready to carve. They reckon a blast of wind bashed the door into the beef and rolled it onto him. Forced him down onto his knife. They reckon he stabbed himself.'

Lex could picture it, even though he didn't want to.

'Is there anything I can do?' he asked.

Sue shook her head. 'No, she's got the church around her now, giving her support. That's where she belongs. With her own folk.'

The funeral was surprisingly large. Lex was amazed at the scores of cars parked outside the church when he drove up in the Volvo. He wandered up the hill with all the other quiet, serious-faced people and found a standing space down the back of the church. Several people he didn't know nodded at him as they passed. He was surprised and wondered what it meant. Perhaps that was what people did at funerals in the country.

The church was packed. Lex hadn't imagined Henry to be so popular. He'd seemed such a difficult person, loaded with arrogance and uncomfortable edges. Whenever Lex had bought meat at the butchery, he'd watched Henry lording it over his assistant, glaring at him and waving instructions with hands as meaty as steaks. He couldn't forget the patronising way Henry spoke to his wife whenever he was ordering her about, and the fear and submission in Helen's eyes.

Helen was there, of course. She was down the front, stiff and straight in black, with the boy holding her hand. Lex saw her glance over her shoulder at the crowd and then quickly turn back to the front again. There was fear in her eyes. Henry was still in control.

The coffin was polished wood, sleek and expensive. It was long, for a long man. It reminded Lex of Isabel's coffin. But hers had been white and obscenely small. He'd cried when they chose it. He didn't want to bury her under the ground, away from the sunlight.

Isabel's funeral had been big too—huge crowd, tiny coffin. Jilly had insisted on a church service, even though they weren't religious. Something about concern for Isabel's soul, just in case there was a heaven up there. She didn't want to think about Isabel missing out and burning in purgatory. But Lex knew that purgatory was here on earth, being left behind with the terror and the grief. Isabel had only been dead a week and it was already destroying them.

Before the service, everyone had wafted around outside the church, patting him on the shoulder and calling it a tragedy. There were tears, an endless tide of them. The memory of being engulfed by hugs. People gripping him as if they were drowning, when it was really him that was going under. The thought of going into the church and watching that tiny coffin throughout the service had withered him. He didn't think he could do it. Didn't think he could sit there knowing that Isabel's tiny fragile body was lying in there. Already decomposing, no matter how the funeral parlour had tried to disguise it. Death was supposed to be for old people, for people worn out with life, their bodies broken and past their use-by date. Isabel's life had barely started.

In the church, he'd sat stiff by Jilly. She was a red weeping mess, seeping constant tears. But Lex's tears were locked somewhere inside him and he couldn't even reach out to hold her hand. Jilly's mother had to be the prop for her that day. Provide the support that Lex couldn't. He ought to have been strong for her. But everything inside him was broken, and without the scaffolding of his meagre self-control he'd have collapsed beneath the weight of a feather.

The service had passed in a blur. Lex remembered nothing of it—none of the soothing words that must have flowed from the eulogy, no recollection of the colourful flowers that must have adorned the church to signify new life and resurrection. All he remembered was the coffin. The shiny white wood, the handles glinting gold, the terrible thought of burying his child deep under the ground.

At the end of the service, he had carried Isabel from the church. When he lifted the coffin from the stand, it was so light Lex thought it might fly away down the aisle, out into the bright day and up into the sky. It would have been better that way. But it ended in the cemetery, with the dull thud of clods of dirt being dropped onto the coffin. Each thud like a hammer battering on his soul. It was as if he were being buried too, the essence of him sealed away in the coffin with Isabel. His heart torn out and interred.

In the Merrigan church, staring at Henry Beck's coffin, Lex felt his heart back within him now, altered, but somehow regrown, thundering with the stress of memory. He saw the minister step up to the podium—a tall man, imposing in his black suit and white dog collar. Elevated above the congregation, the minister stood with his head bowed while the organ burst lustily into 'All Things Bright and Beautiful'. It was incongruous, with Henry's coffin lying there at the head of the church. Nobody sang. And it was too much for Helen Beck. Lex could see her shoulders shaking while she cried.

After the music faded away, the minister raised his head and hands and his voice poured out over a concealed microphone. The service was lengthy and dry, lots of inane preaching, a touch of fire and brimstone, endless talk of love and forgiveness. Lex eyed the door, wishing he could escape. He had come to pay his respects to Henry, strange though the man had been, but he hadn't counted on flashing back to Isabel's funeral and now he was emotionally exhausted and wanted to leave. This was going to be a long haul. But now that the service was under way, it would be difficult to walk out.

To distract himself from the weight of memory and grief, Lex took a look around him. All the Merrigan church-goers were seated in the front pews with commanding views of the coffin. Lex summoned an internal smile. He supposed there had to be some advantage in coming weekly to pay your dues to God. Mrs Jensen and her husband were to one side of Helen, and some other people sat on her other side. Lex assumed they were her parents.

The non-church people were crammed into the back half of the hall. Sue was there, of course. She hadn't been a close friend of the Becks, but she had fostered a working relationship with them, given the proximity of her shop to the butchery. A few of the other people must be farmers who sold meat to Henry. Sue had told him Henry's meat came through the abattoir further up the coast, but it was all grown locally. Henry preferred to have contracts with farmers he knew.

He noticed Sally there too, with Sash and Evan. Sash looked bored and restless. She probably didn't understand what had happened to the butcher, and maybe that was just as well. Lex hadn't known Sally was particularly friendly with the butcher, but he supposed she must have bought her meat from Henry too, like everyone else local. In a small town, perhaps everyone attended funerals.

He searched about for Callista but she wasn't there. He shouldn't be surprised. She didn't like the Becks much. And she probably didn't want to risk running into him after the storm. Lex couldn't believe he hadn't worked it out sooner . . . the fact that she was a Wallace. Everything about the Wallaces and Callista's defence of them made sense now. Lex wondered where his head had been not to notice. Even so, they shouldn't have argued after the storm. He should have held back. He should have quietly asked her to leave and left it at that. But he had been unhinged by the wreckage of the house. And they were both so raw from the storm. He shook his head. He was making excuses for himself. After Isabel's death and the damage he and Jilly had inflicted on each other, he should have known better.

The evening after the funeral was luminescent. The sea was calm and silvery in the late light. Lex left the photo of Isabel on the kitchen bench and went down to the beach. The funeral had reopened all his dark corners, and he had spent the afternoon staring at Isabel's photo, trying to find the shape of her in his memory. Beneath his skin, sadness was welling. It was mixing with the anger that had been boiling slowly there for weeks now; anger at himself for losing his hold on Isabel, anger for forgetting, anger at Jilly, at Callista.

Trying to let his mind slip with the rhythm of the sea, he walked slowly in the wet sand as far as the lagoon. Down by the quiet brown water, he scooped a hollow halfway up a low dune and sat down. In the lap of the sky he watched evening fall. Beyond the sandbar he could hear the muffled crash and roll of the sea. The lagoon lapped peacefully. In the darkening blue-black sky of early evening a few stars blinked. Way across the lagoon, swans whistled and honked intermittently. Occasionally a fish flipped. And always that steady flush and thump of the sea.

Night slowly whispered across the beach. Lex leaned back in his hollow and tried to release himself into the invisible breeze and the cool air. As dark fell, the skies grew larger, until above him the heavens thrust in a dome, spangled with glittering stardust, the arc of the Milky Way. Confronted with the infinite, he felt the smallness of his existence, his own inconspicuous irrelevance.

It must have been the sea that lulled him to sleep, but he couldn't tell where consciousness and sleep merged into the vapour of dreams. Helen Beck swept over him, with her desperate face from the funeral and her white hands. Her eyes were madness—black orbs that sought him, delved into him. Then a different mouth floated over him, softer. A smile he barely recognised, but which somehow knew him. The lips were kind, humorous, comfortable. He ought to know this face. It was so familiar. There was a smooth feeling of generous hands running over him, running through him. Of course. It was Callista. Happiness curled into a dull ache that intensified and slowly split open like a chasm. Cold air, turgid with sadness, gushed up, engulfed him, cleaved him open with a heavy strike. Isabel now, flying over. Her face whipping through the heavens. Grief swamped him, like fresh blood. He felt the horror of Isabel's non-existence and the loss of her. She was being sucked away and he couldn't reach her. He was calling her name, stretching to touch her. But he was clamped to the earth, sinking knee deep in it, while she arced away, deaf to him, transfixed on something else, somewhere else. She was gone.

He was alone in black emptiness. Hollow. There was nothing.

SEVENTEEN

Callista knew the funeral was going on in town, but she didn't want to go. She'd never had much to do with the Becks. Sure, she felt sad for his wife. But then Helen was free of him now, wasn't she? Henry's death might be a blessing in disguise.

She heard a car coming down the hill and wondered who it might be. Her mother hadn't dropped round for a few days. But no, it'd probably be Jordi. He'd know she'd be boycotting the funeral.

The gully was humid this afternoon. The rain that had come with the storm had steamed things up and the air was still. Callista could smell Jordi's sweat as he gave her a quick hug and sat down on the deck beside her.

'What's doin'?' he said.

'Nothing much. Couldn't face Henry's funeral.'

Jordi flashed a smile. 'Didn't think so. Knew I'd find you here. Heard you had a blow-up with Lex.'

'Did you hear the rest? How the house blew in and the bed filled up with glass? It was lucky I wasn't cut to ribbons.'

Callista tried to sound light about it all, but the events from the storm had clotted in her chest and she had been finding it difficult to breathe.

'Thank your lucky stars you were out rescuing Mrs B,' Jordi said.

'I'm still trying to come to terms with it,' she admitted.

'What happened with Lex?'

'He found out my name at the hospital.'

'You didn't tell him?'

'Didn't get a chance.'

Jordi grunted. 'No wonder he threw you out. So the house slips out of reach again.'

'It wasn't about the house.'

'Not even a little bit?'

'No,' she said. 'I'm tired of being alone.'

'So you're over Luke then, and all that?'

Callista smarted. 'What do you mean, over it? Are you over Kate?'

Jordi winced and she wished she hadn't dug at him.

'That's low,' he said.

'I'm sorry. But I'll never be over it. You know that. Didn't you tell me I had to move on? Lex was my chance.'

'Was?'

Tears came, sudden as a spring rain shower. 'He lost a child. And he has a wife.'

'Ah.' Jordi's quick smile was cynical. 'The plot thickens.'

'I think they're getting divorced.'

'Just as well, given that he's been entertaining you.'

'It wasn't like that.'

'What was it like then?'

Callista's tears renewed. 'It was going well. Sort of.'

Jordi's eyebrows lifted.

'He enjoyed the fishing trip. And he's even been talking about getting a job.'

'That's marvellous, now that he's been here three months.'

She ignored him. 'It was only when we got on to Wallaces and whaling that things fell apart.'

'And you complicated it by hiding your name.'

'You think he'd have been all jolly about it if he'd known?'

'It didn't work out too well with him not knowing, did it?'

'Don't punish me,' she said. 'I've been flogging myself enough as it is.'

Jordi frowned. 'So is that why it's over? Because you're a Wallace?'

Callista curled around her knees, miserable. 'It's probably the way it all came out that finished it,' she said. She could remember Lex's face, white with fury. There had been hatred mixed with all that emotion. Hatred and accusation. She couldn't see how they could go back after that. 'Damaged goods,' she said.

Her tears turned off and weariness set in. Jordi went inside and brought out two glasses of water. He sat back down beside her on the lip of the deck.

'Dad asked me to help out on the boat,' he said.

'What's wrong with that?'

He spat on the grass. 'I'm used to going it alone. It's better that way. Nobody relies on me.'

'Barry relies on you.'

'That's different.'

'No, it's not.'

He glared at her. 'I have my own way of dealing with things.'

'And how's that?'

'It's *my* way,' he mumbled.

'I thought the boat would make you happy. Not so lonely.'

'I've got happiness, in my own way. I don't need you interfering in my life.'

'What? It's my fault Dad asked you to help?'

'Mum said you talked to her about it.'

'For God's sake, Jordi. I was only trying to help. Same as you help me. I won't get involved next time.'

'Good.'

'Won't you give it a go?' she said hesitantly. 'You might actually like it. And it'd get you away from the servo a bit. You can't pretend you enjoy it down there.'

He said nothing.

'Please?'

'I'll think about it.'

She put her hand gently on his arm and he let her leave it there for a moment.

'We have our own path, you and me,' she said quietly. 'Our own way.'

Jordi looked at her. 'No,' he said. 'You have your path, and I have mine, Callie. I can't bear the load for you. I have enough of life to carry for myself.'

She watched him sitting there on the step, with his scrawny shoulders squared and his lips firm. There was so much strength in that bony frame and those wild, determined eyes.

'I don't know how to fix things with Lex,' she said.

He glanced at her. 'That's easy. Like the storm. Let it blow over.'

'It wasn't supposed to go this way.'

'No,' he said. 'But life was never supposed to be fair.'

He pulled a joint out of his pocket and lit it.

'I'm done with talking,' he said, taking a drag and passing it to her.

They sat for a long time, breathing the bush, watching the light, and drifting into an easy, mindless haze.

After Jordi left, Callista pulled her paints drawer out from under the kitchen sink. Her good paints were stored there, the expensive ones, the ones she saved for best. Dumping the drawer on the table, she threw aside the dusty old cloth covering it. There was an unexpected tingling energy in her fingers as she rolled a few paint-blotched tubes in her hands. She looked at the paints like they were foreigners, not quite connecting with them. Minutes passed as she went through the contents of the drawer: tubes of oils and acrylics, half-cleaned palette knives, new and neglected brushes, a handful of broken sketching pencils, scraps of charcoal, chips of dried paint.

She allowed time to wash over and through her, and waited for the magic to emerge. She emptied her mind until her focus was centred on the tubes of paint and all she could hear was the whisper of her own tremulous breathing. Beneath her skin large events were waiting to disgorge. Huge dark emotions and happenings were brewing. Thoughts and visions shuffled across her mind: order and disorder, love and terror, fear and disappointment, loss. Flashes of angst. Lex. The storm. The black wind on the beach that night.

She wiped the dust from her palette and cracked off the dried clots of paint. It had been a while. More carefully now, she went through the paints. Some were useless, dried out from the last time she had frenzy-painted and forgotten to twist the lids on tightly enough. What a waste. But there was enough.

The old excitement welled in her fingers and tickled in her chest as she began squeezing colours onto the board: black, blue, violet, white, red, yellow. From those she could mix the strong steely blues and turgid purples that she remembered in the sky before the storm as it thickened with furious clouds and stretched itself vertically and horizontally in the escalating winds.

She clunked a canvas onto her easel. Frantically, her hands scattered amongst the brushes in the drawer, scuffing over stiff tips and shakily selecting large sizes. Everything within her was coarse and urgent.

It was then, with a handful of brushes clutched in her left hand, that she caught sight of her reflection in the mirror. The wildness in her eyes almost frightened her and she noticed the panicked thumping of her heart.

Slowly she placed the brushes on the table. She lifted the mirror down and set it on the easel. Staring at herself, she slipped off her clothes and stood squarely naked in front of the mirror, resting the palette on her right arm. She dipped and swirled one brush, coated it in black. Wildness surged in her, primitive and strong. She dabbed the black on her breasts, covering the generous bulges of creamy flesh, then made a sludge of grey on the palette and slicked it over her nipples. Concentrating, focused on colour, she mixed blue-black and swiped it repeatedly over her abdomen, up to her chin, dots of it over her face.

Panic blossomed.

She squeezed out more black, painted her arms and legs with it. Then another large squeeze of black slathered thick and slick onto the V of her pubic hair. She caked it—feeling hate and dread and fear and loss and loathing, the choke of grief, rising from the ground up through her feet, blasting out through the top of her head. Her hands were trembling. Her chest constricting. Shivers of horror ran down her back.

She reached skywards as she coated her fingers. Her heart pumping. Eveything breaking out of her, swamping her in black.

Then all collapsed to silence, and she fainted on the floor.

Evening woke her with its cold touch. Her body was stiff but light. The paint was caked and congealed all over her. It was going to be a task to get it all off in the shower. Colours cracked as she shifted to a sit. She pulled up on a chair. The cold had seeped deeply through her and her movements were awkward. But she climbed the steps on feet that seemed unweighted, and the shivering could have been happening to someone else.

After the shower, with skin scrubbed red, she drank a contemplative coffee out in the peaceful dark of the deck. Bush sounds eased through her, the smell of the trees at night, the crackly, busy quiet.

Then she removed the mirror, replaced the canvas on the easel and meditatively linked with the storm inside herself so that it could begin the slow process of showing its face on canvas.

EIGHTEEN

Sash came around the day after the funeral. While Lex was putting the dishes away, she sat quietly on the couch playing with two Barbie dolls. Mrs B was due home within the next couple of days and Lex hadn't finished fixing things at her place yet, so he was a little impatient with Sash for turning up when he wanted to get things done. He felt guilty too, for being annoyed with her. She asked so little of him, playing there by herself, immersed in her imaginary world. After he'd tidied up, he sat down on the couch and watched her.

'What game are you playing?' he asked, trying half-heartedly to be interested.

'Families.'

He stared out the window for a while then tried again to engage with her. 'Which one's the mummy?'

'This one.' Sash lifted a Barbie with a glittery purple dress and thick blonde hair.

'Of course,' Lex observed. 'Mummies dress like that all the time. Which one's the dad?'

'This one.' Sash raised the other Barbie, naked with obvious plastic breasts.

'How can you tell that one's the dad?'

'Her hair's cut short.'

'Who are the kids?'

'Me and Evan. I don't have enough Barbies so I just have to pretend.'

'Sorry. I'm not up on these things. You'll have to forgive me.'

She stopped playing and looked at him for a moment. 'They said stuff about "'forgive" at church yesterday. "Forgive" and "sins". What does that mean?'

'Sins are when you do something that you know is wrong.'

She nodded. 'Like when I hit Evan.'

'Something like that.'

'What about forgive?'

'Well, you forgive someone if they do something wrong to you or hurt you, and they're sorry, and you want to let them know you're okay with that.'

Sash frowned. 'I don't want to forgive my dad. I'm not okay with what he did.'

'That's all right. Sometimes it takes time to be ready to forgive.'

She went back to playing her game.

'What's happening?' Lex asked.

'The dad has been away from home for a long time and has just come back again. See, they're going to kiss and make up.' Sash pressed the dolls' faces together. 'And then they're going to get married again.'

'I see.' Lex's heart crushed in his chest. Poor kid.

'My dad's not coming back home,' Sash said. 'I think he's forgotten me.'

'How could he forget someone like you?'

'He forgot my birthday. That's what I can't forgive him for yet.'

Lex turned cold. He tried to be light, shift the topic a little. 'Did you just have a birthday?'

'Yes, I just turned six. But my dad didn't send me a present. He didn't even send me a card.'

He looked at her, feeling useless. 'It's pretty hard to understand,' he said. 'But sometimes grown-ups get so caught up in their own lives and troubles that they forget things that are usually important to them. Even birthdays of people they love.'

He ruffled Sash's hair and went to make a cup of coffee. He felt sick. What choice did a kid have when a parent walked out? Sure, kids were resilient. They coped because they had to. What did they understand of the complexities of adult relationships? Thank God his relationship with Jilly hadn't come to that. But then, perhaps Isabel had taken flight before it did. What had happened to them after she died? It was as if the foundation of their entire relationship had died with her. Jilly had blamed him. She'd flayed him with words until he was stripped to the bones. At first he hadn't responded. He'd just watched this alien person battering him, until one day his teeth had started talking, using the same language as her—the language of the doomed; cruel things that couldn't be taken back. Between them they crushed the soul of their relationship, that fragile shell of mutual respect. Past that point, there was no fixing it.

Frank brought Mrs B home the next day. Lex saw the car pull up and rushed out to help, but Frank was already guiding the old lady towards the house with a hand beneath her elbow. She looked weak and frail, her face thinner and paler than usual, her back more hunched, as if life was getting heavier.

'They kept me in bed too long,' she was saying. 'It's no good for the bones, wasting away in bed. Old people like me need to be up and about.'

'You needed to rest, Mum,' Frank said, nodding at Lex. 'They were worried about pneumonia.'

'I can breathe, can't I?' she snapped. 'It's obvious I don't have pneumonia.'

'You were bruised after the fall.'

'Yes. Well, I suppose that's true.' She turned to Lex. 'Lad, it's good to see you. Can you come over for a cuppa shortly? After Frank sets me up in bed? They've softened me up so much in hospital my legs are like jelly.'

Lex waited at home for thirty minutes, reading yesterday's newspaper, then he went back to see her. Frank was wandering around the yard piling up sheets of corrugated iron that had blown around in the storm. He waved when he saw Lex.

'Just let yourself in. She's in her room. Her cup of tea will need a top-up by now.'

Lex went in via the front door. He found the teapot on the kitchen table and carried it tentatively down the hallway. He'd never been this far into the house before and somehow it felt like an intrusion.

'Mrs B,' he called. 'It's Lex.'

'This way, lad.'

He followed her voice into a dim bedroom. She was propped up with pillows on a big old four-poster bed. The curtains were drawn and the lamp beside the bed lit the room in dull sepia tones.

'More tea?' he asked.

'Please.' Mrs B indicated her cup on the bedside table. Her face was shadowy and haggard in the subdued light.

'Can I open the curtains?' he asked.

'Want to see what the storm's done to me?' she said.

'I already know what it's done to you.'

'Open them,' she said. 'So I can see what it's done to *you*.'

Lex dragged the curtains back and sat on a chair near the window. Mrs B's eyes regained some brightness as she burned them accusingly into him.

'Where's the girl?' she asked.

'Who? Callista?'

'Yes.'

Lex hesitated. 'We had a disagreement.'

Mrs B's lips pressed together into a flat line. 'What about?'

'I didn't know who she was.'

'You didn't know she was a Wallace?'

'No.'

'Does it matter?'

Lex stiffened. 'Yes, I think so.'

'You *think* so.'

'It matters,' he said firmly. He'd thought Mrs B would be nicer to him after the accident.

She pressed further. 'Why does it matter?'

He thought she ought to know why it mattered. It was obvious and he wasn't going to spell it out for her. She was being difficult and provocative after a forced week in bed. He was surprised when she started laughing.

'And are you telling me you came to this with no baggage?' she cackled.

He almost managed a smile. 'None, of course.'

The old lady squinted at him. 'How did you know I'd gone over the cliff?'

'Your headlights flashed through my window. You must have been all over the road. It's amazing they let you have a licence.'

'You should have tried driving in that,' she said. She leaned back against her pillows and lifted her cup to take a sip of tea. 'So,' she said. 'The argument.'

'Not worth discussing.'

'You're very quick to write the poor girl off.'

'Poor girl!' He gripped the arms of his chair and leaned forward. 'Hardly.'

Mrs B tut-tutted. 'So much anger.'

Yes. She was right. *So* much anger. He was seething with it. It burned through his trousers, burned him off his seat, pushed him to lean out the window trying to feel the breeze on his face. He could explode in this room.

'Anger is good,' Mrs B said.

'Good?' Lex turned back to her, disbelieving.

'Yes, good,' she said. 'Anger means healing.'

He snorted. 'Anger means anger,' he said. 'Callista lied to me.'

'And have you been entirely honest with her?'

She kept pressing him with these invasive questions. He looked away. 'She knows everything now.'

'Everything,' Mrs B echoed.

'Everything she needs to know.'

Mrs B sighed and set down her cup on its saucer. 'I need to tell you about the Wallaces,' she said. 'So you can understand some things.'

'Not now.'

'Why not? It won't wear me out, if that's what's bothering you.'

'You should rest.'

'Rest! I've been resting for a week in hospital.'

'I'll bring you back some dinner tonight. When Frank's gone,' Lex said. 'We can talk then.'

'You make sure you come,' Mrs B said querulously.

'I wouldn't want to see a sick woman starve.'

Lex walked off some of his anger on the beach then he cooked a chicken curry for dinner and took it around to Mrs B's at about seven o'clock. She was sitting at the kitchen table in a blue dressing gown.

'I feel better already, being at home,' she said. 'Frank helped me have a bath, and then he was happy to leave me for the night knowing you were bringing me some dinner.'

'Good,' Lex said. 'We'll be sure not to wear you out too much so I don't have to carry you back to bed.'

Mrs B's eyes flashed at him. 'I won't be letting the likes of you carry me.'

He smiled.

'What have you brought me?' She tried to peer into the pot.

'Chicken curry,' he said. 'Mild. It's my specialty.'

'What else do you cook?'

'Chop and three veg. But don't hassle me. I'm learning. My wife used to do all the cooking.'

'Wife.' Mrs B raised her eyebrows. 'That's the first mention.'

'Well, it's out in the open now, isn't it? After the storm.'

'Does she know?'

'Yes. Callista knows.'

'Ahhh.' Mrs B nodded to herself. 'The argument.'

Lex served some rice and then the curry. 'How much does an old woman eat?' he asked.

'Not as much as a strapping young lad like yourself.'

'A bit too strapping these days, Mrs B,' he said. 'But not young anymore. I'm coming up to thirty-nine this year.'

She snorted. 'Don't complain till you have cause to, lad. It's boring when the young indulge themselves.'

He smiled and pushed a plate towards her. 'I'm indulging you tonight.'

'No.' She wagged her head at him. 'This evening's talk is a necessity. Perspective is what an angry young man like you needs. And perspective is what you'll have by the time you leave here tonight. I'm going to tell you about the Wallaces and me.'

'You don't have to tell me, Mrs B.'

'No, but I want to.' She took a mouthful of curry and nodded approvingly. She waved her fork at him. 'You bought more than a house when you became my neighbour. You purchased a history. There's love and death and more than one betrayal in those walls. And I'm mixed up in it all.'

She ate quietly for a while then set her fork down. There was something about the deliberate way she did it that let Lex know this wasn't going to be a casual chat.

'The Wallaces bought the land here a long time ago,' she said. 'Must have been the late 1800s. Vic's grandfather bought it when he was passing through with a boatload of whale oil to sell in Sydney. But nobody lived here till Vic's father inherited the land and brought his family up from Eden. Vic was just a boy then. He helped his father build the house . . . I've told you all that before.'

She forked more curry into her mouth and chewed on it thoughtfully. 'Vic was a wild young lad. Tall and well-built.' She glanced at Lex. 'He caused a serious flutter when he first showed up at the school room. We local girls thought he was mighty handsome

. . . Not that he was at school for long. Only a couple of years, then he was old enough to start working the logging gangs with his father.'

'You fancied him,' Lex said, teasing.

Mrs B glanced at him. 'Oh, of course. We were all keen on him . . . That was the problem. We out-did ourselves trying to impress him.'

Lex smiled. He imagined Mrs B would have been a feisty young woman.

She laughed a rusty, self-conscious laugh. 'I certainly got his attention a few times. Seems I was always pulling off some wild stunt to catch his eye—climbing the highest trees, swimming the river on the coldest days.' Her eyes narrowed. 'But it was Queenie that won him over. I might have been gamest, but she was prettiest.'

He watched her tired old face. 'You win some, you lose some,' he said.

'Yes.'

She retreated to quiet reflection while she finished off her curry.

'So Vic and Queenie married young and headed west,' she said, picking up the story again. 'Vic was restless and adventurous and wanted to go whaling. He was sick of working on the logging crews and his grandfather's tales of whaling were thick in his head. So off they went . . . They were gone for close to fifteen years.'

She went quiet, staring at some place up in the corner, roving somewhere in the past. It had been a big day for her, coming home from the sanitised cocoon of the hospital.

'I'll make some tea,' he said, clearing the dishes away.

He washed the dishes, boiled some water and filled the teapot. When he sat down, she smiled at him wearily.

'You're a gem.'

'We can leave this,' he suggested.

'No, let's finish it. I'll forget where I'm up to if I stop now.'

Mrs B told him many things. She told him how she met her husband, Ted Brocklehurst, about a year after Vic and Queenie left for the west. Ted was a good man, she said, a hard worker and a man of principle. He ran his father's dairy while Mrs B worked at the cheese factory. When they'd saved enough money, they bought the block of land at the Point and built their home. Not long after that Ted started to lose his mind. He couldn't run the dairy anymore and the farm had to be sold. Ted's parents gave Mrs B his share of the money, knowing that she'd need it. And almost as soon as Ted stopped work, he worsened rapidly. It must have been brain cancer. He was only thirty-seven years old, but within a few months he couldn't do anything for himself and Mrs B was nursing him full-time.

That's how it was when the Wallaces came back, Mrs B said. Vic came back to fix up the house, while Queenie stayed in Albany so the kids could finish the school year. The old house was too far gone to live in, so Vic pulled down what was left of it and started over. By then, Ted was rotten with the madness. On the days he could get up, she had to lock him in the house so he wouldn't wander over the cliffs. He lost weight quickly and it was lucky she was strong enough to lift him in and out of bed. They were hard times. It wasn't something she had expected to happen so early in her life.

She had talked a lot with Vic while he was building the house. Most nights after she'd fed Ted and put him to bed, Vic would come over and she would cook him dinner. Sometimes he'd help her lift Ted out of the bath so as she could dress him, then he'd lift Ted into bed for her. She was thankful for the company. She was so lonely in those days—still young and energetic, nursing a husband who could only talk nonsense. And Vic was like a breath of fresh air—so full of life. She didn't think she'd have survived Ted's decline without Vic. He was there for months working on the house before his family could pack up and come back east. Mrs B used to go out on the porch to tend to Ted and there Vic would be, slick with sweat, working without a shirt, sawing or hammering.

They were both lonely, Mrs B said. So it had to happen. All those long evenings over dinner telling stories.

She was three months pregnant when the house was finished and Queenie and the kids finally came over to join Vic. Everything between her and Vic ended straightaway. And nobody guessed. People thought Ted had fathered a child just before he died. They used to say what a comfort it must have been for Mrs B to have Frank as a reminder of Ted. But Vic knew, of course. She would see it in his eyes sometimes—passion that neither of them could express. It was a line they couldn't cross while Queenie was still alive.

And when Queenie died, it should have ended happily ever after. But Mrs B had been too shocked by Queenie's death to chase after Vic right away. Queenie had been a close friend of hers and it seemed wrong to be making designs on her husband when she was barely in the grave. Often Vic came over for dinner and sometimes Mrs B would see him looking at her, waiting for her to say something. But she let the months go by, biding her time till it seemed decent. It was a mistake, she said. After a while the light went out of his eyes, and it wasn't long after that he brought Beryl home. Mrs B tried to talk to him, but by then it was too late. Beryl already had a hold on him.

When Vic died, he left everything to Beryl. It was a whitewash for the Wallace family. Beryl had persuaded him to sign appropriate documents several months before his health started declining. When it came to appeals, the Wallaces didn't have a leg to stand on. And they weren't aggressive people. Jimmy and his wife, Cynthia, let it go passively. Jordi and Callista had been upset because the house was their family heritage after all. But Beryl's documents were watertight. And Beryl figured she deserved it after nursing Vic to his grave. There was no negotiation as far as she was concerned.

At the end of it all, Mrs B stood up and emptied the dregs of her tea in the sink. She looked tired and washed out and Lex was glad it was over.

'Go to bed,' he said. 'You're tired.'

'Yes,' she admitted. 'It's a wearying thing. And I still get steamed up over it.'

'Somebody should have lynched Beryl,' he said.

Mrs B smiled faintly. 'It's a wonder I didn't kill her myself . . . But really, killing Beryl wouldn't have fixed things. You can't force a heart to feel passion that's not there . . . And I can see now it was probably for the best. People might have guessed about my Frank if they'd seen Vic and me together. And that would have been humiliating for Frank. I raised him to love Ted, even though he never knew him.'

She stopped and looked at Lex seriously.

'You're wondering why I've told you this, lad, aren't you? Not even my Frank knows it, and he never will.' She frowned and set her mouth. 'What I want you to know is this. I have never regretted those few beautiful months with Vic when Ted was still alive. I lived what was in my heart and dared to love, even though it was wrong by most standards . . . I'm not saying that I did right to have an affair with my friend's husband. I'm still ashamed of that, even though Queenie is long dead. Where I went wrong was in not opening my heart to Vic after Queenie died. I was too careful. Too wounded, and too concerned about propriety.'

She reached out and touched Lex's hand lightly. 'I'm telling you this, lad, because you're wounded too, like I was. And wounds like yours take a lifetime to heal, I know it.'

'I lost a child, Mrs B.'

'I know.'

'Did she tell you?'

'The Wallace girl? No. Old folks like me just know these things. Loss like that is so large you wear it all over yourself . . . I saw it in you when you first came here. Your walk is grief, lad. And there's a great sadness in your eyes. It makes you vulnerable.'

She paused and Lex thought he saw tears in her eyes.

'But, lad,' she continued, 'life passes by quickly, and when you're old like me you see that loving and caring and giving of yourself are all that matter . . . I want you to know there are some bits I'd do differently if I had my time over. I don't want you to make the same mistakes I did.'

For a moment she leaned shakily against the sink and it seemed as if she had drained herself completely. Then she nodded at him. 'That's the view from inside this old body of mine. For what it's worth.'

NINETEEN

Lex talked to Sue about work possibilities and she gave him the names of some farmers. Within a few days he had a job at Ben Hackett's dairy farm on the other side of the river. He had to do the evening milking four times a week and help with odd jobs around the farm, including fencing, spraying and fertilising. It was a steep learning curve and it meant he had to learn how to drive a tractor and how not to be scared of cows.

Ben Hackett had a sixteen-stand herringbone shed. His herd was mostly Friesians, but he had a few old Jerseys with doe eyes and hellish-looking horns. Lex was scared of all of them at first, but the Jerseys scared him most—they knew how to slyly hook him when he let his guard down. The first milking session was the worst—and the funniest according to Ben. The cows filed in wide-eyed and toey, their cloven hooves tapping on the wet concrete as they shoved and shuffled into position.

'They'll be a bit off today,' Ben said. 'They get edgy around strangers.'

He swung the gates to and stomped down into the pit in his gumboots. The milking machine was already sucking and slurping rhythmically.

'No matter, they'll get used to you soon enough. And soon you'll know them all by name, or be making up your own names for them.'

Decked out in faded blue overalls, Ben walked along the line of cows, brushing clods of dirt off their udders and slipping the suction cups onto the teats like they were extensions of his own fat fingers. He had thick round arms like ropes and a ruddy brown face from too many days in the sun without a hat.

'They've all got their own personalities, same as people. Some will like you and some won't. Watch out for that one.' He straightened his back and pointed to one of the Jerseys glaring impatiently into the shed. 'That's Brownie. She'll hook you, she'll kick you, and she'll toss off the cups and make your life hell. I should get rid of the old bitch, but she's too damn good a milker.'

He swung a set of cups to Lex. 'Here, you have a go.'

Lex took the dangling, pulsing cups and it was like holding something alive. Ben pointed him to the hairy pink udder of the next cow. She was stamping and swishing her tail and jiggling with impatience.

'Don't muck around,' he said. 'Whack them onto her. It's easy.'

Lex tentatively brushed the back of the cow's bag and carefully wrapped his hand around one of the teats. It was surprisingly leathery and tough, hard and wrinkly. The cow stamped again as Lex shakily directed a cup up near a teat. The suction grabbed at it and the teat sucked half in, so that it coughed and choked and the cow stamped repeatedly.

'Here.' Ben shoved in a big hand. 'This is how you break the suction. Just fold the line like this.' He folded the rubber tubing that the cups hung from and they fell away immediately. 'It hurts them a bit when the teat's kinked in the cup like that. Now straighten her up like this and slip her on nice and quick.' The teat sucked smoothly into the cup. 'Now you do the others.'

Lex's attempt was clumsy, but he managed without annoying the cow too much. Her tail swished but she stood patiently.

'They'll have to put up with a lot from me,' he muttered.

'Don't worry, mate,' Ben clapped him on the shoulder. 'They're patient buggers. It's their job. Just get it right before you tackle the tricky ones. We'll get you trained up in no time. You'll be doing the lot by yourself before the week's out. Now, let's give her another try. Then we'll get you on the tractor. You're a challenge, mate. I've never had to get a city slicker up to speed before. It'll be the making of you.'

It all went okay until Brownie finally pushed her way in. Lex was starting to get the feel of slipping the cups on without dragging on the teats. He was also getting the hang of breaking the suction of a set when a cow was done and hooking the cups off in one movement. Ben showed him how to watch out for the milk flow slowing in the line. There was a clear bulb at the base of each set of cups where the lines from the four cups joined together. When a cow was letting down, the milk swished and sloshed and spun in the bulb. Near the end of her run, the milk would slow to a dribble. That was the time to get the cups off and dip the teats if they had any cracks in them, to prevent mastitis.

Then in came Brownie. She raced into the shed with some other cows and jostled and horned her way to a bail. Ben was scowling as he hitched the gate closed and locked them in.

'Old bitch,' he yelled above the din of the milking machine.

Lex was just shaking out a set of cups to milk the cow beside her when Brownie shot out a stream of runny shit straight onto his head and shoulders and all over the cups he was holding. He tried to shake the gooey mess off the cups and looked around for a tap. Then she doused him in a shower of piss.

Ben was above the pit, bent over the gate laughing. He laughed so much he wheezed.

'I'm caked in it,' Lex cursed, shaking off wet clods of dung. It was warm, green, fibrous and unpleasantly wet. 'It's in my ear.'

For a moment he thought he was getting pissed on again, but it was Ben turning a hose on him. Head down, he took the spray and used his fingers to wipe the muck out of his hair. Ben continued to choke with laughter. He looked so goddamned amused that Lex started feeling annoyed.

'Here, let's clean you off and then get you up to the house for a shower. Glenda will find you a spare pair of overalls.'

'A hazard of the trade, hey?'

'It happens to everyone.' Ben's eyes were crinkled and merry. 'And she's an old bitch that Brownie. But you know—it was worth keeping her all these years just for that!'

A week into Lex's new job, Ben came down to the shed near the end of milking. He waved and yelled over the click and suck of the milking machine. 'Come over to the house after you finish. I want to ask you something.'

Lex finished up, hosed down and checked the vat temperature. He liked the quiet of the shed after the cows had gone. After the hose-off, it smelled sweetly milky and it was cool in the still shadows. Ben's rubber gloves were big on his hands as he hooked the crud and swill out of the drain, chucked it in the crap bucket and tossed it out of the shed. He could see the last straggling cows making their dozy way down the lane out into the paddock. They were pleasantly mellow after milking, compared with the stamping steady waiting of before. It must feel good to offload an udder tight with milk.

He flicked the lights off and walked up to the house. It was a white weatherboard place, surrounded by Glenda's neat garden of red geraniums and purple hydrangeas. The back porch was a mess of boots and hessian sacks thrown down for the dogs. Their gouging toenails had scored deep marks in the back door. It was the kind of thing Glenda overlooked so long as the front was tidy and there wasn't too much old machinery or junk left lying around the sheds. She was nervous about snakes coming up near the house or getting into the chook pen.

Lex kicked his boots off and banged on the door. Inside, he could hear Ben's loud voice on the telephone competing with the radio. He opened the door and waved Lex in, phone still hooked to his ear.

'Come in, mate, have a seat.'

Lex stepped carefully in his socks on the shiny linoleum and sat at the kitchen table. Ben wound up the call and swung open the fridge.

'Here, have a beer. Glenda's in town doing the shopping.' He flicked the ring-pull off a cold tinnie and pushed it across the kitchen table. 'I wanted to talk to you about the Show.'

'The Show?'

Ben leaned back and took a long haul on his beer. He threw his empty can in the bin and opened another.

'Merrigan Show. It's in a couple of months. I fancy putting a cow in it, and one of my bulls. What do you think?'

Lex shrugged. 'I don't know much about cow shows.'

'I figured you wouldn't. But I thought you might scrub up better than me to lead them around the ring.'

'Are you kidding? The bull will make mincemeat of me.'

'Nah. He's got a nice brass ring in his nose. You give that a good yank if he's getting a bit excited and everything'll be fine.'

'That easy, you reckon?'

'I'll take that as a "yes". Great. That's tops.' Ben took another swig of beer. 'I wanted to ask you something else too.'

'What's that?'

'We need someone to MC the Show Girl competition.'

'Why? What happened to your last compere?'

'John Watson says he doesn't want to do it any more. Says he's got enough on his plate with all the other announcements.'

'Why me?'

'Thought we might get somebody new involved. And it looks to me like you've got it in you.'

'Thanks for the vote of confidence.'

'So that's a "yes" too, is it?' Ben slapped him on the back. 'That's the spirit. You'll be great. I can see you've got potential.'

Lex laughed. 'That's a big word for a country chap.'

'I'm full of vocabulary,' Ben said. 'Now, let's drink to the Merrigan Show.' He looked pleased.

'Come on,' he said, hauling himself out of the chair and pulling two more beers out of the fridge. 'Get your boots on. I'm taking you over to meet Trevor Baker next door. Said he'd be practising the wood chop this evening . . . and we're not talking firewood.'

Ben led Lex over the boundary fence, dodging a hot-wire at mid-thigh level on the way. From behind one of the sheds they could hear the thunk of axe on wood, a steady rhythmic frenzy. There was a clunk and a loud splitting noise.

'He's a real gentleman,' Ben declared as they cornered the shed and saw Trevor Baker snorting a glob of mucus out of his nose.

'Ahh, bugger off, Hackett,' Baker growled, but his smile was wide in his heavy sweaty face and he engulfed Ben's hand with a huge hairy paw.

He was more bear than man—tall, thickset, massive hairy shoulders half-covered by a baggy blue singlet, a stout belly sagging over his trousers. Lex was surprised by his spindly legs and absent bum. He was all front and top heavy.

'This is my new man, Lex Henderson,' Ben said.

'City name for sure.' Trevor spat on the ground. 'But we'll try not to hold it against you.'

Lex accepted the extended hand and felt his knuckles crushed. Trevor Baker was the local wood-chopping legend. He had won the event at all the local shows for the past seven years and was the undefeated champion.

Lex pointed to the shining head of the axe. 'Looks like you've had a bit of experience with that thing.'

'Yeah. Too many years chopping wood for Mum,' Baker spat again. 'Hey, Hackett. Give us a hand with this log, will ya? I need one more round before I finish off for the night.'

The two farmers rolled the log up and heaved it onto the rack.

'Horizontal chop's my favourite,' Baker said. 'Let's mark her up.'

He pulled a piece of chalk out of his pocket and scratched a few lines on the log. Then he lifted his axe off the ground and ran his thumb along the blade. Taking a measured backward step, he lined himself up at arm's length from the log, placed the axe head gently on the ground in front of him, stretched and gripped the handle. Then, with a sharp breath, he jerked the axe into a smooth upswing and hacked down into the log, right on one of his chalk marks. Lex and Ben stood swigging beer while Baker puffed, grunted and cracked his axe into the wood. He made quick work of it, chopping the log neatly in two.

'I'll have my money on you at the Show,' Ben said, draining his can.

'Dunno, mate,' Baker said. He hitched his trousers with his thumbs and readjusted his balls. 'I'm getting older and my handicap's creeping out. Been winning this thing for too long.'

'Nah. The whole town's behind you. Merrigan's off the map if you don't win it. And Lex here has offered to lead the bull for me this year too.'

Baker laughed as he packed his axe into a wooden box. 'You're a bastard, Hackett.'

'He'll be fine. I've got the old feller quietened down this year. He'll be a picnic.'

'Let's get some beer and drink to survival then.' Trevor hoicked some phlegm and spat again. 'Hackett told me you met Brownie.'

On the way home, Lex stopped at the pub to buy a six-pack of beer. The tinnies with Ben had whetted his appetite and he reckoned, despite constant nagging twinges of regret about Callista, he could manage just a drink or two at a time now, without blowing out and drinking the whole lot. As he was paying up, he remembered the fridge at home was empty. If he ducked quickly back into town, he might just make it to the butchery to pick up some sausages before closing time. It'd have to be snags and mash for dinner tonight.

After Henry's death, Helen had taken over the business. Everyone had expected her to sell the butchery to Henry's assistant, Jake Melling, and move back to her family in Eden. But the shop closure had been very temporary. Helen had cropped her hair short, donned an apron and reopened the doors, keeping Jake on part-time to prepare the meat and teach her the trade. According to Sue, the ladies of the church were outraged. Apparently, butchery was men's work. And so was running a business. Mrs Jensen was telling everyone that Henry would be turning in his grave if he knew what Helen was up to. Sue thought it was a laugh that Mrs Jensen was prattling on in her usual underhand way while Helen simply got on with the job.

When Lex dashed into the butchery, Helen was just closing the door of the coolroom.

'What can I do for you?' she asked.

'I was hoping to grab a few sausages for dinner. But it looks like you're all packed away.'

'Yes. It's a bit difficult to bring anything out now.'

'Doesn't matter,' Lex said. He'd have to make do with toast and cheese instead. His disappointment must have shown on his face.

'If you're stuck, there's a roast cooking at my place. I live just around the corner,' Helen said.

'Thanks, but I wouldn't want to impose.'

Helen stretched a thin smile onto her face. Even the blood-red chillies on her apron failed to detract from her usual paleness.

'You wouldn't be imposing,' she said. 'Henry always liked to ask people around at closing time. I'd be carrying on the tradition.'

Lex hesitated. He didn't particularly fancy the idea of making conversation with Helen Beck, but a roast sounded very appealing.

'All right then. I appreciate the hospitality,' he said.

It wasn't the best night for a roast. The kitchen was hot and sticky, and Helen was like a knot of prickles. There was a tight-lipped tension about her, as blunt as her clipped short hair. Lex sat down at the kitchen table and watched her bang the kettle beneath the tap, gush water into its neck and crash it on the stove.

'Tea or coffee?' she asked.

'Tea will be fine. Standard white with one.'

He looked around the kitchen while Helen measured tea-leaves into a silver teapot. The room was dominated by stark white laminex and linoleum; it was soulless, scrubbed bare of character. There was a tidy bowl of fruit on the table and a loudly ticking clock on the wall above the stove. The only suggestion of dinner was the faint fatty sizzle and smell of meat seeping from the oven.

Helen clattered a teacup and saucer on the table in front of him and poured the tea with an unsteady hand. There was a bang somewhere down the hallway.

'Mum. I'm home.'

'That's Darren,' Helen said. 'He goes up to his grandparents' place after school.'

Lex turned and saw the boy staring at him from down the corridor. The kid's face was anxious, poor thing. His father had only been dead a few weeks.

'Come and meet Mr Henderson,' Helen said.

The boy came listlessly into the kitchen and slumped down at the table.

'Hello, sir,' he said, without interest. Then to his mother, 'What's for dinner?'

'Roast tonight.'

Lex realised Helen was watching him sip his tea, her eyes dark and unreadable. He wished she would talk. It wasn't up to him to lead the conversation. He was the visitor. He thought of Callista and realised how much he missed her. It was going to be a long dinner.

'How was school?' Lex asked the kid. Anything to break the silence.

'Good.'

The boy checked his mother wasn't looking and picked his nose.

'Got any homework?' Helen asked.

'Did it at Grandma's,' Darren said. 'Can I watch a video?'

Helen glared at him. 'We have a visitor.'

The kid sighed and hung his head.

'What's your favourite movie?' Lex asked.

'*Star Wars*,' Darren said.

Lex raised his eyebrows at the boy and gave him a small smile. 'What do you reckon about Darth Vader?'

'He's cool.' The kid's face lit up.

'Darren.' Helen was stern and the kid's shoulders sagged.

'I'm not allowed to watch it,' he said. 'Mum says it's too violent.'

Dinner was served at seven sharp. Helen slid the plates onto the table, and Lex was about to pick up his knife and fork when he noticed her staring at him, her hands folded in her lap.

'We have to say grace first,' Darren said.

'Of course,' Lex mumbled. 'I forgot.'

He bent his head and made sure that he echoed the 'amen' at the right time. He was starving and he was dying to tuck into the food even though it was appallingly hot in the kitchen. The meat smelled delicious.

They ate in silence, knives and forks clicking on their plates. Lex could hear the clock ticking above their heads. It was one of the most uncomfortable meals he could remember. When it was over, he thanked Helen profusely and took his leave. She offered him dessert, and he felt rude turning it down, but the atmosphere in the kitchen was stifling and he couldn't wait to escape. Helen disappeared into the house after she had seen him out the front door, but Darren followed him to the gate.

'Which do you reckon is the best *Star Wars* episode?' the kid whispered.

'I like the one where Luke Skywalker blows up the Death Star,' Lex said. 'What about you?'

'I like the third one. When Annikin turns into Darth Vader. I saw it at my friend's place. Mum doesn't know.'

Lex winked at the boy. 'I reckon you'll survive the violence,' he said. 'What do you think?'

The kid grinned and ran back inside.

★

The next morning, having a coffee at Sue's café, Lex knew he was in trouble. Sue was cross. He listened to her crashing around in the kitchen and thought of his mother on her bad days. He waited for her to come out to refill his coffee, and when she did her body language was stiff and impatient.

'I'm sorry for breathing,' he said.

Roughly she sloshed more coffee into his cup and thumped the coffee pot down on the table.

'You don't get it, do you?' she said. 'You haven't worked it out yet. Living here isn't about running and hiding. It isn't about taking what you want and then slinking around like a skunk hoping nobody notices.' She whipped a cloth out of her apron pocket and started working hard on the adjacent table, wiping and polishing. 'This place is about community and respect. We're all interconnected here. We all rely on each other in some way. You need to make better judgments, Lex, or you won't get the support you want when you need it.'

She flicked the crumbs out of the cloth onto the floor and stuffed the cloth back in her pocket before she went on.

'You were more than halfway to making it after you saved Mrs B in the storm. People have been talking favourably about you. I saw them nodding to you at the funeral. That's acceptance, even if you didn't know it. But right now you're heading straight back to where you started. On the outer.'

She was puffing now, her face was red and her voice excited. 'There,' she said. 'I've said my piece. I've always liked you, Mr Henderson. But this takes the cake.'

'What are you talking about?' he said.

'John Watson saw you going home with Helen Beck last night.'

Lex looked down at his coffee and noticed that Sue had spilled half of it into the saucer while she was topping it up.

'Here, give me that.' She reached for the cup. 'I'll fix it up for you.'

She came back with a fresh cup.

'Now it's time to fix yourself up. You keep away from Helen Beck. She doesn't need your interference. She's lost and confused enough as it is. You leave her to the church folk. They understand her.'

Lex defended himself. 'I didn't do anything. I accepted a kind offer to dinner and then I went home. Nothing happened.'

'I don't want to hear your explanations,' Sue said. 'You keep away from her. There are some things you oughtn't to meddle with and Helen Beck is one of them. Now take my advice and leave it alone.'

'Thank you,' he said. 'I'll take your advice.'

He finished his coffee and drove home, stung with disbelief. One innocent meal and everybody in Merrigan had him hooked up with Helen Beck. There were still many things he had to learn about living in this place.

TWENTY

At home, in the late-summer stillness of the gully, Callista painted a fury of colour onto canvas—exploring, experimenting, drawing out flashes of light and insight. Over the past weeks, working through the storm series had evolved into a journey of emotions. What she put into her paintings was more than her observations of mood and light. It was more than her anger and frustration with Lex, more than her grief over their clash in the shattered house. Grief was in fact cumulative, she discovered. One grief opened the vault of past unreconciled grief, and it all wound together into a new and complex thing.

On top of that, yearning shot itself through everything: yearning for those days of colour when she and Luke had been beautiful, yearning for knowledge of the child that had been lost to her during its short journey of creation, yearning for what she had hoped for with Lex.

While she painted, Callista learned more about disillusionment. The taste of Lex's concealment was bitter. She struggled to imagine him as the owner of a wife. Of course he had a history, but knowledge of this could only bring disappointment. With all his past hurts, she could never have him just for herself. Even if she could resurrect the fragments of their relationship, he would always be partly owned by someone else. And that was painful.

Entangled with this was her disillusionment with herself for not having the courage to be forthright. If only she had been stronger, she could have told Lex who she was. The truth was that without honesty their relationship had been emotionally bankrupt. Together they had been like a shallow and murky lagoon. The storm had broken their banks and what little they'd started with had drained away. They had begun with nothing and ended with nothing.

The house at the end of the road had been a large part of the problem. It had been their nemesis: Lex's unwitting purchase of her family history and Callista's powerlessness to change that. Revisiting the house at the Point had stirred a myriad of memories for her. Grandpa. His life there with Queenie. Running barefoot with Jordi among the heath. Baking cupcakes in the kitchen. Queenie smiling over their curly brown heads. The light shimmering through the windows. Grandpa's whaling stories. Humpbacks beginning to roll by over the years.

None of this could be shared with Lex. Not ever. She had tried to show him an alternative viewpoint on whaling. Not because she necessarily believed it herself. But she had to try to persuade him because if he could not accept a different view he could not accept her. Truly, she had failed all round.

With a canvas on the easel, failure was not something she could contemplate. She pushed thoughts of Lex aside and worked through the moods of the storm, drawing out its texture. Thinking. Painting. Visualising. Working with sensation. Driving through the maze of her emotions.

It was an obsession. She could think of nothing else. Food became something she indulged in when she felt weak. She drove up the coast and bought canvasses with money borrowed from her mother. When one canvas was too wet to work further, she set it aside and put another on the easel, moved into the next phase of the storm, its next mood.

She couldn't remember ever working like this before. It was like a re-creation. Like a reworking of the colours that made up her own complicated personality. And she liked it. Within the mire of all that bruised and boiling sensation, there was the birth of a new rose for her. And its name was confidence.

But today she was feeling distracted and it was annoying her. Helen Beck had rung a couple of weeks ago and asked her to do a portrait of Henry. It was a commission for the church and there was good money behind it, but Callista couldn't motivate herself to start it. She was making good progress on her storm paintings, but this commission was going to cause her trouble. She had flicked through the photographs Helen had given her and she knew Henry wasn't going to come easily.

The problem was his eyes—what was in them, and also what wasn't. He was supposed to be a devout, passionate man of the church. And yet what Callista saw was a man who was arrogant and intolerant. Compassion was missing, and kindness and humility and tenderness. The underlying issue was that she didn't like him. Never had. She had avoided him, preferring not to run up against his abrasive personality. Of course she'd known him. You couldn't grow up in a small town like Merrigan without knowing people. But he had left high school the year she started, so he could slot into the family business. No need to stay at school when he was needed in the shop. And Callista's family didn't eat meat or go to church, so they rarely saw him.

Helen Beck was another matter. Callista had always felt sorry for her, suppressed as she was beneath Henry's patriarchal glare. They had never been friends, but Callista had watched Helen shrinking during her marriage to Henry. She had watched the fear growing in Helen's eyes. Often she had wished she could reach out to the poor isolated woman, buried in the church and in Henry's dominance. But she knew better than to interfere.

When Helen had come to her with the photos, Callista had wanted to reject the job. Yet how could she, when this poor woman's entire life had been rejection. So she'd taken the photos and said she'd see what she could do, knowing at the same time that she couldn't do it. How could she possibly paint Henry in a sympathetic light?

Several times she'd fanned out the photos of Henry on a table and tried to begin by sketching him, first in pencil and then in charcoal. But the drawings were flat and unrewarding. Her heart wasn't in it. She couldn't get inside him and didn't want to. And as each day went by with Helen's down payment sitting on the windowsill above the kitchen sink, Callista's guilt grew. She would have to do something proactive. She'd have to go and talk to Helen.

That evening, she drove the Kombi into town, bought a bottle of red wine with twenty dollars of Helen's money, and knocked on her front door.

'What's that?' Helen asked suspiciously, as she let her in.

Callista followed her down the white hallway to the kitchen. 'Sacramental wine,' she said, sitting down at the table. 'Don't you ever do communion?'

Helen's lips pulled back with distaste. 'Not out of a bottle.'

'Have a glass anyway,' Callista said.

Helen took two tumblers from a cupboard and placed them on the table.

'How are you going?' Callista asked.

'All right,' Helen said with a tight smile, flicking her eyes away quickly. 'We're managing.'

Callista knew that meant Helen was barely hanging in there. She had heard all the outraged gossip going round town about Helen taking over the butchery. Mrs Jensen was promoting Helen's takeover as scandalous. Silly old woman. Callista hoped it wasn't affecting business, but, apart from the pitiful array of prepackaged sausages at the supermarket, there weren't any other options in town for buying meat.

'How's the portrait going?' Helen asked.

Callista hesitated. 'I don't think I'm much of a portrait artist. I'm having quite a bit of difficulty getting going on it.'

'Aren't the photos good enough?' Helen's face sharpened with concern.

'They're fine. But I'm frustrated. That's why I'm here. I've tried a few sketches, but I'm struggling. I didn't know Henry well enough.'

'What do you want me to do?'

'Drink this,' said Callista, pouring some wine into one of the tumblers. 'It's lubricant. To help you talk. Don't worry, I'll have one too.' She poured a second glass. 'Here's to portraits.'

She offered her tumbler to clink and they sipped. Helen looked unsure.

'Call it an investment,' Callista said. 'I'm hoping it will help me get to know your husband.'

'He'd be cross with me, drinking this.'

'But he's not here. You can do what you want now.'

'I don't want to do anything wrong.'

'Does it feel wrong?'

Helen glanced up and the suggestion of a smile touched her lips. 'I feel like having another sip.'

'Do it then. Be outrageous.'

'What do you need to know?' Helen asked, one glass down. She was already flushed and a little unsteady.

'Everything except the saintly. That's the boring stuff. I know all that. I read the obituary the church put out.'

'You did? How did you get a copy? They were only supposed to be for the funeral.'

'John Watson was handing them out at the newsagency. They were on the counter, so I took one. I hope that was okay.'

'It would have been nice if he'd asked me first.'

'Your husband was a local personality,' Callista said. 'Perhaps John thought he was doing the right thing.'

'Perhaps . . .'

Helen drifted off somewhere, floating on wine, and Callista wasn't sure how to press on.

'Look,' she said. 'I want to do this painting for you, but I'm having trouble with it. I need to know more from you. I need to get inside your husband's skin.'

'That sounds a bit strange.'

Callista shrugged. 'Maybe, but it's the only way I can paint.'

Helen sighed. 'What can I tell you?' she said. 'My husband was a very good man.'

Callista stared at her for a moment then topped up both the tumblers. This was probably a hopeless mission, so she might as well enjoy the wine. She'd love to tell this woman what everybody really thought of her holier-than-thou husband, but it'd be too cruel. Even though the man was dead, Helen still wouldn't betray him, despite his substandard treatment of her while he was alive. At least the poor woman was released from all that now.

'Perhaps Henry could have spent more time with his son,' Helen was saying. She gave a small strained laugh and fluttered her eyes nervously away from Callista. 'I'm trying to think of some of the not-so-saintly things you said you were looking for. He . . . Henry . . . was very serious about his job and he was also very devoted to his church duties, so I think, perhaps, Darren might have missed out sometimes . . .'

Callista drank more wine and tried to look interested. Internally, she was rolling her eyes. Was this the best Helen could think of?

'Perhaps, also, Henry might have sometimes been a little indiscreet about his donations to the church,' Helen admitted. 'I think perhaps he may sometimes not have been as wholesome in the giving as God intended. A little boastful, maybe. But then he was very proud of his efforts to support the church, and there's nothing wrong with that . . . being proud of your service to God . . .'

Callista nodded and tried not to yawn. She noticed Helen take a deep breath as if she was psyching up to something.

'All right then,' she said with a small frightened smile. 'I'm going to be very daring.'

She looked directly at Callista, and even before she spoke Callista knew it was a step in the right direction. Helen looked stronger.

'I hope you won't be too shocked if I tell you that Henry enjoyed making love.' Helen's face paled and her fingers tightened around the tumbler. 'And he was very good at it . . . Is it wrong to talk about this?'

Callista laughed. 'No. It's just what I need to hear. When is sex ever wrong if it's good?'

Helen took a nervous sip of wine. 'I suspect Henry probably felt guilty about how much he enjoyed it. Our church says it's only supposed to be for procreation. But Henry definitely quite liked it.' Helen blushed. She stopped and glanced at Callista. 'You're not horrified?'

'No. This is all normal stuff.'

'I can't think what else to tell you.'

'Have some more wine.'

Helen giggled. Her cheeks were starting to fizz red from the alcohol. 'This feels so naughty,' she said.

'But you're having fun,' Callista said. 'It beats communion, doesn't it?'

Helen nodded and took another careful sip. 'Have you ever taken communion?' she asked.

Callista snorted. 'Even if I could get my blackened soul through the front door of the church, I don't think the minister would have me.'

Helen shook her head over-emphatically. The wine was exaggerating her movements. 'I'm sure he'd take you in,' she said. 'The church is the house of the Lord, after all.'

The wine was enhancing the evangelising, not drowning it as Callista had hoped. 'I think I'm doing fine just as I am,' she said.

'Not according to Mrs Jensen.' Helen's eyes widened as she realised her gaffe and she covered her mouth and giggled. 'Oh dear. I'm not being very tactful, am I?'

'Since when was Mrs Jensen ever tactful?'

They laughed together.

'You know,' said Helen, wobbling a little drunkenly. 'There are some things I could tell you about Henry that would turn your toes.'

'Really?' Callista topped up Helen's glass again. 'I don't believe you.'

'Oh yes.' Helen wagged a finger at Callista. 'But the story I have isn't very nice, and it might change your opinion of him, so I don't think I can tell you.'

'Surely it can't be that bad.' She handed the glass to Helen.

'Yes, it is bad.'

Helen took a few more sips of wine, her face pale. She had loosened up as Callista had planned, but she was so wrought and tense, Callista wished she hadn't asked. She wished she'd just painted the bland portrait this tortured woman was looking for.

'You don't have to tell me this, you know,' she said. 'It was unkind of me to pry.'

'No,' Helen said, eyes wide with stress. 'I really should tell it.'

Callista filled her wine and looked at Helen. 'Okay,' she said. 'I'm ready. Nothing you can say will shock me, so don't worry about that.'

Helen smiled faintly, and then it all came out in a rush, as if she had been waiting for years to release everything she'd been holding so tightly within.

It had started two years after Darren was born. Henry had suddenly become serious about having more children. Before that they had been trying on and off, just on the chance that Helen might fall pregnant. Which she didn't. Then two years after Darren, Henry decided it was time. Time to get on and fill all those rooms upstairs with children. They had a moral and religious duty to provide God with lots of little Christians. That was why they had married, after all.

For several months they tried to get pregnant. Henry was very persistent, and each night after dinner, once the kitchen was clean and they had showered, he insisted they make love. He wasn't going to miss a chance. He said it was 'God's work' and that there should be no rest. Then one month Helen's cycle was late. She was just four days overdue and Henry was convinced she was pregnant. He made her cups of tea and sang hymns around the house with all the sunlight of heaven in his eyes. Then, of course, Helen wasn't pregnant. She was afraid to tell him. Afraid to face her judgment. He had been waiting for so long.

So she waited all evening, until Darren was in bed, and told him when they were in the bedroom where she knew Darren couldn't hear them if Henry raised his voice in anger. But Henry didn't yell. He was silent, and Helen waited while he stared at her, disbelieving. Then his face changed and she knew she had to get away. She tried to escape into the bathroom, but he caught her and pulled her back. He hit her and tore her clothes off. He took her violently on the bed. That was the first time it happened like that, but it wasn't the last.

Helen stopped abruptly, looking alarmed.

'That's enough,' Callista said. 'You can stop now.'

'Can I?'

Helen looked so pathetically grateful. Callista was horrified she had pressed her into this. Then Helen turned even paler than usual and swayed to her feet.

'I feel ill,' she moaned. 'What's happening?' She ran to the bathroom and vomited. 'It's Henry!' she said between spasms. 'He's punishing me.'

'No,' Callista said. 'It's the wine. I didn't realise you'd drunk so much.'

Helen clutched the bowl and heaved again, crying. 'God will never forgive me.'

'God *will* forgive you,' Callista said. 'What Henry did was wrong. No woman should be treated like that.'

Helen slipped to the floor, unable to stop weeping.

'Come on.' Callista helped her to her feet, found a bucket in the laundry and took her upstairs to bed.

Knowing about Henry didn't bring inspiration. It brought only anger and disgust. Every time Callista pulled out the photos intending to get started, she wanted to kill him, to hurt him somehow, as he had hurt Helen. Henry's violence was the most putrid thing she could think of. She remembered Luke kicking her on the stairs as he left, like she was a dog. And now there was Helen, powerless beneath a man with righteousness and the wrath of God in his spine.

There must be some way for Helen to be empowered now that Henry was gone. But Callista was appalled to see in herself that same powerlessness, even beyond Luke. She had tiptoed around Lex's edges like a mouse, afraid to tell him who she was. The old powerlessness was still with her too. Had she learned nothing from Luke?

And yet lately her painting had given her new life. It was a fresh feeling, vital. The storm paintings had sung out of her, even though they had been hard work. Ridiculous as it sounded, it had been glorious creating moods of colour and light. The brush had felt strong in her hand. The colours were beautiful.

But Henry was something else. Each time Callista's anger passed, it left her weak and lethargic. She tried to set him aside, attempted to block out the black emotions he stirred in her. But he nagged at her and depressed her. Eventually she was backed so far into a corner trying to flee that she realised she had to confront him. That he wouldn't wait. She couldn't paint the commission for Helen until she started another painting of Henry. There was so much of him she had to purge in order to master the painting that Helen needed. She had to work on the truth before she could muster a convincing lie. The decision felt good. She could hide the work afterwards. No one need ever see it.

She set up a canvas and started on Henry. She would paint him lit starkly with white light against black. For wasn't that how he was? A man of studious contrasts: black and white, good and evil, life and death.

With fresh insight after Helen's revelations, Callista now understood how to paint him. She used her hatred, the new anger at Henry Beck, and directed it all at him. The black and white was potent. No subtle shades of grey for Henry. She pulled him out of darkness in a way he would have understood: in stark sharp lines and rigid boundaries between black and white. Henry Beck was the clot of all the negative emotions she had carried through her life.

She kept at him doggedly, building up his features, shaping his face. And now, finally, she could paint his eyes.

TWENTY-ONE

On the way home from work one Friday, Lex saw a young woman along the highway looking for a lift. She was standing by the 100-kilometre sign with her pack propped up against the signpost. He started to slow down. She was wearing torn-off denim shorts and a black singlet top with a low neckline, dusty hiking boots and creamy-coloured woollen socks. Lex took it all in, admiring her relaxed, unself-conscious, semi-seductive pose. Her legs were long and brown and appealing. As he pulled up he saw her hair was twisted into a mop of dreadlocks with beads sewn in like little nests. Her face was brown and heavily freckled.

She yanked open the back door of the Volvo, threw her pack in and slammed the door. Then she hauled the front door open and swung into the front seat beside Lex. There was an air of slackness about her that he couldn't name. Nonchalance? Confidence? Youthful ignorance? Youthful arrogance? He put the car in gear and pulled out onto the highway. The girl rolled down her window and crooked her elbow out.

'How far are you taking me?' she asked.

Lex was uncomfortably conscious of the taut muscularity of her thighs and calves just a hand's breadth away from the gearstick. There was not a hair on her legs. It was a long time since he had been this close to a young female body.

'My turn-off is about six kilometres down the road.'

'Bullshit! Why did you pick me up then?'

'Does your mother know you're out hitching on country roads alone?'

'What's it to you?'

'You're lucky I'm a nice guy. There's plenty around that aren't.'

'Thanks, Dad,' she snarled. 'Let me out then.'

She swung open the door while they were picking up speed on the highway. Lex was surprised but didn't slow down. He knew she was bluffing and he wasn't ready to let her out yet. She was interesting.

'Want some dinner?' he asked.

She pulled the door shut. 'I suppose I have to eat. Not much open around here.'

'Nothing. Next town's about forty ks away.'

'And you were going to dump me six ks out of Merrigan. Thanks a lot.'

Lex wasn't sure quite what he had intended to do. 'So is that a "yes" to dinner?' he asked.

The girl grunted impatiently. 'Do you want me to beg?'

He swung the Volvo onto the Point road. They hammered too fast onto the dirt and skidded slightly on the corrugations. The girl's open window sucked in the dust. In silence they drove through the bush and then over the rolling hills towards the sea.

'Do you live at the end of the earth or something, man?' she said, finally winding the window up.

'The name's Lex. Lex Henderson.'

'Shit. Fancy name. Are you descended from royalty or something?' She laughed. It was hard and detached, like she'd already lost something of herself in the few years of her life. 'I'm Jen. I suppose we'd better get to first names since you're going to feed me. And, by the way, I'm vegetarian. Can you cope with that?'

Lex rolled his eyes. 'It'll stretch me, but I'll give it a go.'

They pulled up on the grass outside the house. It was a calm evening, with the sea a blue-silver and the light melting to apricot on the horizon.

'You going to take me to Eden after this?'

'I'll think about it. Depends on how well you behave yourself.'

'Scoutmaster.' She pulled her pack out and followed him inside. 'Nice spot,' she said. 'Except for the trash-heap next door.'

'My neighbour's too old to fuss over tidiness.'

'Looks like it. You should clean it up for her—an able-bodied man like yourself.'

Lex wasn't sure he felt comfortable about her reference to his body. And he wasn't sure he liked her critical young eyes checking out his belly and thinning hair. He gave her a beer then started rustling around in the pantry for vegies to chop. While he worked in the kitchen, she poked around the bookshelves and squinted at Callista's paintings on the wall. He admired her easiness as she wandered around the house, touching things and exploring like a child.

'Not a bad set-up,' she said, glancing his way. 'You on your own here?'

'Most of the time.'

'That sucks.'

She grabbed a book from the shelf, sat on the lounge and spread her arm along the back of it, drinking beer and staring out to sea. She made no effort at conversation and no offer to help with dinner. The silence didn't bother her. She read the book intermittently, like she was waiting at a bus stop.

When dinner was ready, Lex laid two bowls of pasta on the table.

Jen didn't look up from her book. 'Mind if I just sit here with it on my lap?'

He sat down at the table and chose not to answer.

'Okay,' she said, standing up on those long lean legs. 'I'll eat with you.'

They ate for a while in silence.

'Are you studying?' he asked to break the silence.

'Nah. I'm an activist.'

'What does that mean?' He masked a smile by plunging a forkful of food into his mouth.

'I demonstrate.' She was gobbling her food. 'This is good,' she said, mouth full. She waved her fork around as she spoke. 'When there's an important social issue going down, like . . . I dunno . . . logging, abortion, social injustice, higher fees for students . . . well, I'm there.' She stuffed more food into her mouth. 'I was studying law. But it was too boring, and then I got busy demonstrating. Too many issues to make a contribution to. Plus they give you good food and somewhere to sleep.'

'Who's they?'

'Whoever's organising the demo. Especially if it's at an out-of-town location. That's why I'm heading to Eden. Logging demo. But they're not so good on the transport side of things. If you don't catch a lift with the first load heading out of town, you have to make your own way down.'

'So you're a woman on a mission.'

'You could say that. Saving forests this week.'

Food kept disappearing into her mouth. Lex had never seen anyone eat so fast.

'Are there any seconds?' she asked.

'Help yourself.'

She leapt up with her mouth still full and came back holding the pot. He watched in disbelief as she set it on the table and ate directly out of it with her fork. The eating involved such measured concentration there was no room for talk. Then she looked up him with a smile that twisted her mouth.

'You think I'm sexy, don't you?'

Lex didn't answer. He hadn't anticipated this switch in the conversation.

'Ever had sex with a young woman?' she asked.

He laughed. 'Yes. When I was young.'

Jen was annoyed at his humour. She obviously didn't like being laughed at.

'In my experience, older men are pretty keen on younger women.'

'Not all older men,' he said. 'How old do you think I am?'

She shrugged. 'I dunno. Fifty?'

It was a payback dig.

'Close,' he said. 'How about you?'

'Twenty. But I've seen a lot of life.'

She was as defensive about her age as he was.

'Want to try it?' she asked.

'Try what?'

'A young body. Then you can take me to Eden.'

He stood up and cleared the table. 'I'm a bit beyond teenagers.'

'Why did you pick me up then?' she asked.

Lex stood the pot in the sink and ran cold water into it. He wasn't sure why he had picked her up. 'You looked like you needed a good feed,' he said, scooping up the keys to the Volvo. 'Let's go then. Get this over and done with. Call it my contribution to the conservation effort.'

He dropped her in Imlay Street near the phone booths. There were plenty of bright lights, but he felt a bit guilty about abandoning her alone and at night, although she seemed unconcerned.

'Your taste in music's shit,' she said, after she had dragged her pack out and slung it on the footpath.

'Thanks.'

She smiled. 'Catch you in another lifetime. Maybe you'll break out next time. Sex can be just for fun, you know.'

'Thanks for the advice,' he said dryly. 'No doubt it'll carry me into a wild and wonderful future.'

She tossed back her dreads and laughed. 'Now you'll remember me every time. I have that effect on people.'

She was so full of brash confidence. Lex rolled up his window and cruised down the street. He was still feeling a little guilty when he U-turned down the end and came back through town to head home. Jen was where he'd left her, sitting on top of her pack jabbering into a mobile phone. So much for isolation, she'd be fine.

He had just turned onto the highway when he remembered the Eden whaling museum Jimmy Wallace had mentioned on his tour. He was all the way down here, he might as well stay the night and go to the museum in the morning.

He checked into a motel.

The Eden Killer Whale Museum was on Imlay Street at the far end of the shops. It was easy to find; a building painted creamy-white, with a short white lighthouse beside it. Perched on the edge of a steep hill, the museum looked out over the moody grey waters of Twofold Bay, the old whaling grounds, a fitting place for a memorial to the past.

Just after opening time, Lex paid his money in the quiet foyer. He was amazed at how cheap it was. Only six dollars. Something like this would be significantly more expensive in Sydney. And, being a weekday, there was nobody else around. He'd have the entire place to himself. He took the brochure from the lady at the front desk and wandered into the display hall.

Two things confronted him immediately: the long skeleton of Old Tom, the killer whale that used to assist the whalers, and a full-size replica of an old-time whale boat.

Old Tom's skeleton transfixed him. It was hard to extrapolate from the smiling skull and the long stretch of vertebrae to the picture of a killer whale on the placard on the wall. The skull could have belonged to a large porpoise. The flippers looked like stubby hands, and the main feature of the killer—the long dorsal fin—was missing. In life, it was a slab of cartilage. Therefore, in death, it was absent from the skeleton. Lex just couldn't see this string of bones as a formidable killer whale, or orca, as people preferred to call them these days.

He walked around the length of the skeleton, running his hands along the wooden bar that fenced him off from it. On the far side, he read the placard and then moved forward to inspect Old Tom's teeth on that side. They were large white pegs and Lex could see they would have been mean weapons. The interesting thing was that Old Tom's teeth were worn where he had taken a line from the whale boat many times to help tow the whalers quickly out to sea when there were whales about. The killer had wanted to hurry up the process of landing a meal.

In the corner by Old Tom's skull was a box that was playing a recording of killer whale calls. Lex stood by the box a long time, reading and rereading the wall hanging about Old Tom and letting the sounds wash through him. They were very different from the calls he had heard from the humpbacks off the Point. The killers were much more conversational: trills and squeals, reverberating clicks, repetitive hollow whines, grinding noises. He listened to the calls as if hearing these voices over and over might help him understand what they were saying, as if it would help him understand the link between these whales and the whalers. A relationship of mutual benefit. A symbiosis.

Eventually, he wandered back around to the whale boat and the series of framed photos along the wall. The boat was long in this room, and it seemed large until you imagined it out on the sea, with six oarsmen, a harpoon on board, and a whale at least two to three times bigger than Old Tom alongside. Once Lex added an image of waves and a vision of enormous uplifted tail flukes, the boat became small—a meagre weapon against a whale. In his craziest dreams, Lex couldn't imagine himself out there, rowing across the stormy bay trying to make ground on a pod of travelling whales. He'd be terrified. When this boat came near to a whale, the harpoon would be fired, and then, if it made fast, the boat could be towed all around the bay and out to sea, until the whale became exhausted and was sufficiently weakened by internal bleeding to slow down. Then it would be the job of the headsman to lance the whale—the final blow.

The whole escapade was susceptible to great risk and danger. When the harpoon was fired, a leg could be caught in the rope and an oarsman dragged out to sea and drowned by the whale as it dived or swam away. An injured whale could lift its tail and splinter a boat in one slap. Inclement weather could sink a boat on its return. At any time a person could be lost overboard. It wasn't a job somebody would do for fun.

Lex moved along the photographs on the wall. Some of them were enlarged prints of the photos in his *Killers of Eden* book. He stared into the faces of the whalers, trying to understand them and what had driven them, what had made them choose this as a way of life. There was a photo of two men with boat spades standing on the bloated upturned belly of a dead blue whale. The men looked like council workers leaning on their spades at a roadside construction site, except that theirs were specially designed chisels to gouge into the flesh of the whale and cut it off. Flensing, they called it. Another photo was of the try works, and the large pots that the blubber was shoved in to boil it down so the oil could be collected. The place must have had a stench that would rival a morgue.

Lex looked at those men, and there was nothing in their faces that explained it all to him. They were the faces of normal men. Men that were struggling to make a living in a time of hardship. They looked like anyone who worked with a shovel in the sun. They looked like anyone who rowed a boat, or laboured to make money. They looked like ordinary people who had families, ate food, drank water, sweated, toiled, feared, hurt. Any one of them could have been him, if he had lived in their time, in their town, in their situation. None of them looked like the devil. They weren't gruesome murderers who loved to kill. They were men doing a job. And it was a job that was hard.

He walked from the whaling exhibit into the room about local shipping history, passing cabinets of items retrieved from wrecks along the coast. He stood at the window and looked out at the sea. While he had been indoors, the clouds had split to a clear blue morning, and the sea stretched wide and flat to the horizon. He squinted into distance. This visit to the museum hadn't been quite what he had expected. Instead of it reaffirming his irritation with the old whalers of Eden and with Vic Wallace, he found much of his anger was gone. Dissolved. He realised that all people had to come to terms with their history, and that it could not be escaped from. Even these men, with their normal faces, had to carry the burden of how they had lived their lives. They had to come to some truce with themselves about how they had conducted themselves, the risks they had taken, the fear and grief they had caused their families.

When he looked at it this way, Lex could see that he was no different. He too had history that he needed to come to terms with. Somewhere ahead he must find his path to absolution.

TWENTY-TWO

It took a whole week for Callista to psych up to ringing Alexander Croft at the gallery. She knew she was procrastinating, but every time she looked at the phone she started shaking. What if he said no? She couldn't face it, after all this work.

When she finally picked up the phone and dialled his number, her hands were sweating and there was a nervous wobble in her voice. She was embarrassed by his lengthy pause when she told him the theme of her paintings. It was obvious he doubted she could produce a collection of substance. During that long moment, her fragile confidence wilted and she scorned herself for even trying. Only *known* artists exhibited at Alexander's gallery. Artists with established names. Artists with clout. Not wishful country yokels like herself. With their heads in the clouds.

She knew Alexander was being kind when he offered to come and have a look at her paintings. His high-pitched nasal voice smoothed over her discomfort. He said he needed a private viewing to assess whether his gallery would offer the best venue to display her work. Callista was aware that it was a marvellously kind and polite deception. She almost refused him, knowing that she was wasting his time.

Alexander came—as she knew he would—in his shiny silver four-wheel-drive, which he parked near the dam wall beside the

Kombi. He picked his way across the grass in smart shoes and clothes, and arrived tight-jawed at the foot of the verandah.

She met him quickly and invited him to take the large inelegant stride up onto the deck. The house in the gully seemed an embarrassment. She could see he was annoyed for having played so far into this charade to save her ego. They made a feeble attempt at small talk then Alexander straightened himself in a business-like manner.

'Let's get on with it then, shall we?' he suggested with a small smile that fell short of his eyes.

For a moment, Callista thought she might not be able to go through with it. She knew exactly how it would happen. She would set up the first painting and Alexander's opinion would be immediately obvious. He would try to hide it, but his disdain would be evident. Of course, he would be careful to give the painting due regard—he was sufficiently shrewd to know about artists and their tender egos. No, a hurried brush-off would be cruel. Having come this far, he would be tactful and kind, but unable to hide his pity. Then he would recommend another gallery that would be more suitable for her work. She would thank him for his trouble, usher him to his car, wave goodbye with false cheer, and file the paintings under her bed.

She hesitated while Alexander jiggled impatiently, and then something crystallised in her and she knew she had to finish it. Quickly now, she glanced at the level of the sun and placed the easel where she knew the natural light would fall kindly on the canvases. She indicated to Alexander where to stand. Then she set the first painting on the easel and stepped away. It was a vulnerable moment and she forced herself not to look at him. Instead she stared out at the tangled green of the bush and tried to slow her breathing and the anxious knocking of her heart.

Alexander remained silent.

Somewhere down along the gully the wonga pigeon whooped. Callista waited a minute or so then she removed the painting, still without looking at Alexander. She placed the second painting on the easel and stepped back. Again she gazed into the gully. In the clarity of those minutes, the birdsong seemed amplified and nature thickened all around her. It was the same as usual—that brief feeling of hope turning sour. She had been kidding herself, of course, that one day she'd make it. But really, country markets were the limit of her talent and she should never have dreamed beyond them. After all, wasn't that why she had stayed in Merrigan all her life? Pretending it was her love of open spaces that held her here? If she went to the city, she would be confronted with knowing what she had really known all along. That she was a no-hoper, hiding under a costume of alternativism. It was a shield for underachievement. It made being average okay. Misery looped over and over in her chest. It was a shame she couldn't spare herself this last.

Over fifteen minutes she shuffled through most of her paintings. At the end of it, she walked inside and poured two glasses of wine with shaking hands. She handed a glass to Alexander. He was still examining the final painting. His face was very still and serious. It was worse than she had expected. This silence. This saying nothing.

'Well,' he said, finally looking into her flushed face. 'You *have* been busy.'

She watched his thumb quietly stroking the stem of his wine glass.

'Is that the lot?' he asked.

'There are a few more.'

'We'd better see those too.'

Callista rushed back into the house trembling with shock. This was good. He wouldn't ask to see more if they were terrible. Her hands quivered with excitement as she shyly set up five more paintings. Now she lost her restraint and checked Alexander's face searchingly to gauge his reaction to each one. He was frustratingly unreadable.

'Any unfinished?'

'A few.'

'Finish them.'

She went to move inside.

'I don't need to see them now.'

'Of course not.' She stopped, confused.

'Here,' he said, handing her the wine glass. 'I'm done with this.'

He reached out then to shake her hand and she thought she saw surprise and perhaps a new respect in his eyes.

'They're good,' he said. 'You've got yourself an exhibition. We'll exhibit in a couple of months. About the middle of April. You'd better leave the framing to me.'

Callista felt tears brimming.

Alexander stepped back and looked at her shrewdly. 'There's something more, isn't there?'

'Not really.'

'No, come on. You're working on something else, aren't you?'

She hesitated. 'How can you tell?'

'Call it experience,' he said with a small smile. 'There's a certain tension about artists when they're wrestling with a new challenge.' He waved a hand over the storm paintings. 'You've conquered this theme. No, there's something else. Out with it.'

'I have been working on a portrait.'

He raised his eyebrows and folded his arms. 'Who?' he asked. 'Who is it?'

'Henry Beck.'

'What, the butcher that stabbed himself in the storm?'

'Yes.'

'Come on then. Bring it out. Don't keep me waiting.'

Callista brought out the official portrait of Beck, the commission for the church that she hadn't yet delivered to Helen Beck. She sat it on the easel.

'You're kidding me.' Alexander snorted. 'What's this?'

'This is the commission. For his wife.'

'The fake, eh? You have something else.'

'I'm not sure I should show you. It was just something I had to get off my chest. I couldn't exhibit it. His wife would never forgive me.'

'Uh huh. Is she a friend of yours?'

'There are some things you just don't do.'

'Come on. Bring it out.'

Callista went back inside and fetched the real portrait of Henry Beck. Her heart was thumping. Slowly she carried it out and set it up on the easel. She heard Alexander draw breath, then silence.

'Interesting,' he said eventually.

'I can't exhibit it.'

'Not here perhaps,' he said slowly. 'But there are some competitions we could enter it in.'

Callista paled. 'It was just for me . . . it was never meant . . . I think I should just put it away.'

He patted her on the arm. 'You'll survive it. Sorry, but you can't just lock it away. Give it to me when you're finished and I'll deal with it for you.'

'I can't. I'll paint something else.'

'But you won't be able to. Not like this. You'll be trying to paint a lie. Like the commission. And you won't be able to find the passion. You have to have enormous excesses of emotion to paint something like this. When everything in you comes together in a painting like this, you have to set other people's feelings aside and reap the accolades.'

'I can't do it.'

Alexander smiled. 'I'll work on you.'

TWENTY-THREE

Merrigan Show Day, Lex arrived early to set up his stage for the Show Girl competition. John Watson was already there with Sue's husband, Geoff, tacking and taping royal-blue fabric around the edge of the stage to fancy it up. Lex offered to help, but they waved him over to a plastic box full of leads and wires that had been dumped on the stage.

'See what you can make of that,' John Watson said. 'Looks like a pile of spaghetti to me.'

Lex lifted off the lid of the box and looked inside. After months chipping away at building a new life, here at last was something familiar. He placed a hand on top of the cables and microphone gear, feeling the texture of the wires beneath his fingers. A tinge of sadness swept through him. He picked up a handful of coiled cables and set them on the stage. The gear was old. He hadn't seen this sort of set-up for years. But it looked functional and reasonably robust. And everything had been neatly coiled and stacked away. He should be able to get organised pretty quickly.

He screwed the microphone stands together and hooked in the microphones. Then he plugged connecting wires into the mikes and ran the wires out to the amplifier and speakers that had been set up at the front and rear corners of the stage. By the time John

Watson and Geoff had finished, he was trying to locate the power source so he could test the microphones and speakers.

John Watson looked up at him. 'Didn't know you had a practical bone in your body.'

Lex shrugged. 'It's pretty straightforward. Even Mrs Jensen could work it out.'

'I doubt that.' John Watson frowned at him assessingly. 'Trevor Baker will bring over a line for you from the power source. They run it from that shed just over there.'

He left to attend to some other job, and Lex set up the table and three chairs at one side of the stage for the judges. While he was unfolding the chairs, he glanced around the showground, wondering if Callista might be out there somewhere. He hadn't seen her since the storm and over the past few days his blood had started fizzing as he contemplated the possibility of running into her.

He was still staring out across the grounds looking for her stall, when Mrs Jensen arrived carrying a white tablecloth across her arms. She nodded at him as she passed the cloth up.

'I hope you're going to do yourself up before the competition,' she said.

'I've got a suit in the car.'

'Just as well. This is a very important event. I hope you'll do our girls justice.'

'I'll try.'

'When you're finished setting up you could pop over to the food pavilion for a cup of tea. It's over there.' She pointed to one of the corrugated iron sheds around the periphery of the arena.

'Thanks,' Lex said. 'I'll see if I have time.'

After she left, he hooked everything up to the power. Then he switched on the mikes and checked the sound levels. He was busy taping the wires onto the deck with masking tape so nobody would trip over them when John Watson came by to check on him.

'Looks like everything's set up,' John Watson said, surprised. 'How did you do it?'

'Beginner's luck.' Lex ducked his head to look at his watch. 'Nearly eight o'clock,' he said. 'Better get a cuppa before the action starts.'

Mrs Jensen and Mrs Dowling were fussing over the iced-cake exhibits when Lex walked into the food and craft pavilion. Considering it was just an old shed, he was impressed with the job they had done to decorate it, with banners on the walls and streamers strung across the steel joists. Mrs Jensen saw him come in and waved him over to a stand where an urn had been set up along with dozens of cups and saucers all lined up in neat rows. He found a tea bag and poured himself a cup. Then he wandered around the pavilion for a closer look.

Tables were set up in long rows across the pavilion displaying all sorts of food arrangements: fruit cakes carefully sliced to show the even distribution of their fruits, plates of scones, preserved fruits, various medleys of home-grown vegetables, loaves of home-baked bread, schoolgirl cupcakes. He was stunned by the array of local crafts too—knitwear for babies, jumpers, hats, carefully stitched dresses, items of turned wood, model aeroplanes, cars.

He watched a woman setting up a spinning wheel in one corner of the shed. She was wearing a pair of old fawn trousers and a purple cheesecloth top. He was sure he'd never met her before, but there was something about her that looked familiar. He couldn't work it out. Something about the way she moved. He watched her screwing a few parts of the spinning wheel together then he wandered over to the iced-cakes display where Mrs Jensen was still organising tablecloths and the location of prize cards.

'It looks fantastic, Mrs Jensen. You've done a great job.'

She straightened up and looked at him down that hooked nose of hers. 'We've quite a bit of talent in our local community, as you can see.'

He followed her along the table.

'Here are the bridal cakes. Just look at the lace work on this one. Sharon Morris does a spectacular job.' Mrs Jensen paused to glance at him. 'That's Barry's wife. From the service station. She wins it every year.'

'What do you do with the cakes after?' he asked.

'Most of them are sold. What else can you do with them? Sharon takes photos of hers and keeps an album.'

'Do you do the iced cakes as well?'

She snorted. 'No. I'm better at the fine knitting and the cross-stitch, though it's getting harder these days with my eyesight starting to go.'

At the end of the cake tables, they had a clear view of the far corner of the shed. Lex could still see the woman down there, laying out wool in an old wicker basket.

'Who's that?' he asked.

Mrs Jensen looked at him with surprise. 'I thought you'd know,' she said, lips slightly compressed. 'That's Cynthia Wallace. She does the spinning demonstration every year.'

'I see.' Lex tried to hide his discomfort. No wonder the woman had looked familiar. He could see it now. She moved just like Callista and dressed a little like her too. She even pinned her hair back behind her ear in the same way. Thinking of Callista made his heart curl over in his chest.

'I'll just put my cup back,' he said. 'Where can I wash it?'

'Here, let me take it.' Mrs Jensen took the cup. Her eyes were measuring him up. 'You go over and say hello.'

He'd planned on going straight back outside, but he had little choice now that Mrs Jensen was watching him. Pausing to look at various exhibits, he made his way towards the spinning wheel.

'Hello,' Cynthia said brightly. 'You're here early. I didn't know they'd opened the gates.'

'I've just been setting up the stage. For the Show Girl competition.'

'Oh.' Cynthia looked confused. 'Have they given you a job?'

'Yes. They've asked me to be MC.'

She frowned and looked at him closely. Lex wondered what she was thinking, whether she had worked out who he was.

'I'm Cynthia Wallace. I don't believe we've met.' She stretched out a slender brown hand that could have been Callista's, only it was more weathered and wrinkled.

'Lex Henderson.'

Cynthia smiled. 'Ah,' she said. 'I've heard a lot about you.'

He flushed. 'I guess you would have.' He wasn't sure what to say.

'I hope people haven't given you too much of a hard time about buying that house,' she said, pushing some more wool into the wicker basket. 'The locals are inclined to be a bit forward with their opinions. They can make people feel uncomfortable at times.'

He flushed again. 'I'm sorry.'

'Don't be.' She stood straight and stretched her back. 'It isn't your fault. I mean, how could it be?' She was frowning slightly as she looked up at him. 'So they've asked you to MC the Show Girl?' She was sizing him up. 'That's a big call.'

'Yes, it is for a city chap. I'll have to jump through a few hoops to impress them.'

'Forget about impressing them. Just enjoy yourself. Everyone will have a better time then.'

'And what about you? Doing the spinning?'

'I can do it in my sleep. In fact, I often have done. When the kids were small. But that's a long time ago.' She smiled at him again. 'It *is* nice to meet you, Lex, after all this time. God knows, sometimes when Callista talked about you I thought I'd be meeting an ogre.'

'I can be an ogre on my bad days.'

'And can't we all. Callista included.' Cynthia frowned. 'I'd like to say she got that from her father. But you know how it is. She's probably more like me.'

Lex laughed. He liked this sunny, warm woman. There was a lot of her in Callista.

'I hope you'll come out to our place for a drink sometime soon, if Callista ever gets around to asking you.'

Lex felt uncomfortable again. 'Yes, well, we'll see how it goes.' He wondered again how much she knew, and realised glumly that she probably knew everything. It would be like that in a country town. And Callista was her daughter. He ought to be wise to it by now.

'Make sure you catch up with her today,' Cynthia said, smiling kindly at him. 'Things might take a turn for the better. She's had a spot of luck. But I can't tell you. She'll want to tell you herself.'

He wondered what could have happened. 'I suppose I ought to make sure everything's ready,' he said.

'Yes, and I've got to get some more wool out of the car. Spinning all day it seems like I need the wool from sixty sheep to keep me going. Good luck with the Show Girl.'

Callista set up her stand on the far side of the showground, where she was well away from the noise of the carnival rides and could get a full view of the events going on in the arena. She loved the Show. She had been coming every year for as long as she could remember. It was a big day for the local community. Just about everyone she knew from around town had a job of some kind. Her father always spent the day on the ground in the arena marshalling competitors and Cynthia would be setting up her spinning demonstration in the craft pavilion. Jordi was down at the servo pumping petrol. He was usually tied up there all day, with all the extra traffic in town.

She'd heard that Lex was to be MC for the Show Girl this year, and at first she had laughed, imagining him all tongue-tied and awkward up there in front of the microphone. But then she'd had a surge of sympathy for him. Even after their blow-up, she didn't want to see him make a fool of himself. And she had to admit that she missed him, that she thought of him often, and that she had spent many days waiting for him to phone her in the gully. But the phone call had never come, and now she was unsure how she'd feel when she saw him today. Whether she'd still be angry with him, or whether seeing him would unlock the yearning within her that had subsided to a dull ache in recent times.

Earlier she had spotted three men fiddling around on the Show Girl stage, and her heart had skipped, knowing Lex must be among them. But she didn't go over and say hello. It was best she kept her distance from him.

At least it looked like they were going to be lucky with the weather this year. The sky was a bit overcast, but the clouds were high and thin and might even burn off to sunshine late morning. She sat down and poured herself a coffee from her thermos. The crowd should start to pick up soon, and she liked to sit back and people-watch.

Just before eleven, Callista hooked a rope across the front of her stand and headed for the stage. The Show Girl contest was always held at eleven o'clock, giving enough time for the crowds to arrive, have a bit of a look around and get in a few rides, maybe buy a show bag or two. It should be particularly interesting this year with Lex trying to fuddle his way through as MC. Callista felt a little nervous for him.

A crowd had already gathered in front of the stage and she spotted Lex standing off to one side holding a sheaf of papers. The girls were in a nervous flurry behind him. He was dressed in a dark blue suit and yellow tie and her heart squeezed as she looked at him. She saw him turn away from the girls and check his watch. Then he walked up the steps onto the stage. He stepped up to a microphone and adjusted it with a quick swivel of his wrist. She noticed he did it expertly, without looking. And his eyes were roving over the audience calmly. There was something strange about this, something about him that looked too comfortable.

'Good morning, ladies and gents,' he said. 'Welcome.'

His voice was smooth as silk over the speakers. Quite soft, but clear, sexy almost. He wasn't nervous at all.

'Welcome to the Merrigan Show Girl contest. It's an event many of you have been waiting for.'

As he spoke he swivelled his head to check the crowd, the judges, all without losing contact with the mike, his voice mellow, soft, thrilling. Callista's heart turned. He must have done this before.

'I'm Lex Henderson,' he said. 'And I'm going to be your MC this morning.' He smiled and waved a slow arm in the direction of the girls, who were watching him anxiously from the base of the stairs. 'I've already met and spoken with the young ladies who are our contestants today. And I'll soon be introducing them to you. But first I want to tell you a little about the Show Girl event.'

His introduction was a departure from the ordinary and Callista wondered what he was planning. Mrs Jensen would be doing a back-flip, but Callista suspected Lex knew exactly what he wanted to do. As he paused, he glanced at her and gave a small, very private smile. She realised he was enjoying himself and she couldn't stop herself from smiling back.

'Traditionally, girls from local families around Merrigan enter this event when they turn eighteen. So really, it's a coming of age. A very big event. A day of great excitement for everyone in Merrigan. And rather than viewing this event as a competition where only one girl is the winner, I want you all to mentally step back from that concept and instead think about the Show Girl event as a debut of wonderful young talent, and a celebration of the freshness and enthusiasm of the young ladies of our region.'

Callista liked it. It was a clever start. She watched Lex at the microphone, hands hooked inside his pockets, eyes shifting calmly through the crowd. As she glanced around the audience she saw that the Merrigan community was watching him too—astounded. Even Mrs Jensen was nodding with approval. Callista realised she was proud of him.

'Usually at this event the girls stand up one by one and talk about themselves and their lives,' Lex said. 'But this year I'm going to use a bit of poetic licence to help the girls along and make it a bit more fun for them. We're going to have a chat, a casual interview if you like, just to get the ball rolling. The first young lady I'm going to introduce you to today is Frannie Baker.'

He turned and beckoned to a tall thin girl with long hair, who stepped meekly onto the stage.

'Welcome, Frannie.'

While the audience clapped, Lex leaned forward and quickly tweaked the other microphone to the right height for her. Frannie looked scared. But Lex was speaking to her very softly.

'Here,' he said. 'Step forward. The mike won't bite. That's it. About two inches off. Stay close and just speak normally. There you go.'

'Hello. I'm Frannie Baker.' The girl smiled at the clarity of her voice. She looked suddenly beautiful. 'I live with my parents on a dairy farm on the flats out from Merrigan.'

She hesitated and stared nervously into the crowd. There was an awkward silence. This was usual for the Show Girl contest. Nothing was different, after all. But then Lex slipped in quietly.

'There's more you can tell us about your family, isn't there? I've heard your dad is quite famous locally.'

'Oh yes. He *is* famous. There's my dad.' Frannie pointed. 'Trevor Baker. He's the local wood-chopping champion. Defending his title today. Go, Dad!'

The crowd clapped enthusiastically and Trevor waved his fist in the air. Frannie smiled. She went on to tell everyone about Trevor's history as the local wood-chopping champion and all about his training sessions. How the whole family supported him—saved up to buy new axes for his birthdays. It was great listening. Frannie relaxed and the story flowed out. Then she stopped again, out of steam.

'What about *you*, Frannie?' Lex asked. 'What are your plans for the future?'

The girl blushed and then shyly outlined her hopes to study teaching and get a primary class at the local school so she could teach the kids more about environmental issues. There was a lot the local community could do, without jeopardising their livelihoods, to protect their farmlands and the river and coastline, she said. Changing attitudes at school was the best place to start. The crowd stood silent, listening intently. When Frannie left the stage she looked happy, and the crowd followed her with their applause.

The next girl was Tracey Dowling. Mrs Dowling's niece. She was small and mousy and she gaped at the microphone, obviously terrified. But Lex was there again, asking her to tell them about the funniest thing that had ever happened to her.

The girl thought for a moment, then smiled at him shyly. 'Well, there was this one time that I could tell you about, when we were kids . . .' she said.

Lex nodded encouragement and Tracey smiled again.

'Well, on this particular day, Dad was taking us all down the paddock in the tractor, and we were sitting up on the hay bales in the back, for the cows in the back paddock . . .'

She hesitated and the crowd was silent, willing her to go on. She cleared her throat.

'Well, one of our paddocks is really steep. We live at the base of the hills, you see. Not on the flats like Frannie. And we'd had a lot of rain that year, so the ground was really wet and slippery. And when Dad turned the tractor down the hill, it started sliding, so he yelled at us all to get off. Then he tried to turn the tractor around, but it kept on sliding.' Tracey's face lit up with excitement. 'And it went faster and faster down the hill with Dad standing up and jumping up and down on the brakes trying to slow it down. But the brakes locked, you see, and he was tearing down the hill, still standing up and hanging onto the steering wheel.' She started to giggle. 'And then, near the bottom of the hill, it looked like he was going to crash, so he did this huge dive off the tractor. And all I can remember is seeing Dad flying through the air while the tractor swung off into a patch of blackberries.'

Tracey stopped and smiled behind her hand. 'The funniest thing is that up till then Dad had been having a war with the blackberries. He sprayed them every year. But since they saved his tractor, he's left them alone. And now we make jam from that blackberry bush and enter it in the Show each year.'

Laughter and applause rippled through the crowd and someone called out, 'Has the jam ever won?'

Tracey blushed. 'Not yet,' she said. 'Mum's not the best at making jam . . . it's always too runny.'

And that was the way it went with all ten girls in the contest. Lex guided them through their nervousness and managed to tease a good story out of each of them. And he did it quietly and unobtrusively, so none of the girls realised how he had manipulated them into bringing forth their best. At the end he handed over to the judges and stood aside. He glanced at Callista, met her eyes and looked quickly away. He knew he was caught out.

The winner's sash was awarded to Frannie Baker. Not that it mattered. All the girls were jubilant.

Afterwards, Callista tried to find Lex behind the stage, but he had already gone. Only John Watson was there.

'Where's Lex?' she asked.

'Gone to get ready for the Grand Parade.'

'What was that performance?'

'He's a surprise, isn't he?'

'Yes. It looks like he's handled a microphone before.'

'Who is he?' John Watson asked.

Callista stared out across the arena, looking for Lex's familiar figure. 'I honestly don't know,' she said.

The Grand Parade was at two thirty and it was Callista's favourite event. It was usually a sedate but stately affair, with cattle plodding around the arena in long snaking lines flicking their tails, goats being tugged along with sashes draped over their sway backs, and kids trotting by on pretty plaited-up ponies. She waved to Frannie Baker passing by in the back of a ute wearing the Show Girl sash over her shoulder. It was the same every year—just a different face in the ute. The Grand Parade was a nice way for everybody to show off their stock and their successes.

She poured herself a coffee and sat back to watch. She was also checking the crowd to see if she could spot Lex. She wanted to talk to him, ask him some questions about the Show Girl contest. Surely he'd open up to her now that all this time had passed since the storm and there was nothing else to hide.

Callista always wondered how they managed to organise the Grand Parade so it ran so smoothly. There were so many animals and exhibitors out there. Her father and the other marshals did a great job bringing all the different groups onto the grounds and keeping all the potential clashes separate. She was amazed there weren't horses bolting everywhere, given how pumped on oats some of them were, and how little control some of the riders seemed to have. And all those cows that spent most of the year grazing in a paddock—it was incredible they could walk so calmly around the arena as if they did so every day of their lives.

But this year all wasn't going so well. At the far end of the arena, Callista noticed a ruckus developing. Among an alarmed scatter of animals, a bull was pulling a man around. It was a large Friesian bull and the man was obviously struggling for control even though he was tugging and jerking at the nose ring. She watched the bull cavorting on feet that seemed to have grown springs and wondered what was going to happen.

The bull let out an eerie bellow and ran backwards, tugging his handler along with him. Cows and horses swayed out of line and broke away, dodging the bull's leaps and twists. For a moment the bull stopped, and there was a tense and anxious lull. Then it lowered its clunky head, turned and took off around the outside track. A child screamed as her pony bolted. Goats skittered. One of the harness horses reared in its traces, then spun crazily away while the driver cursed and tugged at the reins. Bedlam descended.

The man tried to run with the bull, but tripped and skidded along in the gravel, still clinging to the lead rope. When he gave up and let go, the bull took off even faster, running dangerously through a line of shying horses. The man, wearing brown trousers and a filthy white shirt, stood in the centre of the track and watched. The Grand Parade was in disarray.

The bull ran headlong into Frannie Baker's ute and knocked her flying over the edge. Then it paused, shook its head and staggered sideways before raising a trot and then a slow canter with its head carefully held to one side to avoid stepping on the rope. A farmer pulling a trailer load of prize-winning hay behind his tractor finally manoeuvred his rig across the main track and blocked the bull's run. It propped to a flesh-juddering halt and buried its nose in the hay—eyes still white and wild. Another farmer vaulted the fence and grabbed the lead rope.

The Grand Parade was over.

As the crowd dispersed, the man in the brown trousers dusted himself off and headed for the side fence with his head lowered. He vaulted shakily, landed badly and slipped onto his right hip, adding a grass stain to the elbow of his filthy shirt. He lay sprawled on the ground just along from Callista's stall. Now that the bull was captured, the whole event actually seemed quite funny and she laughed until the man stood and looked her way.

It was Lex.

His face paled, but he hobbled towards her anyway, rubbing his hip and then glancing at the scrapes on his palms.

'Did we kill anyone out there?' he asked.

'No,' she said. 'But it was scary for a while. Do you have any skin left?'

She pushed him into her diminister's chair. 'Like a beer? I've got some on ice.' She leaned into the back of the Kombi, twisted the lid off a stubbie and placed it in his grazed and rope-burned right hand.

'Sore?'

'Just a bit.'

'Whose bull?'

'Ben Hackett's.'

'That bull played up last year. You've been had.'

Lex sat quietly for a while. Callista watched him scanning her beach paintings and then he looked at her, lengthily.

'So, how are you?' he asked.

Her heart contracted. 'I'm good,' she said.

She opened a beer for herself and sat down on the grass beside him, just behind the stall.

'So what was that?' she asked.

'What was what?'

'The Show Girl thing. All that confidence with the microphone.'

'Yes,' he said. 'I thought you might ask about that.' He sipped his beer slowly, stalling.

'So?'

'I've done a bit of radio journalism in my time. A few interviews.'

'Just a few?'

'Probably more than a few.' He glanced at her and looked quickly away. 'I've done a bit of print media too. In my time. Nothing to rave about.'

'They certainly asked the right person to MC the Show Girl then, didn't they?'

'Maybe not. I've given the game away.'

'It doesn't have to be a game, Lex. People aren't going to crucify you just because they know what you do.'

He set his empty beer can on the grass and glanced at her.

'I've got something for you,' she said. 'I'll just get it. It's in the Kombi.'

She pushed herself up and went round to the front door. On the seat was an envelope Alexander had given her yesterday. It contained the invitations to her exhibition launch. She hesitated, then slipped her hand into the envelope and pulled one out. She went back and handed it to Lex.

'What's this?' he asked.

'Read it.'

She watched him as he scanned the invitation.

'This is great,' he said. 'Fantastic. I'll be there.'

He was plainly delighted for her. Callista smiled and looked shyly away.

'This is important, isn't it? It means a lot to you.' His eyes were bright.

'Yes,' she said. 'The storm gave it to me. And you—in a bizarre, abstract sort of a way. I suppose I should thank you for that.'

He was embarrassed. 'Well, whatever,' he said. 'I can't wait to see your paintings.'

'I'm nervous,' she said. 'It's like putting my life on the line.'

Lex reached out to take her hand and squeezed it.

'You'll be okay,' he said. 'I know it.'

At home after the Show, Lex took a couple of beers down to the beach and sat watching the surf roll in. There was a gannet fishing far out over the waves. He watched the bird cruising over the surface of the sea, then climbing high in the air before folding its wings and plunging like a spear into the water. It was cool on the beach. The late afternoon sun had little warmth. But Lex lingered, and with each breath the sourness at Ben and his bull eased and washed out with the surf.

It had been good to see Callista again. Could you call it good luck to land at her feet? Or was it just another of life's ridiculous coincidences. Thank God it hadn't been Helen. He had seen her walking around in the crowd too, with Darren. And Sally, wandering around with Sash and Evan while they dipped into their show bags. Country events were just a bit too parochial. And he was never going to live down the Show Girl event. People had been all over him after that, telling him how talented he was, asking where he'd learned to use a microphone. Shame he couldn't stop himself once he got up on the stage. But at least the girls had a good time.

The gannet had moved on. Lex watched the waves curling and the spume whizzing off their tips as they peaked before crashing. His body felt like it had been mangled beneath a roller. Slowly, the late light of evening fell, and some sort of resigned calm. Today the beer was a hollow companion, but it brought a kind of mellow warmth in the chill of the afternoon.

He had enjoyed meeting Callista's mother, Cynthia. He liked her. She was warm and earthy, direct, yet humble. You'd always know where you stood with her. If her daughter could overcome a few complexities, she would have similar qualities.

Lex tilted his bottle and took another mouthful of beer, thinking. What was it that he wanted from Callista, he wondered.

It was the smell of her hair that he wanted, that sweet apple shampoo. The warmth of her back, turned against him in sleep. Her concentrated look as she lay buried in a book on the couch. And the less specifics too. Plates for more than one to wash up. Two wine glasses on the bench. Loose long hairs on the bathroom floor. Coming home to the smell of dinner cooking. Arms around him. Sitting quietly on the beach, like this. Sex. Lazy conversation. Another body in the house. Female complexity.

Yep, all of it.

TWENTY-FOUR

Opening night was a Saturday and Callista buzzed with a ticklish excitement. She had argued with Alexander for an early afternoon opening, after the local shops closed. But he had insisted on evening. He said he knew best about these things and she ought to leave it to him.

Looking in the mirror, Callista felt like a stranger. She had never thought of herself as plump, but in these clothes she felt like too much woman. Breasts and hips and curves. The woman in the boutique that Alexander had recommended up the coast had decked her out in a snug white shirt fitted around the waist, dark stockings and a short, close-fitting brown skirt with scant excess fabric. The mascara she had carefully applied made her eyes look large and round, and the red lipstick emphasised her full lips. With her freshly washed curly hair dancing in ringlets around her face, she was sure it was all too much.

Then there were the shoes. It was with regret that she looked at them now before putting them on. They were fine, strappy and high-heeled—like nothing she had ever owned before. She doubted she could even walk in them. What stupidity had made her buy them? At the shoe store she'd been sent to, the young girl had looked at the outfit and pulled these shoes off the shelf. Callista had tried them on quickly for size. She was acutely aware of her incompetence in such high heels. It felt like she was on stilts.

'Yes, these will be fine,' she'd said, feeling the girl's knowing gaze.

'Special occasion?'

'Yes.'

'Wedding?'

'No, no, nothing like that.'

'Surprise party?'

Callista looked at her, alarmed. 'Maybe. I guess. Kind of.' She *would* be surprised if anybody bought any of her paintings.

'Come on. What is it? I need to make sure I'm matching the shoes to the occasion.'

'It's an exhibition opening.'

'What sort?'

'Art. Paintings.'

'Oh, you're making a trip to the city.'

'No. Apparently the city is coming to the country. And I can't go dressed like this.' Callista had waved a hand over her usual garb of cheesecloth skirt and loose blouse.

'Maybe not. Whose paintings are they? Anyone I'd have heard of?'

'Definitely not. They're mine.'

The girl had struggled not to look surprised.

'You're quite right,' Callista had said. 'I don't look particularly talented.'

'That's not what I was thinking.'

'And I'm not sophisticated either. It all comes from up here.' She tapped her forehead. 'And through here.' She waved her left hand. 'It's a bit of a joke really. Thinking I can dress up in this lot and fool a city crowd. Once they see me trying to walk in these things, it'll be game over.'

The girl had smiled kindly. 'I'm sure you'll pull it off.'

'I'm not so sure.'

'City types aren't as swanky as they make out. It's all show.'

Yes, Callista had thought. They need to cover the emptiness.

Now she looked at the shoes and quickly stuffed them in a string bag. She slipped into her old boots and a worn grey coat and dashed for the Kombi.

She pulled up at the far end of Alexander's car park and strapped on the shoes before getting out. There was no doubt she was an embarrassment. It was obvious she had no idea how to walk in these things. She shuffled across the gravel, feeling knock-kneed and mincing.

Stepping out along the walkway past the gallery windows, she caught a glimpse of herself reflected in the glass. It was a shock. Despite the unpolished walk, she looked like some smart leggy chick from out of town. She had never felt long-legged, sexy or busty before, but the girl striding along in the reflection, with gently bent knees and a red pouty mouth, was bordering on sophisticated. Quickly she glanced away. Best she didn't look. The image scared her. If she thought too long, she might flick the shoes off into the thicket of grevilleas and run flat-footed out of here.

Alexander caught her hesitating at the door. He appraised her with a quick professional eye then gave her a friendly hug. 'You look gorgeous.' He hooked his arm through hers and led her across the room to his office to pour her a glass of champagne. 'Thank *God* you didn't go to Beryl's. I would have had to call in someone to second for you this evening.' He gave her a fond, coquettish smile. 'They looked after you in that little boutique, didn't they?'

Callista remembered the sales girl's nod when she'd said Alexander had sent her. She guessed now that he had called ahead with a few hints and ideas.

'I feel like a freak.'

Alexander clinked his champagne flute against hers. 'But my colleagues from Sydney will love you. And that's what counts. When your shoes start hurting about eight o'clock, just remember you're doing it for show, to manipulate their money out of their hip pockets.'

'I would have thought paintings had to sell themselves.'

'Ah yes. But image helps.'

'I hate it.'

'I know. But you really do look gorgeous.'

Callista stood with her back to the gallery. She was afraid to look, and it was too dark anyway, with the shadows of early evening falling over the unlit space. Alexander watched her twisting the stem of her glass nervously between her fingers. He topped up their glasses.

'You'll need more of this. We need to have you relaxed before they all come.'

'Are you expecting many?'

'Hordes,' he said, rolling the word deliciously. 'There's at least a dozen waiting in my house already.'

Callista glanced nervously over her shoulder towards the door. 'You're kidding.'

'Scouts' honour. They're in there drinking wine and discussing the Sydney art scene.'

'Why not have them over here?'

Alexander's smile spread across his face. 'Waiting for the right light, darling. I've placed all the spotlights for night-time. And you never get a second chance to make a first impression.'

'Just the dozen from the big smoke?'

'God, no. They're coming in cars and aeroplanes as we speak. Merrigan airfield is going to make Sydney International Airport look like a country strip.'

'You're teasing, but I'd better drink more champagne anyway. I'm not used to being a showpiece.'

He laughed. 'That's where you're wrong, darling. You're a showpiece every day of your life with that gorgeous face and smile. Just as well you don't realise it.'

He set down his champagne glass and walked past Callista into the gallery.

'Are you going to come and take a look?' he said. 'It's time to light up. Only fifteen minutes to opening.'

She followed him nervously into the darkened space. He stopped her in the middle of the room while he went for the light switches. In rapid succession the gallery lit up with soft light that was sufficiently bright on the paintings but created surprising warmth in the rest of the room. Sudden excitement set her heart fluttering as she glanced around. The paintings leapt at her, alive and arresting. They were good. And Alexander was a master.

'Cat got your tongue?' he asked, a pleased smile curling his thinnish lips. 'And keep those wide round eyes for the buyers, will you. They're wasted on me.'

By seven thirty the room was crowded and buzzing. Conversation bounced noisily off the bare wooden floors and walls and mounted a cascading sense of excitement. Bodies shifted around the room, mingling, chatting, laughing, perusing. Smartly dressed Sydney people wandered among the jovial Merrigan crowd who were mostly wearing their usual garb of wool knits, floral dresses and flannelette shirts.

For Callista it was like riding on a wave. People surged constantly towards her and around her, congratulating her, shaking her hand, wanting a piece of her. Swanky city men eyed her cleavage, the curves of her figure. They pressed close. Flushed pink with excitement and champagne she tried not to notice, allowed it to happen, so that interest flashed in their eyes and they swung into a second perusal of her paintings. It was just what Alexander wanted. She worked hard to play the game.

Red 'sold' spots quickly appeared on the title tags. Alexander moved smoothly through the crowd, smiling and nodding, passing comments with the suits from the big smoke, accepting their handshakes, topping up glasses.

In between city onslaughts, locals swarmed around Callista, patting her on the back, smiling proudly and declaring her 'our Callista', like she was another exhibit on show. The room was packed. Almost the whole town was there. Even Helen Beck, slinking shyly between the exhibits with Darren's hand gripped tightly in hers. Mrs Jensen stalked around the room looking important, her husband Denis shuffling along behind her. Sue was busily engaged in conversation with John Watson. She was too much of everything tonight—too large, too bright, too loud. But it didn't matter in this room, thick with people and atmosphere.

Even Jordi popped in for a while. He darted furtively around the paintings, inspecting them closely, then left like a shadow after a brief wave across the room. Her parents had made an effort as well. Jimmy had clipped his beard and borrowed a suit from someone in town, and her mother had scoured all the shops in the region to find something that was her style but not too hippie. She looked proud and radiant in a long loose orange dress with a low-cut neckline.

Then there was Lex. He was smooth and neat in jeans and a white casual shirt. But he was too often by the bar, refilling his glass and watching her intensely. She knew he was agitated by the men close around her, by the invasive fingers placed on her shoulders, the eyes on her breasts. Every time she looked around the room, her eyes clashed with his. There was tension in his shoulders, anger in his cheeks. She made her eyes flow by him, as if she had barely noticed him. Otherwise, how could she hold him off? How could she keep him away?

She was afraid of him tonight. With all that wine on board and the jealousy smouldering in his eyes, he could ruin it. She hoped she could trust him not to stage a scene if he got too drunk.

'What's with Mr Henderson this evening?' Alexander asked, refilling her glass.

Callista watched the bubbles fizzing and popping.

'We were together a while ago.'

'Ah, the jealous ex-boyfriend. He doesn't like you getting all this attention, eh? Do you think I can persuade him to buy something? He ought to have city money. Unless he's spent it all in the bottle shop.'

'That's a bit unfair.'

'I hear he kept them in business when he first arrived in town.'

'Alexander, you've become a gossip.'

'And I'm loving it.' He pecked her on the cheek. 'There's so much intrigue in this little town. Who'd have ever imagined.' He leaned in close to whisper in her ear. 'I'm going to give my friends a private viewing of Mr Beck after this.'

'You're not.'

'I just want to seek their opinions.'

'I should never have shown it to you.'

'But you did. And you'll just have to trust me.' He smiled and tickled her chin and moved off through the crowd to tackle Lex.

When Lex arrived at the gallery, there was a tight knot of city people around Callista. Alexander was introducing her to a cluster of visitors, all dressed in suits. Lex smiled quietly to himself. Callista looked like a scared rabbit in the spotlight. For a while he stood at the edge of things, watching her as she smiled and shook hands with people. She was unbelievably stunning. He had never seen her with make-up before.

Then Sue found him.

'Lex. How are you doing tonight?'

'I'm good,' he said.

'Heard you took a tumble at the Show.'

'Ben Hackett's damned bull.'

'What a shame. Perhaps somebody should have told you about that.'

'Perhaps they should have. The country grapevine let me down.'

Sue laughed and moved on to collect another glass of champagne.

He stood by himself a moment, smiling at various people in the crowd who waved at him, then Sally tapped him on the arm. She was wearing a large skirt and a long white T-shirt. He imagined this was about as dressed up as she could manage.

'Have you seen the paintings?' she asked.

'Not yet. I've just arrived.'

'They're amazing. You won't recognise the place.'

He smiled. 'I thought the idea of landscape paintings was that I *should* recognise the place.'

She rolled her eyes. 'What I'm saying is they're good. She's incredible.'

'Where are the kids?'

'I left them with Merv, my new fella. You know how it is . . . not much fun coming out to something like this with kids hanging all over you . . . Have you got a drink?'

'No. I'd better get one.'

He found a glass of wine at a white-clothed table. It was too full so he sucked off the first inch quickly, feeling the cool moisture condensed on the glass. Politely, he skirted a conversing circle of people he didn't know and swung out into the crush to view Callista's paintings.

As he stood in front of the first of them, he felt time stop. The painting was of his beach, the headland illuminated by a flash of lightning that shattered a menacing purple-black sky. He could almost feel the wind whipping up the sea and lacerating the clouds. This was a shock. He hadn't expected Callista to be so good.

Slowly he moved around the room from painting to painting, waiting for the crowd to shift so he could get a clear view of each of them. The collection followed the lifetime of the storm and then its retreat to impossibly calm seas beneath a steely grey sky with stray shafts of creamy light cutting through onto restless surf. Then there was a series of works depicting a range of ocean moods: chopped by fresh winds, frisky in bright light, calm at dawn, reflective and still at dusk, silvered by moonlight.

The exhibition was more than the storm. It was a celebration of light over water and the dark powerful moodiness of the sea. It was a festival of movement, of shadow, of tone, of change. Callista had married herself with the light. She was excellent.

The final painting was one he recognised. It was the quiet sunset moon over water that he had seen at Callista's house that first time he had visited. He clearly remembered the soothing pinks and mauves. He remembered her distraction and withdrawal when he had pulled this painting out. It seemed such a long time ago, when all was unknown and everything was possible. It was hard to believe he had made love with this woman, had shared his body and his bed with her. Yet he barely knew her. He had hardly scraped the surface of her. And it made him feel suddenly urgent. He needed her. He needed to know her, to have her, to discover her rich complexity. His feelings surprised him. They were hot, bloody and intense, and came from deep within his chest. The distance to her across the room was like a gulf. Inside him anger tumbled and he wondered if he was too late. It all seemed so far away.

He left the paintings and moved back to the wine table, found a space at the edge of the throng. He watched Callista across the room, couldn't keep his eyes off her. Those men around her, they were wearing their interest in their eyes. He saw their hands intruding on her space, watched them pushing too close, trying to possess something of her. It made him angry, the way they moved in on her like that, as if she was something for sale too. There were invitations, he was sure. He saw her blush often and turn away.

Alexander came over with a small, knowing smirk and a bottle to refresh his glass. Callista must have told him they had been lovers. It made him feel small.

'What do you think?' Alexander asked, pouring a glass for himself.

'She's magnificent.'

'Yes, isn't she?' Alexander offered to clink glasses.

'Wine's good too.'

'I see that you're enjoying yourself.'

'And holding it like a gentleman.'

Alexander turned his back on the room briefly. 'You should consider buying one.'

'I'd have to ask her which one she'd like me to have.'

'But then she'd have to give it to you. And that wouldn't be fair.' He topped up Lex's glass and looked him daringly in the eye. 'Which one do you think she'd choose for you? Surely you know.'

'Perhaps I don't know her as well as I thought,' Lex said, with a smile like plastic. 'But thanks for the suggestion. I'll think about it.'

Alexander moved on to mingle strategically with his guests, and Lex drank. He drank through the opening speeches, through the escalating noisy conversations as wine loosened tongues and wallets, just as Alexander had planned. He drank close to the bitter end, when the crowd thinned and people drifted off to their cars in the crammed car park. He drank, watching those men from the city standing too close to Callista, touching her while she laughed and smiled and avoided his eyes.

Callista left finally, after having a nightcap champagne with Alexander and giving him a delighted hug. The gallery lights switched off as she stepped onto the walkway, but he left on the outside light for her so she could find her way to the car. She knew he would go straight back to the house where there was more entertaining and more drinking to be done with his guests.

Alone in the silver night, the ache in her legs and feet reminded her of the strappy shoes and she bent to pull them off, then the stockings, which felt tight and unfamiliar against her legs. Her feet spread gratefully on the wooden walkway and she felt pleasantly reconnected with herself as she padded towards the car.

Lex was waiting for her in the car park. She saw the Volvo palely illuminated at the far end and the shadow of him leaning up against its bonnet. Without pausing she walked softly to the Kombi, opened the door and slung the shoes inside. Her heart was galloping. How would he be with her after all that wine and all those men?

She felt rather than heard him arrive beside her, swift across the car park, but she didn't turn around. There was the sound of his breathing, deep and slightly ragged, and then the touch of his hand on her hair, infinitely gentle. She turned.

'You looked stunning tonight.' His voice was soft and low.

'It was Alexander,' she whispered. But he placed a finger across her lips to hush her.

'Your work was magnificent,' he said, his finger sliding down her cheek. 'The world was taken by you.'

His hand crushed gently into her curls and he kissed her, lightly at first, and then urgently as they pressed against each other, their breathing suddenly quick, their bodies alive. They grappled against the car, feeling the contours of each other, the tightness in their bodies, the need.

'They all wanted you,' he whispered against her neck. 'But none as much as me.'

They grasped each other with a wild desperation and made love, bent over the front seat of the Kombi, with the moon silver on Lex's back and the faint stars sailing like jewels in the clear cold sky. It was passionate, but bittersweet. Callista felt like she was flying, and she didn't know what she wanted it to mean—this embrace with Lex. With the spin of the exhibition whizzing within her, she was surprised to find she wasn't sure whether she wanted it to be hello or goodbye.

PART IV

The Stranding

TWENTY-FIVE

Lex didn't hear from Callista for about a month, maybe six weeks. It was a torrid time of hope, doubt, fear and worry. He had come home from the exhibition aflame with passion for her and keen for a fresh start. Seeing her paintings had kindled something in him. Something basic and incredibly clear. He was ready for her. Finally.

He rang a couple of times and left messages on her answering machine, but she didn't ring back. Haunted, he visited Alexander's gallery and meandered amongst her paintings, trying to absorb something of her. It was pitiful and he knew it. And Alexander was onto him. He could see it in his smug smile.

'Any closer to a decision?' he asked each time Lex visited.

'Still working on it,' Lex would say gruffly.

'Better hurry and make a choice or you'll miss out.'

At least two-thirds of the paintings had been sold. But they were still on the walls, waiting out their three-week time slot. When Lex dropped by in the last week of May, the walls of the gallery were clean. Everything had gone. Alexander walked back out to the car park with him.

'You'd never know she'd been here, would you, now that the paintings have been taken down. But she'll exhibit here again. If you want to buy anything you'll have to wait till next time.'

Lex left another message on her machine and waited for her to call. Eventually his fluster subsided to melancholy, then irritation, then bitterness.

She rang finally on a Saturday evening, at the finish of a slow day thick with overcast skies and cool autumn winds. Lex stood by the window with the phone, looking out at the murky clouds and the iron grey waves riding in.

'Sorry we haven't caught up,' she said. 'It's been so busy. Alexander had some work for me. I've been up to Sydney with him a couple of times. Interviews for commissions.'

'He didn't mention that when I was down at the gallery,' Lex said, offhand, but his heart was thumping and he was swinging somewhere between hopeful and cross. 'Has he been lining you up with some of those men from the opening?'

'Yes. But it's not what you think.'

'Are you sure it's your paintings they're after?'

'For God's sake, Lex. Why this sudden concern for my soul? I think I'm big enough to take care of myself. Anyway, I have more good news to share with you . . . Alexander wants to enter one of my paintings in a portrait competition . . . It's one I did of Henry Beck.'

'I didn't know you were painting him.'

'There are a lot of things you don't know . . . But enough about me. What have you been up to?'

'The usual. Just the cows and me.'

'I thought you liked the cows.'

'Yes, I do—in a milky, manurey kind of way. And there's not much else on offer in Merrigan, is there? Unless I want to sign on as a garbo.' Lex couldn't stop himself now. The words rolled out of him, fast and twisted. 'No, I couldn't do that. And it would just be a lateral career shift really. From cleaning away shit in the shed to hauling people's shit to the tip. No, I'd miss the cows too much. And Ben. He's such an entertaining bastard.'

He stopped. A silence thickened between them.

'I was going to suggest a walk early tomorrow,' Callista said. 'There's a beach I wanted to show you. But maybe you don't feel up to it.'

'When?'

'Early would be best.'

'Like how early?'

'Around dawn.'

'It's not my best time of day.'

'You'll be right. Bring a coffee.'

'It'll take more than that to put a smile on my face.'

'I'm sure the weather will cap it off for you then. They're forecasting wild conditions.'

'Great. I'll pack some whisky and a hot water bottle.'

'Just try to bring a warm heart. Forget the rest.'

Lex woke in the pre-dawn and flicked back the curtains. It was a steely grey morning and the sky was streaked with dark wind-whipped clouds. Lovely! Just the day for a walk. In the bathroom, he grimaced in the mirror and flipped a washer across his face to wake himself up.

Silence sat fatly in the kitchen—that hollow sensation of quiet that belongs to loneliness. He tried to ignore it and shuffled around making coffee and pocketing some snacks. Why was he getting up so early to go for a beach walk? He could walk on the beach any time.

The headlights of the Kombi flashed through the front window. Pity Callista was so punctual. He'd have nothing to gripe about, apart from the cold. He poured his coffee, tied his boots and pulled his fleece and Gore-Tex out of the cupboard. On the way out he turned off the lights.

Callista swung open the passenger door for him. 'Hi.'

He folded himself into the seat, saying nothing, taking special care with his coffee.

'Not talking yet, I see.'

Lex could feel her smile in the dark.

'Old bear.' She gave his arm a squeeze.

'Be careful of my coffee.'

'I hope it thaws you out.' She tossed his gear onto the back seat.

As the Kombi roared onto the road, Lex saw a light on in Mrs B's house. Shame they had woken her. He didn't like to think of disturbing her restless sleep. She always looked so tired these days.

'Don't forget to watch out for roos,' he grunted, as the Kombi skidded on the gravel up towards the forest.

'You forget. I've driven this road more times than you.'

'Spare me. I'm not up for a Wallace history lesson this morning.'

Callista laughed and Lex smiled quietly into his coffee. It was good to see her.

On the highway, they drove south in silence. The countryside was muted in the low light of dawn. Fog lay in scattered blankets in gullies and across the low-lying flats. Occasionally the shadowy hummocks of grazing cattle appeared in paddocks alongside the road. There was nobody else around.

'Who bought the painting?' Lex asked. 'That sunset one with the moon over the water.'

She glanced sideways at him. 'Actually, I don't know who bought it. I didn't ask.'

'You know I liked it. You could have saved it for me.'

'I wanted to let it go. I don't need it anymore.'

'But I liked it.'

'It's my past. And I needed to let it go.'

He lapsed into silence. This wasn't how it was supposed to go. Here he was feeling anxious and unsure around her. He wanted to feel confident, positive, hopeful, but he had forgotten how to be at ease with her. The exhibition and all this time without seeing her had shaken him.

'I'm glad things are going well for you,' he said after a while.

She smiled across at him. 'I can't believe it's so good. These commissions Alexander has lined up for me might just generate enough money to keep me going. That means I may not have to do the markets anymore. It's the first positive break I've had in my life.'

'Really? You've had to wait thirty-three years for a positive break?'

She glanced at him then stared back out at the road. When she spoke again her voice was slow and soft. 'Actually, I did have one other break. But I miscarried.'

'I'm sorry,' he said quietly.

'You don't have to be. I can deal with it now.' She was trying to be brave, but her cheeks were flushed and there was a tight edge to her voice. 'It wasn't as big as your loss,' she said.

'It was just as important.' Lex reached out a hand hesitantly and placed it on her knee. Even in the dim early light, he thought he saw tears flash in her eyes.

'Please don't be nice,' she said. 'It makes me feel like I have to be strong.'

She drove slowly through a heavy fog patch. 'I was pregnant when I painted that painting you liked. That's why I didn't want you to have it. I don't want it in my life.'

She flushed nervously and glanced at him sideways, as if she had said something significant. Then she drifted into silence, driving on autopilot. Lex studied her profile carefully. What was she saying to him? That she couldn't have both him and the painting in her life? Did that mean she was saying she wanted *him*? His hand was still on her knee. She hadn't brushed it off.

The highway curved around a lake and through a stand of spotted gum. The fog was wet and the wind heaved in the tops of the trees. Lex could feel the Kombi being buffeted by the occasional blast. They must have driven thirty minutes south when they turned off onto a sealed road that wound through cleared farmland and down over a bridge spanning a stream. Then the road climbed a little, heading towards the coast through the green pastured landscape. On a rise, they turned onto a gravel road that soon crossed a cattle grid and deteriorated into a grassy track.

There were three gates to open. Lex did gate duty between coffee sips, leaving his cup inside the car and pushing the Kombi door out into the snatching winds. Patches of mist curled over him as he struggled with the third gate. The air was wet on his face and his fingers were stiff working with the cold hard wire. He was already damp and shivering when he clambered back into the van. But Callista smiled at him across the space between them, and that was enough for now. She clunked the Kombi back into gear and drove on.

The track eased around a hilltop, past cows resting beneath a tree, and then swung over a ridgeline to finish beside a tiny cemetery overlooking a wild ocean beach. Callista parked the Kombi across the hill just below the cluster of weather-worn headstones and they sat looking out while thick sheets of mist rolled in from the sea.

Lex shivered. 'What is this place? A burial ground for madmen?'

'I love it.' Callista's face was flushed bright. 'Hardly anyone comes here. Sometimes, when you stand on this hill, there's so much fog it's like being in heaven.'

'Or hell. It looks miserable out there.'

'You can stay here if you like. I'm going for a walk.'

She tugged her woollen hat and raincoat from beneath Lex's things on the back seat. He watched her wriggle into her coat behind the steering wheel and pull her beanie down on her head.

'You coming or not?' she asked.

He looked at the shifting mists for a moment. 'I'm out of bed. I might as well come.'

Out of the Kombi he yanked his coat on, fighting with the winds. 'Okay, let's do it then,' he said, snugging the hood onto his head and ramming his hands into his pockets.

Heads down, they hunched into the wind and skidded down a steep sandy path diving off the edge of the grass down into the dunes. Curtains of sea mist slid up over them and dampened their faces. Just before they broke out onto the beach there was a pocket of quiet in a hollow behind the last dune. Lex wiped the wet from his nose and lips with an old hanky he found screwed up in one of his pockets.

'Wild, isn't it?' Callista's cheeks were red and her eyes fizzing.

'You're mad,' he said. 'We'll be sandblasted out there.'

'Sometimes it's blowing a gale up on the hill, and then you get down on the beach and it's dead quiet.'

'Yeah, right.'

He took her hand and they strained up over the last dune.

Out on the beach, the wind fetched them. It swirled and then slung into their faces, drawing tears. Lex glanced down the beach, trying to feel Callista's passion for the place. But it was desolate and all he could muster was an empty reluctance. It was the most godforsaken beach he had ever seen. The sea battered at the sand like a great foaming beast and hunks of seaweed were strewn thickly all the way from the water's edge to the high tide mark just below the dunes. Gusts of wind threw angry blasts of sand against their coats.

'Let's go back,' he suggested. 'We can light a fire at my place and open a bottle of champagne.'

Callista shook her head. 'No, you drank enough champagne at the opening. And this suits my mood today. Just give me fifteen minutes.' She hooked his arm and pulled him into the blast.

The sea gushed high up onto the beach, reefing at the sand. They had to walk in the soft upper margins of the beach where all the sea rubbish had been deposited—chunks of tangled fishing nets, faded plastic bottles, broken buoys, dried-out mutton-bird carcasses, broken cuttlefish floats, mounds of seaweed. It was heavy walking. They battled down the beach, leaning into the wind, the sand whipping across their legs.

Further down, they passed a dune-locked lagoon, ruffled to a light chop. Intermittent sheets of sea mist made it difficult to see and the sand kept kicking up in the fitful wind, forcing them to screen their faces. Lex pulled back a little on Callista's arm.

'Wait,' she said, stopping and craning down the beach. She unhooked her left arm to shield her face from the onshore wind barrage. 'What's that?' She pointed. 'There's something down there on the beach. Way down. Can you see it?'

Lex wiped away salt-stung tears with a wet wrist and peered through the fog. There was something down there, but he couldn't make out what it was and it looked a long way to walk in this awful weather.

'Just some rocks,' he said.

'No, it doesn't look right. Let's go a bit further.'

He shrugged and pressed forward with her again. The mist thickened to drizzle and they didn't bother to look up for several minutes. Callista stopped again as a wind gust picked up the curtain of drizzle and cleared the beach briefly.

'I think it might be a whale,' she said.

'I hope not.'

'It's probably dead. Washed up in these winds.'

'Let's go back,' Lex said. 'That bottle of champagne's calling.'

'No, we'd better check first.' Callista's jaw and her hold on Lex's arm were firm. 'It might have been washed in last night. It could be alive.'

'And what then?'

'I don't know.'

She pushed on down the beach, but Lex didn't want to go. He had a bad feeling about it. Something to do with her determination and the fact that it might be a stranded whale. There was a collision happening in his brain, but he gave in and caught up, striding along with her, head tucked down into the wind. The mist sank over them again, wet and cold. For a while they could barely see more than ten metres in front of them. Then the wind swept the mist up and flicked it over the dunes.

They were much closer now. And it did look like a whale. A humped shape wedged in the sand, half-slumped in the water with waves riding over it. Shiny and black. Huge. Lex saw its tail rise slightly out of the water. Damn. It was alive.

Callista strained into a run, dropping Lex's arm and labouring through the wet sand, but it was impossible to move quickly. As they approached, the whale lifted its tail flukes and slammed them down agitatedly. Water went everywhere. Poor bastard, Lex thought. It's trying to get away.

He stopped as the whale jolted a pectoral flipper in the air, waved it wildly then dropped it with a slap against its side.

'Don't get too close,' he yelled, stepping back and lapsing to shocked silence.

The whale was a spectacular animal, enormous. Lex was awed by its size. He was appalled by the hunched shape of it, swamped in the sand. From head to tail it must have been close to ten metres, slick and black on the back, stark white under the belly and jaw. It was lying on its side, head towards the beach, and he could see the great pleat-like grooves running from beneath its lower jaw down its chest and belly. He had seen all this before, swimming with the whales off the Point, but never like this. It was wrong to see a whale this way. Its body seemed twisted somehow, collapsed on itself. In the water they were rounded and buoyant.

He squatted, his heart pounding, wondering if there was something they could do to ease its breathing. But he couldn't think of anything. He studied the knobbles that studded the whale's great flat head and jawline, then he moved even further back as it raised its pectoral flipper again, flashing the white underside briefly before slapping it down. The whole scene was surreal. They shouldn't be here. The whale shouldn't be here. The poor bugger, it was fighting to breathe again. He saw its body wall rise and slump as air whooshed out through the blowhole.

'What can we do?' Callista walked wide around the whale to its other side. She was clasping her hands and twisting them anxiously. 'Oh, I can see its eye,' she called. 'Poor thing.' She walked back to Lex, distressed. 'Do you think it can be moved?'

'God knows,' he said. 'It's so bloody enormous.'

He watched the whale trying to suck in another breath. It made a wheezing sound through its blowhole and its entire body seemed to heave with the effort. He was horrified. The poor thing was suffocating and they were powerless to help it.

'Dad knows about this stuff,' Callista said. 'We'll have to go and get him.'

She paused, looking with dismay over the long stretch of the whale's back. Lex watched her face, feeling dread slither beneath his skin. His heart tripped. He knew what was going to happen. He could see it all before him.

'Could you go?' she said. 'I think I should stay here.'

'Hang on a minute.' He reached anxiously for her arm. 'We need to talk about this.'

She looked at him with blank incomprehension. 'It's decided,' she said. 'You go, I'll stay.'

'That's not what I'm talking about.'

Confused, she pushed aside a strand of wet hair that had escaped her beanie. 'What *are* you talking about then?'

'We need to talk this through,' he insisted.

'Talk what through?'

'We need to discuss what we're going to do.'

'We need to get help.'

He shook his head. 'You're not hearing me. We need to discuss our options.'

Callista had been stamping around in the sand. She stopped and looked at him, eyes wide with distress. 'Options? What do you mean, *options*?'

His heart rolled with angst. 'The first option is to go and get help.'

She stared at him. 'There's another?'

'Yes.'

'I don't want to hear it.' Breathing hard, she looked back at the whale.

'Have you been to a stranding before?' he asked.

'No, have you?'

'I know a bit about what happens.'

Her tension cracked into laughter. 'What, from reading novels, from movies?'

'From my past life in radio. I did a few stories on strandings. Some interviews with biologists.'

'And that makes you an expert on whales?' She glanced at him wildly, her disbelief escalating.

He reached for her arm. 'Do you know what's going to happen when we go back into town and call your dad and National Parks?'

'We'll stop wasting time and get this rescue happening, that's what.'

'You think it's going to be that straightforward? We bring in the rescue team, roll the whale back into the water and everyone lives happily ever after?'

Callista was outraged. 'You're being patronising.'

'Listen to me,' he pleaded. 'Look how big it is. It's going to take something more than the tide to shift it. They'll need to use heavy machinery and that's going to be stressful. There'll be people everywhere, machinery, lots of noise. And what's going to happen in the end? It'll probably die. Not to mention the rush there's going to be on this place. A whole horde of lunatics making life difficult. It's going to be awful. Do you understand?'

She frowned at him, disbelieving and cross. 'What's the second option then? I want to hear you say it.'

'The second option is to walk away and let the whale die in peace.'

She glanced at the whale then turned to him, eyes like daggers. 'You call this peace? Dying of suffocation?'

'If we get a rescue happening, it isn't going to die peacefully.'

'It might not die!' she yelled. 'Hasn't it occurred to you that a rescue might be possible?'

He shook his head. 'Don't kid yourself. It's delusion.'

For a long moment, Callista stared at him, anger making her body stiff. 'I thought you'd have more compassion,' she said, her voice tight, 'after your daughter.'

It was the lowest possible blow. Lex was so stunned he almost staggered. What was this woman doing? Did she have any idea what she'd just said? And how completely she had crossed the line?

'This has nothing to do with Isabel,' he said, livid.

Callista paled and stepped back, as if afraid he might strike her. 'I'm sorry,' she said. 'But this is about life and death too, isn't it?'

He stared at her, still not quite recovered. She clearly had no idea how much she had winded him. 'This is about pain and suffering,' he said, jaw tense with anger. 'And this is an animal.'

'You think that makes its suffering any less?'

'No. But we could make it worse.'

'This whale is alive, Lex, and I'm not going to walk away. It's stranded on one of my beaches and I refuse to stand here arguing about what to do. For God's sake, neither of us knows anything about whale strandings. Let's get the experts in. People who know about whales. Some *do* survive, you know.'

He was too battered to fight further. Callista was crazy hell-bent on rescue, and she wouldn't listen to what he was trying to tell her. 'All right,' he said. 'I'll go along with it. But are you sure that's what you want? Even if the experts say it's going to die, the public will expect a rescue effort. They won't allow the whale to be euthanased.'

'I'm sure they wouldn't do anything inhumane,' she insisted.

'I'm glad you're confident of that. Because I'm not.'

There was a determined wildness in her eyes. 'It's about giving the whale a chance.'

Lex gave up. 'Okay then. I'm going.'

The drizzle closed in again, pattering on their raincoats.

'What are you going to do?' she asked.

'Call Parks.'

'Thank you.'

She turned away from him and started walking towards the whale. Lex watched her go. In the seeping grey mist she looked small and cold and lonely. He hesitated a moment, delaying the immensity of his decision to help her in this task. It didn't sit easily with him. And he was arrested too by an odd mix of concern, confusion and fear for her. He wanted to tell her not to try anything stupid, not to get too close, that she could be injured, that he cared about her. But he said nothing and started powering back up the beach.

As soon as Lex was lost in the drizzle, Callista felt isolation thicken around her. Turning her back to the weather, she tugged her coat-hood over her beanie and sat in the wet sand about ten metres from the whale, just beyond the foaming lick of the tide. There was time now for that rapid surge of anger and panic to subside and slip out with the backwash of the waves.

She was embarrassed she had let slip that comment about Isabel. It had been a terrible insensitivity. No wonder Lex had been upset. Despite her shock and angst about the whale, she had gone a step too far. And the more she considered it, the less she felt he would be able to forgive her. What a shame they hadn't been able to come to some sort of understanding before things had deteriorated so far. She realised there was as much distance between them now as there had ever been. It was hopeless. One step forward, two steps back. Would they never find a way to get it together?

Perhaps she ought to let it go.

Miserable, she examined the slumped mass of the whale. It looked so wrong hunched on the beach with the waves sloshing around it. So enormous and heavy, its body skewed and partly bogged in the sand. It was a humpback whale. That much she knew. Living on the coast all her life, it was impossible not to know humpbacks. Back when she was a kid, sighting a humpback from Grandpa's house at the Point had been a rare event. Now sightings were part of a visit to the beach, at the right times of year.

She closed her eyes and folded herself inside her coat. No, you couldn't be a Wallace without knowing whales. It was heritage. Whales and the sea had coloured her childhood. Grandpa made sure of that, threading his whaling stories through her early days at the Point so they were as familiar as the winds that raked the heath on the headland. She remembered his faraway look when he searched the horizon for signs of whales, pipe clamped between his teeth. He had never talked about killing whales, but dwelled instead on tales of epic chases, following great bold whales through wild southern seas. He had so entranced them with his tales they felt like they were there with him, floundering around on deck in stormy weather trying to keep sight of a pod.

As a child, Callista had never thought about the end point. Grandpa never mentioned that. It was only when she grew up and became more politically aware that she realised exactly what Grandpa had done and what he had been involved in. She understood it had been his job, but still hadn't been quite convinced. Surely, it had been his choice to go all that way west so he could go whaling. Times had already moved beyond the age of necessity. There were other products that could be used instead of whale. He must have wanted to do it. That had been hardest thing to rationalise—that he had chosen to kill whales for a living. Despite all those tales of adventure, she couldn't overlook the bottom line. But how could you tackle an issue like that with a grandparent? Someone you loved, who had always been an important part of your life. How could you question and denigrate the very root of their existence? Especially when they were ageing, when they'd moved beyond their past and were powerless to change it. No, she had decided that it was her responsibility to make things better for the future. It was for younger people to carry the load. God knows her father had paid for it in the guilt he had carried through his life.

Hot tears stung the stiff chill of her cheeks. There really was no escape from the past. Perhaps her attachment to this rescue was her attempt to make amends for Grandpa's history.

She stood up and inspected her beach companion. She watched the whale's back rise and fall with the huge shuddering effort of breathing. She could hear the hollow gush of air exiting the blowhole after each breath. Rolling up her trousers, she walked into the water and around the whale's head. She could see its heavy-lidded eye rolled unblinkingly open. Crouching down a little, she moved slowly towards the whale's flat head. Close up, the knobbles along its jaw were surprisingly gnarly and its white throat was beautifully riven with furrows. The sweeping curve of its mouth ended just beneath the eye, and the whale lay with its mouth half-open, exposing the baleen on one side like a great fine comb. Every now and then while Callista squatted there, the whale slowly hefted its pectoral flipper in the air, waved it briefly and let it slap back down with a crack onto its exposed upper side. The other flipper must be buried in the sand somewhere beneath that great heavy body. She hadn't realised how long the pectoral flippers were—great knobbled paddles for slicing through water.

As she stared at its eye, the whale heaved a deep grinding moan that seemed to reverberate hollowly through the water and underneath her feet. It was the depth of wretchedness. Callista began to sing, tears wet on her cheeks. Tremulous sound rolled forth from her chest—a haunting undulating coo that was more reassurance for herself than it was a song for the whale. It was so lonely on this awful beach.

She splashed out of the water and lay down on the sand, listening to the crashing thunder of the sea and the agony of slow breaths and occasional moans from the whale. Time became the long spaces between exhalations. She was useless and superfluous. She could not share the whale's pain. She should have gone with Lex. Her presence was as relevant as a grain of sand.

Forever seemed to pass and the drizzle eventually lifted.

Suddenly she couldn't bear it any longer. She stood up and wandered along the beach, kicking over kelp piles and fractured cuttlefish floats. About a hundred metres away from the whale she sat down and looked back at it. Maybe they should have walked away and let it die. But what sort of peace was this? Beached and struggling to breathe, with seagulls hovering around trying to take a peck wherever they could? Why should this creature die a painful lingering death on the sands? Was there any harm in trying to help it back into the sea even just to take its final gasp among the deeper swell of black waves far out? Was it any worse than this?

Callista straightened and walked back towards the whale. No, they had to try something. It was the right thing to do.

TWENTY-SIX

Lex stopped the Kombi outside the newsagency. It was the only shop open in town this early on a Sunday morning—close to eight o'clock. He bent his head onto the steering wheel for a moment, struggling with his next move. Then he shrugged off his wet coat, threw it in the back of the van and walked into the shop.

John Watson was sorting magazines behind the counter. A cup of steaming coffee was perched up on the till.

'Can I pay to use the phone?' Lex asked, not bothering with casual chat.

Watson looked mildly surprised by his bluntness, but handed the phone over with its coiled length of extension line.

'I need a phone diministery too. Do you have one?'

Watson gave him the white pages and watched with clear assessing eyes. Lex had never been sure whether this man liked him or not. His manner was neither friendly nor unfriendly. But Lex's performance at the Show hadn't helped things. It had made Watson suspicious of him. Lex could see it in the way Watson watched him as he leafed through the phone diministery. He found a National Parks number, called through, and then dialled the emergency after-hours contact given on the recorded message. A man's voice answered the phone.

'I want to report a stranded whale,' Lex said, looking straight at John Watson as he spoke. 'Yes, it's still alive . . . No, I don't know the name of the beach, but I can take you there . . . My name's Lex Henderson . . . So you'll come down? I'll be at the Merrigan newsagency. How long? . . . okay, see you in half an hour.'

He passed the phone back. 'He has to make some calls first,' he explained.

'Which beach?' Watson asked.

Lex described it to him.

'Sounds like Long Beach. Were you by yourself?'

'No. With Callista Wallace. She's still there.'

'You'd better call her old man.' Watson handed the phone back and wrote a number on a piece of paper. 'You'll be needing him as well. And what about the girl? In this weather?'

'She'll be okay. She's a Wallace, isn't she?'

Watson laughed.

'Does this happen often 'round here?' Lex asked as he dialled the number.

'Not as long as I can remember. But Wallace is whales 'round here. He'll want to be involved.'

He disappeared out the back and came back with a second mug of coffee which he placed on the counter. 'Cold day,' he said. 'This might help.'

Half an hour later, the Parks ranger pulled up outside the newsagency. Lex and John Watson watched him climb out of the white Toyota and slip a mobile phone into his back pocket.

'That won't be much use to him down at Long Beach,' Watson said.

A new easiness had emerged between them with the cup of coffee.

The ranger looked up and down the street then walked into the shop. 'Hi there,' he said. 'I'm looking for a guy called Henderson.'

'That's me.' Lex set down his coffee.

'Jack Coffey.' The ranger reached forward to shake hands.

He was a tall man, lean, with wide boxy shoulders and a long, pointy nose. Broken vessels crisscrossed his thin-skinned brown cheeks. He had a face that had seen too much weather. Lex figured he was late forties. Probably midway through a lifelong career in Parks.

'We'd better get going,' Lex said. 'The whale's in pretty bad shape. It's going to be a hell of a job to get it back in the water.'

'Sorry.' Coffey jingled a bunch of keys in his pocket. 'We have to wait for my boss to arrive.'

Lex shrugged and John Watson refreshed their cups of coffee which they drank while Jack Coffey walked outside for a smoke. They watched Coffey hook out his phone and walk up the street. About five minutes later he came back looking flushed and stressed.

'So what do you reckon?' Lex asked. 'Can we go?'

'My wife says we should. She says bugger the boss. But I dunno . . .'

'It's your call,' Lex said.

Coffey went outside for another cigarette. It was then that Lex heard the distant thrumming of a helicopter.

'That didn't take long,' he said.

'What is it?' asked Coffey from the doorway.

'Could be part of your rescue team or it could be the media.'

'The media? How would *they* find out?'

'One of your crowd would have been instructed to notify the press. If we wait any longer we could have the *Sydney Morning Herald* following us out there.'

'Okay, we'll go,' Coffey said. He stubbed out his cigarette on the door frame and threw it towards the bin.

Jack Coffey gripped the steering wheel in silence as Lex directed him off the highway and across the farmlands. He bounced the vehicle too fast over the potholes and they almost struck a cow meandering across the track.

'Watch out!' Lex cursed. 'Look where you're going, man.'

'We should have waited,' Coffey said. 'They'll slaughter me for not following protocol.'

'There's a protocol?'

Coffey nodded, his brow a thicket of wrinkles. 'It's a step-by-step thing. Who to contact, what to do. My head will roll for this.'

'The end of a beautiful Parks career, eh?'

'We should go back.'

'Forget it. We're here. Pull up over there,' said Lex, as they crested the ridge below the cemetery.

Coffey surveyed the long stretch of beach way below. The wipers flicked spots of drizzle off the windscreen and far down the beach they could just see the dark shape of the whale. Lex climbed out and pulled on his wet coat. The wind hadn't relented. He watched Coffey ferreting a plastic raincoat out of the back of the Toyota. Then they walked to the edge of the dunes.

'Is there any other access?' Coffey asked.

'I think this is it.'

They stood in the wind and spattering rain and looked down the beach.

'How will we get equipment in? Machinery?' Coffey said.

'Carry the equipment from here, I suppose. They'll need to bulldoze a track for machinery.'

'That'll take hours.'

'Are these things ever easy?'

'I'll be honest, mate,' Coffey said, 'I know bugger all about strandings. This is the first one I've been to. I'm just the lucky sucker on duty this weekend. So I get to be first at the scene. Fact is, I have no authority to make decisions about anything. I just fill in till the head honchos arrive.'

Lex nodded. 'Who are they?'

'Fellow called Peter Taylor. Nice guy, actually. Seems quiet and reserved but he's tough under pressure. Won't stand for bullshit.'

'There's going to be plenty of that here,' Lex said.

'Plenty of what?'

'Bullshit.'

'You know a bit about strandings?' Coffey asked.

'Not much. But I *do* know that it's going to be one hell of an ugly affair once the media and the public arrive. Which they will.'

'What do you think'll happen?'

'I'm just hoping the poor damned whale dies before they all get here. I suppose you'd better call your boss then.'

Coffey reached inside his coat and pulled out a packet of cigarettes. He squinted down the beach. 'Think I'll have a smoke first. What's another five minutes if I'm going to lose my job and the whale's going to die anyway?'

Sitting stiff with cold by the groaning bulk of the whale, Callista saw vehicles lining up on the hill near the cemetery. She watched tiny figures scurrying like ants down the hill onto the beach. The wind had dropped and everything was peaceful. Over time, the cold had seeped deep into her bones. Each shuddering breath and wretched moan from the whale had hollowed her out so there was no longer any feeling in her body. It was surreal. She felt so dislocated she could be hanging on the wind like those evil seagulls that kept drifting by, trying to find an opening on the whale's succulent flesh. The dark figures dashing down the beach seemed completely irrelevant. She stood up and walked slowly in the opposite direction.

A camera crew was first to reach the whale. Callista heard their hoarse shouting voices.

'Get the tripod rigged up, will ya? Gotta get some close-ups quick as we can.'

She sprinted back along the beach to stop them. They were right inside the whale's space, angling for the best view. Worse than the seagulls. She stepped in front of the camera and tried to push it over.

'What do you think you're doing?' yelled the presenter.

The cameraman cursed. 'Get that chick out of the way.'

They shoved Callista aside onto the sand.

'Sorry, love. We're just doing our job.'

'You're too close,' she said.

The presenter shielded her out of the way while the cameraman spun around the whale shooting footage.

'Just get everything you can before they get here and we'll do the voice-over later,' the presenter called. He strong-armed Callista up the beach. 'Just keep out of the way, girlie.' He twisted his grip on her arm and smiled menacingly. 'And remember, love. It isn't *your* whale. It belongs to the public.'

A strong voice broke into their exchange. 'Let her go.'

Jimmy Wallace's blue eyes were steely and the presenter released Callista immediately. Jimmy was accompanied by another grey-bearded man and Callista sensed an instant shift in the control of the situation. Authority had been assumed.

'Sorry, fellas,' Jimmy's companion said. He was thickset with short grey hair and his beard was clipped short. 'I'm Peter Taylor. National Parks. You'll be allowed access, but not that close.'

The cameraman reluctantly lowered his camera and stepped back.

'You've got a zoom lens,' Taylor said. 'Come on. Move back. The whale's raising its tail. Sign of stress.'

Callista stood aside. Glancing up the beach, she could see the rest of the Parks contingent trudging slowly towards them laden with boxes and backpacks. She wondered whether Lex was among them. But her father and Peter Taylor were approaching the whale to assess its condition, so she stopped looking for Lex and watched them as they moved slowly around the stranded animal. Taylor's voice carried on the wind.

'What's the sea floor like 'round here? Steep or shallow?'

'She's a pretty rough beach,' Jimmy replied. 'Changing all the time. Lots of rips and gutters, a few sandbars.'

'Confusion? Misnavigation?'

'It's a possibility.'

'Aren't they heading north right now? Shouldn't they be moving further out to sea?'

Jimmy nodded. 'Yep. Not sure why this one came in so close.'

'What the hell is it doing here? Have there been any electrical storms to knock it off course?'

'Not recently. But you never know what's happening out to sea.'

The men moved in and squatted to check the blowhole. The tide was going out and they were able to get close without getting wet. Jimmy seemed to be counting time intervals between breaths. After a while the two men moved to the far side of the whale and Callista couldn't hear them any more until they were walking back towards her.

'I'll call the vet,' Taylor was saying. 'Then we'll talk access. We'll need heavy machinery, a digger of some sort. And we need to get a track bulldozed in here. What's available locally?'

'We'll have to get onto Trevor Baker,' Jimmy replied. 'He drives an excavator part-time for the local council. And he might know how to find a bulldozer.'

Taylor nodded at Callista as he hurried past to see if he could get mobile phone reception from the nearby dunes. When he was gone, she turned to her father. In his wet-weather trousers, bare feet and knee-length oilskin he was the only one who seemed to belong here. His eyes narrowed with concern as he looked at her, but she thought she saw a quick smile flicker across his face.

'How's the whale going?' she asked.

'Hard to tell. There's not a lot to go on. Did you happen to count respirations while you were waiting?'

'No. I didn't think of it.'

'Doesn't matter. Any impressions?'

'I think the breaths are slower now. Less frequent than when I first arrived.'

'Anything else?'

'It was groaning a lot at first.'

'Less now?'

'I think so.'

Jimmy shook his head. 'Not a good sign.'

'Do you think there's a chance?'

'I don't know.'

Callista searched her father's eyes. 'What's going to happen, Dad?'

'There's a protocol,' Jimmy said. The wind was rippling in his soft grey beard. 'Taylor will follow that. It's only one whale, but it'll still cause a sensation. There'll be other people arriving soon. Maybe crowds. Tricky stuff. Lots of emotions.'

'How do you know?'

'I do more than run whale tours, kid. They put me on the Whale Response team 'round here. Been to a few lectures. They reckon I know a bit about whales.' He glanced along the beach. 'Here comes that feller of yours. They saw those shoulders of his and gave him a canvas tent to carry.' He winked. 'Mother of a job.'

Callista recognised Lex's walk as he laboured down the beach. Even beneath the weight of the tent there was still that familiar spring in each slow stride, as if he could walk into the infinite without stopping. His shoulders were hidden under the sagging tent bag and his head was bowed forward a little into the wind. He dumped the tent on the sand and came up to join them.

'How's it going?' he asked, avoiding Callista's eyes. He seemed distant, uncertain.

'Not sure, mate,' Jimmy said. 'We're waiting for Taylor over there to see if he can get on to the vet. Then we need to discuss logistics.'

Callista wondered if Lex would ever summon the courage to look at her. And then he did and she felt her stomach tighten with distress. It seemed like hours since they'd argued and there was so much space between them now. She wasn't sure whether the distance could be crossed.

'Are you okay?' he asked.

'Fine, thanks.' She could feel her father's eyes on her, questioning. She scanned the grey-bellied skies. 'Do I hear a helicopter?'

'Probably,' Lex said. He was searching the sky to the north.

'They'll be offloading more gear to bring down. I'll have to pitch the tent and then give them a hand.'

He headed back up the beach.

'What happened?' Jimmy asked.

'He wanted us to just walk away and do nothing. Leave the whale on the beach to die.'

'A fair idea to consider.'

'That's for experts to decide. Lex knows nothing about whales.'

'Perhaps not.' Jimmy slung his backpack onto the sand and pulled out a thermos. 'Here,' he said, pouring her a strong black coffee. 'You could probably use this.'

She accepted the mug and took a sip, grimaced at the bitterness of the brew.

'Where's Jordi?' she asked. 'I thought he'd be here.'

'He's bringing the boat in and tying her up at the wharf. We might need her later.' Jimmy scratched his beard and examined the sky. 'If the weather doesn't deteriorate too much and the whale holds its condition, there's a chance we might get it back out in the water by the end of the day. We'll need the boat then to herd it further out so it doesn't get washed back in.'

'The end of the day?' Callista felt a worm of doubt turning in her belly.

'That's about as fast as things go at events like this.'

She looked into her father's calm blue eyes. His gaze steadied her, as it always had, the peaceful acceptance about him, his ability to slow things.

'Give me a job then,' she said. 'Or I'll go mad watching.'

Jimmy smiled. 'You can be my scribe.' He handed her a pad and a pencil. 'We have to document everything that happens and all the decisions we make, including the time, so cranky members of the public can't hassle us about our actions later on.'

'There's nobody here who's going to cause trouble, other than the journalists.'

'No, but they'll come.'

'That's what Lex said.'

Jimmy flashed an ironic, red-lipped smile. 'Maybe he knows something after all.'

Taylor wanted to keep activities at a distance from the whale, so Lex and Jack Coffey unfolded the tent about a hundred metres further up the beach. While they were laying it out, the weather whipped up and the canvas lifted and billowed in the wind. Even at this distance, the whale was agitated, belting its pectoral flipper over and over against its side. Lex winced as he watched the whale struggle to raise its flukes, but the receding tide had bogged its tail in the sand.

Pitching the tent was a challenge. Pegs were useless in the sand, so they improvised and filled plastic bags with wet sand to anchor the corners and the guy ropes. It wasn't a large tent—maybe three metres by four—but it provided shelter from the squally weather that kept drifting in from the sea. Once it was erected, two rangers moved in and set up radio equipment so communications could be established between the beach and the hilltop.

After the tent was secure, Coffey lit a cigarette.

'You haven't lost your job yet,' Lex said.

'Not yet. But Taylor's face was thunder when he saw me on the hill. They won't sack me till next week. They need all hands on deck today.'

'There's a chance you'll redeem yourself.'

'I'll need to do something spectacular.'

'We're in the same boat then.'

'How come you're in trouble?'

Lex nodded towards Callista who was standing with Jimmy by the whale. 'I suggested we just leave the whale on the beach. Leave it to nature.'

'Not a bad idea.'

'It wasn't appreciated.'

Coffey shrugged. 'That's women. It's the nurture thing.'

Lex glanced along the beach towards the hilltop where he could see the chopper setting down again. 'We'd better go for another load, I suppose.'

Coffey chucked his cigarette in the sand and ground it with his foot. 'Penance,' he said. 'Let's go.'

They trudged up the beach in easy silence. As they settled into a rhythm, Lex looked up and noticed a group of young people hiking along the sand towards them. They were scruffy and dreadlocked. The great unwashed. Always among the first to arrive at a scene. Lex had been concerned that casual volunteers might come poorly equipped for the weather conditions, but this group looked well rugged up in plastic wet-weather gear and warm beanies. The front-runner was a young guy with masses of dreads draped across his chest in the wind.

'Hey,' he called out to Lex and Coffey. 'How's the whale going?'

'We're waiting for the vet to arrive,' Coffey said, stopping to shake hands with the guy. 'That might have been him in the chopper that just landed.'

'We're here to give a hand,' the guy said. 'I'm Jarrah.' He waved a hand at the group coming up behind him. 'We've just come up from Eden. Heard on the radio there was a whale stranded up here.'

'News is out already then. We need all the help we can get.' Coffey pointed down the beach to where Taylor and Wallace were standing near the tent. 'Speak to one of those grey-bearded fellows down there. They'll give you a job.'

'Thanks.' Jarrah gave a friendly wave and continued on.

The rest of the group was approaching. There was a girl among them who was staring hard at Lex.

'Don't I know you?' she said, stopping and pulling off her beanie to scratch her head. Her dreads flicked out in the wind.

Lex recognised Jen and quickly lowered his head to continue walking up the beach.

'Yes, I do know you,' she yelled. 'You're the guy who gave me a lift to Eden. Hey, guys,' she called to the rest of the group, laughing. 'This is the guy I told you about who picked me up on the highway outside of Merrigan. Fed me up a treat, but couldn't take it any further. Turned me down.'

Lex stopped, mortified. His day just kept falling apart. And Jack Coffey was looking at him curiously. He summoned a casual smile.

'That's what happens when you get close to forty,' he called to the girl. 'It's quality you're looking for, not quantity.'

Jen laughed. 'Pay that one,' she said. 'What a surprise. I didn't expect to see you again this lifetime. Now we'll be working together.'

'Great.'

Lex glanced at Coffey and they recommenced trudging up the beach. They could hear Jen still laughing as she scuffled away with her mates.

'Not much chance of redeeming yourself today then, mate,' Coffey observed.

Lex shook his head. 'You do the right thing and you still get in trouble,' he said.

'That's life, mate. That's life.' Coffey slapped him on the shoulder.

As they approached the hill, the humming of the chopper escalated to a shriek and it took off, blades thwacking the air. They watched it lift quickly into the grey sky and buzz over them, heading down to make a high pass over the whale before banking steeply and heading north further out to sea. Climbing the dunes, Lex and Coffey met three men skating down the sandy track carrying toolboxes and backpacks. They were grim-faced and obviously in a hurry, not stopping to speak, but they nodded as Lex and Coffey stood aside, puffing, to let them pass.

'Reckon that was the vet,' Coffey commented between gasps. He was leaner than Lex and faster up the hill.

'What's the time? Things seem slow as hell around here.'

'It's after eleven,' Coffey said.

'At least they can get a proper assessment done now.'

'What will they do if the whale's not going to make it?'

'They'll have a go anyway. The public won't stand for euthanasia.'

'Why not?' Coffey asked. 'What's so bad about a humane death?'

'It's a whale,' Lex reminded him. 'On the animal scale they rate right up there. It'll be all stops out for a rescue attempt.'

'You're not impressed, are you?'

'I don't want to see it die. But I don't want to see the poor thing dragged through some epic rescue that was doomed from the start.'

They trudged slowly to the top of the hill where more gear was waiting to be transferred to the beach. Lex surveyed the gear and divided it mentally into loads. This would keep them busy for a while, even with the assistance of the other rangers. His stomach growled.

'How are you going? I'm hungry.'

'Starving, mate, starving.' Coffey lit a cigarette.

Lex propped his hands on his hips and waited for his breathing to ease. 'Can I use your phone?' he asked. 'I'm going to see if I can rustle up some tucker.' He dialled diministery assistance, then punched in the number they gave him. 'Sue,' he yelled into the phone.

'Is that you, Mr Henderson? Where are you? You sound like you're in a cyclone. Are you in on this whale rescue too?'

'It's wild out here. I thought John Watson would have filled you in by now.'

'He's right here with me. We're in the shop. Discussing you lot over a coffee and a chocolate brownie.'

'That's cruel, Sue. We're dying of hunger out here. There's no food and it's going to be a *long* day.'

'What do you want me to do about it?'

'I was wondering if there was any way you could organise some food. There's going to be a crowd down here. I'm sure National Parks or somebody will help cover the costs.'

'Leave it with me. I'll see what I can do. I might pop up to the church and see if Mrs Jensen can organise a team.'

'The church, Sue! I thought you'd forgotten where it is.'

'Yes. It's amazing what one can do in times of emergency. How's the whale going, anyway?'

'Not great.'

'Should I invite the minister along to pray for you?'

'Why not? We could use a miracle.'

TWENTY-SEVEN

Callista took on the job of keeping the whale covered with wet towels. Taylor and a group of about six men had tried to roll it onto its chest so it could breathe more easily, but the sand held tight and all they achieved was a few stressed air-blasts from its blowhole. Then the whale let out a wrenching moan that brought everyone to a sickened full stop. At that point, Taylor decided they should only carry out basic supportive therapy until the vet arrived.

The reporters were happy smoking and chatting, and Taylor didn't want too many people working close to the whale, so Callista offered to lay out the towels on her own. Near the tent, she rolled up her trousers and took off her boots, grabbed an armful of towels from a pile that had been dumped on a tarp, and strode into the shallows. The water was grippingly cold. It was difficult to wring the wet towels out with stiff cold hands, so she gave up and hauled them heavy with water towards the whale.

She approached cautiously, moving around to where she could see the whale's eye so it knew she was coming. Even so, it raised its flipper half-mast and tried to wriggle in the sand. Beside the great animal, her heart beating fast, she placed the pile of wet towels on the sand and carefully shook the first one out to lie over its back. This was the closest she had been to the whale and she was surprised by the surge of emotion that swamped her. The poor animal was making small scraping movements with its flipper back and forth across its side. Gently, tentatively, she placed a hand on its back, half-expecting it to shudder at her touch, but it lay still and its flipper stopped moving. The skin was smooth and surprisingly firm, rubbery almost. For a while she stood there with her hand against its skin, breathing empathy through her palm. Then she draped the first towel carefully, avoiding the blowhole.

Moving slowly, she covered the whale's back and then moved around to the belly side to complete the job. The grooves running along its throat and belly arrested her, great deep furrows in parallel rows. She had seen photographs of these pleats billowing out to create a huge throat sac when a whale took in large volumes of water while feeding. That was how they caught their food, trapped inside the mouth while the tongue pushed water out through the baleen like a great sieve. She dipped her fingers into one of the grooves and slid them along the long contour of the whale's belly. Then she let her fingers run down across several grooves, tripping from one furrow into the next, unable to believe that she was touching a whale's skin, touching an animal that belonged untouchable in the sea.

Tears came again. Not the first time today, and she suspected not the last. As she leaned forward to press her forehead against the whale's side, it exhaled with a blast and she jolted upright, aware of the upwards jerk of the pectoral flipper just missing her head. The whale's breath was putrid. Like rotting fish. The stench of it sent her staggering out of the water to vomit inelegantly on the sand. She felt wretched. Pathetic. And she hoped Lex hadn't seen it.

When she raised her head, she saw a newly arrived group of people watching her. Great! She hadn't been expecting an audience. Mustering a feeble thread of dignity, she waved at them and walked unsteadily over to where Jimmy was waiting with a cup of water. The new people were volunteers, he explained as she drank. And this might be a good time for her to take a break. She had already put in significant hours on the beach this morning, and these people were fresh and eager. Callista appreciated his tactful offer for her surrender, and was happy to grasp it and step aside.

In the tent, she dried off and pulled on her boots. She was surprised at how quickly the cold had seeped in and stiffened her. She must be a bit overwhelmed by everything—the argument with Lex, the long wait in the cold, the close contact with the whale. It had already been a long day.

Jimmy poured her a coffee and they stood together watching the new volunteers taking turns to wet the whale down.

'What's happening with the machinery?' Callista asked.

'Trevor's onto it, but apparently it's going to take some time.'

'Everything takes too much time.'

'Yep, slow as a wet week. First they have to load the 'dozer and the excavator onto trucks and then drive out here. Trevor reckons the dunes are too steep and unstable, so Ben Hackett's finding out who owns the property backing onto the lagoon so he can get permission to come through that way. He's going to help Trevor drive down here and then he'll bring the excavator through behind the bulldozer.'

'I didn't know Ben drove heavy machinery.'

'He doesn't, but he's used to farm machinery and apparently that should help. Trevor's giving him a crash course. It'll save time. Trevor can't be in two places at once, and they can't raise the other plant operator. He must be away for the weekend.'

A slim dreadlocked girl strode up to the tent to collect more towels. She met Callista's eyes and smiled. It was a direct smile, overly confident, almost brash.

'Are you okay?' she asked. 'I saw you chucking on the beach. Can you believe how bad their breath is?' She grabbed an armful of towels and ran back down to the water's edge.

Callista had to admit that the girl and her friends were doing a good job, moving slowly and quietly around the whale, and working efficiently as a team. The girl was standing back with a spare towel, waiting to briskly dry off a lanky dreadlocked man after each foray into the sea to remoisten the towels. Another pair from the team was watching from a distance, ready to take over, and the others had moved further up the beach where they had set up a small gas stove and a billy to boil.

As Callista watched, the girl hooked off her beanie, threaded her fingers through the mass of dreads and deftly twisted them into a plait which she stuffed down the back of her jacket. She looked young, probably in her late teens or early twenties, and she had a relaxed easiness about her and an aura of confidence. Callista wondered where they had come from.

'Looks like the vet's here,' Jimmy said. 'I'll have to go.'

Callista watched him join Taylor and three men who had just arrived at the tent, but she couldn't hear their conversation because the canvas was flapping and cracking in the wind. The men soon moved towards the whale, carrying toolboxes. One of them, a short, dark, curly-haired man, waved the volunteers away from the whale and Callista noticed that they stepped back slowly and reluctantly. Perhaps they didn't like taking orders from people.

'That's the vet,' Jimmy said. He had come to stand with her again and was observing the men closely, his hands deep in the pockets of his oilskin.

The vet looked too young to have much experience. 'Do you think he knows what he's doing?' Callista asked.

'Apparently he used to work in Tasmania,' Jimmy said. 'They get lots of strandings down there. Multiple strandings that make this one look like a picnic. Taylor says he's good at making decisions, picking winners and losers. That's what they have to do when there are multiples. Decide which whales are most likely to make it and focus on those. They have them dying all over the beach down there.'

'Who are the other men?' Callista asked.

'Whale biologists. From one of the universities.'

'What do they know about strandings?'

'More than me,' Jimmy admitted. 'I've read a lot on paper, but these fellers have had first-hand experience.'

They watched as the vet stepped up to the whale and pulled the towels off. He ran his hand firmly along the whale's back, slipping up and over the pectoral flipper, but the whale didn't move. The vet was obviously concerned about this. He shook his head then squatted near the blowhole and spent some time examining it and timing the interval between breaths. Next he moved further around to examine the whale's eye and mouth. Callista saw him tapping at the corner of its eye and tugging at its mouth. Then he stood up and yelled and clapped his hands. The whale shifted its pectoral flipper slightly, but the vet obviously wanted more. He took hold of the pectoral flipper and wriggled it a bit, lifted it high, let it go and watched it fall back down with a slap onto the whale's side.

'What's he doing?' Callista asked. 'Does he have to hassle it like that?'

Jimmy didn't answer.

They watched as the vet walked into the shallows at the rear end of the whale and pushed at its tail flukes with his gumboot. There was no response. Then he clapped his hands and yelled as he pushed at the flukes again. The whale sucked a quick breath of air and tensed as it tried to lift its tail.

'Can't he see it's buried in sand?' Callista said.

Jimmy said nothing.

The vet gave a small nod, as if finishing a discussion with himself, and joined the biologists just beyond the whale's head. They talked amongst themselves animatedly for several minutes. The vet spoke least and stood looking down at the sand, interjecting occasionally.

Callista saw the slim girl go up to them. She must have asked if they could resume their support work, because the vet nodded and four of the team started replacing the towels across the whale's back. Then the vet came up to the tent looking for Peter Taylor who was up at the dunes making phone calls. Jimmy went to fetch him, leaving the vet with Callista.

He seemed quite shy standing away from her while he waited, hands thrust in his trouser pockets. He shifted from foot to foot, avoiding eye contact, and his agitation made Callista nervous. She wasn't sure yet whether she could trust his judgment. He seemed so uncertain, so unconfident.

'You've got a hard job,' she said. 'I don't envy you.'

'These things are never much fun. I'd rather be kicking a football with my son back in Sydney.' He glanced at her quickly then his eyes skated away.

'How's the whale going? I was one of the people who found it this morning, and I keep hoping it'll be okay.'

'You're just the person I need to talk to.' The vet pulled a notebook and a pencil out of his hip pocket and peeked up at her briefly, then back down at his notebook. 'Have you been taking any notes? Writing anything down?'

'Only for the past hour or so. Respirations, movements, things like that. Before that I didn't have anything to write on, and to be honest, I didn't think of it.'

The vet nodded. 'Anything you can tell me could be useful. Just chat and I'll make notes while you're talking.'

Callista told him about how they'd found the whale, how it was responding then, where the tide had been, what the weather had been like. She referred to the notes she had taken for Jimmy, mentioned the frequency of breaths and moans, how things had changed since early morning. She wanted to talk about her discussion with Lex, and ask the vet what he thought of Lex's so-called options, but she wasn't game and she stuck to the facts.

'Thanks,' the vet said. 'All of that really helps. I can compare your observations with mine and that gives me a gauge of the whale's deterioration.'

'Deterioration?'

The vet gave a small smile. 'They all deteriorate out of water,' he said. 'There's only one way to go and that's downhill. We monitor how quickly they're sliding and that gives us a measure of the chances of survival. By the way, I'm Tim Lawton.' He extended his hand, leaning forward to reach her, reluctant to come closer.

'What could you tell from your assessment?' Callista still felt uncertain of him.

'Things aren't looking too bad,' he said. 'He's hanging in there. Muscle tone's not great and breaths are a bit few and far between, but we'll give him a bit of stimulus soon and try to stir things up a bit. We don't want to hassle him too much, but if we just leave him lying there, he might forget to breathe. We'll keep up with the support treatment too. You guys made a great start getting those wet towels on him, but there are a few other things we can do too, before the machinery gets here. We can hand-dig some trenches to free up his chest and tail a bit. Then he'll feel a bit more comfortable and it might help with his breathing.'

'Do you think he'll make it?'

The vet looked at her seriously. It was the first time he had met her eyes directly. 'It's too soon to tell,' he said. 'There's a long day ahead of us yet. We'll just have to wait and see. Here comes Taylor now.'

Tim quickly filled Taylor in on the whale's status and then asked permission to take some samples. He wanted to try to collect some blood, and also to get a swab from the blowhole. He asked if somebody could take the samples back to the nearest hospital for him. The tests were fairly basic, he explained, but would give him a few hints on how the whale was faring.

Callista watched him pick up his toolbox and walk down to the whale with the two biologists. She was still unsure. She had expected optimism and positivity from him. She hadn't expected him to be so frank. Of course the whale had deteriorated over the past few hours. She knew it. But she hadn't wanted the vet to say it so directly. Then again, perhaps there was little room for coddling people in a situation like this. Everyone had to be prepared for the worst.

Tim stopped several metres away from the whale and pulled some large needles and syringes from his toolbox. He poked along the whale's back down towards the tail, then unsheathed one of the needles. Bending down, he poked around the tail a bit more and then pushed the needle in. Callista looked away, feeling faint. It must be the cold—so many hours sitting waiting on the beach—and the needle looked so large. When she glanced back, one of the syringes was already full of blood. Tim passed it to one of the biologists then he attached another syringe and filled it also. The biologist was busy filling blood tubes. There seemed to be dozens of them.

Feeling weak, Callista sat down and wrapped her arms around her legs. The girl with dreadlocks came over and crouched on the sand beside her.

'What do you think about all this?' she asked.

'I don't know.'

Callista looked at her more closely. The girl's hair was wrapped around her neck like a shawl and it smelled of smoke. She was concentrating hard on the vet's actions, her young face firm and her eyes clear.

'I don't like the way he touches it,' the girl said. 'Do you?'

'Not really,' Callista admitted.

'It's a matter of respect. He's rough.'

'He's doing a medical examination.'

'I don't care what he's doing. He lacks compassion.'

'He's trying to make an objective assessment. That's his job. He's been looking for reflexes, responses, those sorts of thing, so he can tell how far gone the whale is.'

The girl shook her head. 'If he doesn't have compassion for animals, I don't see how he can help.'

'Don't you think we should give him a chance?' Callista said. 'He's seen more whales than we'll ever see. And perhaps it doesn't work to be gentle with an animal that big. The vet said if they leave it alone it might stop breathing.'

'Do you believe that?'

'Yes, I do. It's breathing less frequently than it was this morning.'

The girl looked at Callista with bright level eyes.

'You're straight up and honest, like me,' she said. 'My boyfriend

Jarrah describes it as tactless. But I think there's too much tact around these days.'

Callista tried not to smile. She didn't think she'd ever been as forward and confident as this young girl. But the girl was very serious. She wiped the sand from her hand and offered it to Callista.

'I'm Jen.'

'Callista.'

They clasped hands.

'With a name like that it's no wonder I like you.' Jen looked knowingly at Callista. 'I can pick it. I can see things in people. It's a skill I have.'

She looked around and waved her hand towards Lex who was standing with Jordi watching the vet. 'Like that guy over there,' she said. 'He picked me up on the highway a few weeks ago.'

Callista tried not to tense.

'He's the polite type,' Jen said. 'He hides behind silence. You'd think an older guy like him would jump at the chance to be with a young chick like me. But he was overwhelmed. Didn't know what to do.'

Callista looked at Lex, tingling. 'Not everyone is what they seem,' she said. 'The vet does care. He wants the whale to live.'

They looked back to the whale and watched Tim as he dabbed around the blowhole with a wad of gauze and then dipped inside it with a cotton bud on a long stick, swirling it around. The whale exhaled with a blast. There might be a medical reason for needles and swabs, but Callista felt a surge of nausea. She couldn't watch anymore.

'I'm sorry, I have to go,' she said.

She heaved herself quickly to her feet and walked up the beach.

TWENTY-EIGHT

Looking back later, Callista had difficulty pinpointing exactly when things changed on the beach. But there was a distinct turning point when everything shifted from being casual and interactive to being more organised and controlled. That was the moment at which something was lost. But it was inevitable, and it was because of the number of people massing on the beach.

Word had spread via live-to-air reports on radio and TV, and over several hours the beach had transformed. More tents were pitched further back up the sand, folding tables were set up, generators were fuelled and kicked into life, and more and more bodies scurried back and forth from the hill lugging equipment. The chopper came and went, disgorging gear, and cars crowded the horizon in haphazard disarray.

Sue, John Watson and a contingent from the church arrived with bags stuffed with food—sandwiches, chocolate, fruit, sweets—and thermoses of hot drinks. They came with gas stoves and moved straight into two tents. One was set up to cook sausages that Helen Beck provided. Some of the church ladies, led by Mrs Jensen, organised themselves in the other tent to serve tea and coffee.

More media crews arrived. They closed ranks with the other reporters and hung out in tight circles, badgering Peter Taylor for interviews. Callista was surprised they left the vet alone, but Jimmy explained that Taylor was protecting him. Tim had a more important job to do than performing for the media sharks.

As the crowd swelled, things got worse. Soon there were more than two hundred people on the beach. Cordons had to be set up, and Taylor had to call in more staff to handle the crowd. Another tent was pitched even further back along the beach to greet new arrivals and organise them into groups. Volunteers were briefed and trained and a roster was established so they could assist the vet. But the number of people continued to burgeon and there was insufficient work to occupy them all. Yet it was difficult to turn them away. Even if they couldn't help, people wanted to watch. The mood was anxious. Many people had strong opinions, which they believed were important and deserved to be heard. And as they arrived with all their emotions in their pockets, most of them expected to be allowed to approach the whale, to touch it. Taylor and Jimmy had to explain over and over that it was stressful for the whale to have too many people around.

In the back of her mind, Callista could hear Lex telling her that the public would expect a rescue, that they wouldn't want the whale euthanased. And now, with all these people milling around and the media hovering with cameras and the tents that had popped up all over the beach, she wasn't so sure about balance and objectivity anymore. How would this crowd respond if the vet said the rescue had to be abandoned? Would they all just pack up meekly and wander off home?

From outside the control tent where she was waiting to see her father, Callista could see the vet down by the whale, overseeing support operations. The tide had receded from the whale's tail now, and its flukes lay flat and limp and half-buried in the wet sand. This morning, when she and Lex had first found the whale with the sea still washing around it, it had appeared helpless. But now it was completely marooned, like a washed-up sailing boat left high on the beach after a storm surge.

Around the whale, several people were scooping out trenches in the sticky sand. It was hard work and a good way to keep volunteers occupied, bent over, digging with their hands and piling sand up a couple of metres away from the whale to form the beginnings of a seawall. Other helpers were dousing the whale with sea water. Each time a volunteer approached with a bucket, the whale tensed and lifted its flipper to slash at the cascade of water.

Callista struggled with tears. There were too many people around being too busy. Surely the vet was aware of it. Why was he letting them go on with this?

Jimmy joined her at the back of the tent.

'Can't they just leave the poor thing alone?' she said.

'The vet would prefer it that way,' Jimmy said. 'But the volunteers want to help. And we'd have a riot on our hands if we kept them away. They haven't just come to stand around.'

The whale dashed its flipper again at a volunteer. As the flipper fell, the whale emitted a deep groan.

'Did you hear that?' the volunteer yelled, waving excitedly. 'It's talking to me.'

Callista clenched her hands. 'People have no idea, do they? Has the vet said anything about how it's going?'

Jimmy's clear blue eyes met hers and he smiled kindly but sadly. 'Chances aren't great, kiddo. You can hear it all for yourself soon. He's giving a public address in ten minutes. Down by the volunteer tent.'

'Should we have walked away?'

'It doesn't matter now.' Jimmy gave her a hug. 'I'd better head back. The machinery will be here soon. Probably in the middle of the vet's address. You know how it is.'

Callista joined a cluster of people congregating at the volunteer tent where Peter Taylor was standing on a milk crate holding a loudspeaker. She felt someone reaching for her hand and turned, startled, to find Jen beside her with tears in her eyes.

'I'm so frustrated.' The girl's face was wrought with tension. 'What happened to everything today? It was going fine until all these people arrived. Now none of us can do anything and I'm going mad just hanging around watching.'

Callista nodded, gripping the girl's hand in sympathy. 'My dad's on the rescue team. It's tricky for them—juggling everyone's need to be involved and all their emotions.'

Jen glared around at the crowd. 'I just wish they'd all go away.'

They were interrupted by a short blare of static and then Peter Taylor's voice over the loudspeaker.

'Can I have your attention, everyone, please. I'm Peter Taylor from National Parks. And I'm in charge of getting this whale back in the water.'

He looked so cool and calm standing up there. But Callista knew it must be a nightmare overseeing an event like this with everybody wanting to tell you how it should be done and everyone wanting a piece of the action.

'I have to say how impressed I am to see such a large and enthusiastic public response,' Taylor said. 'But I must ask for your cooperation while you're waiting to help, otherwise our rescue won't be successful. This is a large whale and operations are going to be difficult and risky. I know things are slow, but our biggest hold-up has been waiting for the machinery. Access to this place isn't easy and mobilising heavy equipment on a weekend isn't something that happens quickly. But you'll be pleased to hear that the bulldozer is nearly through to the beach and the excavator's just behind it. Once they arrive, we can start getting the whale in position for a return to the water when the tide comes in.'

'When the tide comes in?' someone yelled. 'But isn't that hours away?'

'Yes,' Taylor said. 'And we have hours of work to do. We have to try to shift the whale onto its chest so it can breathe easier and then we need to get the excavator to work building a seawall around the whale. The idea is to build up quite a large wall. And then, when the tide comes in, we can breach it and the sea water will flood around the whale and float it off the sand.'

Questioning hands went up everywhere in the crowd, and for the briefest of moments Taylor looked harassed by the barrage of people calling out. He held up a hand to stop them.

'Questions afterwards. The vet is going to speak to you first.'

He introduced Tim Lawton and outlined his experience. Then he passed the loudspeaker to the vet and directed him up onto the milk crate. Tim looked small and hesitant as he faced the crowd and Callista found herself hoping he'd be convincing. Everyone needed an injection of confidence at this time. Not more doubt.

Tim Lawton jiggled the loudspeaker then spoke into it tentatively, his voice quavering slightly. But the crowd waited patiently for him to clear his throat and the general mood seemed supportive.

'Folks,' he said, 'it's not a pleasant task I've been invited along to here today. And I'm sorry it's going to be a long day for you all. But unfortunately nothing happens fast at whale strandings. It's hard, because we all know that the faster we get this whale back in the water, the better his chances of swimming away. But first we have to stop and look at where this animal has come ashore. Amazing place, isn't it? Wild and remote. The locals tell me days can go by without anyone coming here. And so we have the access problem that Peter Taylor mentioned. That's our first obstacle.'

He switched the loudspeaker into his other hand.

'The second problem we have to consider is our patient—a stunningly beautiful animal. Enormous, isn't he? He's a humpback. Subadult. He's just nine metres, whereas a mature male should make it out to twelve or more.' He paused. 'Unfortunately, there's still a lot we don't know about strandings. We have a few theories, but most of them apply to social species, like sperm whales and pilot whales and false killers, for instance. But single stranders like this one we see less commonly. Around here, humpbacks head south with their young somewhere between September and November. That's when they're heading down to Antarctica where there's lots of food available over the summer. Come this time of year, the humpbacks head back up north again to breed. But we don't tend to see them as much when they're going north. They tend to swim quickly and further out to sea.

'The thing about humpbacks is that they rarely strand. They're good coastal navigators and they're used to moving in shallow waters close to shore. I've been to quite a few strandings, but I've never seen a live humpback strand before—although I have heard of one, more than a decade ago, up at Peregian Beach in Queensland. What you have to remember is that these events are few and far between. And so we have to be quite worried about this young humpback, and we have to ask ourselves why he's here when he shouldn't be.

'There are a few possible explanations. Apparently the beach here is pretty unstable with lots of rips and gutters. So he might have screwed up his navigation and got himself into trouble in shallow water. But as I said, that's less likely for a humpback than some other species. It's also possible he might have been separated from his pod for some reason and got lost. Or maybe he's sick. Unfortunately, there's not much a vet like me can use to assess a large whale like this. I look at responsiveness, muscle tone, the condition of the skin and blowhole, that kind of thing. And I can get a few hints from blood samples. But I can't tell much about what's going on internally, such as what sort of condition his lungs are in, or whether he has a significant parasite load or some other serious underlying disease. I don't even know how long he's been stranded or how he was when he first beached. And remember, just being out of water compromises a large animal like this. So that means I'm second-guessing. It's not a precise science in any way.'

As she listened, Callista tried to suppress the sinking feeling in her chest. If the vet didn't know what was going on, what chance was there?

'What I can tell you about our whale is this,' Tim continued. 'From what I see, he's still in reasonable condition, even though he's somewhat depressed. Apparently he was vocalising more frequently this morning, and we're not hearing much from him now. So that's not a good sign. But his skin is still in good condition, there's no bleeding from any orifices, he's still making attempts to move, and we're still getting reasonable respirations from him. So, for the time being, I'm feeling cautiously optimistic.

'We're lucky to have such a grey day out here. That means he hasn't overheated, and we've been working hard to make sure he stays nice and cool and that the sand doesn't abrade his skin. Our trench-diggers have been doing a good job, trying to free up some space around his chest so he can breathe easier, and we'll continue with that until release time. So now I want to thank you all for your hard work. And I hope that's all, because I need to get back to some monitoring.'

Tim handed the loudspeaker back to Taylor, and for a long moment the crowd stood quiet, watching him walk back down the beach towards the whale. His dark head was bowed and there was weariness in his stride. Callista had never seen anybody look so lonely.

TWENTY-NINE

Lex was tired from lugging gear for hours. He and Jack Coffey had slipped into an easy camaraderie, mixing humorous stories and joke-telling with long comfortable silences as they slogged up and down the beach with endless loads of gear. Pack-horsing, they called it. Over the past hour they had been ferrying night-lighting equipment. They had shifted the gear without question, but they knew then that the whale might not be released by nightfall, and with increasing length of time there was a decreasing chance of success. They agreed that few of the volunteers understood the magnitude of the event they were involved in.

When Coffey was off helping with other tasks, Lex had walked a few laps of the beach with Jordi. It felt strange striding along the sand with Callista's brother. Beside him, Lex felt like a bear hulked into his Gore-Tex. Jordi was all fly-away bones, his scrawny bare legs poking out from beneath his battered oilskin and his beard puffing over his shoulder in the wind. But he had been affable enough, and it was obvious he wasn't happy with events on the beach and the way the rescue was full steam ahead without discussing the option of euthanasia.

Jordi had chewed the fat as they walked, gauging Lex's opinions and then letting his own ideas slip. The whale shouldn't be here, Jordi said. And they shouldn't be interfering with it. Nature had already taken her course bringing the whale ashore. They should let it be, or finish it off quickly—although he understood there were complications with that. Killing whales wasn't a straightforward task. All these people shouldn't be here either. It annoyed him having to pussyfoot around them. The job belonged to National Parks and they should be allowed to get on with it.

He also commented on the split in the town over the whale. Plenty wanted to see it rescued, like bitch Beryl and Helen Beck. But there were some surprises in the negative camp, including Mrs Jensen. Jordi had thought she'd be a right-to-lifer, for sure. But he'd heard rumours that Beryl and Mrs Jensen were clashing head-on in the coffee tent. Sue and John Watson were a bit ambivalent, but he reckoned Sue wouldn't want to see the whale suffering, and once she got a break out of the sausage tent she'd be a dead-set convert to the negative camp. Watson, he said, was a bit of a cold fish and wouldn't really be fussed which way it went. It'd be better for everyone, Jordi admitted, when the bulldozer got here and a bit of action could get under way. Everyone was going stir-crazy with standing around.

It was the most Lex had ever heard Jordi say. He asked what Jimmy thought about it all, but Jordi clammed up then. All he'd say was that it was Jimmy's job to appear neutral. Even if he wasn't.

Lex had just dumped another load beyond the cordon when he saw Darren Beck slipping around the back of the control tent. The kid must have dodged the Parks staff and was probably trying to get a better view of the whale.

'Oi, Darren,' he called. 'Over here.'

The boy looked back guiltily and slunk up like a naughty dog. Lex was surprised to see him on his own. Helen was usually so over-protective. In fact, it was surprising that she would have come here at all, especially on a Sunday. Lex hadn't seen her among the crowd, so perhaps the kid had come along with Mrs Jensen. He put a hand on Darren's head and wiggled his beanie.

'How are you going?' he asked.

'All right.' The kid was hedging, a bit guarded.

'Lost your mum?'

'Yeah, ages ago. She got yapping to some weirdos with dread-locks. She told me to go and hang out with Mrs Jensen. But that's not much fun . . . You won't make me go back there, will you?'

Lex shook his head. 'No. I wouldn't want to hang out with Mrs Jensen either.'

He hid his concern. It sounded like Helen had somehow become tangled up with Jen and her mob—the ratbag element. Taylor and Wallace had been muttering expletives about them since things had hotted up on the beach, and Lex had seen them earlier sitting around in a tight knot, brooding. They might cause trouble before the event was over. He looked down at Darren standing beside him with his hands shoved in his pockets. The poor kid was all gawky angles, not quite sure of how to be and where he might fit in the grand picture of life.

'Let's get something to eat,' Lex suggested. 'We can dodge Mrs Jensen's tent.'

In the food tent, Sue was busy turning sausages. She was flushed despite the cold weather.

'Mr Henderson,' she said, waving her tongs at him. 'It's your fault we're all caught up in this. I could be at home in front of the fire doing some knitting.'

Lex smiled. 'Now come on, Sue. If I hadn't rung you, you'd have been down here by now anyway.'

'What'll you have, boy?' she said to Darren. 'A sausage or a sausage. They're your mother's snags after all. Not that she'd know anything about it. She's joined the renegades from what I hear.'

'What are renegades?' Darren asked.

'They're representatives of the devil,' Sue said.

'Sue.' Lex tried to check her. 'Tone it down.'

Sue handed them each a sausage wrapped in bread and splattered some tomato sauce out of a squeeze-bottle.

'John,' she called. 'Come over here and tell Lex what we think about all this.'

John Watson appeared at the entrance to the tent carrying two loaves of bread in each hand. 'He already knows,' he growled. 'I don't reckon he wanted this scale of rescue either. It's all about feeding the hordes and keeping them warm to save them from themselves, rather than saving the damned whale. They ought to leave the poor bugger alone to die.'

'I don't want it to die,' Darren said, his face creased with stress. 'My dad would have wanted it to live too. Everything has a right to live.'

'Oh dear,' Sue said quietly. 'The legacy continues.'

'They won't kill it, will they?' Darren looked up at Lex, alarmed.

'No, they won't. Don't worry.'

'What about Callista?' Sue asked. She raised her eyebrows at Lex. 'What does she think?'

'She's not talking to me at the moment. But this morning she seemed pretty keen on getting a rescue under way.'

'A sticking point, eh?'

'You could say that.'

'Are you two ever going to work it out?'

Lex shrugged and Sue shook her head.

'You wear me out,' she said.

Lex ate his sausage in the shelter of the tent, Darren beside him. They watched people file in for food, some of them looking very cold. Perhaps Parks should turn away the under-equipped. It might not be raining anymore, but the bite of the wind was chilly and without proper windproof gear some of the crowd would be getting pretty close to the edge. It wouldn't help morale. Lex was hoping there'd be some significant action soon. Everyone was sick of waiting for something to happen.

A shout up the beach drew them out of the tent.

'The bulldozer's coming,' Darren said. 'I'm going to get Mum so she can watch.'

The boy disappeared and Lex moved to the edge of the crowd where he could see the bulldozer lurch out of the scrub down by the lagoon and turn to begin grinding along in the sand near the base of the dunes. The excavator slowly bobbed and swayed behind it.

It took ten minutes for the machines to reach the tents, and there was a general buzz of excitement and a rush as people scuttled forward for a better look. Among the gathering of bodies, Lex saw Sash and Evan weaselling their way between the legs of adults. They materialised out of the crowd just near him and flung themselves at him with enthusiasm. They were barely recognisable in their over-size raincoats and red woollen beanies. Lex lifted Sash for a hug. Then Sally found them.

'I knew they'd be where they could get a good view of the machinery,' she said. 'Forget the whale.'

'You have to get your priorities right,' Lex said.

'I'm glad they're trying to rescue it,' Sally said. 'Poor thing. It'll be nice to see it swim away. How long has this been going on?'

'Do you really want to know? Hours.'

'Really?' Her face fell. 'That's a shame. It's not looking too good then, is it?'

It was a relief to hear someone make a rapid practical assessment on the basis of good sense.

Sally looked at her children with concern. 'I'll have to be careful about when to take this lot home then,' she said. 'You don't want to protect them from everything. But there are some things you'd rather they didn't see.'

'I want to watch the machines, Mummy,' Sash said.

Sally smiled. 'You can watch the machines, honey. And then, when we get a bit cold, we'll head back home.'

'Thank you,' Lex said.

'What for?'

'For being sensible.'

Sally laughed. 'I'm sometimes capable of it on a good day.'

Callista watched as Peter Taylor and several other staff wrapped blankets around the bucket of the excavator, tying them on with ropes.

Then a small posse of volunteers dragged inflated mattresses down the beach and pushed them in against the whale's belly. A large flat sling was placed across the mattresses. The plan was to roll the whale onto the mattresses and then pull the end of the sling beneath the tail. On its chest, the whale should be able to breathe easier. And once the sling was in place it could be used later to help pull the whale out to sea after refloating. A harness would also be strapped around the pectoral flippers to help with this.

Peter Taylor had tried to make the plan sound straightforward, but, reading her father's face, Callista knew it was ambitious. Jimmy was not somebody who stressed easily, but he was tense today.

In the cab of the excavator she could see Trevor Baker, quiet and red-faced. He wore his tension like a coat, his big hands tight around the controls. Jimmy's job was to direct machinery operations and Callista could see him giving hand signals to Trevor to guide the excavator into position. It was going to be difficult; the excavator was already sinking in the sludgy sand.

On the far side of the whale, volunteers continued to press the inflatable mattresses up against its belly. The whale lay still, but it raised its pectoral flipper as the excavator approached and flailed wildly in the air, slashing the flipper against its side like a flashing black and white windmill. Then, somehow, the whale arched and managed to drag its massive tail out of the sand. As the huge flukes crashed down violently, the volunteers staggered backwards. Callista felt sick with fear. Someone could be killed if they lost balance and fell the wrong way. She wished there was another way. But she knew it was this or they'd have to shoot the whale.

Trevor tried to hold steady as he inched the excavator towards the whale, but occasionally the machine jolted and clanked and the engine revved throatily. At first, the whale struggled, but after a few minutes it slumped and lay still. Callista wasn't sure which was worse: the stress of watching the whale react or seeing it give up.

When the excavator was close, Trevor lowered the bucket and jiggled it down onto the sand beside the whale's back. With the blankets wrapped around the bucket to prevent trauma to the whale, this was going to be a difficult manoeuvre. But eventually Trevor managed to dig the bucket into the sand and then use its flat side to push slowly upwards. With the assistance of another group of volunteers, the whale finally rolled onto its chest. Trevor backed the excavator away and more mattresses were buttressed against the whale to maintain its position. Taylor was calling out, asking if the sling was visible, and a couple of volunteers tried to find it, but it must have bunched up beneath the whale's belly as it rolled. Another strategy would have to be used to place the sling.

Jimmy huddled with Taylor and Trevor Baker discussing what to do next. It was unfortunate it had to be like this—one wretched step at a time, with impromptu meetings to discuss and adjust strategies. It made the rescue appear less than professional. But nothing about this event was predictable and Callista hoped the positive support of the crowd would persist. In truth, the whole process was horrible. No matter how carefully each step was planned, something could go wrong.

She heard someone call out.

'What's going on?'

Jen's friend Jarrah ducked under the cordon and strode up to a ranger.

'Aren't they going to brief us on what's coming next?' he yelled.

Jen was there too, just behind the cordon. 'Let Jarrah help,' she demanded.

'I'm sorry,' the ranger said, grim-faced, trying to encourage Jarrah back under the cordon. 'This is a bad time. We can't have anyone approaching the whale right now.'

'Ah, you bastards.'

Jarrah knocked the ranger over, but at that moment the sound of the excavator revving up again hooked everyone's attention back down the beach. The excavator was clanking slowly down towards the water to start digging a seawall and some Parks rangers were pulling another sling across the sand.

Suddenly, barefoot and with dreadlocks flying, Jarrah dashed down to where Taylor and Jimmy were standing with the vet. Callista saw her father's surprised face when Jarrah elbowed in on their discussion. From Jimmy's gestures she knew he was angry, but a solution was quickly reached. There was too much urgency to waste time.

Two men were placed on each end of the sling. Jarrah was one of them. Callista hoped his inclusion wouldn't send the wrong message to other would-be helpers. But nobody else tried to make a break down the beach. Shouldering the weight of the sling, the men carried it down beyond the reach of the whale's tail. Then Jarrah and his partner crossed behind, dragging one end of the sling wide. They laid the sling flat on the ground and tried to slide it beneath the whale's tail, but the whale wouldn't move.

After another huddle to discuss tactics, the excavator was recalled. Trevor revved the engine to frighten the whale in the hope it might lift its tail, while Jarrah and the other men stood alert, holding up the ends of the sling, waiting for the right opportunity. For a long minute it seemed nothing would happen. The whale lay still. Then Trevor jerked the machine to make a loud clank and the whale arched and thrashed its tail wildly, alarmed by the noise. Quickly the men dragged the sling forward. It was a desperate and perilous move, but they pulled the sling safely into position beneath the tail.

As the men headed back to Taylor, Jarrah paused, his body tight with the desire to do something more. Ignoring Taylor, he moved quietly forward and pressed his cheek against the whale's back. Callista felt the crowd around her breathing with empathy, breathing their own hopes through Jarrah as his hands slid gently over the whale's sides. For several moments, Jarrah stood there unmoving, despite Taylor impatiently calling him away. And, watching him, Callista started to cry. Whatever she had hoped, this rescue was awful for everyone. Perhaps a quiet death on the sand would have been preferable to this after all.

★

When the crowd finally dispersed up the beach, Callista hung back, avoiding the swarm of people. Further along the cordon she saw Lex. He waved as he came towards her, and she knew the expression on her face would tell him how terrible she was feeling about the rescue. But just as he reached her, a man walked up to them carrying a microphone in his hand.

'Hey. Lex Henderson.' The guy swung the microphone over his shoulder and grabbed Lex's hand in an enthusiastic shake. 'I heard you were down here. What's happening, man? How did you get caught up in this? It's been a long time.'

'Shane.' Lex sounded reluctant. 'I knew someone familiar had to turn up.'

'What are you doing down here? We lost you, man. Nobody knew where you went. You living 'round these parts?' Shane laughed loudly. 'Apart from whale strandings, there can't be much going on around here. You must be going mad.'

Callista watched, wondering at the relationship between them. Friends or acquaintances. It was hard to tell. Lex had pocketed his hands and his face was closed down.

'It's not so bad,' he said. 'But you wouldn't understand, breezing through like journos do.'

Shane smiled, but his eyes swung to Callista, assessing, presumptive, almost rude. He continued with overdone friendliness.

'Is this a friend of yours? Hey, I'm Shane Maxwell. An old buddy of Lex's.'

He offered her his hand, but it felt intrusive.

'This is Callista,' Lex said. He moved closer to her. 'Her family runs the local whale-watching tours.'

Shane's face expanded too kindly. 'Hey. You must be the chick that found the whale. I heard about you down at the newsagency this morning. That's great.' He reached down to switch on his microphone and recording unit. 'Can I ask you a few questions?'

Callista pushed aside Lex's blocking hand. 'Sure,' she said. 'Let's go and get a cup of coffee.'

At the coffee tent, Mrs Jensen and Beryl were deeply engaged in discussion. Callista heard them from outside and she checked Shane before he entered the tent.

'There are too many of us here,' Mrs Jensen was saying.

'What do you mean?' Beryl huffed. 'It's only natural for people to want to help.'

'It'd be easier for the rangers if none of us were here. Then they could get on with deciding what they should do.'

'What are you saying?' Beryl sounded outraged. 'You can't possibly think they should kill it?'

'If necessary, they should. I can't help thinking that all of this is going on to keep the humans happy.'

Beryl snorted. 'What would the minister say if he heard you talking like this?'

'Do you think this is what God wants? To see an animal tortured?'

'This is a rescue,' Beryl snapped. 'Both God and the minister would want to see this whale saved. You've lost your mind, Mrs Jensen. It must be the cold.'

'Well, you've lost your heart, Beryl. They always said you had no heart when you took that house away from the Wallaces. And now I'm inclined to believe it.'

There was icy silence.

'Perhaps you'd better go home.' Beryl's voice was thin and tight. 'Half of Merrigan is down here. I'm sure someone won't mind taking your place.'

Callista grabbed Shane's arm and walked into the tent. She saw the women rearrange their faces into polite smiles.

'What will you have?' Mrs Jensen asked, staring at the microphone and recording unit slung over Shane's shoulder.

They both accepted coffee and Shane thanked Mrs Jensen humbly. He could certainly put it on when he wanted to. Perhaps that was a skill all journalists cultivated; anything to get people onside if there might be a story in it. She followed him to the base of the dunes and sat with him on the sand. He drank his brew silently and seemed casual enough, but his sideways glance was an attempt to peer inside her and work out who she was. She didn't like it.

'What do you want to know?' she asked.

Shane threw back his head and laughed. He had yellow teeth like a horse. He must be a smoker.

'It's not whales I'm interested in,' he said, watching her keenly. 'It's Lex. I want to know what he's been up to these past months. Looks to me like he's lost his mind, moving down here.'

'What's it to you?' Callista asked.

'I know him well. At least I used to. And I know his wife.'

'I thought they were getting divorced.'

'Ah. So you do know something about it.'

'He doesn't let on much.'

'I'm not surprised. He had a pretty shit time before he disappeared and came down here.' He looked at her. 'Are you his girlfriend?'

Callista shrugged and Shane watched her keenly.

'You are, aren't you? You're Jilly's replacement. I know Lex's wife well.'

'I see.' Callista steadied herself. 'I don't imagine I'm anything like her.'

He laughed. 'Nobody's quite like Jilly. She's some lady. Fearsome.'

'I'm no match for her then.'

He shook his head. 'I'm not so sure about that. She's a hard woman. Demanding. Challenging. Gorgeous, actually.'

Callista felt suddenly weary. She really didn't want to hear about Lex's past relationships. She moved to leave but Shane waved her back onto the sand.

'Does he speak about her?' he asked, more gently now.

'No. I think he's trying to delete the life he had before he moved here.'

'That explains a few things. Nobody's heard from him back home. He just disappeared off the face of the earth.' Shane frowned and hesitated for a moment. 'Did he tell you about the child?'

'Yes. Eventually.'

'Bloody awful, watching the two of them fall apart after that. Lex didn't cope at all. He took to the whisky. And Jilly shut him out. She can be as hard as a stone.'

'Perhaps that was her way of coping.'

Shane shrugged. 'I always thought people were supposed to come together in times of grief. Not tear each other apart.'

'Grief as big as that might be hard to share.'

His eyes narrowed as he looked at her. 'Lex was a big-time media personality. Did he ever tell you?'

'No. But we suspected something like that. He starred as MC at a public event just recently.'

'Of course he didn't tell you. He's probably hiding from all that down here too. But he was a high-rating radio presenter back in Sydney.'

'He milks cows down here.'

Shane was shocked. 'That's a comedown.'

'Perhaps it's just different. He likes it.'

Shane shrugged again. 'Whatever takes your fancy. But it doesn't sound like the Lex Henderson I know. I mean milking cows, for fuck's sake! There's not much you can say to a cow, is there?'

They sat in silence for a moment then Shane looked at her frankly. 'You're all right,' he said. 'I like you.'

'You mean Lex could do worse.'

'No. You've got more compassion in you than Jilly.'

'I'm not sure I like being compared to Jilly.'

'Well, no, you wouldn't like it, would you?'

'And I'm not sure things are going too well with your mate Lex and me anyway.'

'Complicated?'

'Always,' she admitted.

Shane nodded. 'He gets hooked up on things and he can be difficult to budge. But he's kind underneath. He can talk for a living, but personally he's hopeless at it. Tends to internalise things. Hide away from himself.'

Callista tightened her lips. Lex was certainly good at hiding away from things.

'Perhaps we should get on with that interview,' she said. 'I'm done with hearing about your mate Lex.'

THIRTY

Lex couldn't help watching Callista and Shane sitting up near the dunes, talking. It made him nervous. Shane could tell Callista anything, and now he wished he'd told her everything himself, right back at the beginning, when the possibility to be direct and up-front was still there. It would have been difficult and painful, but she'd have had the opportunity to be sympathetic and understanding. Now, it would feel more like a confessional, and up there by the dunes Shane could embellish as he wished. Lex was deeply uncomfortable knowing they were talking about him. And he was certain they would be. Shane had that investigative look in his eye. A look of interest that extended beyond the whale.

He was just psyching himself up to join them when Darren Beck arrived breathless at his side.

'They're doing something to Mum,' the boy said. 'They're making her take drugs. You have to help me. We have to get her away from there.'

Lex didn't want to get involved but the kid was desperate, so he followed him along the beach to where Helen was sitting among Jen's scruffy mob. They had blankets draped around their shoulders, and Jarrah was sitting beside Helen, holding a fat joint to her lips. Jen was rubbing Helen's back and laughing as Helen coughed and gagged after taking a drag. Lex felt the boy tense beside him.

'Let's get her,' Darren said, tugging Lex towards them. He stepped over someone's legs to get to his mother. 'Mum. You have to come with me and get a cup of tea from Mrs Jensen.'

Helen looked up at him with glassy red eyes. Lex could see she was already smashed.

'Darren,' she said blearily, patting Jarrah's knee. 'Come and sit down and meet my friends.'

'Mum. They're not your friends.'

'They're nice people, son. Come and sit down with us.'

Helen looked suddenly green. She turned, swaying, and vomited into a plastic bag that Jarrah held open for her.

Jarrah smiled up at Lex. 'She's got the spins. She'll be okay. Just greening out a bit.'

'How about I give her a hand for now?' Lex suggested, stepping carefully into the little circle.

'Sure, mate.' Jarrah didn't resist. 'Is she your girlfriend? She's one hell of a cool chick.'

'She's a bit confused,' Lex said, as he helped Helen to her unsteady feet and took the sag of her weight against his hip. 'It's a difficult and emotional time for all of us.'

Jarrah took the joint from Jen and relit it. 'Want a drag?' he offered.

'No, thanks. I've still got a few jobs to do.'

Jen sneered up at him. 'You do-gooder,' she said. 'Can't help yourself, can you? You had to save me when I was hitching. And now you have to save the poor lady from the nasty greenies and their drugs.'

'The kid asked for help,' Lex said. 'He's worried about his mother.'

Jen's voice followed them as he led Helen away. 'Yes, that's him. And hasn't he got shoulders like an ox.'

Lex deposited Helen and Darren with Mrs Jensen and Beryl. The church ladies were tense and silent from arguing and he figured Helen was in just the right state to sit between them. It'd give them something else to think about. He sat her down with a plastic bag and went to find Shane and Callista. It was best for him to escape any situation that involved Helen Beck. Local gossip had got out of hand so quickly after that time he'd had dinner with her. If Mrs Jensen and Beryl wanted to find a life raft for Helen, he wasn't going to let it be him.

He found Callista near the control tent, focusing out to sea through a pair of binoculars. The distant black shape of a boat was rounding the headland.

'Part of the rescue mission?' he asked.

'Stage two,' she said, lowering the binoculars and looking at him.

'They're not using your dad's boat?'

'Jordi's gone to bring her in. He should be here soon. They'll definitely need two boats. That's the National Parks' shark-cat out there. It's too small to haul the whale out alone.'

Down the beach, Lex could see the seawall around the whale growing as the excavator swung to and fro, shovelling sand. Trevor was working on digging out a channel now, using the scooped-out sand to build the wall higher. It had to be sufficiently high and wide to withstand the press of the incoming tide. If it breached too early, the rescue attempt would be lost. The whale wouldn't cope with waiting until the next turn of the tide for the wall to be repaired.

Lex glanced back at Callista, wondering what Shane had said to her. He couldn't read anything in her face.

'I had to rescue Helen Beck,' he said. 'I've handed her over to Mrs Jensen.'

Callista tensed and lifted her binoculars again. 'I'm glad someone did it,' she said. 'Shame it had to be you. I heard you had a little interlude with her a while back.'

There it was again. One dinner with the woman and he was guilty until proven innocent.

'She asked me to dinner *once* out of politeness. Nothing happened. I do have some self-control, you know.'

'And the girl with dreadlocks?'

Ah yes. That too. 'I picked her up on the highway, fed her some dinner and drove her to Eden.'

'Why did you pick her up?'

Lex clenched his fists, exasperated. 'I'm being honest with you. Nothing happened. Ask the girl. I'm sure she won't hesitate to tell you.' He dropped his fists and gave up. 'Please can you help?' he said. 'Helen's off her face. Stoned. She's been vomiting. And the kid's really upset.'

'Poor wretch,' Callista said without sympathy. 'She hasn't got much idea, has she? Doesn't know what to do without Henry to dictate The Way.'

'Even if you just pat her hand?' Lex suggested.

Callista glared at him. 'Go and chat to your journalist mate,' she said. 'At least you guys understand each other.'

Shane was still at the base of the dunes, smoking and biding time. He saw Lex coming and waved.

'Coffee?' he yelled.

Lex nodded. He saw that Shane had a gas cooker set up in the sand.

'I bring my own stuff,' he explained. 'It's the only way you can get good coffee in the field. I tried that shit the church dames are serving up. Tastes like cat's piss.'

Lex couldn't help laughing. 'Can't say that I've drunk any cat's piss lately.'

While they waited for the billy to boil, they talked Sydney and the radio industry and other inane stuff that took them nowhere. Lex knew they were edging around. Sussing each other out after a long gap in their acquaintance. Finally, Shane poured the coffee and passed him a mug.

'What *are* you doing here?' he asked.

Lex shrugged. 'How's Jilly?'

'Do you really want to know?'

'Not really. It all feels a bit remote.'

Shane laughed. 'You're the one who's a bit remote. Living way out here.'

'It's not so bad.'

'Milking cows, eh?'

'She told you all that?'

'It might entertain you for a while, mate,' Shane said. 'But it's not enough for you. You'll rot.'

'It's not so bad.'

'You belong in the city, mate. They'd have you back at the radio station, you know. Don't you miss all that?'

'Haven't thought about it,' Lex mumbled.

'Yeah? Well, maybe you should.'

'And Jilly?'

'She's like a lost sheep. She got fixed on a rich lawyer for a while, but that went nowhere. I asked her out once too.' Shane winked. 'I reckon she's still waiting to see if you come back.'

Lex gazed out to sea.

'I heard you put in a professional appearance at a local event,' Shane said.

'She told you that too.'

'Sounds like you haven't lost your touch.'

'It was the Show Girl contest at the local show.'

Shane snorted. 'Must have needed your rose-coloured glasses at that one. What was it like? A line-up of dairy cows?'

'Actually, I had fun,' Lex said. 'The girls were fresh and unpretentious. If you staged an event like that in the city, the girls would be falling over themselves trying to be something they're not. It's simpler here. Simpler and cleaner.'

'You've lost it, mate. You're a bloody country convert.'

They sat in silence for a moment.

'How about you?' Lex asked. 'Any developments in your life?'

Shane looked at him hesitantly. 'I hope you don't mind me asking Jilly out.'

Lex shrugged. 'She's fair game now, I suppose. She's not a bad woman. It's just that everything's gone for us now.'

'Can I call that your consent?'

Lex smiled. 'Go ahead.'

Shane started packing away his stove. 'I meant what I said about radio. You should think about it. Your producer's only a phone call away. It's all there for you. Come back and get some meaning in your life. We can't have you milking cows forever.'

Lex grunted. 'The second boat's coming,' he said, pointing towards the headland. 'Phase two will be on soon.'

Shane snorted. 'Soon! Not likely. Tide's still a mile out. And I reckon the whale's had it anyway, poor bugger.' He drained his coffee and looked down the beach. 'What's going on down there?'

He pointed to a fluster in the crowd and Lex recognised the tall figure of the minister flanked on either side by Beryl and Mrs Jensen.

'Looks like the minister's arrived,' he said. 'Just what we need.'

Shane laughed. 'What's he here for? To give a bloody sermon? To this lot?'

'Don't laugh,' Lex warned. 'This is the country. It's likely to happen.'

'Let's go down and watch,' Shane said. 'This could be entertaining.'

They walked down the beach and joined the gathering crowd near the volunteer tent, where Jimmy had set up the milk crate as a makeshift pulpit for the minister to speak from. Lex pitied Taylor for having to deal with this extra complication. He wondered if Taylor and Jimmy had seen the potential for the minister to unhinge things. If the minister didn't choose his words carefully, he could enrage the crowd. But when Lex caught Jimmy's eye, he saw a twinkle there, even though his face was very straight. At least Jimmy was maintaining a sense of humour.

The crowd stood brooding and silent as the minister stepped tentatively onto the crate. He looked a little anxious as he surveyed his audience, and so he ought to, Lex thought. Didn't he realise how patronising he seemed to this bunch of agitated people who had been out in the cold all day? Silly pompous man. What did he think he was going to do anyway? Offer a prayer and deliver a miracle?

The minister cleared his throat and tucked his hands behind his back in typical pulpit pose. 'This is not quite what I'm used to for delivering speeches,' he said, surveying the crowd with a flickering smile. 'At the church we have a luxury podium and a microphone these days, to make my job easier.'

He shifted awkwardly on the box, and Lex was glad he was uncomfortable. Why should it be easy for this man? It hadn't been easy for anyone else today.

'This is quite a different experience for me,' the minister continued. 'I'm generally used to speaking to people who agree with me even before I begin. And I'm well aware that many of you may not have been to church for a long while, if ever. But that doesn't have to matter. I'm not here to tell anyone what to believe in. In fact, now that I'm here, I find myself wondering what I thought I could do. Back at the parish it seemed that a prayer might help. But now I see the size of the task you people have undertaken, I feel embarrassed at my presumption.'

He sought the eyes and faces of everyone around him. He had a knack of making people feel involved.

'Setting my embarrassment aside, I do think it would be useful for us to pray together. Even those of us who are not religious have our own ways of praying. And I strongly believe it could help if we all stand here beneath this great grey sky and offer a prayer in whatever form it comes to us. Prayers from all of us might have the power to change things.'

He paused.

'You see, now that I'm here, I have doubts. Like any of you. Doubts exist even in my job. Who can be sure of the power of God and the kingdom of heaven?'

'Isn't that sacrilege?' Shane muttered. 'Speaking like that. Who is this guy?'

'I've only ever heard him at a funeral,' Lex whispered.

Shane sniggered. 'He ought to be reading the last rites.'

'I believe in the power of enthusiasm,' the minister was saying.

'And the power of collective will. The power of gathered determination. Only our combined energy has the potential to change things. If anything can save this whale, it will be this, our combined energy and our combined prayers. Not my private plea to God. But the power of all of you, pulling as a team, praying as a team, bonding as a team. That is what delivers miracles.'

The minister was definitely warming up. He had softened the crowd and everyone was listening.

'Many of you would not describe yourselves as religious,' he continued. 'But I propose that *all* of you are spiritual in some way. We just have different names for our spirituality. Whether it is God or Jesus or Nature. Whatever we call it, it is all one. We're all part of God and Nature, and that is the source of power that might deliver the miracle we're hoping for today.'

Lex saw the minister smile at someone in the crowd. He followed the smile to Helen Beck, who was standing trembling and uncertain, with Darren gripping her hand. The minister's keen on her, Lex thought, surprised. The poor kid will never escape the grip of the church.

'I want to finish with a word of caution,' the minister said. 'We're all hoping this whale will return to the sea where it belongs. But despite our collective prayers and hopes, there's a possibility the whale might die. And, if that dreadful moment arrives, we may find ourselves thinking that God has forsaken us, or that He has let us down. But no . . . if such a terrible ending becomes our reality, we need to meet it positively, and take its lessons. There are lessons for all of us, both in life and in death. Thank you.'

'Thank Christ for that,' Shane said as the minister stepped down. 'We can only hope he goes home now.'

'I doubt it,' Lex said. 'He'll be here to the bitter end.'

THIRTY-ONE

Callista sat alone on the sand and watched the excavator at work. She could see Trevor Baker hunched behind the controls, shifting the long yellow arm of the machine like it was an extension of his own body. Down close to the sea, the wall rose about a metre above the sand—a barrier to the incoming tide. From there, two walls ran along a channel that Trevor had gouged out as he stacked up wet sand, backing the excavator up the beach as he went. The walls flared out like arms beginning to encircle the whale in an embrace.

Around the whale, the groups of volunteers continued tirelessly. There were so many of them waiting on the beach for a chance to assist. Despite the enthusiasm of the helpers, both the whale and the vet looked tired. Both had a similar dejected slump. Tim's face was tight with exhaustion, black rings sliding their way beneath his eyes. The day had been too long.

Trevor had been working for hours without a break. Close to the whale, he worked more slowly, carefully scooping up buckets of sand and shaping the walls, trying not to alarm the animal with sudden clanks as the machine swung and moved. Eventually, he trundled the excavator up the beach with its arm folded like a claw and its caterpillar tracks clacking on the sand. He stopped it by the dunes, then mounted the bulldozer and began working around the whale from outside the walls, banking up sand to complete the barrier.

By now the tide was lapping at the wall. Taylor and Jimmy were watching it carefully. They emerged often from their tent to walk down to the water's edge and observe its effect on the seawall, eating away at the sand. Further up the beach, several staff members had laid out the harness ready to strap around the whale's pectoral flippers shortly before the wall was breached. But the time had not yet come.

Callista was relieved that preparations were nearly complete. This morning, the end of the day had been forever away. Yet while Trevor had been out there scooping and gouging with the excavator, it had seemed there was too little time to construct the planned sea-barrier. Now, with everything almost ready, they need only wait until the tide crept in far enough, as it would, relentlessly and silently. Then they could breach the wall, watch the water flush in around the whale and watch it float out to sea.

Despite her hopes, she knew it wouldn't be that easy. What she wanted, along with everyone else, was to see the whale out in deeper water and to end this torture of watching it beached on the sand. She wanted never to be involved in a stranding rescue ever again. And she wanted to go home to bed. Cold and fatigue had seeped into her bones and she was weary with everything. She couldn't bear the waiting any more.

She stood up, brushed off the sand and walked away up the beach alone. Striding hard and fast, she walked beyond the tents, away from the grind of the generators, away from the crowds, away from that accumulated fervour and tension, until all she could hear was the soothing rhythm of the waves thumping onto the sand and skimming in towards her feet. Then she stopped and faced the headland, staring up into the grey sky.

As she stood there, Jen came running up.

'I can't take any more.' The girl's eyes were wild and her dreads flicked out in the wind.

'Neither can I. But we just have to wait.'

Jen choked out a sob, angrily swiping a tear from her cheek. 'It's the suffering,' she said. 'And just watching is killing me. Maybe I haven't got what it takes for this stuff. Maybe I should stick to trees.'

Callista looked at the girl, all twisted with frustration, torn by despair. 'It's great that you've been here,' she said. 'You've helped and you haven't caused trouble. That's an achievement, given the strength of your passion.'

'You think so?'

'Yes, I do.'

Jen flashed a sad smile and jogged on the spot for a moment, all pent-up energy. 'I've gotta run,' she said. 'Then maybe I can go back. I have to see this through.'

Callista watched her race off along the beach, dreads flying. She admired her immediacy, her lack of finesse. There was something infinitely wild and attractive about her. She wouldn't have blamed Lex if he had slept with her—all that raw energy and blazing youth.

She turned back, wondering where it was going to end.

As the tide crept in, sloshing along the seawall and gradually eroding its sides, Taylor organised a team of men in wetsuits to assist the whale once the wall was breached. The whale would be weak after such a long period on the beach and they may need to provide physical support to prevent it from rolling and to stop water running over the blowhole. The men could shoulder-up against the whale and help as best they could while the boats pulled it out into deeper water.

Lex was among the chosen. Jarrah too. On the open beach, as the tide inched in, the men stripped naked and tugged on wetsuits, throwing modesty to the winds. Goose pimples pricked their exposed flesh. They shuffled down to the seawall where it expanded to surround the whale. Taylor was down there talking to them, but they were too far away for Callista to hear. She couldn't recognise

Lex amongst the group. All those restless bodies crammed into wetsuits, with coats pulled on over the top. They were black and indistinguishable. They must be cold waiting in the wind.

The tide was licking up along the wall and the occasional wave foamed over it, smoothing the clods of sand. Just beyond the breakers Callista could see the two boats bobbing and rocking on the waves. Jordi was standing astride at the wheel, holding his boat stern to shore at a safe distance from the National Parks' shark-cat.

Something should be happening soon. Her father was down by the water, talking to Tim Lawton, who had donned a wetsuit too and was standing in the shallows with a coat wrapped around his shoulders. They must be assessing the whale's condition. Tim set aside his coat then he and Jimmy climbed the wall, lugging the harness. They slid the harness across the whale's back and secured it beneath the pectoral flippers. Everything was ready.

The boats drew closer. Callista saw a man in a wetsuit lean out over the stern of the shark-cat and climb down the ladder-steps into the water. It seemed to take forever for him to swim the short distance from the boat to shore, his black-hooded head barely visible over the waves. Then he was thrust through the breakers, staggering into the shallows dragging a cable and hook. He passed the hook to Trevor Baker, who was waiting at the water's edge, and Trevor hauled the cable ashore. He climbed over the wall and locked the hook into the tail-sling, while the swimmer towed in a cable from Jordi's boat. Trevor hitched this to the sling as well. Another line from Jordi's boat was hitched to the harness.

Finally, at a waved signal from Jimmy, Trevor chugged the excavator into gear and rattled it down into the water alongside the wall. The boats began to move slowly out to sea, churning up over the waves and gradually taking up the slack in the lines.

When the cables began to tighten, Trevor waited for a nod from Taylor then he swung the arm of the excavator high, its claw hovering a moment before it reached out, splashing into the water, and tore through the wall. The water gushed through, ripping into the barrier. Trevor scooped again to deepen the rift and the wall was sucked away, the water surging through and sloshing around the whale.

Quickly now, the wetsuit men scaled the wall and surrounded the whale, their hands flat against its sides. Their presence, and the water slapping around, agitated the whale and it raised its tail, thumping it down hard against the resistance of the lines. Jimmy signalled out to sea and the boats slowly throttled their engines and started to pull. The wetsuit men pushed.

Callista felt the moments ticking by slowly. Why wasn't anything happening? If the whale didn't move now, the game was over. It would have to be shot. Jimmy maintained his thumbs up and the boats continued to pull. The men in the water beside the whale had their heads bowed with effort as they pushed against all that reluctant bogged flesh. Callista could hear the increasing throb of the boat engines over the thump and swish of the waves. She wondered what it must be like for Jordi, feeling the boat shaking beneath him and the whale still anchored to the shore. Thank God she wasn't out there with him.

Without warning, a pectoral flipper waved in the air and two wetsuit men staggered back. The white underside of the flipper flashed briefly before it slapped into the water. The boat engines growled and water frothed up behind them. And the wetsuit men moved in again and continued to push.

Suddenly the whale arched its body against the pull of the boats. A wave broke across its back and there was a loud blast of exhaled air. A dreadful moan flowed through the sands and up through Callista's bones. She could see her father's face creased in horror, but he was still indicating to the boats to go ahead. He was doing the only thing that could be done. It had to be finished.

Then, slowly, amidst the reverberating tremor of another awful moan, the whale's bulk shifted in the sand. Tim Lawton dashed in and tossed a towel over the blowhole, and the boats maintained tension on the lines. Then the whale was moving ever so slowly, with the wetsuit men still leaning into its sides, pushing. Gradually the whale began to slide backwards into the breakers.

Ecstatic shouting erupted on the beach. People cried and thumped each other's backs, hugged, cheered, jumped up and down, cried some more. The minister threaded amongst the crowd, shaking hands and smiling. Helen Beck wafted along behind him, eyes like black saucers.

Callista watched, but felt separate from all of it, tired and unmoved. It was such an ugly scene—the pitiful helplessness of this great animal being dragged into the water, waves sluicing over its flat knobbled head and running along the downward curving groove of its mouth. Everybody was celebrating as if this was the end, but she knew it wasn't over.

The boats dragged the whale until it was just beyond the breakers where the waves rose up and over its glistening black back. Tim pulled the towel off and shortly after Callista thought she saw a small vapour spout rise.

The wetsuit men remained shoulder-in to the whale. They looked like a mass of black seals, their heads and shoulders bobbing up and down in the water. The whale seemed to be listing to one side. Tim was yelling instructions, getting the men to push it straight using the buoyancy provided by the water. He watched several waves roll in over its back. Then he hollered to the men again. Callista saw the majority of the team cluster along one side of the whale. They ducked their heads low and gouged their shoulders in hard. From the shore, it was difficult to work out what they were doing. Tim was in there too, pushing and shoving against the whale's reluctant bulk, stopping periodically to yell encouragement to the team. Slowly, the men pushed the whale around, fighting against the waves, until it was facing out to sea, looking the way it had to go.

Callista gazed out there too, squinting into a new band of drizzle that had begun to seep from the belly of a low cloud. The grey sea hardly looked encouraging, but to a whale it must look like home—that wide stretch of heaving, rolling water. She'd imagined they'd tow the whale far out to sea, as far out as possible, where it was truly buoyant and couldn't see the shore. She had imagined the sling slipping off as the whale slid into the depths with a flick of its flukes. But Taylor had said they couldn't tow it further, because water could run via the blowhole into the lungs and cause pneumonia. Instead, the plan was to hold the whale facing out to sea until it recuperated enough to swim away. Quick tears flushed onto Callista's cheeks. Was this the best they could do after finally getting this animal into the water? So much trauma and stress to come to this moment—where it was all up to the whale. It seemed hopelessly optimistic. And there could still be hours to go.

Time slipped into a new holding pattern, marked by periodic vapour puffs as the whale huffed air with each breath. On the beach, the crowd fidgeted edgily. Everyone was still charged with tension. Callista too. She begged Jimmy to allow her onto the next wetsuit team he was mustering. But he rolled his eyes.

'We need muscles, kiddo,' he explained. 'Not pumped-up wenches with fire in their bellies. You'll be needed soon enough to warm up these fellers when they come back ashore. That Lex of yours is going to need a bit of mothering. He won't know what day it is. It's freezing out there.'

He was right. Callista was shocked when the first man stumbled ashore, shivering and blue. In the shallows, he staggered to his knees and had to be helped into the shelter tent by several people.

'We need to sort out something for Tim,' Callista heard her father say. 'He'll be hypothermic if we don't do something soon.'

A Zodiac was launched from the shark-cat. It plucked Tim from the water and whisked him away to the boat. Within minutes, he was back, clad in a yellow drysuit. He continued to supervise from the Zodiac while the wetsuit team rotated in and out of the water. As freezing men came ashore, shambling out of the waves into the icy lick of the wind, volunteers teamed up to hurry them into the shelter tent. They peeled wetsuits off and wrapped men in towels and blankets. Steaming hot chocolate was pressed to frozen lips. There was careful monitoring for hypothermia. Mrs Jensen's tea and coffee team and Sue's food team were back in their tents keeping the hot drinks and food coming.

Eventually Callista saw Lex come out of the waves. His lips were dark and he was shivering. Hovering on the edge of the group of assistants who reached for him, Callista observed the tight whiteness of his face and the dark hollows beneath his eyes. His hands were shaking and stiff, awkward with the cold. It frightened her. He seemed distant, vague, unaware that she was there. The other volunteers crowded her out in their enthusiasm to help. They walked him into the shelter tent and their hands tugged at him, unzipping his wetsuit, tugging it off and slinging a towel around him, rubbing him dry. They piled blankets around him.

Callista stayed outside the tent, watching the cluster of black bodies surrounding the whale in the steely grey of the late afternoon. Seeing Lex so debilitated by the cold, she wondered how long they could keep this up. Multiplied by the wind chill, the cold was intense. It would be at least half an hour before Lex could even think about going in again.

THIRTY-TWO

As the day grew late, the cordons were dropped and everyone moved forward to the water's edge. A new heavy quiet fell on the beach. The tide turned and shifted out, and the whale was pushed further out to prevent it wedging in the sand as the water retreated. The wetsuit team continued to rotate on and off the beach, growing colder with each shift. With only an hour and a half of daylight remaining, surely the release time was near.

Eventually, Tim rode the Zodiac ashore to meet with Taylor and Jimmy, and they stood near the tent, punctuating their lengthy discussion with frowns and waving hands. Finally, Tim left the huddle, white-faced, and headed back into the surf. He looked small and lonely as he waded through the waves. The Zodiac scooped him up and rode past the whale and over the swell to the boats.

They must be about to move the whale out at last and Callista was glad. There had to be an end to it, and she hoped it would be before dark. Everyone was cold and weary, and the grey afternoon light was oppressive. Spirits were sinking. She was pleased to hear Taylor's voice again, crackling in the loudspeaker. But he sounded tired and flat and, as he spoke, outlining the plans for the release, Callista felt dread creep through her.

The whale had been in the water recuperating for at least a couple of hours, and Taylor was pleased about this. But he was adamant that decisions had to be made now that dark was coming on. In a perfect world, the whale would be held a few hours longer before being pushed out to sea. But unfortunately, with daylight running out, Taylor wasn't willing to take this risk. The overnight weather forecast was for gale-force winds and more rain, and if the whale was released at night and in a storm, it'd be hard to follow his movements and there would be a significant chance of a restranding. Taylor said the other option was to hold the whale overnight in shallow waters. But he wasn't keen to do that, because the longer large whales were held ashore, the more likely they were to die.

The final option was to release the whale tonight, and soon. Shortly, Taylor said, the whale would be pushed further out and the wetsuit team would come ashore. Once the whale was in deeper water, they would release the harness and move the boats in behind to herd him out to sea. He ought to be able to swim by now, if he was going to make it. And if he was released soon, there'd still be sufficient daylight left to follow him out to sea and keep monitoring him. If possible, they wanted to put a few kilometres between the whale and the shore.

The assumption was that the whale would be able to swim away. Tim Lawton had cautioned that, despite all the rescue efforts, there was a considerable chance the whale might have significant lung damage. He had been breathing fairly regularly, but wasn't as alert and responsive as Tim had expected after a return to the water. Taylor warned everyone that although they were all hoping the whale would swim successfully out to sea, there was a chance he may not.

Lex came in with the last shift, cold and exhausted. He stumbled out of the water on legs that were numb and felt his mind blurring around the edges. Probably a bit hypothermic, he thought, bumbling with the towel that someone handed him. He staggered into the shelter tent before accepting the hands trying to wrench his wetsuit off. He was so drowsy he could just lie down there in the tent and go to sleep. But people kept pushing at him, holding him up and dragging at the sticky tightness of the wetsuit. Strangers' hands rubbed him with towels and insistently pressed hot fluid to his lips, forced him to swallow. Somebody brought his pile of clothes. Normally he'd have been indignant to have someone help him into his trousers, like a child. But this afternoon, it didn't matter.

More hot chocolate. He could taste the drink now. The snugness of his thermals and then the weight of warm layers. Wool. Extra clothes from the volunteer tent. Finally, the cocoon of his coat. He held his arms out and let them help him. He realised Callista was among them, watching him with eyes that were dark with concern.

The others went outside to see if there were other wetsuit men requiring assistance, and suddenly Lex and Callista were alone in the tent.

'What's happening?' he asked.

'We'll have a look in a minute,' she said, zipping up his jacket. 'They've started pushing the whale out into deeper water. The vet's going to assess him out there and see how he's going.'

Lex allowed her to tug woollen gloves onto his hands.

'Good,' he said, sliding his tongue around the thickness of his cold lips. 'That whale hasn't much energy left for waiting around.'

'What do you mean?' she asked.

Lex hesitated. He was spent. Physically and emotionally. He was ground down by the cold and fighting the surf and waiting for the whale to breathe. Who knew how long he had spent with his shoulder dug into the firm flesh of the whale's back, his fingers hooked into one of the throat pleats, trying to hold the whale straight.

They hadn't talked out there. The cold was too intense, the exertion too draining. Each man had been mired in his own internal journey, trying to cope with the magnitude of the whale's fatigue, the apparent impossibility of the rescue. How could he explain all this to Callista?

'The whale's tired,' he said. 'He's sick, and he's tired. Out there, you keep thinking each breath is his last . . . Maybe he hasn't got it in him to swim back out to sea. Maybe he doesn't want to.'

'Don't!' Callista said sharply. 'You can't say that. Everyone has worked so hard to get that whale back out there.'

Her face tightened and it almost made Lex cry to think he may have triggered her again. But he had to be honest. There was nothing to be gained by deluding her. She hadn't been out there. She hadn't felt the weight of all that flesh trying to list sideways in the water. She couldn't know about the tremor that had slid through that great body as they pushed it into deeper water. It hadn't been easy. Lex could still feel his feet struggling to find a foothold on the sandy bottom while the waves pushed through. All they could really do was hold the whale straight, facing seawards.

They had guided the whale out as far as they could. Once their feet were off the sand, they could only bob in the water alongside, while the men near the tail unhooked the sling and let it slip off. They had stayed there, riding the waves beside the whale, until the boats came around behind, rolling wildly in the slap of the waves. And then Lex and the others had swum wide of the boats and back to shore, labouring their frozen limbs into some kind of flailing stroke to slowly inch back into the shallows. There had been moments when he didn't think he could make it, even though it was only twenty or thirty metres to swim. How could he describe all this to Callista without sounding like he had given up?

'I don't know if he's got the will,' he said finally, hoping she wouldn't close him out again.

But she patted his arm and handed him a mug of hot chocolate.

'Let's go and see,' she said. 'You're tired and addled with the cold.'

He accepted that, and followed her outside into the onshore breeze, cold as ice off the water.

It took nearly half an hour to follow the whale a kilometre out to sea. By then, the boats were black smudges rocking against the steely sky. Low clouds, dense as burrs, scuttled beneath the higher cloud mass. A bulk-carrier pushed across the horizon. The pulsing throb of the generators further up the beach mingled with the roar of the sea. And the waiting continued.

On the beach, Taylor kept everyone informed via messages relayed from the shark-cat. Far out to sea the whale had stopped and was resting quietly at the surface. The boats stayed with him to prevent him from turning towards the shore. They would sit there with him until after dark, or until he swam further out. Either he was too tired to swim, or just biding time, storing strength.

Lex left Callista with her father and took more hot tea from Mrs Jensen's tent. It seemed he just couldn't get enough warm fluids into him. Each time he emptied a cup, the cold would return and within five minutes he would be shaking again. He suspected it was as much about reaching his limits as about suffering from hypothermia.

Darren served him in the tent. The boy was wearing a smile almost as wide as his face. He nodded towards the back of the tent where Helen Beck was sitting with Beryl, Mrs Jensen and the minister. The minister was holding Helen's hand. Lex stood holding his tea, wishing he felt comfortable enough to sit with them. Even after all that had passed during his time in Merrigan, he was still hovering on the edges with these people. Perhaps he'd never belong. But maybe in his tiredness he was being melodramatic. He had made friends here: Sue, Ben Hackett, Sally, Mrs B. In his own way he was starting to belong, even if he could never be entirely at ease with the church crowd.

For a long time he stood near them, warming himself with the tea and their quiet conversation. He should be helping to set up the lights, but he was more tired than he had ever been. Exhausted to the bone. It was soothing somehow to remain in the tent among people he knew, even if they didn't encourage him into their midst. They were familiar and he was linked to them by shared experience, and for now that was enough.

Standing quietly gave him space for the first time today to hear a small voice within that had been trying to get his attention all afternoon. There was a worm in him. He could feel it, despite his tiredness, and it was new. Something was settling in him. It was some sort of resolve and acceptance. A way forward that was both heavy and light. For a moment he considered it, then let it ride, allowed it to wash with the burble of conversation around him. He could think about everything tomorrow, when he was fresher.

He ruffled Darren's beanie as the boy pushed past him through the door of the tent.

'Where are you going?' he asked. 'It's freezing out there.'

'I can hear someone coming.' Darren leaned outside. 'It's Mr Jensen.'

Mrs Jensen leapt up and bustled out of the tent. Lex looked outside too and saw Denis Jensen hobbling towards the tent with Mrs B.

'Good Lord, man!' Mrs Jensen cried. 'Have you been sitting up there all day? Of all the silly things to do! I thought you'd have driven home after you dropped me off.'

Lex joined her in helping them into the tent and onto folding chairs. He saw Beryl leap up, flustered, to start making cups of tea. He noticed she was dodging Mrs B's sharp eyes.

'You silly man,' Mrs Jensen said. 'I could have taken a lift home with someone else. And now poor Mrs B has to bring you down here, when she can hardly make the distance herself.'

'I can manage well enough,' Mrs B said in her gravelly old voice. She glanced at Lex and took in his fatigue. With a curt nod, she accepted a cup of tea from Mrs Jensen.

'I was out at the Point all morning just knowing something was going on,' she said. 'I should have listened to my intuition, shouldn't I? But when you get to my age, you're never sure whether it's your intuition or insanity talking.'

She leaned forward on her walking stick and examined them all with fierce eyes.

'Looks like insanity's closer to the truth,' she snapped. 'What's been going on down here? Is this supposed to be some sort of rescue?' She glared at them all. 'I went to town early this afternoon and there wasn't a soul to be seen. The whole of Merrigan is down here, it appears. I had to take myself up to the church to find out what was going on. The minister was the only living soul around.' She nodded at him, still sitting with Helen.

'It's happened before around here, you know. A stranding. Years ago. But not like this.' She waved her arms in the air expressively. 'They blew the last one up. The army did it. And a damned sight more humane it was than what's going on here. Denis and I have been watching it all from on the hill. The poor damned thing being dragged into the water. You should all be ashamed, the lot of you, for being involved in it.'

No one spoke.

'Now,' she said, poking at the sand with her walking stick. 'Where's Jimmy Wallace? If anyone can explain this to me, it'll be him. The Wallaces know more about whales than anyone else around here.'

'He's down at the water's edge,' Lex said.

'Take me,' she said.

Lex took the old lady's elbow and they walked down towards the water where they found Jimmy and Callista together. Jimmy sensed their approach and turned to Mrs B, his eyes meshing silently with hers for several long moments. Not a word was spoken.

'I see,' she said, taking the large rough hand he held out to her.

The old woman's shoulders sagged and the anger passed. Somehow in that wordless exchange, Jimmy had communicated everything Mrs B needed to know. He put an arm around her shoulders and they stood staring silently out to sea for a long while.

Lex left them and scuffed away along the sand until he was alone. He sat down in the congealing dusk, aware of his heart thumping anxiously and goose bumps prickling along his arms. Uncertainty chilled him. He looked along the beach. Everyone else must be feeling the same way. Most people were clustering quietly around the shoreline. They couldn't see much in the late afternoon light. Just the dark shapes of the boats far out, merging with the horizon.

Lex hung his head between his knees and closed his eyes. He could still see the mistiness of the morning as he and Callista had walked down the beach together, pushing into the wind. There had been hope between them then, possibilities, the suggestion of a future. But today had sealed the lid on everything, again, for the last time. In a way, their disagreement over the whale was symbolic of their struggle to find common ground. It surprised him that on the beach today he had been the level one, the steady one, who had seen no sense in continued suffering to fulfil an entirely human will for rescue. He had wanted to find a peaceful end for the whale. But Callista, always so broadminded and practical when it came to emotive issues like modern whaling, *she* had been the one caught up in the mindless race to rescue, the life-at-all-costs approach. It wasn't what he had expected of her. And it had brought them to loggerheads again. He felt the shock of the entire day tumbling inside him.

He was vaguely aware of Taylor's voice scratching out over the loudspeaker again, and then the sudden note of excitement caught his attention. He leapt to his feet and tried to see out into the deepening murkiness of early evening. There was a long pause as Taylor waited for information to dribble in via his two-way radio.

'There's some unexpected activity going on out there,' he said. 'Apparently, the whale's rolling from side to side in the water as if he's testing himself out . . . He's lifted a pectoral fin on each side. Given them a slap . . . Tim says his breathing's fairly regular . . . maybe a bit laboured . . . but he's moving around some more . . . They think he might be preparing to dive . . . They're staying in behind him to keep him pointed in the right direction . . .'

Lex hoped the whale would dive soon. Get the hell out of there, with dark coming on. He imagined the whale rolling down beneath the rising swell, the dorsal fin peaking just before the flukes rose out of the water and then slipped under. He hoped the whale would do it spectacularly and wave those flukes high on the way down. It would be a victory for the whale then, departing like that.

He glanced along the beach to where everyone was waiting. In the gloom, he could see the flare of an occasional cigarette being lit down by the water's edge. There was a dull murmuring of voices and the constant sound of the waves breaking and scuttling into shore. He felt strangely detached. And the sand was getting colder. With everything happening so far offshore, there was a lack of tangibility, a lack of reality. But it was best they couldn't see what was going on out there. Then they could imagine the finale as they wished. The reality would probably be far less liberating.

He thought of Callista and felt resignation settle. A flush of loneliness, knowing he was on his own again. The momentary ache of not knowing where to go. Then Taylor crackled over the loudspeaker.

'We're a bit unsure why the whale's still hanging around. They thought he was going to dive, but he's stopped still again at the surface . . . They're going to take the Zodiac up close to encourage him to head out to sea . . .'

Lex's heart began to gallop. His resignation fled and hope surfaced, intermingled with fear. Taylor's voice came over the speaker, tight and guarded.

'They're up alongside the whale now. They've got the lights on him because it's getting dark out there. Tim's leaning out from the Zodiac to stir him up a little . . . That's good. Apparently, he's responding . . . They say he's moving. Maybe having a bit of a look around . . . Looks like he might swim. . . . They're shifting in to keep him facing out to sea . . . He's moving out, they're telling me, swimming along a bit . . . they're having to follow him . . . It looks like he might dive . . . Yes. There it is. He's done the up-flukes. And he's gone. That's it!'

Lex touched his cheeks with his fingertips and was surprised to find tears there.

The boats followed the whale further offshore, but the crowd was finished with it now. They had the ending they wanted and so the day was over. Everyone milled around under the sudden glare of the floodlights, shaking hands and patting each other on the back. It was a quiet celebration. Now that everything was over, there was a mood of exhausted elation and a weary lack of direction.

Taylor wandered around quietly, shaking hands and saying little. Jarrah slapped him on the back with enthusiastic jubilance and Taylor took his hand, but offered only a small smile. Callista was surprised Taylor wasn't more animated. Maybe he was too tired and had done this sort of thing too often. With the excitement over, nausea swamped her. She couldn't remember ever being so exhausted. She merged with the shadows on the edge of the camp to look for her father. The Parks staff had already started packing away. He would be helping with that.

Jimmy was down near the water's edge, deflating mattresses and looping ropes in large coils on the sand. In the shadows, he looked gaunt and haggard. His motions were mechanical; the deliberate slow movements of a tired, ageing man.

'Dad,' she called. 'Isn't it great!'

Jimmy looked up. His eyes were hollow.

'The whale,' Callista said. 'Aren't you pleased about it?'

Jimmy threw another coil of rope. 'The whale isn't going to make it, Callie. Taylor couldn't tell the crowd, but the poor bugger hasn't a hope in hell. Started bleeding from the blowhole. Erratic breathing. And he couldn't float straight. Kept wallowing onto his side and trying to correct in time for the next breath.'

'There's a chance though, isn't there?'

Jimmy cast another coil of the heavy rope. He stood up a moment with his hands supporting the small of his back and stretched, studying Callista. 'You look awful, girl.'

'I feel terrible.'

He gestured out to sea. 'They'll follow him out another kilometre or so then they'll turn back. When they drop the vet off, I'm going to send you out to the boat in the Zodiac. Jordi'll take you home. I'll be here for hours yet. Have to pack away.'

He finished coiling the rope. 'Is Lex still around?' he asked.

'Somewhere.'

'Good, we'll need his muscles. The crowd will disperse pretty quick now. Nothing to hold them here. Packing up isn't half as romantic as rescue.'

'There's nothing romantic about whale rescue.'

'You learned something.'

'You've left me with nothing positive to take home.'

'Would you have believed me if I put on a smile?'

It was eerie riding the Zodiac out to Jordi in the dark. As they left the floodlit shore, the Zodiac operator gave Callista a spotlight to help him navigate through the incoming waves. Then he asked her to extinguish it and they used the soft light emanating from the boat to find their way over the swell towards it. Jordi hauled her aboard, and waved to the operator who pulled away and zipped off to the shark-cat.

Jordi said nothing, of course. In his brief glance she saw he had knowledge he didn't want to share and she let him keep it. What Jimmy had told her had been enough. Jordi waved her to a seat but she walked past it to the bow and stood there as he swung the boat seawards and set a course to take them out around the headland. Way out there she could see the periodic blinking of the beacon to guide them out from the rocks. For a while she looked down into the water and followed the rhythmic surge of white froth as the bow ploughed through the swell, slicing the black water.

Some distance out a squall closed in. Rain sluiced across Callista's face and Jordi called her to cover, but still she stayed out there. Somehow the punishment of the weather seemed fitting and she wanted to ride through it, even though it was irrational. Her face chilled and the cold rain was like needles on her skin. Jordi called again. But this pain was something that she needed. She couldn't explain why. She stayed out there, feeling the rain run under her hood and down inside her coat.

The squall ended as quickly as it began. Suddenly she was in clear night again, watching the dim beams of the boat illuminating the water beyond the bow. She realised she had lost the beacon in the squall, because suddenly there it was, blinking out of the blackness. It was like life really. The truth was always there, only you lost it sometimes in the murk of your private storms. It took major events for you to catch sight of it again. And then there were moments of vivid clarity when the path seemed so obvious you wondered how you had lost your way.

It was the barriers she didn't understand—when you thought you knew where you were going and then a roadblock appeared, so enormous you couldn't see a way over it. That was how it was with Lex. She needed him to show her where the right footholds were so she could reach him safely. But he was always looking the other way.

Lex returned to the tea tent to a group of weary faces. He had planned to help pack up, but there was another job to do first. This group needed shepherding back to their cars. He'd have to borrow a spotlight from one of the rangers to lead them up the beach. Mrs and Mr Jensen looked overwhelmed by the whole experience. Helen was quiet and subdued, with Darren clamped to her hand, his face white and tired. Beryl was pale and bedraggled, despite the lipstick and the henna, and Mrs B sat stiffly turned away from her on a foldout chair with one hand on her stick, ready to go at first call. Her mouth was a tight line and her old blue eyes flashed into his. She was angry about the rescue. And about the proximity of Beryl. Sue and John Watson were still packing away in the food tent. They would make their own way back. The minister had left earlier, just before dark.

Before taking the Merrigan crew up the beach, Lex tracked down Jimmy. He was dismantling the volunteer tent with two other men.

'I hoped you'd find me,' Jimmy said, setting down a bunch of tent pegs so he could shake Lex's hand. 'We need all the help we can get.'

'I have to take some of the locals back to their cars first. There's a few of them looking pretty weary.'

'We'll be here a while.' Jimmy regarded Lex for a lengthy moment.

'No good, eh?' Lex said quietly.

Jimmy shook his head.

'Does she know?'

'I sent her home with Jordi.'

'Good. Best to get her off the beach.'

Jimmy grasped his shoulder. 'We'll see you soon.'

It was a long march down the beach in the dark. The beam of the spotlight lit a bright circle outside of which everything was cast in the deepest black. Lex instructed Darren to lead the way with the spotlight and he walked just behind, supporting Mrs B and Mr Jensen. Beryl and Helen assisted Mrs Jensen, who was stiff after standing all day in the cold. It was eerie following the bright blaze of the beam with the night slick and black around them.

Lex guided them slowly up the dunes. The cold wind whisked through the grasses and swirled around the cars, everything wet with sea mist. He asked Mrs B if he could bring her car back later, and whether she would mind going home with Helen. He needed a car, and he figured a ride with Beryl wouldn't improve Mrs B's black mood.

Mrs B held his hand tight after he helped her into Helen's car. 'Come over when you get home. I'll have some sherry and hot scones waiting for you.'

'Thanks, Mrs B, but there's no need to wait up.'

'I'll be awake,' she said.

Lex watched them leave, the headlights cutting crazily through the mist as the cars bobbed over the uneven ground until they found the track. Then he turned wearily back down the dunes.

THIRTY-THREE

It was close to midnight when Lex got home. He sat on the couch in the dark and listened to the wind rattling the window panes. The house was cold. It never held the heat well with all those windows. And there was nothing outside. It was black as pitch. He could be nothing and nobody in this darkness and it matched his mood. Apart from the ache in his muscles and bones, there was nothing left in him. It was good to sit with the emptiness, beyond the clamour of emotions. This was his peace.

When he thought of the whale, there was a knot in him. It was tangled somewhere between his chest and his throat and felt similar to thoughts of Isabel. Another battle lost. Callista too. His weariness magnified. How to move beyond this inertia? He could have a shower and go to bed. Wash off the salt and search for something positive in the day. But perhaps he was too exhausted to make any assessments right now.

A light came on in Mrs B's house and Lex remembered the scones and sherry. There was warmth there, at least. And company. Perhaps he should have that shower and go over. Debrief. Purge the day's events. Or perhaps he should say nothing. Mrs B knew anyway. She always seemed to know. He opted for the scones and sherry.

Mrs B lit some candles on the old wooden table and switched off the lights. The flames flicked and jiggled in the breeze seeping under the door. They sipped sherry and listened to the wind banging some loose boards up near the eaves.

'I'll fix those for you tomorrow,' Lex said.

Mrs B grunted and poured some more sherry from her crystal flask with its heavy stopper.

'No rush,' she said. 'They've been thumping away in the wind for years. If I woke up and it was quiet, I might think I was dead.'

Lex watched the candle flame fluttering. The alcohol eased warmly through him, and he focused on the quiet crackling of the fire in Mrs B's old stove.

'What went on there today?' Mrs B asked, after a while.

Lex watched the candle flame in silence.

'The vet must have known,' she said. 'They should have shot the poor thing. Put it out of its misery.'

'It was complicated on the beach.'

'Complicated enough to justify cruelty?'

'It wasn't my call. I wanted to walk away right at the beginning.'

'I'm not blaming you, lad. It's just that I don't understand all that craziness, the lack of judgment. They ought to have known when it was time to stop.'

He shook his head wearily. 'It should have stopped before it started. But I learned a few things out there today, Mrs B. I learned that wildlife is public property. And that whales belong in the realm of the sacred. When a whale is involved, nothing justifies euthanasia. The public owns the whale and the public wants to save it. Pain and suffering don't come into it. Even the vet said it's hard to assess. And if *he* can't say what's going on, who else can make those decisions? And what's objectivity amongst all those emotional people anyway? What does it mean?'

'Did they talk about euthanasia?'

'Of course not. The peaceful death option was over the moment I turned away from Callista on that beach and went back to call National Parks. I knew that's the way it would be. Rescue or burn in hell.'

'The girl was just emotional. She'd have come around in time.'

'I doubt it. She held her stance all day.'

'Do you really think she'd have admitted a turnaround to you? She is a Wallace, after all.'

Lex hesitated. 'She did help me after I came out of the water on that last shift.'

'Perhaps that was her way of giving ground. These things can be subtle, you know.' Mrs B poured some more sherry.

'She was right about one thing,' Lex said. 'Leaving the whale to die on the beach wouldn't have been peaceful either.' He sipped his sherry, working through the events of the day. 'There's more to it too. There's this strange notion that whales are a symbol of everything grand and beautiful on earth. Everything wild and free. I don't know why that is. There's nothing rational about it. Maybe it's because they're so big, and because you can never really see them. And if you do, it's such an awesome event . . . Remember how you and I were blown away seeing those whales close up on Jimmy's tour? You can't kill that, Mrs B. You can't kill people's passion for wild things.'

He paused and slid his fingers around the stem of the sherry glass, watching his thoughts form in the flicker of the candle flame. 'I can see Callista's point now. I can see what she was trying to tell me. If you can't help a stranded whale on your own beach, then what hope is there? If you can't act with passion to save a creature that represents the pinnacle of freedom, then you kill any sense of being able to do something worthwhile in this world. You're left with nothing. And we're already powerless enough when it comes to changing things.'

He stared at the flame. 'It was awful today.'

Mrs B reached across the table and covered his hand with her firm dry grasp. 'I know,' she said.

They drank more sherry. Filling time with quiet companionship until Lex felt sufficiently warm to go home to bed.

★

Lex slept the unmoving, undreaming sleep of exhaustion and woke in the grey morning feeling muscles he never knew he had. He wished he could roll over and re-enter oblivion, but a growling hunger niggled him. He lay on his back and stared at the ceiling, wondering what his feelings would be today about yesterday, whether sleep had changed his perspective, as it so often did. Yet as he lay there going over the day's events, there was little new or satisfying to find in another analysis. Whether he agreed with what had taken place or not, the basic fact remained—they had done all they could and with good intentions. That had to be enough. The ethics of the situation were a separate issue. Ethics belonged to a world of public discussion and debate. Not to any one individual with strong opinions of their own. Even at the beginning, it had never really been his decision to make—the decision to walk away.

In a way, it was just as it had been with Isabel. He had done all he could and with good intentions. However awful the outcome had been, the whale's death, and perhaps also Isabel's death, hadn't been his fault. He felt strangely released. Settled.

After breakfast, he took a hammer and some large nails from the toolbox in the laundry cupboard and went next door to ferret out a ladder from amongst Mrs B's junk. She boiled the kettle while he secured her loose roofing boards. Then they ate leftover scones and drank tea on the verandah. It was disconcerting that a day could feel so normal after yesterday.

'You're brooding on something,' Mrs B said after a while. 'I know it.'

Lex placed his cup back on the saucer. He was surprised how steady he felt on the cusp of this decision.

'When my little girl died from cot death, she was barely eight months old. I lost something enormous with her—a whole life that I wanted to invest in. And it's taken a long time for me to come this far, but now I see that I've gained something from losing her too. She's taught me a lot through grief. So perhaps in a way her life wasn't wasted.'

Mrs B listened to him, kindness flowing from her old blue eyes.

'Yesterday sealed something for me,' he said. 'I love it here. The sea, the sky, the wind.'

Mrs B's lips tightened slightly. 'But you have to go.'

'Is it that obvious?'

'The worst of the grieving is over.'

'Is it always like that? Suddenly you reach up out of this dreadful black hole and you can see light?'

She smiled. 'It hasn't been as sudden for you as you think. It's been very gradual, this seeing the light you're talking about. Don't forget, I've been watching you. You've been healing a bit at a time. That's the way it is with the deepest wounds in life.'

He nodded. 'Today I'm exhausted, but somehow I feel like I have the energy to start living again. Properly.'

'And what do you think you've been doing here, lad?'

'I've been marking time—healing, trying to find my feet again. It was like I was destroyed somehow when Isabel died, and this place has resuscitated me. I've been rehabilitating.'

'You think you have to go back to the city to find this life you're ready for now?'

'I need to go back to get some closure on things and to pick up some old threads.'

'Not every tapestry requires completion in this life. Sometimes it's all right to take up something new. In fact, it's necessary.'

'I have tried here, Mrs B. But I've made too many mistakes.'

'The girl?'

'I think it's done. Over.'

She regarded him steadily with unjudging grey-blue eyes. 'You do what you have to do, lad.'

Callista arrived at the Point in the early afternoon. She climbed the steps slowly and found Lex inside pulling the zip on a suitcase. Books and clothes were all around him in piles on the floor. Panic surged in her throat.

'What are you doing?' she asked.

'Packing.'

'I can see that.'

He tugged the zip closed and pushed the case against the wall. When he stood up, he grimaced.

'My body's a bit the worse for wear today,' he said.

She held her face still as she watched him, her heart battering wildly. She'd come hoping for some sign of intimacy from him. Some suggestion that he was pleased to see her. But everything about him was distant, withdrawn and impersonal.

'So you're leaving,' she said.

'I've decided to go home.'

'Back to Jilly?'

He rubbed at his back, massaging a stiff spot. 'No. That's over. I'll go back to radio. Shane seemed to think they'd have me back.'

Callista struggled to suppress her dismay. 'You never talked about your life much. About being a journalist.'

He shrugged. 'I guess it seemed irrelevant here. I can tell you now if you want. There's nothing much to it.'

'That's not what Shane said.'

'Well, no, I suppose he wouldn't when he's been lusting after my wife and my job for years.'

Callista shivered. 'I thought she was your ex-wife.'

'She is.'

'Shane said you were a celebrity. The life of the party.'

'You have to have a public face to hide behind.'

'What's your real face then?'

He bent over to pick up a loose handkerchief from the floor. 'It's boring. You've seen it. I'm as ordinary as the next person.'

'Why go back then? To all that pretence?' She'd couldn't believe he'd contemplate it.

'It's what I do best.'

'Pretence?'

He looked weary. 'No. Radio.'

'So you'll just slot back into your old life?' She laughed, cynical.

'It'll be different,' he said. 'I'm different.'

Callista glanced despondently around the lounge room. It already felt as if he had gone. There was a coldness in the place that hadn't been here before.

'What will you do with the house?' she asked.

'I'll keep it. I can come down on weekends. And I'll organise my holidays when the whales are due back in spring.'

'And you'll just pop by to visit your old Merrigan friends? It won't be the same, you know. You won't belong any more.'

'I never did, really.'

'That's an insult.' She succumbed to rising irritation. 'When you took the time to engage with people around here, this community welcomed you with open arms. You're already a celebrity here, for doing *real* things—saving Mrs B, the Show Girl competition. Not for spinning superficial chat on talkback radio. Tell me, how many city people are going to stop and talk with you in the street? You won't get any sense of community back there.'

'Radio's a kind of community.'

'That's rubbish, Lex, and you know it. You're talking about a bunch of like-minded people sticking together because they live in a cocoon. A real community is a mixture of people with different opinions. It's a mosaic.'

'Whatever.' Lex looked at her tiredly.

'You're running again, I thought you were bigger than that.' Callista felt sick with disdain. She'd expected so much more from him. All she needed was a sign that he wanted her.

'I'm not running,' he said. 'I belong in the city.'

'You don't really think it's going to be better, do you?'

'Maybe not. But I'll be busier.'

'Filling up your time and your mind so you can't see where you're at.'

'Maybe so, but I can't milk cows for the rest of my life.'

'It's that journalist friend of yours, isn't it? He's run us down. He's painted us as a bunch of yokels and you've believed him.'

'It's not that at all.'

He was shutting down, his face closed and distant. She reached out with everything that was left in her: anguish, receding hope and exasperation.

'There are other things you could do here if you used your imagination. You could start up a local paper. Use your skills. The community would support you. If you hadn't been wallowing in your own problems for so long, you might have thought of it earlier.'

Lex's eyes flashed. 'Callista. Stop.'

'No, I won't stop. I think you've been incredibly selfish. I suppose I should have expected this sort of behaviour from a city person, especially from a journalist. You come down here, use up all the friendship and support of our community, and then you just walk away. We don't deserve that.'

Lex was angry now and she felt a flash of triumph. At least she had stirred a response from him.

'Is that why you're here?' he said. 'To have a go at me? It's not as if I haven't tried with you. But there's no winning whichever way I turn.'

'If that's how you feel, I had better go.'

On the deck, Callista paused to look out to sea where a shaft of light played through a crack in the clouds and silvered a patch of water. Here she was watching the light again, even in a crisis. She stepped slowly down the stairs, her heart tumbling.

'I actually came to apologise,' she said, looking back up at him.

'What for?' His arms were folded tight across his chest, his face blank.

'You were right. We should have walked away, as you suggested. I was wrong to pull all that moral stuff on you.'

'It doesn't matter.'

'Yes it does.'

'There was no right or wrong decision.'

'Did Dad tell you about the whale?'

'Yes.'

'That it's going to die.'

'Yes.'

'Is that why you're leaving?'

'No.'

'Then why?'

He looked at her desperately and she knew he couldn't find an answer.

You don't know what else to do, do you, she thought.

'When will you be leaving?' she asked, carefully masking the tremor at the edge of her voice.

'Tomorrow sometime. Most of this stuff can stay. I'll have to do a few trips over the next month or so.'

Callista looked slowly around at the house, the grass shifting softly in the breeze, the moody grey skies, the slow roll of the waves, and then at Lex, standing quiet and folded into himself on the deck.

'I guess I'll be going then,' she said.

In the morning Callista drove up to Jordi's place. Mist hung wet and grey in the treetops. It dripped from the leaves, damp and cold. Jordi had moved back inside the humpy, where he kept a slow fire burning in the old stone fireplace, more for atmosphere than for warmth. He was sitting on a tattered director's chair, watching the door as if he had been waiting for her. His beanie was pulled down hard over his ears and he was wearing a thick old duffle coat to keep him warm.

'Tea?' he asked, as she scraped the door shut and folded out a chair.

'Of course.'

She sat down with him and watched the dull flames licking lazily at the heavy wood.

'I've only got half an hour,' he said. 'I'm taking out a group of fishermen at eleven. I have to bring the boat in and organise some supplies. They want lunch as well.'

'I won't stay for long. I just wanted to sit with you for a while.'

Jordi poured her a cup of tea then sat the billy back inside the fireplace near the edge of the coals. She felt his eyes on her as she took a few sips, but she evaded him and he said nothing.

He gave her five quiet minutes before he banged down his cup.

'What's wrong?' he demanded.

Callista's breathing quickened. She hadn't expected him to confront her.

'Forget the bloody whale,' he growled. 'There was nothing else could be done.'

'It's not the whale,' she said, feeling weak.

'What is it then?'

'I'm pregnant,' she said, without looking at him.

She stared into the fire, giving in to the sweeping nausea for a few moments before looking across at him. He was watching her, uncertainty written over his face.

'Is that good or bad?' he asked.

'I don't know.'

'I thought you wanted to have a baby. Have you told him yet?'

She shook her head.

'Why not? He should be man enough to deal with it.'

'He's leaving.'

'Where's he going?'

'Back to the city. To his old life.'

Jordi stood up. 'No, he's not. Not when you tell him, he won't.'

'I'm not going to tell him. I don't want him if he's dreaming after something else.'

'Is he going back to the woman?'

'He says not.'

'Do you believe him?'

'Yes. I do.'

'Then you have to tell him. He's a good man. If he's the father, he's got a right to know.'

'What do you mean, "he's a good man"? You've never particularly liked him. Don't stand up for him now.'

'He's got a right to know,' Jordi repeated stubbornly.

'And I have a right not to tell him.' Callista was pale and sick, but adamant. 'I'm not going to make the same mistakes I made last time.'

'What mistakes?'

'Running into someone's arms just because I'm pregnant.'

'Lex isn't Luke. And you don't have to marry him straightaway.'

'I don't have to marry him at all.'

'No. So why are you worried? Why can't you just tell him and see how it goes?'

'See how it goes! Why would anything be different?' She shook her head. 'I won't do it.'

Jordi turned suddenly and kicked his chair over. He kicked it again, hard, against the wall of the shack.

'What is wrong with you two?' he shouted.

Callista had never seen him so angry. Her tears came from nowhere.

'I don't know,' she said. 'Every time we seem to be getting along, some issue comes up and it's like this huge wedge that stops us from coming together.'

'What was it this time?'

'The whale. He wanted to walk away from it. And I wouldn't listen to him. I hung all my guilt on him. I hung everything on getting that whale back in the water.'

'That's the past,' Jordi said. 'You've got *this* now. Can't you see he loves you?'

How could it be so obvious to Jordi, but not to her?

'You've painted your storm,' Jordi said. 'Now let it go. What are you expecting from Lex? Thunder and lightning? Because you won't get it. That's not his way.'

'What *is* his way?'

He looked at her, eyes serious. 'He's steady. As steady as the tide.'

Then he took her hands in his, urgently. She looked down at the black soot on them, the in-ground dirt over his knuckles. And his voice kept coming at her, soft now and insistent.

'There's something new in your life now,' he was saying. 'Something exciting. A new baby. How about that! That's the future. Your future. Your future with Lex, if you want it that way. You can't let the past stand in the way of that. And you'll be all right with him. You've grown. You're a different person now.'

She couldn't stop crying.

'What about his past?' she said. 'It's like some chasm I can't ever cross.'

'Yes, you can,' he said. 'The baby's the bridge. He'll give you what he can when he can. But you have to be prepared to let some of it go. Most of it, if you have to.'

He looked towards the door. 'When's he going?' he asked.

'Today.'

'Look,' Jordi said. 'Listen to me.'

He talked then as if he had been waiting for years for the right moment to come. Observations accumulated over a lifetime flowed out. And more. The wisdom of Jimmy, of Vic, of Mrs B. All the depth behind that silence.

When he was finished, he hugged her and she stood for a minute, wildly uncertain, staring desperately into his eyes.

At last she made a decision and ran out of the hut. She flung herself into the Kombi, slammed the door and started it with a roar, tossing a wave at Jordi through the window. He was standing in the doorway of the hut, watching her with sad eyes, aching for her pain and her indecision. This moment surely was her transition to womanhood. The finding of the strength to be humble.

The old car bounced down the track, clanking over the washouts. She swung it onto the road, skating sideways in the gravel, then floored the accelerator, trying not to take the curves too recklessly. There might still be time. She might make it to the Point before Lex left.

What was it Jordi had said?

You don't have to think the same. You don't even have to agree. Embrace your differences. In the end they're what make you interesting. She should let Lex bring his love to her in his own way—like the tide—slow, consistent, dependable, leaving small unexpected gifts of love, as precious as pearls.

You have all that it takes, Jordi had said. Courage. Persistence. And strength. With the right ingredients, there's always a chance for happiness.

ACKNOWLEDGEMENTS

For helping me find time to write this book somewhere within our hectic family schedule, I thank David, Ryan, Nina and Marjorie. For early readings and constructive comments, my gratitude and appreciation go to David Lindenmayer, Fiona Viggers and Vicky Heywood. Thank you to Fiona Inglis at Curtis Brown for making this happen. Thanks also to Jane Palfreyman for wonderful, sensitive editorial input and to all the other fabulous staff at Allen & Unwin who have helped me. I wish to acknowledge my veterinary colleagues who have shared their experiences of whale strandings at various wildlife conferences I have attended over the years. Their comments and stories have inspired elements of this book.

Thank you to my mother, Diana, for her lifelong encouragement; my father, Jim, for his interest and support. And a special and deeply heartfelt thank you to my husband, David, for his patience, positivity and love. I dedicate this book to him.